Holiday Magic

Books by Fern Michaels:

Sins of the Flesh
Sins of Omission
Return to Sender
Mr. and Miss Anonymous
Up Close and Personal
Fool Me Once
Picture Perfect
About Face
The Future Scrolls
Kentucky Sunrise
Kentucky Heat
Kentucky Rich
Plain Jane
Charming Lily
What You Wish For
The Guest List
Listen to Your Heart
Celebration
Yesterday
Finders Keepers
Annie's Rainbow
Sara's Song
Vegas Sunrise
Vegas Heat
Vegas Rich
Whitefire
Wish List
Dear Emily

The Godmothers Series
Exclusive
The Scoop

The Sisterhood Novels
Cross Roads
Game Over
Deadly Deals
Vanishing Act
Razor Sharp
Under the Radar
Final Justice
Collateral Damage
Fast Track

Hokus Pokus
Hide and Seek
Free Fall
Lethal Justice
Sweet Revenge
The Jury
Vendetta
Payback
Weekend Warriors

Anthologies
Snow Angels
Silver Bells
Comfort and Joy
Sugar and Spice
Let It Snow
A Gift of Joy
Five Golden Rings
Deck the Halls
A Joyous Season
Jingle All the Way

Books by Cathy Lamb:

Such A Pretty Face
Henry's Sisters
"Whale Island" in Almost
Home
The Last Time I Was Me
"Suzanna's Stockings" in
Comfort and Joy
Julia's Chocolates

Books by Mary Carter:

My Sister's Voice
"The Honeymoon House" in
Almost Home
Sunnyside Blues
She'll Take It

Books by Terri DuLong:

Casting About
Spinning Forward

Holiday Magic

FERN MICHAELS
CATHY LAMB
MARY CARTER
TERRI DuLONG

ZEBRA BOOKS
KENSINGTON PUBLISHING CORP.

ZEBRA BOOKS are published by

Kensington Publishing Corp.
119 West 40th Street
New York, NY 10018

ISBN-13: 978-1-61664-929-6

Printed in the United States of America

~ Contents ~

"Holiday Magic"

FERN MICHAELS

*I'd like to dedicate this novella
to all the "snow bunnies" in my life*

Chapter 1

Telluride, Colorado
November 26, 2010
Black Friday

Stephanie glanced at her watch again, making sure she wasn't running behind her self-imposed schedule: 5:50 A.M. They were opening the doors at seven o'clock sharp as today would be the busiest day of the year at Maximum Glide's ski shop, Snow Zone, where Stephanie had been working as manager for almost two years.

With an hour to go before the doors opened, she adjusted the volume on the hidden stereo filling the ski shop with the soulful sounds of Michael Bolton singing "Have Yourself A Merry Little Christmas." She took four large cinnamon-scented candles from beneath the counter, grabbed a pack of matches, then lit and placed each candle in a secure place where it couldn't be knocked over by a customer reaching for something or an accidental bump from a ski. Though there were signs posted at the main entrance and throughout the shop stating NO SKIS ALLOWED INSIDE, that didn't mean that customers always paid attention to the posted rules. She'd brewed coffee and heated water for hot chocolate and bought several dozen donuts for the early risers. Judging by the amount of sugar consumed, shopping must be hard work.

Stephanie smiled, thinking about the upcoming Christmas season. For the next four weeks, Maximum Glide would be packed with vacationers from every part of the world, and, of course, the locals, who came in droves on the weekends. Scanning the shelves one last time, she refolded three bright red sweaters with matching scarves and toboggan caps. The many styles of ski boots on sale were stamped with bright orange stickers. Last season's waterproof gloves were placed next to this season's newest designs. People could decide for themselves if the price difference was worth purchasing the latest style. Personally, Stephanie thought they were pretty much the same except that the current style had a zippered pocket for an extra set of hand warmers.

She adjusted the Spyder jackets and the North Face ski pants, making sure they were evenly spaced on the racks. These were the biggest-selling items in the shop. She'd ordered more than she had last year, not wanting to risk running out before the holidays were over. Last year, the general manager of Maximum Glide, Edward Patrick Joseph O'Brien, who preferred to be called Patrick though privately she always thought of him as Eddie, like that cute kid on *Leave It to Beaver,* insisted that she place the order on her own. After checking her inventory, Stephanie had decided they had enough ski pants and jackets in stock for two seasons. What she didn't know then was that the famous ski shop, part of a resort owned by an Olympic gold medalist, attracted skiers with bushels and barrels of money to spend. She'd ended up placing another order, then had to spend hundreds of the ski shop's dollars for an overnight delivery. A lesson learned. More secure in her position this year, she'd placed her order with confidence, knowing she'd be lucky to have anything left after the holidays. For the moment, Stephanie was sure she'd ordered enough to get them through the busy holiday season. She wouldn't get a day off until after New Year's, but she didn't mind. She needed the extra money this year. With all of the overtime pay, plus her Christmas bonus, she would finally be able to afford the down payment on her very own home, a first for her and her two daughters, Ashley, ten going on twenty, and Amanda, an adorable seven-year-old. She'd been searching the paper for months and had finally found a perfect three-bedroom, two-bath ranch-style house that she adored and could afford.

Last week she'd made a special trip into town to Rollins Realty, who'd listed the property. Jessica Rollins, a smartly dressed woman in her mid-fifties, took her to the house, and Stephanie was immediately smitten. She'd practically salivated when she saw the deep garden tub in the master bath, a luxury she hadn't counted on. When Jessica saw her reaction, she explained that the former owners were avid skiers. Stephanie figured that covered about three-quarters of Colorado's population but knew a good soak in a tub of hot water was considered a necessity after a day on the slopes. After she viewed the house of her dreams, one she could actually afford, she had made a silent promise to herself and her girls: They would have a home of their very own, and unbeknownst to the girls, she planned to surprise them with a new puppy sired by Ice-D, Max's Siberian husky. She intended to keep both promises no matter how hard she had to work.

Placerville was her home now. She'd hated leaving Gypsum, but she was only a twenty-minute drive from Telluride. Grace and Max often made the four-hour drive to visit the resort. They always stopped at the shop to see her, and, of course, Grace wouldn't dream of missing a chance to see the girls. Grace was like the sister and best friend Stephanie had never had.

For nearly two years, Stephanie and the girls had been living in a one-bedroom garage apartment that Grace had found for her when they left Hope House, a shelter for battered and abused women. Grace, along with her new husband, Olympic skier Max Jorgenson, who just happened to own the ski resort where Stephanie worked, had announced yesterday during the Thanksgiving dinner they'd shared that they were expecting their first child. Grace had made jokes about her age, and Max had insisted she didn't look a day over twenty-one. Almost forty, and finally Grace's dream of having a child was about to come true. Funny, how it had all come together. If anyone had told her two years ago she and the girls would be on their own, *happily* on their own, she would have told that person he was out of his mind. Women like her couldn't support two young girls on their own, certainly not without financial help or a husband.

Well think again, buster!

So far she'd proved herself wrong, and she intended to keep doing so. She'd escaped from her abusive husband, high school-sweetheart Glenn Marshall, who was now serving eight years at the State Penitentiary in Canon City, Colorado, a maximum-security prison, for escaping the minimum-security prison he had been sent to when he'd originally been jailed for abuse. Stephanie cringed as she remembered how he'd managed to escape while being transported to another minimum-security facility.

It had been her first week at Hope House, just a

few days before Christmas. She'd allowed Grace to take the girls to see *The Nutcracker* at Eagle Valley High School. On her way back to Hope House, Grace had to take another route because roadblocks had been set up along I-70 in an attempt to catch the escaped convict. She'd gotten lost with the girls, wound up searching for help at the first house she'd located, which just happened to be the home of Max Jorgenson, the famous gold medalist Olympic skier. Stephanie recalled the horror-filled night she'd spent when Grace did not return to Hope House with her girls. Fortunately, Grace and the girls had found Max's log cabin on Blow Out Hill and remained there until the roads could be cleared, but not before Glenn, lost and on the run, also found Max's cabin and the girls. When Max found Grace tied up and the girls frightened to death, he'd made quick work of returning Glenn to the deputies who'd lost him in the first place, but not before delivering a few choice knocks that shattered Glenn's nose. Stephanie detested violence, but secretly she'd been delighted when she heard that Glenn had received what he'd dished out to her on a daily basis. And as they say, the rest is history. Almost two years later, Max and Grace were married and expecting their first child. Stephanie couldn't think of a better gift for the couple. They were made for one another.

Unlike her and Glenn.

Two years ago had found her beaten down and afraid to do anything to change her life. With no immediate family, and no close friends to speak of, Stephanie had resigned herself to a life of misery until she'd read an article on battered women. She remembered the part that convinced her she had to make a change, and she'd best make it fast.

It wasn't uncommon for the abuser to turn his anger on his children. . . .

Stephanie knew then she had to get away from Glenn no matter how difficult it proved to be. Two police officers had escorted her and the girls to Hope House immediately after Glenn's arrest. Since they'd been living with Glenn's best friend and drinking buddy, Stephanie had nowhere to go. Shamed, hopeless, and frightened for her children, she'd swallowed what little pride she had and allowed the officers to whisk them away in the middle of the night. Grace had greeted her and the girls like old friends, made them feel welcome, made Stephanie feel as though she was more than just another woman who'd remained in a bad marriage for the sake of the kids. Grace had set Stephanie on a path that had changed her life, and the girls' lives, too.

No longer did she feel worthless and afraid. The girls were resilient, just as Grace had predicted. Though Stephanie knew they were well aware of Glenn's violent behavior, she didn't allow them to dwell on it. Instead, with Grace's effective therapy, they'd acknowledged that some men hit women, and those that did needed to be punished by the proper authorities. Though Glenn wasn't eligible for early parole, Stephanie knew the day would come when he would be released. Until that day arrived, she would continue to work hard to provide a safe and happy home for Ashley and Amanda.

Melanie McLaughlin, her landlord's daughter, had just finished her last year of college when she answered Stephanie's ad for a sitter, explaining that she wanted to take a break before she headed out into the business world. Stephanie was delighted, and the girls adored her. Two mornings a week, Stephanie had to open the shop early for deliveries, so she'd needed someone to see the girls to the bus stop and be there when they returned. Melanie had been a godsend the past two years. She'd started a computer graphics business from her new apartment, which allowed her to continue caring for the girls. This week, they were out of school for Thanksgiving break. Melanie, ever the trouper, was bringing the girls to Maximum Glide later in the day to spend the afternoon on the slopes.

That night was the official lighting of the resort's main Christmas tree. Stephanie had promised the girls they could attend. It would be a long day for all of them, but fun. And she would see Patrick. He'd asked her out several times when she first started working at the shop, but she'd always told him no, saying she wasn't going to date until her divorce from Glenn was final. He'd said he respected that and would ask again. The day her divorce was final, she called to tell Grace, who informed Max, who then let Patrick know. That evening, he'd arrived on her doorstep with flowers for her, two Disney movies for the girls, and a piping-hot cheese pizza for all. She hadn't the heart to turn him away. They'd been out three times since then.

On their last date, they'd gone to the movies. She remembered the movie was a romantic comedy about a couple who each had six kids and married in spite of the antics the kids pulled hoping to keep the couple apart. As expected, the movie ended happily. Stephanie had enjoyed the movie immensely and remarked to Patrick how wonderful it was that the children finally accepted their new stepparents in spite of their earlier misgivings. He hadn't called since. Something was up with him, though she hadn't known what it could be and didn't ask. He was her boss, and she wasn't going to jeopardize her job by asking him why he hadn't called again. If she were completely honest with herself, she would admit it'd hurt her feelings when he hadn't bothered to call or offer an explanation for his sudden lack of interest in her. Even worse, Amanda and Ashley continued to ask when Patrick was coming over again. She'd put them off, telling them it was the busy season at the resort. They'd accepted her answer, but Stephanie knew it was more than that.

Putting all thoughts of her personal life aside, she inspected the store one last time. Everything seemed to be in place. Last but not least, Stephanie plugged the extension cord into the outlet, filling the small shop with bright twinkling lights on the eight-foot blue spruce. Candy Lee Primrose, a bright and witty high school senior and part-time employee, had spent the day before Thanksgiving decorating the tree. Tiny sets of skis, tiny snowboards, miniature sets of ski poles, scarves, brightly colored mittens, and hats hung from its branches. Fresh pine perfumed the air, reminding Stephanie of the giant pines that flanked her favorite blue run, Gracie's Way.

Glancing at her watch for the umpteenth time, Stephanie booted up the computer, clicked a few keys to record the time, then counted out the cash drawer. The credit card machine was up and running for a change. She replaced the white spool of paper with a brand-new one, then went to the alarm panel and punched in the security code to turn off the alarm.

Twenty minutes later, Candy Lee raced through the back door. "Smells wonderful in here," she said as she removed her snow boots and replaced them with a pair of tan Uggs.

"It does, doesn't it?" Stephanie said as she took in the shop, decorated in all its Christmas finery.

She took a deep, cleansing breath.

Here we go, she thought, *let the season begin.*

Chapter 2

Edward Patrick Joseph O'Brien, Patrick to his friends and family, placed a gloved hand on the dash of his most beloved possession, his bright shiny black Hummer. The love of his life. His passion, his reason for getting up in the morning.

Shit!

He was losing it. Too much cold weather had warped his brain, he figured, as he cranked the engine over. He'd become obsessed with Hummers ever since he purchased this baby two years ago. Couldn't get enough of them. He knew just about everything there was to know about the vehicle. If asked, he could tell you there were six different styles; they were originally designed for the military; some were equipped with caterpillar tracks for use in heavy snow and were nicknamed the Snow-Vee. He could go on and on, and did when asked, but mostly he appreciated their performance in the often harsh Colorado winters.

He adjusted the rear-window defroster, then

clicked on the fog lights as he maneuvered the Hummer out of the narrow drive at the base of the mountain where he lived in a newly constructed log home. Today was usually one of the busiest days of the season at Maximum Glide, where he was the general manager. He wanted to get an early start before he was bombarded with lost skiers, missing skis, snowboarders monopolizing the slopes, and the broken bones that were sure to happen to some poor unlucky souls. Glancing in his rearview mirror, he caught a glimpse of himself. His coal black hair was in need of a trim, big-time. His dark blue eyes were shadowed with gray half-moons. He'd spent too many late nights carousing with the guys. But what the hell? He was a single guy. What else was there to do after-hours? Currently, there was no special female in his life, no woman for whom he really cared. Not really, or at least no one that he would admit to. He'd been out with Stephanie Casolino-Marshall, the manager of Snow Zone, a few times, but he'd put a stop to that going anywhere real quick-like. Not that he would admit this either, but that woman had touched a part of him that had remained *untouched* for all of his thirty-nine years. He wasn't about to involve himself with a woman whose past was as dark as his black Hummer. No way. Women like her did nothing but cause pain and heartache. At least that was what he believed. He'd seen too many of his best buds go down that path. A woman with kids and an ex was pure trouble with a capital *T*.

That last evening he'd spent with Stephanie had sent him running. That damned movie with all those kids and that Brady Bunch happily-ever-after stuff was definitely *not* for him. He'd never asked her out again, and she'd never questioned it. She probably knew she wasn't prime meat on the for-sale market, but hey, that was her problem. She'd been sweet, and in spite of all that she'd been through, there seemed to be a hint of innocence about her. That part had touched him. Before he allowed himself to explore exactly what that meant, he'd boogied his way right back to his old tried-and-true rule. If he hadn't slept with the woman by the third date, she was history. He'd been on four dates with Stephanie and hadn't even kissed her. Definitely time to move on. A vision of dark eyes and long brown hair caused him to veer off the road. And those two girls of hers, well they were absolutely adorable, but kids were totally off-limits for him. No way. His sisters' three boys and one girl were enough kids for an overprotective uncle. Besides, he'd seen what had happened to his sister Colleen. Kids were not on his life list.

"See! This female/kid crap is for the birds," he said. "I'll wreck the Hum if I keep thinking along those lines." He shifted into low gear before turning onto the winding road that led to Maximum Glide. It was still early; the lifts didn't start running until nine. As it was one of the busiest days of the year at the ski shop, he wanted to check in early, make sure Stephanie and Candy Lee had things under control. He didn't want another episode like last year. He'd thought Stephanie had been ready to take over all the duties at the ski shop. Patrick had insisted she order all the stock for the upcoming season. She'd been doubtful, but said she would do her best. And dammit, her best had cost the resort big bucks. Her order was modest, not near enough to cover them for the month of December. He hadn't been too hard on her because she was so damned . . . well, she was so kind and apologetic. He hadn't the heart to scream and yell at her as he was known to do when things didn't run smoothly. Patrick simply wanted to do the best job possible. As general manager, it was his responsibility to make sure his employees knew exactly what their jobs entailed; otherwise, it was his ass on the line. Max Jorgenson and Patrick, or "Eddie" as Max still insisted on calling him, had been friends since they were in their early twenties. While Max was busying making Olympic history, Patrick had immersed himself in college at the University of Colorado, where he'd also received his master's degree in political science, thinking someday he would change the world. Like all young men, he'd had an idealistic view of the world's potential for change, and felt it was up to him to contribute to that change. So after he'd graduated, he went to work for the State Senate. Eight years of dirty politics destroyed his idealistic vision of making a difference. He'd had his fill of self-interested liars, cheaters, and backstabbers who had anything but the interests of their constituents at heart. Leaving a successful career, Patrick spent that first winter out of politics doing absolutely nothing except hitting the slopes. He reconnected with Max. They'd bummed around for a while, then Max married Kayla and hired him to run the resort. For two years after Kayla's tragic death, his good friend had sat on the sidelines, but now he was happily married to Grace, who Patrick thought was the best of the best. A good egg.

Coming from a large Irish family, with four older brothers and three younger sisters, had made him extra protective of women but guarded, too. He knew what little sneaks they were most of the time. Growing up, he'd been the best big brother he knew how to be. Which in his family meant he'd been to six proms, three of them with his youngest sister, Claire, who'd explained she simply needed him to act as her date because the guys in high school were just "totally immature." Which was a crock of crap. Claire had been trying to hook him up with her best friend Lisa Grimes since the first time Claire brought her home to meet the family her freshman year of high school. Patrick was flattered, but she was too young, and she was like a kid sister to him.

Then there was Megan, a year older than Claire. Megan was the family dreamer. She sailed through school without any problems but didn't have much of a social life. Patrick worried about her and told her so. Shocked that he'd felt that way, she revealed that she'd been dating a college man since her sophomore year. When he'd asked why she hadn't brought him home, Megan had clammed up. After much screaming and many threats, Megan had finally told Patrick why she hadn't brought her boyfriend home to meet the rest of the brood. He was married. Patrick wanted to find the son of a bitch and kick his butt, but Megan refused to reveal his name. She'd made Patrick swear he wouldn't tell their parents. He'd reluctantly agreed. Megan reminded him that she didn't pry into his love life, and he should grant her the same respect. She'd had him on that one, but he'd always kept an extra close eye on her.

Three years after Megan graduated from high school, her married lover divorced his wife and made an honest woman out of her. Patrick didn't care much for the guy, now a high school math teacher. He treated his sister and their three boys, Joseph, eight, Ryan, six, and Eric, who'd just celebrated his fourth birthday, extremely well. As long as Nathan continued to do so, Patrick would accept him as his brother-in-law, though not without reservations. Patrick took Megan aside once and told her if Nathan cheated on his first wife, the odds were good he'd cheat on her. They'd been married for twelve years. As far as Patrick knew, Nathan hadn't strayed.

Finally, there was Colleen, only a year younger than Patrick. Married to her high school sweetheart as soon as she'd graduated high school, she didn't bother with college. She'd always made it very clear to the entire family that becoming a mother was her life's desire. And she had. Almost one year to the day after she'd married Mark Cunningham, she delivered a healthy baby girl, Shannon Margaret. Eighteen months later, Abigail Caitlin came along. Colleen couldn't have been happier. Mark had accepted a job with Apple, and they had moved to Seattle. Their life together had been almost perfect until Shannon Margaret became ill. At seventeen, Shannon was in her senior year of high school doing all the exciting things seniors do. Mark and Colleen planned to surprise her with a bright red Hummer as a graduation gift. Shannon had been as much in love with Hummers as he was. A week before graduation, Shannon had complained about being extremely tired and short of breath. Colleen had laughed, telling Shannon her endless pre-graduation activities would wear out a triathlete. Shannon continued to complain over the next few days, but no one really paid much attention. Three nights before Shannon was due to graduate, Colleen found her in a heap on the bathroom floor, almost comatose. She'd called 911, and they'd rushed her to the hospital, where doctors were mystified until the results of her blood work came back from the lab. Shannon suffered from a rare and oftentimes deadly blood disorder, Thrombotic thrombocytopenic purpura. The doctors shortened it to TTP. Her platelet count had dropped to eight thousand, and her red blood count was so low, they'd had to give her red blood cells intravenously. A hematologist was called in. He'd explained to Colleen and Mark exactly what was happening inside Shannon's body. Something had gone wrong with her blood's ability to clot. Patrick was so shocked when he heard she was in the ICU, he didn't really remember the details. Suffice it to say, Shannon died on the very day she should have graduated from high school.

Patrick went through hell for several months, but it was nothing compared to what Colleen, Mark, and Abigail were still going through. No way could he ever withstand that kind of personal loss, hence his desire to stay single and kid-free. He knuckled away an unshed tear and parked the Hummer in his assigned parking place. He slid out of the driver's seat into the bitter early-morning air and jammed his hands in his pockets. His heavy boots crunched against the slush and ice as he walked across the parking lot to the employee entrance of Snow Zone. *Damn it's cold!*

Heavy snow was in the forecast for the weekend. He smiled. Fresh white powder would have skiers waiting in the lift lines for hours. The resort would be especially jam-packed that night as well. It was the night for the Christmas tree-lighting extravaganza. Patrick usually got a big kick out of it, but this year his heart wasn't really into the holiday spirit. His thoughts always returned to Colleen and Shannon. This would be the second year without her.

His parents had retired to Florida after Shannon's death. Claire remained in California, unmarried, a workaholic. She had a successful law firm that took up her every waking moment. She'd flown in for Shannon's memorial service and left immediately after. The rest of the family living in Colorado had gathered at the oldest sibling's house. Last Christmas, his four brothers, Connor, Aidan, Ronan, and Michael, all of whom had married only within the last ten years, and their wives and kids had made a half-hearted attempt at a celebration, for the sake of the kids, but none of their hearts were into the holidays either. Since they were an extremely close-knit Irish family, Shannon's loss had devastated them all. Shannon had been the first grandchild, the first niecc. Nothing would ever be the same again.

Patrick pushed all thoughts of sadness aside. There would be time for those memories later. Before opening the employee door, he scraped the ice and brown slush from his boots on the boot scraper beside the door. He could have gone in through the store's public entrance; he had keys and knew the security code, but he wanted to make a surprise visit. It was his way of checking up on his employees. They never knew when to expect him, kept them on their toes. Max didn't approve of this tactic but allowed it since Patrick ran the entire operation. He'd already spied dozens of early birds waiting patiently in their heated vehicles in the parking lot. Patrick hoped Candy Lee and Stephanie were prepared for the rush.

Entering through the back door, he was greeted by the pleasing scent of coffee and a hint of cinnamon. Before Stephanie or Candy Lee saw him, he made his way up and down the aisles, inspecting the shelves piled high with sweaters, hats, scarves, and a dozen other varieties of clothing that promised to keep their wearers warm. Personally, he never hit the slopes without wearing his Hot Chillys, long johns that truly stood up to the test. He saw that the Hot Chillys display was stocked in all colors and sizes for men, women, and children. Satisfied that there was enough stock to keep the shoppers shopping, Patrick weaved his way through the narrow aisles to the front of the shop. Stephanie and Candy Lee were both sipping from forest green mugs and munching on donuts.

Damn, what did they think this was? Snack time? They should be . . . working, not smiling and eating.

C'mon, Patrick, they have to eat!

He shook his head, hoping to clear his thoughts of any negativity. Today called for a positive attitude. Optimism, his mother always advised, when faced with negativity. Growing up, she'd taught him and his brothers and sisters that they were the masters of their lives, and always had the power to choose between optimism or pessimism. Since Shannon's death, more often than not, he'd chosen pessimism. Maybe it was time to turn over a new leaf? Wasn't Christmastime considered to be a time of goodwill and charity? With his mood suddenly shifting to buoyant while he watched Stephanie laugh as she conversed with Candy Lee, he decided he would choose to be optimistic that day. And it had nothing to do with the image in front of him either. At least that's what he wanted to believe. But deep down, he couldn't deny the simple joy just being in her presence gave him. He felt warm all over as he continued to watch and, yes, admire her. Any man would admire those long legs encased in tight black ski pants that accentuated every curve of her body. A moss-colored Hot Chillys thermal turtleneck clung attractively to her petite frame. She definitely had curves in all the right places. Add the warm brown eyes and hair the color of nutmeg, and Patrick couldn't find a single thing he didn't like about her physical appearance. Hell, he couldn't think of anything he didn't like about her period except for the fact that she was the mother of two young daughters. Amanda and Ashley were as sweet as sugarplums, too. They'd pounced all over him when Stephanie had introduced them. They were very much in need of a father, but he was *not* willing to play that role.

Before he had a chance to make his presence known, Stephanie spied him lingering in the center aisle opposite the front registers.

"Patrick, I had no idea you were coming in this early. Come and have some coffee and donuts before they're all gone. Candy Lee and I concluded that shopping makes you extremely hungry." She smiled at him as though he were the greatest thing since sliced bread. His heart flip-flopped, then did a backward somersault.

"No thanks. I'm only here for a minute. Just wanted to make sure you were prepared for the onslaught." Patrick crammed his hands in his pockets for fear he'd reach out to smooth the unruly curl that clung to Stephanie's peach-colored cheek.

Stephanie placed her mug on the counter and wiped her mouth with a paper napkin covered with snowmen and reindeer. "I think we're more than ready. Between the two of us, we should be able to handle the rush. If we get too swamped, Melanie said she would help out. She's bringing the girls over to ski today."

Patrick wasn't sure how to reply, so he just nodded. Damn this woman. She made him feel like an inexperienced teenager. All clumsy and unsure of himself. He hated the loss of control.

Stephanie stared at him, the smile leaving her face. "Is that all right? If not, I can tell her to forget it. She said she would stop in before they hit the slopes."

Patrick heard the words, but couldn't have repeated what they were if his life depended on it.

"Patrick! Are you listening to anything she's saying?" Candy Lee asked, her voice several octaves higher than normal.

He blinked his eyes, then shook his head. "Uh, yes, I was thinking."

Candy Lee, never one to mince words with Patrick and always getting away with it because she was not much younger than the age Shannon would've been had she lived, came out from behind the counter to stand beside him. She cupped his elbow in her small hand, guiding him to a stool behind the counter. She put a small finger to his lips. She poured coffee, a large portion of Half and Half, and three scoops of sugar into a white mug decorated with Santas. She plated three donuts from the box beneath the counter. A chocolate-covered glazed, a cream-filled, and a French cruller. "Get some sugar and caffeine into your system. You sound really stupid, Patrick. And I don't believe you were thinking either," she added, squinting her bright blue eyes into slits.

Patrick took a sip of the hot coffee, then took a huge bite of the chocolate-covered confection. Damn, maybe Candy Lee was onto something. This was decadent, almost pure bliss. "Stupid, huh?" he said, then finished off the rest of the donut.

"Well, yes. You have that *off* look on your face, you know, like you're *off* in another world or something," Candy Lee explained.

Patrick took a sip of coffee, then bit into the French cruller. He finished it off in three bites before attacking the cream-filled donut. He would have to spend hours on the slopes burning off all the sugary carbs he'd just consumed. When he finished, he wiped his mouth with one of the snowmen-and-reindeer napkins placed next to the pot of coffee. "Thanks for the compliment and the calories, kid. Stephanie, if you get in a bind, call my cell number. I'll send a Maximum Glide employee from the ski school to help out. I can't risk Melanie's getting hurt or injuring someone else."

Stephanie started to speak, but before she could utter a single word, Patrick spoke up. "It's company policy. Sorry."

"Of course, I understand, it's just that Melanie offered. I told her to stop by just in case." Stephanie swatted at the hair clinging to her cheek. "I doubt we'll need the extra help, but of course I will call you if we do." She swallowed, lifted her chin a notch higher, and met his gaze.

Avoiding her direct stare, Patrick glanced at the display of flavored lip balm on the counter for fear he'd give his feelings away.

Feelings? He wasn't going there. No how, no way!

Absorbed in a sudden rush of unwanted emotions, new and *unwanted* emotions, Patrick gave her a disparaging look. After all, she was nothing more than an employee. "I'll expect nothing less. Maximum Glide can't afford another costly mistake."

Much to his surprise, she showed no reaction to his comment. She simply turned her back to him as though he'd said nothing.

He hurried toward the door without another word said. Feeling like the idiot that he was, he started to return and offer an apology, then decided against it. He didn't want her to think he was sorry for his comment. He truly meant it. Maximum Glide was in the red. If he didn't pull off a financial miracle this year, they would all be out of jobs.

Chapter 3

Expert at hiding her emotions, Stephanie was too stunned to reply to Patrick's hateful comment. She'd spent years deflecting Glenn's insults. One would've thought she would be used to such verbal abuse. Too stunned to cry, not to mention how humiliated she was to have Candy Lee witness her being reprimanded, she swallowed back any thought of an outburst.

She tossed her Christmas napkin in the garbage can and downed the last of her now-cold coffee before turning to Candy Lee. It was all she could do to keep from commenting on what a jerk Patrick had acted like, but she knew it was best just to forget about it. And him. He was right. Sort of. She *had* cost the shop loads of money last year. There was no way she would repeat that mistake again this season. With a new sense of determination, Stephanie set out to prove just how wrong he was about her. She was quite capable of working as many hours as needed to see that Snow Zone turned a profit. She didn't care if she had to peddle their wares on the slopes.

As soon as the back door closed, alerting them to Patrick's departure, Candy Lee voiced her opinion. "He can be such a nitwit. I don't know why you let him talk to you like that. You need to speak up for yourself." She sprayed window cleaner on the glass-top counters. "If he doesn't think we're capable of doing the work, he should tell us straight up."

Stephanie thought he just had, but didn't bother saying so to Candy Lee. They had a busy day ahead of them. Whining and arguing would only put them both in a negative frame of mind. She was sure this was the last thing the Christmas shoppers wanted to encounter on the busiest day of the year. They wanted *holly-jolly-ho-ho-ho,* and she would give them *holly-jolly-ho-ho-ho* no matter what.

Wanting to discourage further talk of Patrick's behavior, Stephanie cleared her throat. "He's just doing his job. Forget about it because I intend to this very second."

Candy Lee shook her head. "Well, then you're a nicer person than I am. I don't even know why I work here; well, I need the extra cash but still . . . I was in the storage room the other day and overheard two guys that work the lifts talking about him. I guess Mr. O'Brien chewed them out after four people fell when they were getting off the lift at their checkpoints, which we all know isn't really anyone's fault," Candy Lee stated as she vigorously polished the glass-topped counters. "I'm pretty good on a pair of skis myself, and I still suck ice every now and then."

"Suck ice?" Stephanie inquired.

"Fall down, you know, suck ice," Candy Lee informed her.

Stephanie laughed. "No, I hadn't heard that term,

but do me a favor and try not to use it in front of the girls." They'd seen enough in their short lives. Stephanie was trying her best to make up for what they'd witnessed. She wanted to keep them innocent as long as possible.

"Sure," Candy Lee said. "Though they'll hear it soon enough on the slopes. Especially from the snowboarders. They always cuss and spit. It's so gross."

Stephanie gave a small laugh. "I've heard them more than once myself. I just want to keep the girls away from anything . . . off-color, at least for a while. Now"—Stephanie glanced at her watch—"let's lower the drawbridge and prepare for battle."

At precisely seven o'clock, Stephanie unlocked the main door, where a line of shoppers anxiously waited to spend their money. Stephanie said hello to those she knew, greeted others she didn't, then headed to the register, where she spent the next four hours ringing up ski jackets, ski pants, mittens, hats, and ski boots. It was almost lunchtime before they had a chance to take a break. Tallying up the morning sales in her head, Stephanie figured if this was any indication of how busy the season would be, not only would she be working overtime, she'd prove just how wrong Patrick was about her ability to manage the shop and turn a profit. Plus, she'd have a bit of extra cash, even after putting the down payment on her dream house in Placerville. She would use the extra money to purchase a new bedroom set for the girls.

They'd been without the basic comforts for most of their lives, and for this reason they were appreciative of any gift they received, no matter how large or small. They were good girls, and Stephanie found herself visualizing tucking them into a brand-spanking-new white-canopied bed in their new home. Plus she couldn't wait to see the look on their faces when she

announced they would be adopting one of the pups
sired by Ice-D. They'd begged for a pet for the past
two years, but Stephanie knew it wouldn't be fair to
the girls or an animal if she were to bring a pet home
to the small garage apartment. There was barely
enough room for the three of them as it was. As the
girls grew older, she knew they would want and need
their privacy. A new home with three bedrooms, not
to mention two bathrooms, would be pure heaven for
the three of them and a pet. Angry that she'd wasted
so much valuable time with Glenn, Stephanie figured
she had to make it up to the girls, and a home of their
own would be a good place for new beginnings.

Cheered by her thoughts, Stephanie felt a renewed
sense of purpose. She could manage her life at last,
but this time around it would be on her own terms.
She didn't need a man to take care of her. Look at
where that had gotten her. Actually, Glenn's jailbreak
was the catalyst that had sent her in search of a better
life. Stephanie had learned at an early age that life
wasn't always easy, but at thirty-two, she felt as
though she'd learned enough about life not to repeat
the mistake of allowing a man to have complete and
total control of her life. After her mother flew the
coop to parts unknown, when Stephanie was three,
she'd been sent to live with her mother's older sister,
Aunt Evelyn, who'd loved her like her own daughter.
While they hadn't had much in the way of material
things, Stephanie knew she was loved. Sadly, her aunt
had passed away the year she graduated from high
school. While grieving for the only mother figure
she'd ever known, Stephanie had allowed Glenn to
step in and control her every move. At first she'd enjoyed her newfound lack of responsibility as she'd
spent most of her life caring for Aunt Evelyn, who'd
been severely crippled with rheumatoid arthritis.

However, her independence was short-lived. She and Glenn married right after graduation; he started drinking, and within a year turned into an angry, bitter, controlling man. Having no outlet for his anger, he made Stephanie into his punching bag. And as they say, the rest is history. Though this time around, Stephanie was writing her own story.

Stephanie had a job to do in the here and now, so she pushed all negative thoughts of her past to that little dark corner of her mind, where they remained dormant most of the time.

"Why don't you take your lunch break now. We're staying open until seven tonight. This might be the only chance you'll have. Once the lifts are closed, I expect we'll be swamped."

Candy Lee looked at the Minnie Mouse watch on her wrist. "Okay. You want me to bring you something back? You have to eat, too," Candy Lee informed her in that all-knowing teenage way.

"Yes, that's why I brought my lunch with me. I knew I wouldn't have time to go to The Lodge for lunch today. Now, go on and get back here," Stephanie said, using her mothering tone.

Candy Lee grabbed her purse from beneath the counter, gave a quick salute, and raced out the back door. Stephanie watched her as she tore through the icy parking lot. Had she ever been that young and carefree? If she had, she couldn't pull up the memory. She had new memories to make, and this time around they'd be the kind she'd always dreamed of.

Wouldn't they?

Chapter 4

Melanie held a mitten-clad hand in each of hers. The slopes were always dangerously crowded the first day after Thanksgiving. If she let go of Ashley or Amanda, it would be very easy to lose sight of them. Stephanie had made sure to tell the girls to dress in their neon yellow ski suits; that way they would be easy to spot. Melanie glanced around her, seeing at least a dozen other young children dressed in the same neon yellow suits that her charges wore. *So much for sticking out like a sore thumb,* she thought. Melanie wouldn't let the girls get too far from her sight no matter what.

"Auntie M," Ashley said. Melanie laughed when Ashley called her by the new nickname they'd christened her with after she'd allowed them to watch *The Wizard of Oz* four times last week. "Can we ski on the blue trails today? *Please?* Uncle Max says we're as good as most of the older kids, and their parents let them ski the blue runs."

"Puhleeze," Amanda echoed.

"I guess so, but not by yourselves. I'll go with you," Melanie stated firmly. "There are a lot of skiers out today, so we have to be extra careful."

"Yeah, or we'll get hurt, right? And then Mommy will have to take us to the hospital, and we'll have to stay there cause she won't have enough money to pay the hospital bill, *right,* Auntie M?" Amanda crooned in a squeaky voice.

At five-foot-nine, Melanie had to stoop in order to be at eye level with both girls. She wanted to wrap them both in her arms and tell them she would never allow that to happen. And she had the resources to keep that pledge, having inherited millions from her grandparents. Nor would her wealthy parents allow it. But Melanie knew how badly Stephanie wanted to make her way in the world on her own, so Melanie had carefully refrained from even hinting at her own financial situation.

Stephanie had told her more than once about her life with Glenn. Determined to provide for her children, Stephanie had rules she'd explained to Melanie when she'd first taken the job, and one of those rules was no financial help, no loans, no expensive gifts. Two years ago, Melanie's parents, longtime supporters of Grace's work with battered women at Hope House, had reduced the rent to something that Stephanie could afford. And to the best of Melanie's knowledge, no one, including Grace, had ever breathed a word of this to Stephanie.

Melanie smiled at both girls. "Well, we won't have to worry about that because you're both such good little skiers, I can't even imagine either of you falling down, let alone getting hurt so badly that you would have to go to the hospital. So let's not even think about that. How about the three of us take the lift up to Sugar Hill, ski to Snow Zone where we'll stop in and see your mom, then maybe grab a cup of hot chocolate at The Lodge?"

Both girls nodded in agreement.

They were both worrywarts, something Melanie wished she could change, but time more than anything else would help to ease the fear and anxiety both girls tended to feel. Again, given their start in life, it was a miracle they hadn't suffered anything more than becoming overly cautious where their mother was concerned. Melanie wasn't sure she would've been able to cope at such a young age had her life been as tragic as theirs had been.

"Are you taking us to the Christmas tree lighting tonight, too?" Amanda asked. "Mommy says it's the highlight of the start of the holiday season. What's that mean?"

Ashley looked at Melanie with a knowing smile. "You want me to tell her?"

"Absolutely," Melanie said, bending over to tighten the hooks on her ski boots.

Ashley pursed her lips, moved them from side to side as though she were contemplating the best answer. "Well, it's kinda like the first day of school when the teacher tells the class what she wants us to learn that year, only the Christmas season is short and a lot more fun." She looked at Melanie for confirmation.

Grinning at the complete and total simplicity of Ashley's explanation, Melanie stated, "I couldn't have said it better myself."

"It's sorta like a new beginning, right, Auntie M?" Ashley said.

She continued to be amazed by the girls' perception. They were both exceptionally intelligent for their ages. Melanie knew Stephanie took great pride in her children's education. Many times Melanie had stopped by their apartment only to find the three of them gathered at the kitchen table with a pile of books in front of them studying anything and everything, ranging from science to geography.

"That's exactly what it is," Melanie agreed.

"Then let's go. I wanna ride the lift now. Can I sit in the middle?" Amanda asked.

Melanie stood up to her full height, gazed to her left, where she saw that the lift lines were getting longer by the minute. If they were lucky, they'd have just enough time for one run before stopping in to see Stephanie. "Let's do our safety check first." Melanie had spent most of her life on the slopes but never took her skill or that of the girls for granted. A loose boot buckle or a stray article of clothing could cause a lifetime disability. Melanie wasn't going to allow the girls to get hurt on her watch. No way. They went through their usual routine.

First, they checked to make sure they had all the basics covered. Skis and boots were fastened properly. Pole straps were checked. Helmets and goggles were secure. Gloves were on properly. Since the season was predicted to be one of the coldest on record, Melanie had given the girls foot and hand warmers to place inside their gloves and boots, plus she now put an extra set of each in the inside zippered pocket of their ski jackets. Each of them had a tube of cherry-flavored lip balm in her pocket, along with a granola bar. As an added precaution, Melanie always made sure Ashley kept a pack of waterproof matches inside her jacket. One never knew. At ten, Ashley had been taught a few basic survival skills. Melanie was sure Ashley would never need them as long as she was around, but that was part of being prepared. One must always prepare for the unexpected.

"Sunscreen on our faces, and we're good to go," Melanie said, removing a small tube of sunscreen from her pocket. She made quick work of slathering their faces with the cream before readjusting their helmets and goggles. "Now remember, I'm in the rear, and you two always stay in front of me. If you need to stop and rest, just stop at the side of the run that faces away from the mountain, okay?"

"Okay," the girls parroted.

Melanie followed close behind the girls as they skied to the long lift lines. Dozens of skiers dressed in every color of the rainbow swished in and out of the lanes, racing to get to the front of the lift line. Melanie kept her eyes on the girls as they carefully maneuvered toward the chairlifts. They were moving surprisingly fast today considering it was the first official day of the Christmas season. Throngs of skiers dotted the mountainside, like the lofty evergreens that flanked the trails.

Above, the skies were heavy with slate gray clouds. The wind was frigid, the conditions perfect for a snowstorm. Melanie wanted to take the girls up for at least one run since the weather might not cooperate later in the day. The forecast called for snow, a necessity for all skiers and snowboarders, but Melanie didn't like the looks of the clouds looming above the mountaintops. Since the snowfall wasn't predicted until later in the afternoon, she reasoned they should have time for at least one decent run.

When it was their turn at the chairlift, the trio slid into position directly behind the bold red line, and gripped their ski poles in their left hands as they'd been taught while looking behind them to see the chairlift as it slowed to allow them to take a seat. Once seated with the safety bar down, Melanie commented, "You two are really getting to be pros at this.

It took me forever to learn how to load up without falling."

Since they were going on the blue runs, their ride was longer than normal. It took almost seven minutes for the ski lift to arrive at their designated stop. During the ride up, both girls chatted nonstop, telling her what they hoped Santa would bring them for Christmas. They'd told her about the wall plaques they had made for their mom in art class, and last but not least, they said that their "Aunt Grace" wanted to introduce Melanie to her brother, Bryce.

She couldn't help but blush. She'd seen Bryce at Maximum Glide on more than one occasion. He was the epitome of a true hunk. Melanie thought he fit the image of a ski bum more so than that of a college professor. Lucky for her, they arrived at their stop in time to provide her with an excuse not to answer. But she knew these little mischief makers, and this wouldn't be the last of that conversation. They were relentless when it came to questioning why she wasn't married and didn't have children of her own.

Both girls exited the lift chair with ease, skiing away as fast as possible so as not to block the next group of skiers preparing to exit the lift.

The particular area on the mountain where Melanie was taking them had an elevation closer to thirteen thousand than twelve thousand feet. The air was thin at that altitude, making one almost gasp for oxygen. The temperature was several degrees lower than at the base of the mountain. Wind gusts at this height caused the majestic towering evergreen tops to sway from side to side, their movements producing a soft whisper, a slow dance, with the bone-chilling winds supplying a soft whistle as their music.

Melanie skied to where the girls were waiting. "Are you both ready?" she asked.

Again, they nodded their helmet-covered heads.
Melanie motioned with her gloved hand for them
to begin their descent. They pushed off like two little
thoroughbreds, traversing downward without getting
too close to the edge of the mountainside. Melanie
trailed behind them for several minutes before the run
led to a bowl of intersections leading to three different areas on the mountain. One ski lift would take
them to the very top of the mountain, where they
would find the double black diamond runs. The second lift would take them to the opposite side of the
mountain, where the terrain park allowed freestylers
and snowboarders to hone their acrobatic skills on
half-pipes, rails, ramps, and tables. The third lift led to
the mogul runs, for those hardy souls brave enough to
tackle the minimounds of packed snow that dipped
to the bottom of the mountain at a ninety-degree
angle. The girls knew that they were supposed to wait
for her at the big blue sign directing them back to lift
number one at the base of the mountain.

She weaved in and out of the groups of skiers,
passed a friend who was on the ski patrol. When she
reached the intersection, she searched for the two
neon yellow ski suits. Seeing a small group gathered
at their appointed sign, Melanie made quick work of
poling over to get the girls. When she arrived, she was
a bit surprised to find that neither of the two kids
wearing yellow neon ski suits was Ashley or Amanda.
She pushed off and circled the bowl. Seeing that there
were no pint-sized girls wearing yellow suits, she
stopped once again and scanned the area around her.
Then she skied slowly around the perimeter of the
bowl once again, and she thoroughly searched the
sides of the run, where a grove of evergreens flanked
the trail. Maybe they'd fallen, hit a small snowdrift, or
something, she thought.

Melanie jammed her poles into the snow behind her, trying to pick up speed on the flat terrain. She went from side to side, looking in every possible direction, every gully, and even went off trail, thinking one of the girls might have gone to the woods looking for a bit of privacy in order to use the restroom. They'd done this before, and while Melanie didn't approve of it, sometimes Mother Nature's call had to be answered no matter what. After searching for fifteen minutes, Melanie had a sneaky feeling the girls had decided to go off on their own. This was not good. Not at all. If she didn't locate the girls at the end of the run, she'd have to contact the ski patrol and explain the situation.

What was even worse, she'd have to explain to Stephanie that she'd lost her children.

Chapter 5

Candy Lee returned from lunch in the nick of time. Stephanie had managed to eat a few bites of her turkey sandwich between customers. She'd thought the lunch hour would be quiet, but she'd been wrong again. She'd been so bombarded with customers, she hadn't had time to think. Good thing Patrick wasn't there to witness her poor planning. She took a deep breath, exhaled, and smiled at a young mother waiting in line with two small children clinging to her legs. Amanda still did that at times. Stephanie didn't mind, as she wanted to keep the girls sheltered for as long as she could given that the first years of their lives had been plagued by violence and fear.

She looked at her watch. It was almost one o'-clock. Melanie had promised to bring the girls by. Stephanie felt a shiver of alarm run up her spine but remembered this was Black Friday. The lift lines were probably as busy as she was. If they weren't here in half an hour or so, she'd call Melanie's cell to check on them. Both girls were natural-born skiers, and

Stephanie knew from experience that once they were out on the slopes, it was quite a task to get them to stop for anything. Poor Melanie. She'd take her to dinner and a movie when the holidays were over. Just the two of them. They needed a girls' night out anyway. Maybe she'd invite Grace to join them.

So caught up with the customers coming in and out purchasing everything from lip balm to ski boots, Stephanie glanced at her watch again and was shocked to see that it was already after two o'clock. Worry caused her brow to furrow, but if there was a problem, Melanie knew to call her at the shop. Stephanie continued to ring up sales while Candy Lee restocked and refolded the pile of sweaters on the half-price table. If sales kept up like this, Stephanie might have to call Patrick and take advantage of his offer to send another Maximum Glide employee to her rescue. It was the last thing she wanted to do, but she and Candy Lee could only stretch themselves so thin. Dreading the thought, she looked up as Melanie entered the shop and hurried to the back of the store. Her cheeks were reddened from the wind, her long blond braid hung haphazardly down her back, and her normal cheerful smile was nowhere to be seen. *Emergency potty break,* Stephanie thought as she walked to the back of the store.

"I wondered what happened to you girls. I was about to worry," Stephanie said. "Where are the girls? I bet they're freezing." As Stephanie was about to turn around and head for the entrance to tell her daughters to come inside and warm up, Melanie grabbed her arm and prevented her from taking another step.

"Melanie!" Stephanie shrieked. "What's wrong? Where are the girls?"

Melanie looked down at the floor, where puddles of water had pooled around her ski boots. She shook her head from side to side, then looked Stephanie squarely in the face. "I was hoping they would be here with you. I've spent the past two hours looking for them."

Stephanie felt her heart plummet to her feet and back, then lodge in the back of her throat. She tried to speak but was unable to utter a single word. She shook her head, hoping she'd just imagined what Melanie had said, but the look on her babysitter's face told her she'd heard correctly.

Glenn? It couldn't be!

Melanie must have read her mind. "They're on this mountain somewhere skiing, I'm sure of it; no way did their dad bust out of jail. They were so excited about going on the blue run, I think they simply forgot to wait for me at the appointed area. I saw them ski all the way down, then I lost sight of them for what couldn't have been more than two or three minutes. By the time I got to the meeting point, they were nowhere to be found."

Stephanie felt as though she would simply die. Just die and be done with it. But she wasn't a quitter, especially where her children were concerned. She'd been this route before and would do whatever she had to do to protect her daughters. She wanted to strangle Melanie, but her anger would have to wait. She had to find her children before it was too late. Just minutes ago, she'd heard a snow report, and it didn't sound good. She'd heard a few customers saying they'd heard the lifts were going to close early if the snow report held true.

Springing into action, Stephanie raced to the office, where she grabbed her old skis, poles, and boots. She knew this mountain like the back of her hand. If her girls were lost, she wasn't going to wait around. She was going to find them no matter how long it took. She raced out of the office, shouting to Candy Lee over her shoulder. "There's an emergency. Call Patrick and tell him to send someone over to help you. The girls are lost on the mountain!"

Melanie raced after her. "Stephanie, you can't go out in this weather. The storm is moving in faster than the forecasters anticipated. I've contacted the ski patrol, and they're all out searching for them. They'll need their mother once they're found."

As Stephanie raced out the back door to the snowy parking area, she stopped to lay her skis down on the crusted snow on the path that would lead her to the lifts. She shot a quick glance at Melanie and saw thick tears streaming down her face and knew she was as concerned for the girls' safety as she was. She leaned in to give her a quick hug. "I can't *not* search for them, Melanie. They're all I have," Stephanie said as she buckled her ski boots and slid her boots into the skis' binding. After she heard the required click letting her know her boots were fitted securely into her skis, she pushed away from Melanie, heading to the lift. She poled as fast as she could through the clumps of ice and brown slush. An injury was the last thing she needed.

Arriving at lift number one, Stephanie practically soared to the chair, where she was met by a young boy of no more than eighteen. She'd seen him around but couldn't recall his name.

"We're closing the lifts. Sorry," he said as he stood in front of the chair Stephanie was preparing to get on.

She shook her head. "No, I have to get up there. My girls are lost. The ski patrol is looking for them now." Stephanie saw the look of indecision on the boy's face. "Look, I won't tell anyone you let me ride up to the mountain in these conditions. I have to get

up there, please!" Stephanie shouted. Giant flakes of
snow scattered across her cheeks as she stared at the
boy. Apparently he decided her request was worth the
risk because he went inside his minibooth, and the
chair began to move slowly.

A million thoughts went through her mind as the
lift made its climb to the top of the mountain. What if
they couldn't find the girls in time? With the weather
conditions worsening by the minute, they wouldn't
last long in this cold. Stephanie knew Ashley understood basic survival skills, as she'd insisted that Ashley take a junior mountain-survival class last year
when the child had pleaded with her, telling Stephanie she was old enough to ski the green runs alone.
They'd compromised. Ashley took the class and was
allowed to ski certain green runs, but she had to take
Stephanie's cell phone with her. Why hadn't she
thought to get the girls phones of their own? They
could have called for help. The reception on the
mountain was excellent, so there wasn't an issue
about lack of coverage. Why in the world hadn't she
provided both girls with such a necessity? She remembered when she first arrived at Hope House.
Grace had insisted she take a cell phone, saying she
gave them to all the women at Hope House just in
case they needed to dial 911. Why, why, *why* had she
been so irresponsible? Money, she thought as she
shivered in the bone-chilling air. She'd been so intent
on giving the girls a home of their own, she'd lost
sight of their other wants and needs. Ashley had
asked for a cell phone months ago, and Stephanie had
dismissed it, telling her she was too young for a
phone of her own, saying it was an added expense that
she didn't need. How she wished she'd given in! As
they say, hindsight is twenty-twenty. Little good it did
her to dwell on what she should've done. Now all she

wanted was to find both of her daughters safe and sound. She gave a silent prayer. *Please let them be safe. I'll equip them both with GPS if I find them safe and unharmed.*

The lift came to a slow stop at the top of the mountain. Stephanie practically jumped out of the chair. She whipped down the trail, making the twists and turns from memory, as the snow was coming down heavier by the minute. She wiped her hand across her goggles just in time to get a decent look at the bowl where Melanie had last seen the girls. She knew the girls would never attempt to ski a black diamond trail, so she followed Melanie's route, hoping and *praying* that she would magically find her girls hiding behind a snowdrift, visible only to her. She'd bring them back to the Snow Zone, where they'd sip hot chocolate, warm their hands with the chemical hand warmers they sold at the shop, all the while relaying to Candy Lee how brave they had been. If only, Stephanie thought as she traversed down the last quarter mile of the run, with still no sign of her children. She stopped every few minutes to call out their names, only to have her voice drowned out by the turbulent sound of the wind as it whipped through the towering evergreens.

Tears stung her eyes, freezing against her windburned cheeks as she continued to ski in areas that she knew were off-limits for the girls, but at this point she'd have skied down Mount Everest blindfolded if she thought it would bring her girls back. The late-afternoon sky was overcast, the light flat and indistinct, the snowfall heavy and thick, making visibility almost nil. These were blizzard conditions, Stephanie thought. Why hadn't she paid closer attention to the weather forecast? Why had she even allowed the girls on the slopes, knowing how packed they would be?

She was stupid, her skill as a parent equivalent to that of a teenage babysitter. Her throat was dry, and her heart pounded in her chest as she used every ounce of energy she had left to pole her way back to the lift. She'd seen the chairs as they hung suspended from the heavy-duty cables, empty of passengers. Knowing the lifts were closed wasn't going to stop her. She'd borrow a snowmobile from the ski patrol. She was not leaving this mountain until she found Amanda and Ashley.

Alive. The word skittered through her brain. *Alive. Alive. Alive.* From out of nowhere, Stephanie was filled with a complete and utter sense of peace and well-being. Without knowing why, she suddenly knew her girls were alive. And not only were they alive, but they were fine.

Somewhat shocked by the epiphany she'd just experienced, she debated her next move. With the temperature dropping into negative numbers, Stephanie stopped in the middle of the storm, took a deep breath, and prayed for a higher power to guide her in the right direction. As though controlled by an outside force, she pointed her ski tips in the direction of Snow Zone, where she saw a crowd gathered outside its doors. Briefly, she wondered how anyone could possibly shop when her girls were missing, but then common sense took over. These people had no idea where her children were. For that matter, Stephanie was sure they didn't have a clue about her or her life. And why should they? She was nothing more than a shop manager who couldn't seem to keep tabs on two small children.

Beyond cold and knowing she needed to check in with the ski patrol, Stephanie skied as far as the snow allowed before she stopped to remove her skis, leaving them in the middle of the parking lot. Not wanting to disturb the crowd gathered at the front door, she used the employee entrance. Inside, she hurried to her office, where she dialed the emergency number for the ski patrol. The line rang a dozen times before a recorded message told her to dial 911 if this was a true emergency. What the heck? Wasn't someone supposed to be there manning the phones in case of an emergency? Wasn't that the entire point of having a ski patrol? Were they out searching for the girls? She hit the END button on the phone, then saw her black leather, fur lined boots, which she'd tossed under her desk. She quickly pulled off her ski boots, changed out of her damp socks into a dry pair, and crammed her feet into her warm boots before heading to the front of the store, where dozens of people stood in a semicircle. She would ask Candy Lee if she'd heard anything, then she would go to the ski patrol office to see if there was anyone there with any news of the girls. This was beyond a nightmare. The girls should be enjoying their Christmas vacation. They'd been so excited about tonight's tree-lighting ceremony. How could a day that started out so perfect turn into one so horrid? It actually caused her physical pain to think beyond the *what ifs* and the *if onlys*. She couldn't even imagine life without her children.

She wouldn't go there! *She couldn't.*

Stephanie hurried to the front of the store, where she found Candy Lee and Melanie . . . *smiling.*

How could they even think about smiling at a time like this? She was about to ask that very question when she saw what or rather whom they were smiling at.

Her girls.

Sipping cups of hot chocolate.

Chapter 6

Stephanie was momentarily stunned when she saw Amanda and Ashley seated behind the counter. "Thank goodness you're both okay! What happened? Where, who?" Stephanie cried out. She glanced around her, only to discover Patrick, along with several Maximum Glide employees, grinning from ear to ear. Apparently the two mischief makers had a story to tell.

Overwhelmed by the sheer relief of seeing her daughters safe and sound, Stephanie forced her way behind the counter. Not caring that she was being watched by several dozen strangers, she wrapped an arm around each of her daughters. Tears of relief streamed down her face, and her heart sang with delight as she breathed in the scent she knew and loved so well. The sweet smell of Johnson's Baby Shampoo clung to their long, dark hair. Stephanie gloried in the moment as she recalled her vision of her daughters being alive and well. It had happened exactly as she knew it would. She would leave it at that. After all, it was Christmas, and she still believed in miracles.

Candy Lee handed her a wad of tissues along with a piping-hot mug of cocoa. "You're gonna need this," she said.

Stephanie wiped the tears from her eyes, then took a sip of her drink. "Okay, now I think it's time I heard exactly what happened out on that mountain today."

"Patrick saved us, Mommy! He really did, then he cried," Amanda said. "Right, Ashley?"

Those were the last words Stephanie expected to hear. She caught Patrick's gaze across the group that had gathered around the girls. He smiled. Sort of. Joy bubbled up inside her like an overflowing fountain. She smiled back.

"I don't think he was crying. I think it was just the cold air," Ashley stated matter-of-factly in the way that only a ten-year-old can.

Patrick edged through the crowd, stopping when he reached the girls. "Why don't you tell your mother what happened out on that mountain today. I think she'll be very proud of you two," he added. "And it might help to keep you both out of trouble," he went on, grinning from ear to ear.

Amanda spoke up, "Are we in trouble? I sure hope not 'cause I still want to go to that tree-lighting thing. We can still go, right, Mommy?"

Using a firm-yet-gentle tone, Stephanie explained, "A lot of people were worried about you two today. Right now, I want to know what happened, then we will think about the Christmas tree lighting."

Ashley started to speak, then hesitated as the crowd gathered closer. Suddenly, she seemed bashful, almost as though she were afraid.

Patrick observed her hesitancy. In a boisterous

voice, he spoke directly to the group. "I think Ashley feels a bit overwhelmed. If you're not here to shop, why don't we give the little lady a few minutes with her mother. As most of you know, these children have been through quite an ordeal." Patrick paused as he waited for the crowd to disperse. At least two dozen people left the shop, but not before wishing the girls good luck and congratulating them on a job well-done. The remaining few were Maximum Glide employees. Patrick turned to Stephanie. "If you don't mind, a few of my employees would like to stay and hear the rest of the story since they were part of the search party."

Stephanie looked at Ashley. "Only if you're okay with this?" If she didn't find out soon what her daughters had been involved in, she would take them to her office, where they could have a few moments of privacy.

"I'm okay with it, Mom," Ashley replied.

"Then spill the beans because I don't think I can wait another minute. I've been beside myself with worry the past hour," Stephanie said, in hopes that this would hurry along what was becoming quite a lengthy process.

"We were waiting for Melanie at the sign, but then me and Amanda heard this really loud crying sound. It was by that building where they keep those giant machines that smooth out the snow." Ashley smiled. "Then we just followed the crying. It was inside the building, so we weren't really cold, but Amanda had to use the potty in the corner."

"And there wasn't anyplace to wash my hands either, so I just . . . didn't," Amanda offered.

Laughter pealed from the employees as they listened.

"Go on," Stephanie encouraged.

"We heard where the crying noise came from." Ashley looked at Patrick. "She's gonna be okay, right?"

"Thanks to you and your sister she is," Patrick said. "Now don't keep your mom waiting any longer."

"Once we were inside the building, we just followed the cries. And that's when we found the mommy dog. She was so sad, her eyes had that look you know? So we just waited for her to stop crying, but then I saw a little baby puppy, and there was another one that was trying to . . . get out of the mommy's belly. That's why she was crying 'cause it was hurting her so bad. Amanda covered the baby pup up with her ski jacket."

"And I rubbed her head, too," Amanda informed them.

Ashley laughed at her little sister. "And the puppy was fine. But the mommy was still crying, and that's when I helped her out, sort of."

Stephanie wasn't sure what was coming next, but something told her it was about to make her day.

"I watched those little tiger cubs on Animal Planet. That man helped take the cubs out with his hands, so I just did what he did, and another puppy came out, and the mommy stopped crying. She licked the puppy, and we gave her our granola bars. Amanda and me melted some snow and gave it to her to drink. So once the mommy had both of her pups, she just licked 'em, then she fed 'em. We put our jackets on them, so they wouldn't freeze. I wanted to leave to find Melanie so she could help us with the dogs, but when I peeked out of the shed, I didn't see her anywhere. The snow was really pouring out of the sky by then. And I remembered what I learned in my survival class. They taught us to stay where there was shelter, and, well, that's what we did." Ashley told the story as if it were something a ten and seven-year-old did every day.

The employees applauded loudly, some calling out to Ashley "Way to go!" "You're a hero!" "You can ski with me anytime!"

Ashley appeared surprised by all the attention, so she just smiled as some of the employees stopped to give her a hug before they left. Stephanie watched in amazement as her daughter accepted their thanks in stride as though this were a normal, everyday event. Stephanie wasn't sure exactly what to think right then. How was it possible that her ten-year-old daughter had delivered a puppy? And not only that, she remembered what to do in an emergency situation while in a snowstorm. Tears pooled once again. She was extremely proud of both girls for using their heads in this situation when most children their age wouldn't have had a clue as to what to do. And where and how did Patrick fit into the picture?

"I can't tell you how proud I am of you both. I'm sure the dog was grateful you two showed up when you did, but that still doesn't get either of you off the hook for not waiting for Melanie. She was worried about you, and so was I. You both know how I feel about knowing where you are at all times, right?"

The girls nodded in unison.

"But what about helping others? Didn't you tell us that's what good, decent people do?" Ashley asked, a puzzled look on her face.

Oh boy. Stephanie didn't think now was the time to get into the moral of this lesson. She would wait until they were home, where they could discuss this in private. For the moment, she was simply relieved that they were alive and didn't seem to be fazed in the least by their experience.

Stephanie needed to know Patrick's role in finding her daughters. Since it didn't appear as though he wanted to tell his side of the story, she turned to face him. For a second, she was flustered. He was so sexy, with his windblown raven black hair just a shade too long. And those blue eyes. Well she knew she could drown in them if given the opportunity, but it wasn't the time. "How did you find the girls? And before you say anything, let me say thank you."

Patrick chuckled. "It was by sheer luck, trust me. When Candy Lee called me and told me they were missing, and with the storm worsening by the minute, I didn't want to take a chance on using the snowmobiles. I took the lift up to the garage, where we store the Snow Cats. I found them there caring for the dogs. I loaded the pups and the girls into the cab, and brought them here before dropping the dogs off with a friend of mine who's a veterinarian. I stopped back by to make sure you'd found them. End of story."

"I can't thank you enough. I was beside myself with worry," Stephanie said, then stopped. "I know you don't have children, so you probably haven't a clue what it feels like knowing you might not see them again, so thanks, Patrick. You can't imagine how much this means to me."

"As long as you don't get any funny ideas about the future," he said.

Shock at his remark yielded quickly to anger. Not caring that he was her boss, and not caring that he was the man who'd just saved her daughters from being stuck out in a blizzard, Stephanie found she was practically breathless with rage. How dare he? And in front of her daughters, Candy Lee, and Melanie! She swallowed the vile words she wanted to sling at him before she made a fool of herself. Taking a breath, as much as she was able to, Stephanie spoke, letting her eyes convey the outrage and fury she felt. "Mr. O'Brien, trust me, any 'funny ideas' I may have had about you have been completely erased from my memory. If you don't mind, I'm going to take my girls home so they can change their clothes, then we're going to the Christmas tree lighting." She walked to the front of the store, where she flipped the OPEN sign to CLOSED.

"You can't do that! We've got two more hours before it's time to close up shop. In spite of what you may think, there are people still out there who might want to visit the shop before they call it a day. You can't just leave. There is money to be made, and I expect you to stay here and do your job. Or else," he added.

Knowing Patrick had about as much tact as a rattlesnake didn't excuse his smart-ass comments, and for once in her life, Stephanie refused to allow a man to browbeat her into submitting to his demands. Without giving it another thought, she shot back, "Or else what?"

She knew her remark caught him off guard just by looking at him. His nostrils flared like those of an angry stallion. She was familiar with Patrick's reputation as a tough and demanding boss, but that didn't prepare her for the words that spewed from his mouth.

He rubbed the dark stubble on his chin and lowered his voice. Standing as close to her as possible, he said, "Or else this. How about you take the next four weeks off work. Spend some quality time with your children."

Stephanie felt the blood rush to her head, settling in her temples only to pound like a jackhammer.

Before she even had a chance to respond, Patrick leaned next to her, and whispered in her ear, "Without pay."

Chapter 7

As though she were on autopilot, Stephanie hastily took her daughters' hands and practically pulled them off the stools they were sitting on as she raced to her office. Rage consumed her, then the feeling left as quickly as it came, humiliation coming in its stead. She'd lost all her wind, all of her spark, in less than a few seconds. Like a deflating hot air balloon, every emotion, every word, every thought drifted out with each exhalation.

She removed her purse from a bottom drawer and grabbed her car keys from a hook on the wall. She quickly scanned the small space, searching for anything of value she might be leaving behind. Fortunately, her pride was visible only to her.

"What just happened out there?" Melanie whispered.

Stephanie shook her head. "Not now. I have to get out of here."

"You want me to take the girls?" Melanie asked. Realizing the enormity behind the innocent comment, Melanie swallowed. "I mean I can take them to the Christmas tree lighting with you, help out."

"Thanks, but I'd like to spend the evening with just the girls. I'm sorry, it's not you, it's . . ." She looked down the hall at the front of the store, where Patrick could be seen bossing Candy Lee around.

Melanie followed her gaze. "I see. Then I'll just go on. You call if you need me for anything, no matter what, okay?"

Melanie's words jolted her back to reality, the reality that she really did need a friend right now. "No, don't, I mean don't go off by yourself. Come with us to the Christmas tree lighting. I think I might need a friend tonight." There, she'd said it. She'd actually taken Grace's advice. When you need help, a friend, a hug, ask for it.

Melanie instantly brightened. "I was hoping you'd say that. I don't want you and the girls to be all alone tonight."

Stephanie nodded, then walked to the employee exit, Amanda and Ashley trailing behind. "You want to ride with us?" Stephanie asked as she stepped out into the frigid evening air. Snowflakes swirled in the bluish glow beneath the lights in the parking lot. Icy wind whipped the ends of her hair as she walked across the almost empty lot to her car, a car in such pitiful condition, it almost made her smile. She'd scrimped and saved for three long months so that she could have a car of her own. She and the girls used the public bus system, but the buses didn't take them through the drive-thru at McDonald's, nor would a bus be there when they had the sudden urge to go out for ice cream. She'd been so proud of herself when she bought the car, her first major purchase with money she'd earned on her own. But as she fumbled through her pockets for the keys she'd placed there minutes ago, she saw the vehicle for what it really was. An almost-twenty-year-old hunk of junk just barely making it. Sort of like me, she thought as she unlocked the back door for the girls.

Surprisingly, neither girl had uttered a word since they'd witnessed Patrick whisper those harsh words to her. Then it hit her! They weren't talking because they were *afraid!* Even though they hadn't actually heard his words, they knew their import from the way in which she was behaving. How could she be so blind? They'd spent so many years living on pins and needles with their father that it was second nature for them to behave this way when they saw a man and a woman together who didn't appear to be on the best of terms!

For this, she was mad. Madder than she'd been in a very, very long time. Anger pulsed through her veins, throbbing with each thought that raced through her head. Thankful no one could read her mind, she took another deep breath before getting behind the wheel. It wouldn't do for her to be distracted in this weather, especially with the girls in the car. She looked in her rearview mirror. "Are your seat belts fastened?"

They nodded.

Melanie slid into the passenger seat, and Stephanie was glad she'd invited her, or rather that she'd accepted Melanie's offer to come along. The younger woman reached across the seat and clasped Stephanie's cold hand with her gloved hand. "We can talk later," Melanie said.

Stephanie gave a slight nod.

"Let's get these future veterinarians home so they can change clothes. Then I think we should all go out for pizza after the Christmas tree lighting." Stephanie glanced in the rearview mirror again. Both girls were smiling, and in that very second all was right in her world.

As she pulled out of the parking lot, Stephanie's thoughts drifted to the enormity of what had just taken place at Snow Zone. This was the worst time in the world for it to happen, but she'd try and put it out of her mind for the rest of the evening. She owed it to the girls to at least try to act as though everything were normal. It wouldn't be hard, as she was an expert at that type of behavior.

Amanda was the one who broke the silence. "Mommy, can we go to Burger King instead of having pizza?"

Kids, Stephanie thought as she carefully guided her old Ford down the narrow road that led off the mountain. "I think you should ask your sister."

"So do ya?" Amanda asked Ashley.

"Mommy, tell her she needs to speak in complete sentences. When you're in fourth grade, Mrs. Yost won't allow you to speak that way if you're in her class. Right, Mom?"

"I suppose that's true. But you didn't answer Amanda's question," Stephanie said in a teasing tone, amazed that she could still banter back and forth with her girls given the dire situation Patrick O'Brien had just put her in.

"Burger King is fine, but the only reason Amanda wants to go there is so she can get that Dora the Explorer toy they're putting in the kids' meals," Ashley explained. "She's too big for that stuff."

"And you're too big to sleep with that crummy old rabbit that you've had forever. Right, Mommy?" Amanda asked. She was at the age where she needed her mother's approval for almost everything she said. Most of the time, it was funny, but at that moment,

Stephanie was trying to drive carefully in near-blizzard conditions, and it wasn't funny.

Melanie leaned over the front seat. "Let's allow your mom to concentrate on her driving. Okay, girls? The roads are very slippery right now."

"Is that right, Mommy?" Amanda asked.

Stephanie couldn't help but laugh. "Yes, Melanie is right. How about we play the quiet game until we get home. Whoever wins gets a double-dipped chocolate-covered ice-cream cone."

She was met with silence. She smiled at Melanie. "Both of them always win this game," Stephanie explained.

She knew the girls wanted to talk, but they were also very competitive. They'd bite their tongues if they had to.

The rest of the drive to the garage apartment was made in silence. Stephanie wanted to enjoy her night with the girls because, from the look of things, it might be a while before she had a free night. Since she was out of a job, she would have to hustle to find something so late in the season. While she had her savings for her down payment on the house, she didn't want to dip into them unless she absolutely had to. She still had high hopes of giving the girls a home of their own for Christmas. She might have to sacrifice the white canopied bed, but that would be okay, as long as they had a home of their own.

Stephanie parked the Ford Taurus next to the outside stairs that led up to their apartment. The girls knew the rules of the quiet game. Once they were inside the house, they could talk all they wanted. Both shot up the stairs like bolts of lightning.

"I think the quiet game is about to officially end," Melanie said as she waited for Stephanie to unlock the door. Both girls barreled through the door.

"I am not too big to sleep with my bunny rabbit. Mommy said she slept with a stuffed Tasmanian Devil until she was fourteen, so there!" Ashley said in a huff.

"Well, then, it's okay if I want the Dora Explorer prize in the kids' meal."

In response, Ashley rubbed Amanda's shoulder. "I guess it's okay. I was just teasin' with you anyway. I like Dora, too, just don't tell anyone at school. Pinkie promise?" Ashley asked.

Both girls locked their pinkies together, then shook their hands. "Okay, so let's go change. I want to see the tree, but first I want something to eat. We never had lunch today," Ashley explained to her mother.

"I'm sorry. We'll make up for it at dinner, now both of you change into something warm and brush your teeth and comb your hair before we leave. You've got ten minutes, or we'll miss the Christmas tree lighting."

They ran inside their bedroom, slamming the door behind them.

Out in the galley kitchen Stephanie poured glasses of Coke for her and Melanie.

"Want to tell me what sent you racing out of Snow Zone today? I know that conceited idiot said something to anger you," Melanie said before taking a sip of her Coke.

Stephanie debated not telling her, but she needed a friend. Even though the girls had managed to get away from her today, she trusted Melanie to the nth degree. "He told me to take the next four weeks off. Said I needed to spend the time with my kids. Then he added that my extended leave of absence would be without pay."

Melanie's mouth opened and closed several times

before she was actually able to form words. "That sneaky, low-life creep! How could he?"

"He's the boss, something he seems to like to remind me of all the time, that's how." Stephanie took a long pull from her glass of Coke. "I used to think he was a really nice guy, just a little rough around the edges. Now I think he's a mean, hateful SOB who needs to get a life."

"I can't believe he would do that to you, especially this time of year. Not only is the Snow Zone going to be swamped, but you have two children to buy Christmas gifts for."

"Yes, your thoughts mirror my own. But you know what angered me more than anything?"

"You're gonna tell me," Melanie stated.

"The girls were afraid. They knew that I was upset after speaking to that self-important jackass. It was like old times. When their father started ranting and raving, they would always clam up, hoping not to anger him. That's the exact way they acted today when Mr. Patrick O'Brien got up on his high horse and gave me the boot. He can fire me, give me a leave of absence, whatever he wants. He's the boss. But what he can't do is frighten my girls! I won't allow it, and I don't care if he fires me for leaving early today. They've seen enough already."

"Do you think you should bring Max in on this? After all, he is your real boss, and Patrick's, too. He *owns* Maximum Glide, and I bet Grace would have a thing or two to say about Patrick's pissy managerial skills, not to mention his treatment of you."

"No, I don't want to do that. Besides, I think this is personal. You know Patrick and I went out a few times; it didn't work out for whatever reason, and it's as though he's had it in for me ever since. I don't want to involve Max, and certainly not Grace, in her condition. I will handle this, but thanks for offering. It's nice to have a friend go to bat for me." Stephanie put a finger to her lips, stopping further conversation. The girls were waiting at the front door.

"We brushed our teeth and our hair just like you said," Amanda informed her.

Stephanie bent over to give each of the girls a kiss on top of their shiny brown, nicely combed hair. "You're good girls," she added. And they were. Other than an occasional disagreement over something inconsequential, the girls got along remarkably well.

"Then I say it's time we go to see that giant evergreen that is going to light up Maximum Glide. Are you two ready?"

"Yes, yes, yes!" Ashley cried as she stomped down the stairs.

"Be careful, those steps are slick," Melanie said, then took Amanda by the hand and walked with her to the bottom of the stairs before she slipped and fell. That was the last thing Stephanie needed at this stage of the game.

Once they were loaded back in the Taurus and the girls were safely buckled in their seats, Stephanie relaxed. She knew how much the girls had been looking forward to that night. No matter what issues she had to deal with after the day's events, she was a mother first. A fun night out with the girls would make what she knew she had to do much easier.

Chapter 8

Patrick sent Candy Lee on her way along with the rest of the Maximum Glide employees. He'd already been there for over an hour, and from the looks of things, it appeared that the weather had driven away whatever onslaught of customers he had expected. Stephanie had been right about closing Snow Zone even though her reasons for doing so weren't. She couldn't just take off whenever she felt like it. She had a responsibility to Maximum Glide and to him. While it wasn't he who signed her paychecks, without him she wouldn't have such a cushy position at the resort. It usually took an employee years to be promoted to a management position. And because she was good at her job, he'd given her the benefit of the doubt, and after last year's screwup, he hadn't demoted her. She was loyal to a fault, always on time, and never complained when he asked her to do things that normally a stock boy or girl would do. She did an excellent job no matter what he asked of her. She even cleaned the employee bathrooms every evening before she left.

He was still kicking his own rear end for the comment he'd made about her getting any "funny ideas" about their future. Where the hell that had come from he didn't know, but he'd kick his own butt a hundred times if he could take back those words. Stephanie hadn't even hinted that she wanted anything to do with him after their last movie date. It was *he* who'd decided she wasn't top-quality pickings on the meat market. Patrick sighed. If his mother or his three sisters even had an inkling that he'd referred to a woman as meat on the market, all four of them would string him up like cattle, then use a cattle prod on him. He didn't really think of women as "meat." It was just something the guys said when they were trying to be macho. And he always wanted to blend in when he was with the guys. Max was the only one who really knew him, knew that he was more than the image he presented to the world. He was educated and quite brilliant, but that didn't always work on the slopes, though he had to admit it had been a blessing dealing with suppliers and a few angry guests. He knew what worked financially and what didn't. Max trusted his judgment, but he knew Max would be mad as a hatter if word of how Patrick had treated Stephanie got back to him. As much as he hated to eat crow, he was going to have to serve himself a very large portion and swallow every bite as though it were the rarest of caviar.

He hadn't planned on attending the Christmas tree lighting, but knowing that Max and Grace would be there, not to mention Stephanie and her two kids, he figured it wouldn't look good if the manager of the resort didn't put in an appearance for what was widely billed as the kickoff to the Christmas season at Telluride. Plus, he didn't want to give Stephanie the opportunity to corner Max and Grace, not before he had a chance to explain to them what had happened.

Knowing another hour wouldn't make or break the day's sales, he quickly went about the business of closing the shop. Candy Lee had restocked all the shelves before she left, telling him that someone had to do it if Stephanie wasn't there. She went on to tell him what a great manager Stephanie was and that she wouldn't blame her one little bit if she just up and quit. Someday he was going to tell that kid to keep her thoughts to herself. But he liked her, she reminded him of Shannon back in the day. Candy Lee had . . . *moxie,* and he liked that about her. He secretly wished some of it would rub off on the store's manager. She was just a little too compliant at times. Not that he would admit it, but today she'd really surprised him when she walked out in the middle of her shift. Took a lot of guts for her to do that. He probably would've done the same thing had he been in her position. Which he reminded himself he wasn't. He'd had a job to do, and he did it. He could've left out that part about the future, but it had just rolled off his tongue. Why it had rolled off his tongue was something he did not want to think about. No how, no way. He liked his life as it was. No complications, no children to complicate the complications, certainly no children to break his heart into a million tiny pieces the way Shannon's death had left Colleen, Mark, and Abby. That was just too much pain for one man to tolerate.

He turned off the computer systems, did a batch report on the credit card machine, and counted out the cash, checks, and traveler's checks. After that was finished, he tallied up the day's total sales and was extremely impressed. Stephanie usually made a bank deposit on her way home from work. He'd do it because he felt he owed it to her. Once he had all the required checks stamped with the account numbers on the back of them and deposit slips made out, he stuffed them into the bank bag.

Since all the normal closing duties were finished for the day, Patrick walked back to the office just to make sure there wasn't anything there that needed his attention. He opened the door, peered in, and saw nothing out of the way. He ran his hand along the length of the wall searching for the light switch when the flashing green button on the answering machine caught his eye. Dammit, he couldn't leave without listening to the messages. They might be important, and with Stephanie not there to take them, he'd have to intercept them in case there was something that needed his immediate attention. He pushed the PLAY button. A monotone female voice said, "You have fifteen messages."

"What the hell?" He hit the forward button several times as most were calls from suppliers, customers, and other departments at Maximum Glide. He was about to click the STOP button when he heard a soft, but businesslike voice speak as though the woman were in the room.

"Hi, Stephanie, it's Jessica Rollins. I have some good news. I'm pretty sure the owners on the Placerville property are going to accept your offer. If Lady Luck stays on your back, I might be able to close this deal before the end of the year. Call me as soon as you can. I think you and your daughters just might have a Merry Christmas after all. Oh, before I forget, the bank wants to verify your employment. Talk s—"

The machine stopped.

Patrick flicked the light switch back on. He opened a drawer in search of something to write on when he was completely taken by surprise. In the top drawer was a pile of gold ribbon, and a movie ticket stub. He picked it up to read the title of the movie. He let the soft gold silk run between his fingers, then dropped the two items back in the drawer where they belonged. This wasn't good at all. Really it wasn't. Though he broke out into a grin as wide as the bunny run. She'd kept the ribbon from the box of candy he'd bought her, and the tickets from the movie they'd attended on their last date. It was *that* movie that sent him running for cover. She'd probably put these things in the drawer the next day and forgotten about them. Women did that. Saved things that had no meaning or value whatsoever. Stephanie must have forgotten she'd left them there. Should he take them to her, or should he just leave well enough alone? He didn't want her to think he'd been prying through her desk drawers, but he'd needed something to write on so he could remember Jessica Rollins's message. He found a blank Post-it. He played the message once more, wrote it down as best he could, then crammed the paper in his pocket. This Jessica hadn't left a number, but Patrick figured if Stephanie had been dealing with her, then she already knew her phone number. He closed the drawer again, turned off the light, and left through the employee exit.

He'd left his jacket in the Snow Cat; hopefully, one of the guys would remember it belonged to him and return it. Those Spyder jackets cost big bucks. The parking lot was completely covered in snow. What he wouldn't give for a snow tube just right then. He'd sail across the parking lot like a bat out of hell. He had a quick flash of two little girls in bright yellow ski jackets and wondered if they'd ever experienced the pure joy of sliding in a parking lot on fresh-fallen snow.

Something told him they hadn't had much fun in their lives. It caused a lump to form in the back of his throat. *Damn! I'm not cut out for this.*

Yeah, those girls were as sweet as hot cocoa laced with the finest whipped cream. Whcn he'd heard they were missing, he about jumped out of his skin though he didn't tell that to anyone. Riding the lift up to where the Snow Cats were stored had been his first priority. He knew if he took a Snow Cat out, first he would be in an all-terrain vehicle that would take him to any part of the mountain, double black diamonds and all. Also, it was equipped with bright lights and had a kick-ass heater. Lucky for him and the girls, and the dogs—he couldn't forget the mother and her pups—he hadn't had to go far. And now it seemed all was as it should be.

He jumped into the Hummer, cranked the heat up as high as it would go, then carefully made his way out of the parking lot. The snow was still falling, but it wasn't nearly as thick as it had been earlier that afternoon. He needed to go home for a quick shower and a change of clothes. He'd make sure to give Stephanie the message from her realtor friend, then he would apologize, tell her how sorry he was for being such an . . . a dope, then he'd tell her she could come back to work first thing in the morning. Once that was out of the way, he could breathe freely again. Hell, he might even ask Stephanie and the girls out to a movie. There were all kinds of G-rated movies out at Christmas. Maybe he would take Megan's boys along. One big happy family.

He shook his head as he traveled down the salt-covered road.

One big happy family!

He couldn't believe a thought like that had even entered his head! *What the heck is going on here?* It must be the holidays. Maybe he was supposed to enjoy them this year. It was just so hard without Shannon. When his family was together, it was so obvious a link was missing. Shannon was the first grandchild, the first niece. She was just the first. And, sadly, she was the first to die.

Tears filled Patrick's eyes, blurring the road in front of him. *Damn!* He wanted to be happy; he just didn't want all the pain that came with it. Knowing he couldn't have one without the other, Patrick figured he would always be the uncle, the good friend of a friend. He didn't have what it took to be a father figure. To anyone's child. He didn't know a diaper bag from a baby bottle. Well, yes he did, but it wasn't something he wanted in his daily life. That was all. Or was it? And was he just afraid to take the leap?

Chapter 9

The crowd gathered smack-dab in the middle of Maximum Glide. Hundreds of people had faced the cold weather to attend the Christmas tree lighting. A thirty-foot evergreen was placed directly in front of the main offices, the site of most of the day's comings and goings. Ski lessons could be arranged in the building to the right of the giant tree. To the left, children under the age of three could be left in the capable hands of Bunnies and Babies, the day care offered by the resort. North of the tree was The Lodge, where one could eat breakfast or lunch, or simply sit by the raging fire that never seemed to burn out in the giant fireplace. South of the tree were the ski lifts that took men, women, and children to the other forty-six lifts that covered the mountain. Tonight was like a scene from a Charles Dickens novel. Snow twirled like tiny ballerinas in the chilled night air. Mock gaslights wearing bright red bows flanked the main street on both sides. The shops stayed open, all displaying brightly colored lights and Christmas trees decked out in all the finery of the holiday season. The odor of mulled cider emanated from several of the shops, along with the earthy smell of burning wood.

Stephanie held her daughters' hands in hers as the three of them walked through the festive village that made up Maximum Glide. Melanie walked alongside them. The four were silent as each took in the fairy-tale-like images that lit up the resort like something right out of a magical storybook.

As expected, it was Amanda who spoke first. "Mommy, this is the most beautiful place in the whole wide world! I never want to leave here. I bet when Santa comes here, he doesn't want to leave either, right?"

They all laughed.

"I'm sure he doesn't, but he has many places to go all over the world. Still, I'm sure it hurts him just a tiny bit to leave this very special place," Stephanie said, as they continued their leisurely stroll down the main street, taking in all the brightly decorated windows and people dressed in their warmest, most colorful outdoor wear. It really was beautiful, Stephanie thought. It would be equally beautiful in its raw form, too. No lights, no flashy decorations, just the tall trees with the scent of evergreen perfuming the air, along with the clean freshly falling snow. Yes, she mused, that would be just as beautiful.

"What time do they light the tree?" Ashley asked excitedly. "I can't wait. I know it's just a tree, but it's so big!"

Stephanie and Melanie looked at one another over the girls' toboggan cap-covered heads. They laughed. "Seven o'clock, right on the dot. And it's ten minutes till, so we'd best hurry over so we can get in as close as possible. I don't want you two to miss anything."

"We don't want to either, Mommy. Right, Ashley?" Amanda singsonged.

"*Right,* Amanda. You know what I'm going to wish for when they light up the tree?" Ashley asked in a firm voice.

"I haven't the first clue," Stephanie said. "Why don't you tell us."

"I'm going to wish that Amanda would stop saying, 'right, Mommy,' 'right, Ashley,' 'right, Melanie' all the time."

Stephanie looked at Melanie, who could barely contain her laughter. Amanda, on the other hand, looked as if she was about to cry.

"It's okay, honey. Your sister is just doing what big sisters do." Stephanie fluffed the ball on top of her toboggan cap, hoping this wouldn't turn into an all-out verbal war between the two.

"Santa Claus doesn't tell me what to say, right, Mommy?" Amanda asked in her squeaky-I'm-about-to-cry-voice.

"Of course not. You're the only one who can decide what words come out of that sweet little mouth of yours. Look"—Stephanie pointed to the tree a few yards ahead of them, hoping to distract her younger daughter—"they're about to light the tree. Come on, let's hurry."

Without another word, the quartet weaved their way through the throngs of people clustered around the giant tree's perimeter. They were able to find a spot about six feet away. Stephanie figured that was as close as they could get without actually trampling on toes, strollers, and, looking down, the largest boot she had ever seen. Her eyes followed the boot to the calf, then the knee, all the way to the thigh. Why did this look familiar to her? Before she knew what was happening, the boot man snatched Amanda right out of her grip and hoisted her on top of his very broad shoulders.

Patrick!

"If you'll follow me, I've got the perfect place to view the tree," he said.

Stephanie was about to tell him to back off when Melanie shook her head and pointed to the girls. They were so excited, the sparkle in their eyes could light up half the giant tree if needed. She mouthed okay and inched behind Patrick, with Ashley sandwiched between her and Melanie.

Patrick guided them through the crowd without too much pushing and shoving. On the opposite side of the street, Stephanie spied what she knew to be a giant boom lift, or a cherry picker as some referred to it. She couldn't help but grin. She glanced behind her at Melanie, who wore a grin as big as the tree. Ashley hadn't said a word since Patrick had come in and literally swooped Amanda onto his shoulders. Not that she could've been heard through the sounds of excitement coming from the groups gathered around the center of the resort.

"Let's hurry, we have about two minutes to climb up in this thing," Patrick said.

"This will hold our weight?" Stephanie asked cautiously. Up close, the machine didn't look that big or steady.

"I'm one hundred percent sure," Patrick attested. "I wouldn't risk it if I wasn't."

Was that supposed to be a dig of sorts, she wondered, as Patrick opened the glass door. Did he think she'd taken too big a risk when she'd allowed Melanie to take her girls skiing on the mountain? She figured if he had, too bad. It wasn't his concern how she raised her children. She told herself if he really knew her, he would know the last thing she would do would

be to place her children in danger. A small voice reminded her that was exactly what she'd done when
she'd remained married to an abuser. *But that's for
another time. Tonight, I simply want to enjoy being
with my daughters and Melanie.*

Trusting he knew what he was doing, Stephanie allowed Patrick to lift Amanda inside the boom. Ashley
wasn't nearly as excited as her sister about climbing
into the small bucket.

"Mommy, is this safe?" she asked.

"Absolutely," Stephanie replied in her most reas-
suring voice. "I would not allow you inside if I
thought otherwise," she added.

"Well, okay then," Ashley said, allowing Patrick to
assist her.

Patrick placed Ashley next to Amanda on a small
seat. He grabbed Stephanie's hand to help her take the
giant step leading to the inside of the bucket. Sparks
shot up and down the length of her arm as he held her
for what she thought was a minute too long. She felt
out of sorts for a few seconds. She stood behind the
girls, then Melanie climbed in. Once they were all securely in position, Patrick spoke up.

"I'm going to be operating this thing. It'll only
take a minute to reach the height you'll need to view
the lights. Just try not to jump around too much,
okay?" Patrick said.

"You're not gonna watch the lights with us?"
Amanda asked.

"I'll see them from below, kiddo. Now let me close
this door and get all of you ladies up in the air,"
Patrick said. He gave Stephanie a small smile before
closing the door.

She wondered if this was his way of making up to
her for the way he'd talked to her at Snow Zone. She
wasn't sure, but again, for the girls' sake, she wouldn't

question it, at least not just then. There would be plenty of time later for her to think about and rehash the day's events.

Before any of them could utter a word, they were lifted in one giant swoop. Patrick had positioned the boom so that they were able to view the tree at its midpoint. They could look up and down, yet they weren't so close that they couldn't see the people below them, too.

"Oh, Mommy, this is the best fun ever," Amanda said.

"Okay, let's watch," Stephanie said.

Within a matter of a few seconds, the giant evergreen lit up . . . just like the Christmas tree in Rockefeller Center!

Hundreds of red, green, blue, and white lights clung to the tree's branches, illuminating the entire perimeter around the tree. From somewhere there was a drumroll, then a giant silver star as big as a car tire sparkled, completing the ceremony.

"Wow," Ashley said. "This is so way cool from up here."

"And I'm not even scared, right, Mommy?" Amanda informed them.

"See, she's doing it again!" Ashley pointed out.

"Girls, now isn't the time. Let's just enjoy the view before Patrick puts us down."

A few minutes later, Patrick lowered the boom to the ground. Once they stopped, he stepped out of the cab, opened the door, and let them out into the frigid night air.

"That was the coolest thing ever, thanks," Ashley said.

"Yep, it sure was. Mommy thinks so, too, right?"

"Amanda," Stephanie chastened, "it was wonderful. Now, what do you girls say to Mr. O'Brien?"

Quizzingly, Amanda said, "That we want to do it again."

They all burst out laughing, even Stephanie.

"That's not what I had in mind," she said as an afterthought. Her girls knew their manners. Or at least she thought they did. Apparently tonight, that knowledge had taken a leave of absence.

"Thank you, Mr. O'Brien. That was very thoughtful of you to think of us," Ashley said in her most prim and proper voice.

Again, the adults laughed.

"You two are very welcome. That tree sure is a sight to behold, huh?" Patrick said as he gazed up at the rainbow of colors.

"Do you wanna go to Burger King with us?" Amanda asked. "We didn't have lunch today when we were with the pups. I am starving, and Mommy says we both can have double-dipped ice-cream cones because we didn't talk on the ride home."

If there had been a giant hole somewhere, Stephanie wished it would swallow her up right then and there. She was really going to have to start explaining to Amanda exactly what social manners were. She realized her daughter was only seven, but she had to learn sometime, and it might as well be now, before she totally humiliated Stephanie.

For once, Patrick saved her from Amanda's eagerness. "I'd love to, but I need to go to Claude's to see how the pups are doing."

"Oh, I want to go with you," Ashley said. "I've been so worried about them. Can I go with Patrick, Mom? Please?"

Stephanie wasn't sure exactly what had gotten into her girls, but she was really going to have to sit them both down and discuss manners with them.

"No, you may not. And please don't assume that

Mr. O'Brien has to invite you just because you want to go. That is very rude."

"I tell you what I'll do if it's okay with your mom," Patrick said to both girls. "As soon as I leave Claude's, I will call your mom with a pup report. Maybe later this week, if it's all right with your mom, I can take both of you girls to see the pups." Patrick looked at Stephanie, shot her one of his killer smiles, and her heart turned to mush, but only for a second. She remembered just how hateful he had been to her that afternoon.

"I'll think about it. I'll certainly have enough time on my hands to do so," Stephanie said directly to Patrick.

Patrick looked at his big brown boots. "About what I said today—"

"What's done is done, Mr. O'Brien. Thank you for offering the pup update. You can call my cell as soon as you have word of their condition."

With that, Stephanie took both girls by the hand and led them away from Patrick, his promises, and whatever it was he had been about to say.

Chapter 10

Two weeks later . . .

"Well, I for one think he owes you at least a bit of loyalty. You've worked your rear off at that place for two years, and this is what you get? Laid off during the holidays?" Melanie took a sip of her coffee. "I still think you should have told Max and Grace at the tree lighting."

"I know you do. It stinks, but it is what it is. I didn't want to spoil their evening. I'll be fine as long as the deal on the house goes through. I've already filled out all the paperwork; the deposit is being held in escrow; now all I'm waiting on is the bank. And you know how banks are. They take their good old easy time. Jessica said if I was lucky, I'd be moved in before the end of the year, but I don't see that happening. Not with the holidays coming up."

Stephanie and Melanie had just returned from walking the girls to the bus stop. Since her forced leave of absence had begun, they had spent almost every day together. If anything good had come out of her layoff, it was her close friendship with Melanie.

They'd taken the girls to the movies twice, three times to McDonald's, and once they'd gone out for pizza at a new pizza parlor in town called Izzy's. Melanie wanted to take them to see a Christmas play in Denver this weekend, but Stephanie really couldn't afford the tickets. Melanie had told Stephanie it was her treat, but Stephanie, who had no idea just how well-off her friend was, said that was too much. Instead, the four of them were planning to see *A Christmas Carol* at the high school in Placerville. It was free to anyone, and Stephanie knew the girls would get a kick out of it. Ever since Grace had taken them to see *The Nutcracker* at Eagle Valley High, they'd fallen in love with live performance of any kind.

"I know you can't wait to get out of this little place, but I think I will miss it when you and the girls leave," Melanie said as she gazed around the three-room garage apartment.

"Then you should ask your parents to rent it to you," Stephanie teased. "I'm sure they would give you a decent rate. Not that they haven't given me a good rate. I didn't mean to imply that they hadn't. I know what they could really get out of this place if they wanted to rent it as vacation property."

"I don't see that happening. They've loved having you and the girls here. I don't think the place has ever looked quite as homey."

Stephanie had tried her best to make the small, cramped area into a home. She'd painted the walls a warm butter color and sewn cream-colored drapes to cover the large picture window in the living area. She'd spent two weekends putting new tile in the one and only bathroom. She'd been quite proud of herself, too. She'd taken a course on installing ceramic tile offered at the local hardware store and found it really wasn't all that hard to do. She'd borrowed the wet saw and cutters from Max, and the tiles she'd chosen, a creamy beige, were on sale. She'd asked permission first, and, of course, she'd been given complete and total discretion over the apartment. She was told to make it her own, and that was exactly what she'd done.

The kitchen wasn't much bigger than a closet, but Stephanie had left her mark there, too. She'd wallpapered the one wall with tiny butterflies, bought an inexpensive set of pale yellow canisters at a discount store, and added a sheer yellow curtain over the window above the sink. The table had been there when she moved in. Stephanie now knew that it had been a tenth-anniversary gift from Melanie's father to her mother many years ago. Solid hard rock maple with four matching chairs. She'd purchased yellow checkered cushions and matching place mats after she'd polished the deep honey-colored wood to a mellow shine. It was homey, just as Melanie said.

Stephanie had been hesitant about putting up a tree that year, hoping by some sheer force of magic that she would be in the new house, and they would have Christmas there, but she hadn't told the girls about the house, so she'd had to decorate the small artificial tree she'd purchased the first year they lived there. The apartment couldn't hold much more than that, but she and the girls had decorated wherever possible. They'd tied red and green ribbons on all the doorknobs, and on the handles on the kitchen cabinets. They'd strung cranberries and popcorn on thread and draped it on top of the curtain rod in the living room. Baskets of pinecones they had gathered covered every available surface. Amanda had cut out shapes of stars and Christmas trees from red and green construction paper and taped them all over the walls. Not to be outdone, Ashley had used all the aluminum foil in the house making angels and taping them to the ceiling. That had been quite the task, but they'd all enjoyed themselves. And now their little place sparkled and shone, ready for the holidays.

Though it was expensive and not in her budget, Stephanie had bought the girls each a cell phone for Christmas. Remembering those few hours of fear on Black Friday had left her shaken, more so than she'd let on. She'd purchased cards with a limited number of minutes and would instruct the girls that the phones were only to be used in case of an emergency, but she didn't see that happening, at least not with Ashley. She was starting to talk on the phone with her school friends, and Stephanie knew she would want to fit in with the rest of her classmates by texting and talking on her new cell phone. When Grace and Max had asked what they could give the girls for Christmas, she'd told them to buy them minutes for their phones.

"Thanks, we love it here, it's just not big enough. You know what it's like when three girls share a bathroom?" Stephanie teased.

"I've witnessed it with my very own eyes," Melanie informed her.

"Yes, I suppose you have. I'm just lucky they're still young. Can you imagine what it would be like if they were teenagers?"

Melanie laughed. "I don't even want to think about it."

They chatted for a few more minutes. As Melanie was getting ready to leave, the phone rang. Stephanie hoped the girls were all right. She still didn't feel one hundred percent secure when they were out of her sight.

She raised her index finger to Melanie, indicating for her to wait a minute.

Melanie stood by the door.

"Hello," Stephanie said into the phone, her voice tinged with a bit a fear. "Jessica! It's great to hear from you." Stephanie paused, then nodded to Jessica, who, of course, couldn't see her. As though she were moving in slow motion, she sat down on the kitchen chair.

"That's not true," she cried vehemently. "I don't understand," she trailed off, her voice laced with disappointment. "Yes, of course. I don't know what to say except it's simply not true. I'll have to call you back," Stephanie said as she tossed the phone on the table.

Melanie walked across the small living room back to the kitchen. She sat down in the chair she'd just vacated. "You don't look so hot. Are the girls okay?"

"I hope so. That was Jessica Rollins on the phone. She said she just got off the phone with the bank." Her eyes pooled with unshed tears. "They've denied my loan."

Melanie reached cross the table for Stephanie's hand. "How can that be? Jessica said the hard part was over. I thought they'd already approved the loan, that it was simply a matter of signing the final papers at the closing." Melanie appeared to be as dumbfounded as Stephanie. "Did they offer an explanation? Did Jessica say what happened to change their minds?"

Crestfallen, Stephanie nodded. "Jessica said banks don't give loans to people who are unemployed."

Chapter 11

"Out of a job? What is she talking about? You're not out of a job," Melanie said again, as though saying it would make it so, at least as far as Jessica Rollins and the bank were concerned. "I don't know where they got their information, but I sure hope you find out."

Depleted of whatever energy she'd had, Stephanie got out of her chair and stood at the sink looking out the window that overlooked the long, winding driveway leading to her apartment. She cleared her throat and wiped her eyes on a tea towel. "I know where it came from. It's obvious."

"You think Patrick is behind this?" Melanie stated the obvious.

Stephanie turned around to face her. "Who else would stoop so low to do something like this? I think he's still upset at me for not allowing the girls to go to Claude's with him to see the puppies."

"I don't think he's that vindictive, or juvenile. I know he's not the most classy guy in the world, but I really don't believe he would stoop to this sea urchin level."

Stephanie sniffled into the tea towel, not caring that she'd painstakingly embroidered the butterflies on it late one night whcn she'd had a hard time going to sleep. "You don't get it, Melanie. The guy has it in for me. He thinks women like me are nothing but trash. I know what I'm talking about, trust me."

"Well, I never trust anyone who says 'trust me,' but I can tell you this; whatever makes you think you're trash and whatever 'women like me' are, I would be honored to walk in your shadow, Stephanie Casolino-Marshall. What you are is a decent hardworking woman who wants nothing more than a better life for her two daughtcrs than she had. What you are is a loving, giving, caring mother and friend. Now I know you're not going to like this, but in this instance I'm going to tell you, too bad. I'm calling Max myself. This childish behavior from his manager, and I use that word loosely, has to stop." Melanie reached for the phone in the center of the table.

Stephanie placed her hand on top of Melanie's. "I really don't want you to call Max or Grace. It will seem as though I'm taking advantage of their friendship. And thanks for saying all those nice things about me. You're a good friend, you know that, right?"

"Yes, I know that, and thanks. But friends don't sit by and allow their best friends to get kicked in the butt when they're already down." Melanie held her hand up as if to ward off any further comments from Stephanie. "Go take a shower, wash your hair, and put on some makeup. Not that you need it with that peaches-and-cream complexion, but do it anyway. Then when you're finished, get that black pant suit out of the back of your closet. The one you wore when you applied for your mortgage. No, on second thought forget that. Get the tightest, sexiest pair of jeans you own and top them with that bright red sweater I gave you." Melanie was on a roll. "Don't say another word because I'm not listening. Go on, get in the shower. You have one hour to sexy up."

"Sexy up? That's a new one," Stephanie said.

"Yes it is. And that's because I just made it up. It's mine, an original, so don't think I'm going to let you take credit for it. Now get in the shower, or I will toss you in there myself."

"I'm not sure if I like you this way. Bossy and all."

"If you don't get out of here and get in that shower, I will show you what bossy is. Now *git,* and I don't mean perhaps. Now! Remember, you've got exactly one hour."

Stephanie gave up. "Okay. I guess I need to shower, but for the record, I want you to know that I will be okay with this."

Melanie shot her arm out like an arrow pointing toward the bathroom.

"Okay, okay," Stephanie whined before locking herself in the bathroom.

Melanie waited until she heard the shower running before she picked up the phone. She knew that Stephanie's pride was on the line, but right then she didn't care. What she cared about was that someone had caused her dear friend to lose out on her dream. Whether it was intentional or not didn't really matter at that point. It only mattered that Stephanie had worked harder than anyone she knew just to save a few thousand dollars for a down payment on a home for her and her children. In today's fast world of give or I'll take, Stephanie was a rare breed. And what was a huge sum to Stephanie was chump change for Melanie, who had way more than enough to make a real difference. For the first time in her twenty-four years, Melanie felt like this opportunity, to do something really, really special for people she loved, was a gift to herself, not the other way around.

She hit *69 on the phone to get the last incoming number. She scribbled it down on a magnetic pad stuck on the front of the refrigerator.

"Jessica Rollins, please," she said when a young woman picked up the phone. "And tell her it's a matter of life and death."

"Oh my gosh," the young woman said, "I'll take this call to her myself."

Melanie thought the girl deserved a raise.

"Thank you," she said.

A minute later, Melanie had Jessica Rollins on the phone. She made quick work of telling her what she needed and when she needed it. The woman was more than willing to jump through a few hoops to make her wishes come true. When they finalized their plans, Melanie dialed the number to the office at Maximum Glide.

A voice she didn't recognize answered the phone. Melanie wasn't sure if it was a male or a female either.

"Mr. Edward Patrick Joseph O'Brien, please. Tell him it's a matter of life and death." Melanie liked this new role of taking charge, sort of like kicking ass and taking names later.

Two seconds later, the man himself was on the phone. "This is Patrick."

Melanie rolled her eyes. She was sure the man deliberately downplayed his intelligence.

"Patrick, this is Melanie, and we have a problem." Just for meanness, she waited a few seconds before continuing. Let him wiggle in his britches.

"Is it Stephanie, or the girls?" he asked.

More meanness. "All of them."

"Tell me where they're at, and I can be there in minutes," he replied anxiously.

Again, she let him stew. She knew it was mean, but it was her way of getting even over his putting Stephanie on that unpaid leave of absence.

"Melanie, tell me what's wrong. Please!" He shouted so loud she had to hold the phone away from her ear.

"I need you to listen, and I don't want you to interrupt me. Is that clear?"

She heard an intake of breath over the phone line. "Okay. I'm listening."

Melanie made fast work of telling him what she wanted and when she wanted it. He complied as fast as Jessica Rollins had. *Maybe graphic design isn't my calling after all.*

Thirty minutes later, Stephanie was showered, dressed, and looking like a million bucks.

"Now, I want you to get in my car. We're going out for lunch."

"Melanie, I know you're trying to cheer me up, and I really do appreciate it, but I have to be here when the girls get home." She looked at the clock on the stove. "And that's in two hours. I don't see how we can go out to lunch and actually enjoy ourselves in such a short period of time."

"Did I say we were going to enjoy ourselves? Hmm, I don't believe I did. Now go."

"Well, I hope you know I feel like a fool, all dressed up, looking so silly, just to eat lunch. And we'll have to go to a fast-food place because that's all I have time for. And I won't take no for an answer, not where my girls are concerned," Stephanie said adamantly.

"I've arranged for my mother to be here when they get home." She really hadn't, but she would. "You have way too much blusher on. Go wipe some off before we leave. You look like Ronald McDonald."

"I *really* don't like this side of you."

"Tough. Go wipe your cheeks. Now."

Stephanie turned around and headed for the bathroom.

Melanie called her mother and explained the situation. She was more than willing to help out. She said she would be waiting at the bus stop for the girls and from there she would take them to Chuck E. Cheese, if Stephanie didn't mind, of course. Melanie assured her she wouldn't but reminded her mother not to forget to take her cell phone, because Melanie knew Stephanie would want to call and check on the girls.

Stephanie came out of the bathroom as soon as Melanie hung up the phone.

"If I didn't know better, I would think you were up to something. But I don't know better, at least not today. So let's just have lunch and enjoy ourselves before the girls come home. It might be fun just the two of us for a change. We can order junk food."

"Yes, and we will as soon as you get in the car." Melanie practically shoved her out the door. "I told you my mother would be here just in case we ran a little late, and you're going to have to trust me on this one."

"And you want me to trust someone who says she doesn't trust people who say trust me?"

"Did I say that?" Melanie asked, as they loaded into her Lincoln Navigator.

"Yes, you did."

"Well, I'm telling you now that you have to trust me. You don't have to like me, just trust me."

Stephanie took a deep breath. "Turn the heat on, it's freezing. I really wish you would tell me what's going on. I don't like surprises."

"Tough," Melanie said as she maneuvered down the long, winding drive. Evergreens topped with a heavy layer of snow flanked the sides of the drive. It never failed to remind her just how beautiful Colorado really was.

Exactly twenty minutes later, they pulled into the main parking lot at Maximum Glide.

Stephanie looked as though she were ready to do battle. "What are we doing here? This is the last place I want to be right now."

"Tough. It's where you need to be. There is someone here who wants to talk to you. Now get out, or I will carry you over my shoulder like a sack of potatoes."

"I'm not sure I want the girls to see you like this. It might scare them," Stephanie teased.

"Right! They love me any way I am, and we both know that."

"Yes, they do."

As they trudged across the parking lot, snow crunched against their boots, the sound barely audible over the crowds on the mountain. The previous week's blizzard conditions were long gone. In their place the sun was as bright as butter, the sky as blue as a robin's egg, and the snow as white and clean as freshly beaten cream.

They hurried inside the main offices because even though the sun was out, the temperatures were still in the teens.

"We're having lunch in Patrick's office. I told him to order in from The Lodge," Melanie explained.

"I don't know why I agreed to this, but remind me when we leave to wring your neck."

Melanie tapped on Patrick's door, then opened it before he had a chance to tell them to come inside.

Just as she had commanded, there was a table set

for *two,* an exquisite crystal vase with one single yellow rose, and a bottle of Cristal chilling in a bucket of ice.

Stephanie glanced at Patrick, then back at her friend turned harridan. "Tell me this isn't what I think it is."

"It isn't," Melanie said. "Enjoy lunch."

She hurried out of the office before Stephanie even had a chance to ask what was going on. She saw the table, the rose, and the champagne.

"Please, come in and have a seat." Patrick motioned to the chairs, which Stephanie recognized from The Lodge.

"Just so you know, I'm not here because I want to be. Melanie seems to think this is . . . I don't know what she thinks, but let's just get this over with."

"You sound like you're headed for the guillotine."

"It's probably not as bad," she responded, then sat down in the chair Patrick pulled out for her. Surprise, surprise. She didn't know he had manners.

"You can tell me that when I'm finished with what I have to say. I took the liberty of telling Jack to wait on our food. You might not want to be in the same room with me when I say what I need to say, something I should've said a long time ago, and I would have if I'd had the guts to admit it to myself. But better late than never, so here it is."

"Look, if it's about my job, I probably shouldn't have walked out the way I did. I was just so worried about Amanda and Ashley, then you made that comment about . . . well, you know what you said. I was embarrassed and just wanted to leave. So if you're going to apologize, then fine. I accept."

"Actually, this isn't about your job at all. As a matter of fact, it has nothing to do with this place." He took a deep breath, raked his hand through his dark locks, then took another deep breath. "I come from a very large Irish family. I have three younger sisters and four older brothers, and my sisters have three sons and two, uh, one daughter. My brothers have a number of children also, but this is about my sisters and their children and me. About how it's my job to protect them."

"Okayyy," Stephanie said, still unsure what this was all about.

"This is hard, okay?"

"Sorry."

"Two years ago, my sister and her husband lost their daughter, Shannon."

"I'm so sorry, Patrick, I had no idea." Stephanie still didn't know where this was leading, but she was calmer, knowing it had something to do with his family. Family she could handle.

"She was seventeen. . . . She had this rare blood thing called TTP. She died the day she was supposed to graduate from high school. Our family hasn't been the same since. *I* haven't been the same since. It's been a nightmare for my sister, and their younger daughter, Abby. It took about a year before the shock wore off. I . . . This isn't coming out the way I want it to."

Patrick reached for her hand, and her first thought was to pull hers away, but when she saw the look in his blue eyes, she stopped herself. Sadness blanketed his face.

"I swore that I would never allow myself to get in a situation that would make me suffer a loss as great as Shannon's death. I saw what my sister went through, what she'll go through for the rest of her life, what I couldn't protect her and my oldest niece, my parents' oldest grandchild from, and I decided that wasn't the life for me. If I didn't get too close to anyone, I wouldn't get hurt. Typical cliché, but true. Then you and your girls came along. I tried not to like you, I tried not to like your daughters, but that's impossible. I've been trying to figure out a way to tell you this without putting my foot in my mouth, or ticking you off, and as luck would have it, Melanie called and told me what I knew but wouldn't admit to."

"When did Melanie become such an authority on everyone?"

"She's observant, and she's smart. A little mouthier than usual, but I'm glad she chose me to use as an example. What I'm trying to say is I have very, very strong feelings for you, and your girls. Do you think it would be possible to give me another chance to do things the right way?"

This was the last conversation she'd ever expected to have that day. And with Patrick, of all people. So there was a heart beating inside that massive chest after all. Stephanie grinned.

"I suppose I could, but there would have to be conditions."

"Anything you say," Patrick agreed, then squeezed her hand.

"Anything?" Stephanie asked.

"Whatever it takes," he said, his eyes boring into her as though it were the first time he'd actually looked at her.

"Let's hit the double black diamonds, first," Stephanie said, feeling more lighthearted than she had in years. She actually felt like having fun for a change. She didn't worry about the girls because she did trust Melanie even though she had told her she shouldn't. That day Stephanie was simply going to enjoy being in the company of a man she thought was the sexiest boss alive.

Patrick stood up, pulled out her chair, then took her in his arms. "I haven't even kissed you."

"Then let's not waste another minute," Stephanie said just before his lips met hers.

Epilogue

Christmas Eve

The knock at the door sent both girls racing to answer it. Melanie was stopping by to bring them their gifts. They'd been acting like two Mexican jumping beans ever since she told them.

"Girls, let's remember our manners," Stephanie said.

Both girls slowed down and opened the door.

"You're not Melanie," Amanda said.

"Amanda, that's rude!" Ashley said, stepping aside to allow Patrick to come in out of the cold. "We're trying to teach her manners, but I think it's going to take a long time."

"I'm still learning myself. It just takes some people longer than others," Patrick replied.

"Patrick, I thought you were Melanie," Stephanie said, though she wasn't unhappy that it was him. They'd been out four times in less than two weeks. He wasn't the man she'd thought; he was more. Loving, funny, and kind. He had the patience of a saint where the girls were concerned. She'd never been happier.

"Yeah, speaking of Melanie, she called me and told me she couldn't make it until later, something about her car. Said she wanted me to give you this." Patrick reached inside his leather jacket and pulled out a thick manila envelope.

"Oh, that must be the gift she wanted to give to the girls."

"I'm sure of it. Why don't you open it?" Patrick asked as he invited himself to sit at the small table in the tiny kitchen.

"Well, it's not for me," Stephanie said. She was surprised that Melanie hadn't wrapped the girls' gifts since she knew how much they loved shiny paper and fancy ribbons. But maybe she hadn't had time.

"Actually, Melanie said it was for you *and* the girls, so I think it's okay to go ahead and open it."

By that time both girls were hanging all over Patrick. He lifted Amanda onto his right knee and Ashley onto his left. "Go on, Mommy, open it!" Amanda said.

"Oh, all right, but I wish she hadn't . . . Well, okay, I'll just open it." Stephanie had knitted a sweater and matching scarf for Melanie and a hat and gloves for Patrick. She had been hesitant to dip into the deposit money, which had been returned to her after the purchase of the house fell through, so gifts from her this Christmas were handmade.

She used a fingernail to open the top of the envelope. She pulled out several official-looking papers. She skimmed through them, looked over at Patrick, who had her girls sitting on his lap as though they'd been doing that their entire life.

She looked at the papers again. And again. Then it finally hit her.

Melanie's gift to her. Tears filled her eyes and coursed down her cheeks like a waterfall. She could hardly speak. She thought she must be dreaming. But it was what it was. She didn't know how it was possible, but somehow, some way, Melanie's gift to her and the girls was the deed to an unencumbered piece of property, the little house in Placerville.

"This is the best present we've ever gotten, right, Patrick?" Amanda asked.

They all laughed as the girls told their mother about Melanie's surprise and how it was possible. And how Melanie had said that, for the first time in her life, she knew the true joy of Christmas giving.

And a surprise it was, a complete and utter surprise.

For the first time in her life, Stephanie and the girls would truly have a home of their own, thanks to the incredible generosity of a loving friend.

"A Very Merry Christmas"

CATHY LAMB

To Cindy, Todd, Mitchell, and Cara Everts.
Thanks for the drift boat rides down the Missouri
River, the opportunity to tease the fish,
and the water gun fights.
Most of all, thanks for the laughs.

Chapter 1

"It's the holiday season so I don't want to have to shoot you." I drummed my red fingernails against the long, polished bar, hooked my cowboy boot on the rail, and eyed the drunken fool who had crawled up on the stool next to mine like an inebriated sea urchin. "But you're pushing it, buddy."

Through the dim light of Barry Lynn's bar, a bar that has been around for over a hundred years and has the bullet holes to prove it, I could tell that he had gotten all dressed up in his fancy-pants fly fishing gear to head out to one of Montana's world class rivers and pretend he was a "real man" out in the wilds. He had probably flown in on a private jet, and was looking for a little hee-haw before going home to his mansion and his pampered life.

"Honey," he said, pushing a hand through his blond wave, while I studied his buffed fingernails, "you've got a face that could cause Jesus himself to sin."

I refrained from smashing my unbuffed fist into his nose for that rude comment. "Jesus himself created this face. I can assure you he's not going to sin. You, however, may cause me to sin when I knock you off your stool. Now *back off.*"

Out of the corner of my eye, I could see the Three Wise Women, as they had dubbed themselves about ten years ago, waiting for me in our usual corner, near the Christmas tree, past the pool tables, by a window we opened up to the moonlight when the heat from many bodies became too suffocating. The discussion topic tonight: "Would marriage be easier if the couple lived next door to each other and not *with* each other?" Plus Vicki was bringing all of us Gracious Journals to write in, whatever that was.

The inebriated sea urchin sighed heavily, shook his head, then leaned toward me, his whiskey breath encircling my head. "Okay, honey, but I gotta get your name." His three other middle-aged, fleshy buddies were now laughing at him from a nearby table. "Your name, then I'll leave you alone." More whiskey breath. *"Your naaammme."*

"My name's Mary Magdalene." I could feel my temper triggering. It did not take much. I knew it was because of my past.

"Your name's Mary Magdalene?" His eyes opened wide, then his face got contemplative. He was trying hard to think. *Think, brain, think!* "I've heard that name before." His brow furrowed. "Are you famous?"

I stared at a bullet hole in the ceiling and wondered who shot off her gun. Hey! Maybe it was a woman who was being hit on by a whiskey-breathing idiot.

"You look famous." He shook his head, baffled. "You got that, I dunno. Charisma. Something about you. Special-like. Original. You're a thoroughbred. You know what I mean?"

"So I'm a horse to you?"

The mirror above a row of liquor bottles behind the

bar gave me a brief look at myself. Full mouth, "a mouth that looks botoxed but it's not," Hannah, one of the Three Wise Women told me. High cheekbones. Brown eyes that seemed abnormally large to me. Long hair that is straight and black with a white streak running from a widow's peak down the full length. My father said it was a birthmark blessed upon me from my ancestors, who about "swam over here from Italy, they were so desperate to come to America."

My mother, the rebel daughter of a proper, titled, English family, who fell head over heels in love with my father when he was on leave from serving in the U.S. Army, and ran off with him when she was twenty, called it my Wisdom Mark. "It would be wise if you were not quite so tough, dear. When we English say to keep a stiff upper lip, we do not mean 'give someone else a stiff upper lip.'"

The sea urchin slouching next to me said, "Nah. You're not a horse, but that white streak is sexier than hell. I would like to bite it."

"If you attempt to bite my hair, I will knock your teeth into your beer."

I said this politely. My mother would have been proud of my restraint. ("If you feel your temper rising, Meredith Jean, make yourself some tea.")

The sea urchin laughed, obviously not taking me seriously. "I love a tough woman, and you Montana gals, man, you rock in that department. You gals can take down a bear."

He must think we "gals" are stupid. No woman I know would try to take down a bear unless she wanted to be eaten. "I need a beer and a sledgehammer Barry Lynn, please," I told the owner of the bar.

"One beer and a sledgehammer coming right up," she called. "How 'bout a staple gun, too? Sometimes those are handy."

"Bring 'em. This one is going to need more than usual."

"Now, Miss Mary Magdalene," the drunken sea urchin said, oblivious to our conversation, "How 'bout if you join me and my buddies? Why I have never seen a woman wearing a red cowboy hat with rhinestones before. Never. And you got eyes like a cat. Lemme buy you a beer."

"No. Leave. Your breath is enough to set fire to this building."

"Come on, sugar . . ."

"I'm not interested and my name is not sugar." I picked up my cowgirl hat and put it on my head. It was well worn, and fit perfectly, the way I liked them. "Last time I'm gonna warn you. Go back to your hole and your rich men friends with the snarky smiles who are pretending to be fly fishermen, with your bottle of whiskey, and drink yourself into a stupor. I have no interest in drunken men who are so weak they can't approach a woman, sober, make intelligent conversation, and then invite her to a dinner in a fancy restaurant to show her respect."

The door opened to the bar and a burst of cold, snowy Montana air swirled around. I idly glanced around wondering which neighbor was coming on in. My breath caught in my throat.

There he was.

I could almost hear the sleigh bells ringing and jingle bells jingling. Following that I heard an echoing gong, my own brain warning me that he was trouble.

Total trouble.

Logan Taylor. Born in Copper, Montana, about three hours from Telena, a self-made millionaire, various businesses in five states in highway development, electrical something 'er other, real estate, ranching, et cetera. Hard scrabble childhood. He was about eight years older than me, but even as a kid growing up on a farm outside of town, I'd heard about him because every athletic team he was on won some state championship or other. He'd had a tough reputation, too, a fight or two or three or more, all reported in the newspaper because of who he was.

The man was a Montanan through and through and had recently built a log cabin outside of Telena. He was huge at about six feet five inches tall, with blondish hair, shoulders a thousand Christmas angels could dance on, and sharp eyes that didn't miss a whit.

Every time I'd seen him in town the last weeks, I'd ducked into a store, a church, one time a government building, and I steer clear of government buildings like I steer clear of the black plague.

My attention was re-caught by the drunken sea urchin.

"I'll take you to a fancy restaurant," he slurred. "I got enough money to buy every fancy restaurant here in this town and the yachts here, too. Let's go right down; you turn me on . . ."

And that's when the drunken sea urchin made a herculean mistake.

He reached out a hand and tried to stroke my white streak, knocking off my cowgirl hat. I caught his wrist, leaned in, and said, quite calmly, "Don't touch me, you overgrown leech."

He laughed in a slimy way. "But I wanna touch you, you look so soft and tender and I want to—" He said something disgusting in my ear, lifted up his other hand to stroke me again, and we were, at that very moment, finished. All done.

I heard Howard and Norm, brothers, generational ranchers, Ivy League educated, World War II vets, sitting next to me at the bar, suck in their breaths.

Howard said, quite slowly, "Son, that was a poor choice."

Norm said, "If I were you, I'd start running. That would be right now. Run. Run fast, run long, but run."

The Three Wise Women cackled. Hannah yelled, "Okay, everybody, prepare for the show. It's going to be almost better than my speech on mathematical derivates."

I heard scattered applause as I seethed. My past has given me a lot of anger.

"Why do men think saying disgusting things is a turn on?" I asked him. "Why do men try to touch women without our permission? Why do men think they're sexy when they're drunk? Why do men continually tick me off?"

I didn't contemplate these questions for very long as I squared my red cowboy boots and brought a fist up into the sea urchin's jaw. He went flying off the stool and onto the floor, flat on his back.

I heard one of the Wise Women, Katie, a mother of four yell, "That was impressive, Merry Meredith. Even better than last month's hit."

Another Wise Woman, Vicki, who owns one of the largest ranches for miles around, said, "Hormones, hormones, don't mess with the hormones. Why don't men get that?"

After a second's shocked hesitation, the sea urchin scrambled right back up to his feet. He said something else nasty to me, called me a bad word, then yelled, "What the hell was that for?"

"What was it for?" Barry Lynn drawled, slamming a sledgehammer and a staple gun on the bar, she's so funny. "She told you to back off many times. She's not interested. Did you need that in eight languages? Did you need a banner? You're not that good-looking; why would a woman like her want to be with you?"

"Now that's a little unkind, Barry Lynn," Norm said. "He's soft looking, pasty, a city folk with a snake for a spine but . . ."

"It's not unkind, it's accurate," Barry Lynn snapped, thunking the sledgehammer. "He's got a gut, a weak jaw, sloping shoulders. . . ."

They began to argue about the man's looks.

"By cannons and guns, Barry Lynn is correct," Howard intervened. He likes to use expressions with weapons in them from his former military days. "The man is a numbskull, and a lady shouldn't have to hit a man to get him to back off. Do you have no brains?" he asked the sea urchin, not insultingly.

"What . . . what the heck? I've got brains!" the sea urchin said, red and flustered.

"Show me," I told him. "I'd like to see your brains."

The drunken man's friends had gotten up from their table, hopefully to restrain the sea urchin, and not to come after me, but that part was unclear. I would take them on, too, if I had to. I would enjoy it. I'd had a tough week with my bed and breakfast business, with Jacob who was playing piano obsessively, and with Sarah who had been brought home by the police again. A bar scuffle, skinned knuckles, and a broken hand from fighting might do me well. Let out some of my flaming hormones.

The drunken sea urchin then made mistake number two. He charged toward me, all heated up, and I had to swing my fist once again, right into that weak jaw of his, and there he went, flying onto his back, rattling his disputed brains.

The drunken sea urchin swore, and his friends came to a dead halt. Why they had simply wanted a roll in the sack, a little hee-haw! Some warmth in their beds! They'd spent a fortune coming up to fish, and they wanted dessert to go with their fish dinners! Why couldn't these Montana women understand that!

"Norm, that rich boy does have a weak jaw and sloping shoulders . . ." Barry Lynn said.

"His jaw is slack because he's scared; his shoulders slope because he's drunk and frightened; his gut is large because of general laziness. . . ." And there they went, arguing again.

That's when I heard a voice right beside me. It was low and deep and gravelly and yummy. "Get out," the voice said to the sea urchin and company.

Logan Taylor, huge and rather menacing, grabbed the man's shirt and yanked him straight up, up, up, I am not kidding, up until that man's toes were off the ground. "Get out," he said again, teeth clenched.

The drunken sea urchin struggled and wiggled like a worm dancing on a fish hook. "Put me down." He stared into Logan's eyes then swallowed hard and whispered, "Please. Please put me down. Please."

"Uh, could you, uh, put him down?" one of the pasty-colored men friends said to Logan, nervous-like.

"Yeah, he's uh . . . We'll take him out," another one said, also nervous.

"How come you don't know how to treat a lady?" Logan asked him, jaw hard, giving him a shake. "Why is that?"

I suddenly envisioned Logan in the doorway of a humongous, iced, decorated gingerbread house, waving at me. I conjure up humorous images with food which, in this instance, made me super mad. "You know, I didn't need help," I snapped to Logan.

Logan turned to me, the sea urchin's toes dangling, clearly confused. "I'm sorry?"

"What am I to you? A damsel in distress? Do I look weak? Do I look helpless?" I could feel my temper getting hotter. He was playing right into a very sore, sensitive spot for me. I could handle this myself, and I did not need help.

He eyed me, from the tip of my white streak down to my red cowboy boots. "No, you don't look helpless, but I wasn't going to stand by and let this jerk come at you."

"Why not? I'd hit him twice. I was getting ready to do it again and then you had to jump on in and interfere." I glared up at him.

"I jumped in," he said, still holding the sea urchin, who had a stunned, petrified expression on his face, "because I can't tolerate men treating ladies badly and that's what I saw. I apologize for not getting here sooner." He glared at the man. "You're not a gentleman, are you?"

The sea urchin nodded. "I am," he whispered.

Logan shook him. "You're not a gentleman, are you? Be honest."

The sea urchin squeaked out, in sure, sea urchin fashion, "No. I'm not."

"I'm handling this situation," I said. "I could have taken on him and his friends with the fancy schmancy fishing outfits and pale, fleshy faces by myself. I didn't need you to take over here."

"I was trying to help you."

Man, up close Logan's eyes were green with flecks of gold. His photo periodically in the newspaper had not picked up that goldenness. Black lashes, lines fanning out from the corners of his eyes. *He was hot.*

"Help me? I don't need help." I was steamin' mad.

"Ya gotta understand, Logan," Barry Lynn called out, playing with the sledgehammer. "Men hit on Meredith all the time. She handles the situation, and we move on. It's our entertainment. Second only to my annual toy drive. Reminder to everyone: Christmas is less than six weeks away. Start buying new toys. Bad economy, and we got a lotta kids who need a Christmas this year. I need bikes, especially. Now a bunch of you got a lotta money, and I want to see you carrying in armloads of toys and bikes. Put 'cm right under the Christmas tree in the corner. Don't forget, if you don't give toys, you get suspended from my bar for one year."

Out of the corner of my eye I saw beer mugs being raised. That was our way of agreeing. No one wanted to get suspended from the bar; that'd be a tragedy.

Logan shook his head. "No, we don't move on. First this guy"—he shook the sea urchin, who was now gray with fear, and Barry Lynn was right, the shoulders sloped—"is going to apologize, and then they're all going to leave, then we'll move on."

One of the fleshy face nervous friends said, "Uh . . . look around. We're sorry about this. We're not from here—"

"Gee, now that's a surprise!" Wise Woman Vicki said, exasperated. "You're as out of place as a pink flamingo would be on my ranch."

"Logan, the only thing Meredith needs help with is her cowgirl hats." Wise Woman Katie called out. "She's got a definite cowgirl hat shopping problem."

I raised an impatient eyebrow at Logan's expression. "All we ladies have a vice. I happen to like my cowgirl hats. Different colors, different styles . . . for different days, different moods." I knew why I'd started my slight obsession with pretty cowgirl hats. It was to deflect attention away from something else about me that wasn't pretty, not pretty at all. "Sometimes I'm in a bad mood so I wear black; better moods mean I pull on my pink hat with the brown ribbon. You know how it is."

He shook his head. "No, I don't."

"Can you," the sea urchin squeaked, "can you let me go? Please?"

Logan dropped him. I stuck my cowboy boot out and caught him on the way down so he landed on his buttocks.

"Now that you're on your buttocks, listen up," I said, leaning over. "I didn't want you to hit on me. I didn't ask for it. I told you to back off and you didn't and I had to smell your drunken whiskey breath. That grossed me out. You touched the streak of hair my daddy says I got as a blessing from my ancestors. That triggered my temper. You flicked my cowgirl hat off my head. That pissed me off. Don't treat a lady like a tramp, you got that, fleshy face? We're not your toys, we're not your playthings. We're not for your amusement. We are people, with brains far brighter than yours. And for the record, I'm not impressed with your money or that you could buy all the fancy restaurants in town. We have no yachts in Montana, by the way. Braggarts annoy me. Braggarts are insecure. I can't stand insecure men. If you can't present yourself to a woman without bragging, you ain't a man. Got that?"

He nodded. "Yes, ma'am," he whispered, stricken.

"Leave now," I said.

"No," Logan said.

"What?" I straightened up.

"I said no."

"No what?" I put my hands on my hips. I don't like to hear the word "no." I'd heard it way too much during a certain part of my life, and now I won't tolerate it.

"No, he's not leaving until he apologizes."

"Good idea," Barry Lynn said.

"Splendid," Howard said. "He needs to say he's quite sorry. He was ungentlemanly. Came off like a bomb."

"I do believe that's correct," Norm said. "An apology is in order."

"And you three." Logan glared at the sea urchin's friends. "You're going to apologize for allowing your friend to harass a lady without interfering and hauling his butt out of here before she got offended."

The three friends gaped at Logan. He did make an impressive figure. Towering. Strong. Not happy. Toughened face. Cowboy boots, of course, worn and scuffed. Jeans. My, he had a nice butt.

"I told you I can handle this situation," I said, indignant, though I did admire the butt.

"I'm handling it now."

"No, you're not. You can't waltz into this bar and take over. I'm going to finish this up myself."

"You can finish this after me."

What? No. "No, I'm finishing it my own way."

"After me, lady with the cowgirl hat obsession. An apology is needed."

The sea urchin and his friends tried to slink out. Not a good idea. The Three Wise Women formed a line, as did a bunch of other Montana men and women, arms crossed on their chests.

"Yeah, what do they think this is?" Wise Woman Katie said. "They come to Montana in their fishing costumes, guts spilling over, go to the local bar and hit up a woman without an apology? Sorry, I agree with Logan here."

"But I don't want their apology. I want them to leave so I can drink my beer and do the Gracious Journal Vicki brought for us."

"It's a Grateful Journal," Vicki said, so helpful. "You write down what you're grateful for."

I glared at Logan.

He smiled down at me from his great height. "I'm grateful that I like your hat."

"I don't care what you like," I said, sulkily. "Don't expect me to fall all over you with thanks, because I won't."

"I didn't ask for your thanks."

"You're not going to get it."

"Okay, okay," one of the friends said. "We're going to leave. If you all move out of the way, this will end peacefully."

"Apologize," Logan commanded.

"I don't have to apologize," one of them stuttered. "I didn't do anything wrong, Mervin was assaulted, and if you people don't move, I'm going to call the police."

Laughter.

He blushed.

"Half the police force is right here, son," Norm said. "Yun, would you care to get involved in this unfolding incident?"

Lieutenant Yun shook his head. "Nope."

"And I'm going to call my lawyer!" another friend said.

More laughter.

"Call him! Tell him to bring his gun," Katie the Wise Woman dared. "I'd like to see your lawyer's tiny gun. I'd like to see your tiny guns, too. Your guns are teeny tiny, aren't they?"

"I think his guns are about as big as the guns on a rat I saw in my barn the other day," Vicki said, pushing back her brown and gray ponytail. "My cat ate the rat."

"Statistically speaking you have no chance of winning this in court," Hannah said, squinting her eyes behind her glasses. Hannah is a math professor at the college in town. She is obsessed with mathematics. On Friday night she goes online and does math problems with people around the country. "It was self-defense."

Logan Taylor looked at all four of the men. "This is the last time I'm going to tell you that Meredith here needs an apology. I'm counting to three. One, two . . ."

"We're sorry! We're sorry! We're really, *really* sorry. Oh, man!"

"Lady, I'm sorry, okay? I'm sorry I hit on you—"

"Apology not accepted," I said. "But can I show you my left hook?"

They scurried out faster than you can say, "Merry Christmas."

I glowered at Logan.

He grinned at me.

"Could I have a moment of your time, please?" I asked.

He was *so* hot.

And I was *so* going to completely, utterly ignore that delicious fact. If I didn't it would lead to nothing but more pain. I knew that.

I knew that.

"Come on, you testosterone-driven cowboy oaf. Get outside so I can give you a piece of my mind." I stomped out.

He followed.

Chapter 2

I live on the top floor of a three-story brick house built in 1889 that I bought about a year ago and transformed into my bed and breakfast/morning café business.

When I'm in my bedroom with the peaked roof I can see all over Telena and to the Elk Horn mountains. I feel like I'm in a very tall, old tree house with a claw foot tub.

My bedroom is a lovely place to temporarily lose my mind. I decorated my four-poster bed with a light yellow flowered comforter, and a mountain of white pillows, with white lacy material draped over the posts. I have a white dresser and desk and a pile of books to read by my nightstand. How would Logan look in my bed? I smashed that thought because then I would have to deal with his look of disgust when he knew what I know about myself.

Also on the third floor are two other small bedrooms for Sarah and Jacob, my sister's kids who have had too much heartbreak in their lives and now live with me, a living area with French doors to a small deck, and a bathroom.

My home has a coal chute through which, obviously, coal used to be funneled. I have an old carriage house on the property that used to house, obviously, horses and a carriage. The home has a short stair rail because people were much shorter when this home was built, wide, ornate white trim, and eleven-foot tall ceilings on floors one and two. Downstairs there is one guest bedroom, a parlor with a piano and a fireplace, a sun-filled dining area with a fireplace, and a kitchen. On the second floor there are four bedrooms that I've decorated with four-poster beds, wooden chests, old-fashioned wallpaper, stacked hatboxes, and armoires.

I have named my bed and breakfast, "Meredith's Bed and Breakfast," because at the time, in the midst of a stress tornado, I couldn't think of anything more clever.

I did some research, and my home has more history in it than a history book.

It was built by a Jewish businessman. He had five daughters and a wife. One of his girls ended up marrying the boy who lived directly behind this house; another left town with a convict. Apparently he was a handsome convict.

A railroad executive also lived here with three different wives, who all predeceased him. He had nine kids, a timepiece, and a top hat. I have framed that photo in my entry. A mine owner lived here, alone, and he apparently fancied the ladies. A millionaire lived here for two decades and never left the house. Three sisters bought it at one point. One owned a bar; one worked at a church; one was a doctor who provided birth control to Telena. They had many "gentlemen" callers. It was also once a popular house of "ill repute," as confirmed by an old newspaper article. The madam in charge was named, no kidding, Hearty Tallfeather.

I bought it from a woman who wanted to move outside of Telena and start a farm. I heard she had over two hundred chickens at one point and sold eggs and garlic to all the local stores. They called her the Egg Lady. I also heard she told people what was going to happen in their futures. She wasn't a fortune teller, she was a "future predictor," her words. Popular lady.

Sometimes, I think, with these old houses, that the previous owners' spirits all somehow stay in it. Their lives, their memories, their problems and tears, laughter and joy, their fears and their hopes are still here, somehow embedded in the walls, the chandeliers, the original wood floors.

So when I hear a pitter patter of feet and no one is home, I shrug my shoulders. When I hear a horse whinny or the creak of carriage wheels, I don't think anything of it. When a hint of twenties music tra la las for a second, I shrug it off. When I hear two women whispering and see nothing but a lace curtain floating in the wind, I know I'm not losing my mind.

Maybe someone with a long, ruffled skirt, a pink parasol, and black button-up boots, had her heart broken by a fickle young man . . .

Or maybe she's running in, only to change clothes, grab her bonnet, and catch the first train out of town to start a whole new life in California. . . .

This is what I do know: My old, history-laden house will stand long after I'm gone.

Maybe I'll come back and haunt it.

That night I dreamed of the accident.

The pavement beneath my back was cool and wet

from rain, the moonlight shining on the underside of my parents' car, which was completely flipped over and in a ditch.

My breath felt constricted, as if it was being cut off, pulled away from me, my body weakening, freezing.

"Meredith! Where are youuuuuu?" my sister sang out, then giggled, still stumbling around near the car. "What a trip! How fast do you think we were going?"

I heard a motorcycle engine, then a man was leaning over me, his white shirt a beacon in the darkness. His eyes were intense, but somehow calm, too. Through the razor-edged haze of unbelievable pain and shock, those eyes held me steady.

"Stay with me, stay with me," he yelled. He pulled off his white T-shirt and ripped it into pieces. I had no idea why he did that, nor did I understand what he was doing with my left leg which felt as if it was on fire. I didn't understand why a half naked young man with a beard was leaning over me, the pain too excruciating to think through. "You're going to be fine."

In the distance I could hear my sister giggling, laughing. "What a ride! Where are you, Meredith? Wasn't that fun?"

No, it had not been fun. Leia had picked me up from a friend's where we'd been studying for a final. I was eighteen. She was twenty-one. I hadn't known she was drunk when I got in the car and she sped off.

I felt the edges of my eyes go dark. "It's getting black," I whispered. "Why is it black?"

He swore, finished working on my leg, then held my face with both of his hands. "Don't look at the black. What's your name?"

I tried to tell him my name, but the pain, which had been shooting up and down my body, like a speeding train stuck in forward then reverse, reached my head.

I think I screamed, I think it was me, or maybe the scream was stuck so deep in my mind I didn't open my mouth to let it out.

"What's your name?"

I shook my head as I heard him swear again, although I knew he wasn't swearing at me. He was huge I noticed, his shoulders blocking out the moon, as he propped me up with his arms.

"There's a light in my head," I told him. It was white and gold and moving. It was so pretty. So safe. It reminded me of the star on top of our family's Christmas tree.

"No!" he yelled again. "Get back from the bright light. Look at me, look at me."

My sister, off in the distance giggled again, that giggle bouncing off the trees. "Whoa! Whoa! We flipped and flipped!"

I looked at those eyes, inches from my face, as my breath seemed to swoosh out of me, leaving me alone, my whole body floating, the pain finally subsiding, a golden glow wrapping me up tight. My last memory was of him reaching for the bottom of my sweatshirt and ripping the whole thing in half. I was vaguely embarrassed about this young man seeing my boring beige bra, and then there was nothing but the stars and they faded quickly and everything else went completely black.

The bad sort of black. The sort of black that says, "This is it. Welcome to heaven."

"I quit. I won't tolerate this one second longer. I have tried to organize you people, tried to inject a sense of solemnity into the Telena Christmas Concert Series, to bring it to a righteous level, but I can no longer volunteer my precious time, unless you all agree to my vision of how the concert must go." Ava Turner stuck her fierce bosom out under her prim sweater.

I resisted the urge to roll my eyes to the back of my head and leave them there. I was sure the other ten people in the community room at the library did, too. I envisioned sour grapefruit surrounding Ava like a hula hoop.

"I have been the director of the Telena Christmas Concert Series for two years," Ava puffed. "And I can't have my authority questioned."

I heard three people groan. One sniffed. One said, under her breath, "And I believe I have the authority to arrest you for being obnoxious." (That was a police officer named Pauline.) Val Porter, eighty years old and as outspoken now as she's been for the last seventy-eight years, according to those who know her, said, "Oh, my donkey's butt. You aren't a dictator, Ava. We're a committee, we decide together."

"Together?" Ava said, her voice pitchy. "This is not a hippie movement. I am the director. You may make suggestions, but I am the ultimate authority and I will make the final decisions about the content of this concert."

"Yes, together," Val croaked. "We gotta change things. Our numbers have been dwindling since Chit Holcomb quit running it three years ago, bless that handsome gentleman."

Chit, seventy years old, widowed for ten years, and a retired oil exec, had decided to move to Arizona during Montana's winters because, he said, "I figure that if I'm in and out of two states I have a better chance of finding me a wife. I'm still sexy, don't ya think, Meredith?" I assured him he was, and he ate the strawberry waffles I'd cut up and arranged in the shape of a sports car for him.

"Bless Chit," Pauline murmured. "And bless me, because I want to handcuff that Ava's mouth."

"Our numbers were lower last year but we had a better audience, a more educated, cultural group who knew how to appreciate a high class concert," Ava sniffed.

"It was boring," Howard said, matter of fact. "Boring. All these solemn, sad Christmas songs, all classical music, no fun, no laughter, no skits. It was a defeated battlefield."

I thought Ava was going to pop. "I am bringing class to this sleepy town, class. Chit did not have the musical background that I have, the prowess for directing and choral training. We need hymns, not banging on drums. Melody, not rap. A serious choir, not a hard rock concert. No skits. *Class!*"

"Unless we offer free beer, we are going to lose even more people if we don't make radical changes to this infinitely boring concert series," Barry Lynn said. "We can't afford to lose the tourism. All of our businesses need people."

"Are you saying my concert won't bring people in?"

"I think I saw more drunken elves in my bar last year than you had people for *our* concert," Barry Lynn said. "Word got out that it was a funereal affair; all that was missing was the pallbearers, dead body, and incense, and they didn't buy tickets."

"Well, I never!" Ava huffed, fierce bosom out again.

There was a tight, tense silence. "I think, Ava," I said, trying to be gentle, which can be difficult for me, "that we need to, well, modernize things, appeal to a broader audience, make sure that the younger people are excited about coming, the families, the college-aged kids—"

"This is not a family event—"

"It should be!" Barry Lynn shot out. "It's Christmas, remember, Ms. Scrooge?"

The arguments went on and on until I was nauseous and Ava stuck that fierce bosom out under her prim sweater one last time and declared, "You've spoken then. I am walking right out that door and once I leave, that's it. I will no longer be your director. I cannot possibly support this outrageous idea, this radical Christmas concert, this abomination. You'll ruin my reputation!"

She grabbed her purse, chins wiggling with righteous indignation, and pointed her finger in the air, slowly heading toward the door. "Once I leave, that's it!"

I waited to see if anyone would move to stop her.

She slowed her walk, still pontificating, as she reached for the door handle. "If I step through this door, you'll regret it."

Still, not a movement.

"This is your last chance. Without me this concert series will fail!"

Not even a wee flick of a wrist or bat of an eye.

Ava blushed bright red, turned on her heel, and slammed the door.

All was quiet for about two seconds, then Pauline patted me on the back. "You'll make a great Christmas concert director, Meredith."

"Me?" I said, stunned.

"Yes, you will," Howard mused. "It will be an extraordinary event. It'll be the bomb. The bomb of all concert series."

I puzzled over that one. The bomb of a concert series?

"Who votes for Meredith?" Barry Lynn said, raising her hand. Those hands shot into the air before I could say, "My Santa, you sure are fat."

"Oh no. Heck no."

"Ho, ho, ho!" Pauline said.

"Jingle bells," Barry Lynn said.

"Oh no," I said again, feeling panicky. "I can't."

"You can!" Val said. "You're going to make a beautiful Mrs. Claus, darling. Have you thought about who should be Mr. Santa Claus? We'll need a Mary, too, mother of Jesus!"

"Not me." I was appalled. "Someone else!"

But the "someone elses" were already getting slices of the Shot and Stirred Strawberry Angel Cake I'd made and that was that.

I, Meredith Ghirlandaio, whose bed and breakfast business was struggling, who worked almost all the time, a whacked out woman who was trying to handle two troubled kids, was elected director of the Telena Christmas Concert Series.

"This is delicious, Meredith," Howard said. "Divine."

I buried my head in my hands.

Why did Logan Taylor's manly, smiling face dance in front of my eyes?

No sane person is up at 1:00 in the morning decorating a Christmas tree in her dining room with pink and white angels and pink lights. No sane woman thinks nonstop about a man unless she is losing it.

I must be losing it.

Logan. Taylor. Taylor, Logan. Meredith Taylor. *Oh, stop it!*

Why did he have to have such a romantic name? Why did he have to be huge and tough-looking? Why did he have to have a chest that I wanted to lie on?

Why did he have to have a gravelly voice that oozed through my body?

Why did I keep replaying our last encounter in my head . . . ?

"Hello, I'm Logan Taylor."

I ignored Logan's outstretched hand. We were outside the bar, which was where I'd yanked him after getting rid of the sea urchin and friends. The snowflakes drifted down, and it felt like we were in one of those sappy Christmas TV specials. Except the heroine in those movies is not generally in possession of a red-hot temper and a powerful right hook.

"I know who you are, Mr. Macho. I don't need rescuing. This is Montana, remember? Or, have you spent so much time out of state you forgot? Women ride tractors through snowstorms, hunt, and shoot rattlesnakes out of the ground if they get too close to the house. Barry Lynn runs this bar and has broken up fights with modern day warriors. My friend, Katie, gave birth to all her kids without drugs, and my friend Vicki runs one of the biggest cattle ranches in this state."

"I haven't forgotten," Logan drawled, grinning at me. "My mother's family has been here for four generations. I have an aunt who could shoot a mosquito from fifty feet away and a great grandma who could guzzle any man under the table and then wrestle a calf to the ground. I am well aware of the strength and courage of women here."

"Then you were doubly in the wrong to interfere. That was an obnoxious show of testosterone and maleness."

He raised his eyebrows at me, and I could tell he was trying not to smile.

"Do you find me amusing?" I snapped. *Can desire knock a woman to her knees or is that only in the sappy Christmas TV specials?*

His smile became wider. "Yes, Meredith, you are somewhat amusing. But you are many other things, too."

"How do you know my name?"

He hesitated. "I've heard of you."

Oh, darn it and Christmas bells! What did the man know? "And?" I snapped.

"And it's a pleasure to meet you."

I crossed my arms. "Why, you truck-sized male? Why is it a pleasure to meet me?"

He stepped closer, and I tried not to swoon, but golly gee, if mistletoe had dropped right out of the sky at that second, I would have been hard-pressed not to make a grab-and-kiss gesture.

Nothing wimpy or pale or weak about Logan Taylor.

Such a man!

And he will judge you harshly, exactly like all the others, so put a lid on this brief foray into passion, I told myself. *Don't set yourself up.*

"It's a pleasure to meet a woman who can deck an obnoxious drunk, wears a red cowboy hat, and has an attitude. I hear you bake well, too. Thick French toast with homemade raspberry syrup that's to die for. An Italian omelet that brings shame to all other omelets. Cinnamon rolls with a secret recipe."

"I like decking obnoxious drunks, and I like my red cowgirl hat, and my omelets are lighter and fluffier than anyone's. I will never tell the recipe for the Ghirlandaio Family Go-Go Cinnamon Rolls, but I don't have an attitude." Instantly I envisioned cinnamon rolls circling Logan.

"Yes, you do."

"I defended myself against a leech and *I* have an attitude?"

"Perhaps it was the way you defended yourself." Those eyes, those green-gold eyes twinkled at me. No kidding. There was twinkling going on here!

"And how's that?" I was still ticked off.

He paused, and the smile disappeared. "Fearlessly. Confidently. With total control. Almost as if you were used to it."

"He touched my hair!"

Logan's eyes examined the white streak through the black. "You don't like your hair touched?"

"Not by him."

He nodded, serious now. "I understand. The man was a disrespectful, rude creep. Had I been there earlier, I would have removed him from your presence immediately so you wouldn't have had to deal with him."

"I can protect myself," I said, but it was weak. So, okay. Maybe it was a teeny tiny bit romantic for a man to be protective, to want to rescue me from a situation. Was it anti-feminist to think that? "All right, tough guy, nice meeting you, stay out of my business and my life, don't ever try to rescue me again, and a Merry Christmas to you." I turned to go back into the bar, but he caught my arm.

"All right, tough lady, it was nice meeting you, too. I won't get in your business again until at least tomorrow, I won't interfere with your life unless you invite me or I invite myself, and a Merry Christmas to you, I'd like to see you again."

No. Definite no. That would be a disaster. "Why do you want to see me again? I haven't been pleasant, I yelled at you, called you a testosterone-driven cowboy oaf and told you not to treat me like a damsel in distress. That doesn't usually lead people to want to see others again."

He was so close now that if it hadn't been snowing, I was sure I could have felt his heat. My, I did love his cowboy hat. Cowboy hats are so earthly, Americanly sexy.

"Here's what I know already, Meredith," he said, his voice soft. "I've never seen a woman in action like you before." He chuckled and that chuckle ran down my spine in an earthly, Americanly, and sexy way. "You're a tough lady, and smart. You stood up for yourself, fought for yourself, and stayed cool the whole time. You're articulate, even when you're knocking a man on his butt."

"I wanted . . ." I was getting all confused again. "Honesty is the best policy." I cringed. Honesty is the best policy? What was I? A school teacher?

"Sure is, and I'm being honest here. I like how you don't filter what you're thinking; I like the way you dress with all the different cowboy hats I've seen the last two weeks; I like the sound of your voice, and your smile. I wanted to introduce myself before this, but couldn't quite catch up to you." He winked.

I inhaled sharply. Yikes. He knew I'd been avoiding him!

"I like your independence, too." He grinned again, his green eyes smiling at me, inviting, welcoming. "Are those good enough reasons? Can I take you to dinner?"

I pinched myself as a haze of lust started swirling around me. This, I had to call a halt to. I needed to reject before I was rejected.

"No, they're not good enough reasons. Look here, testosterone cowboy. I don't want to go out with you. What's the point? I go to dinner with you a couple times, you want to swing me into bed, and then that's that, you go back to your 'work' in whatever state that's in now. You want a Montana sweetie, don't you? You want a little hee-haw like those drunken fishermen in there, but you wrap it up prettier, isn't that right? I don't do that type of thing."

All vestiges of a smile were now gone, his face hardening. "I don't either, and that's not what I meant." I did not miss the sharp anger lacing through those words.

"Good. Because I'm not that kind of lady."

"I never thought you were, Meredith," he bit out, shoulders back as if I'd hit him. "I was asking you to dinner because I thought we'd have great conversation if you could refrain from decking me. I thought maybe we'd laugh, and I could get behind that nail tough exterior you wear so mercilessly. I could get to know you, without the armor. Would I want to take you out to dinner a few times, throw you into bed, and then leave? No. That's not in the plan. *I'm not that kind of man.* Do you always judge people so harshly?"

"I judge what I see."

"You judge what you see?" His eyes narrowed, and he did not look so gentle anymore. "So, let me get this right. I come into the bar, step into a fight you're having with one man, which is soon going to be four men, I lift the man off his toes, make them all apologize to you, and you've got me pegged as a man who will flip a woman into bed and then drop her when I move on? Have I got that about right?"

I nodded. Gall. Wasn't I right?

"Well, guess what, Meredith, with the white streak in her hair and a dangerous right hook, you're wrong. Entirely wrong."

We glared at each other in the silence of the

snowflakes. This argument would not fit into one of those sappy Christmas shows.

"Damn, but you are going to be difficult, aren't you," he muttered. "Not a moment's peace will I have with you."

"What do you mean by that?"

"I mean, Meredith Ghirlandaio, that I'm going home, to my ranch, outside of town, and I will see you soon so that you can begin torturing me with your difficultness."

"What are you talking about? I'm not going to see you soon—"

Logan Taylor wrapped one arm around me, drawing me close from chest to knee, put his hand on my cheek, tipped my head back and said, "I would really like to kiss you, but I won't. You're a classy lady, and first we're going to date and I'm going to treat you like a lady should be treated. Then, when you're ready, and you ask me to, I'm going to kiss you and that'll be the start of us."

"Us?" I said weakly, breathlessly, and I cursed myself for it. Where was my tough cowgirl attitude?

"Yes. Us. But it's too much for tonight, my lady Meredith, so, good night."

He released me, and all his warmth was instantly gone. Poof. I leaned against the wall of the oldest bar in Telena with the bullet holes to prove it, and attempted to breathe.

I was in trouble. No doubt about that.

Chapter 3

Two days after going weak in Logan's arms, I sat next to Jacob at the piano.

"Hi, Jacob."

Jacob took his hands off the keys and placed them in his lap. I dropped an arm around his shoulders. He was rigid and stiff at first, but then leaned into me.

"Everyone talked about how beautiful your Christmas songs were this morning." That was true. There was a reason that on Saturday and Sunday mornings we were packed for breakfast from 9:00 to 1:00. Jacob, a piano genius at age twelve, usually played about three and a half hours then. People called asking when he would play. My answer was always, "He'll play when he feels like it." I looked at his tip jar. "Looks like you made another haul of money."

Jacob had a mop of brown hair and huge brown eyes that showed every emotion he was feeling. Unfortunately, he hardly spoke. When I asked him why he loved piano, he said, "I like that I can make music with my fingers."

When I asked him why he liked to play for hours every day, he said, "Because then it's just the piano and me, not me and my loneliness."

When I asked him how school was going, he said, "Not so good. The kids think I'm weird." He had not made friends this last year here. "No one likes me. I'm always alone at school unless the kids are bugging me. I'm invisible."

Jacob and Sarah's childhood had so far been lousy. Though their mother, Leia, and I were born and raised here, Leia had left and wandered from city to city after high school. She had two boyfriends who produced Jacob and Sarah and who had both taken off into the wild blue yonder.

Our parents tried to visit with their grandkids as much as possible, when they could locate their daughter. I came and got them for three weeks every summer and took them to stay with me in New York, starting when Sarah was five and Jacob was three. They had been so happy to see me, so tearfully grateful, it was gut-wrenching. No child should be that pathetically relieved to be away from his or her mother.

Leia had finally settled in a small town in Idaho for about six months, before she declared, "I cannot be a mother for one more minute. I have to live my life. My spirit is crushed, my inner soul is crying for freedom, and I know my destiny isn't here. I'm sorry, kids." She left the kids with a neighbor and called me. "Sorry, Meredith! They like you better anyhow."

She was sorry. Sorry. Well, good golly, apology not accepted, you selfish she-devil. I smashed down that well of anger that flowed against my sister for numerous, complicated reasons.

My parents, both doctors, prepared to leave a new medical clinic for kids that they'd helped to open in Africa to take care of their grandchildren. I didn't see that happening. Leave all those kids? No. So, after a long, long argument, and a gale of tears, I quit my chef's job in New York City, packed up, and flew out to Leia's.

"I'm sorry, my sweet daughter," my father wept. "I'm sorry for all that Leia has done to you. We could not control that girl. I know your teenage years were so hard with her moods, her rebellion, her tantrums, and then with the accident, honey. She was dropped on her head by the nurse when she was about a day old. Maybe that's what caused all this."

"It's my fault," my mother groaned. "In every single generation in my family line in England, there is one girl who is so naughty, so very naughty, and your sister is it. It's the royal curse, I know it. I have drunk so much tea over that girl."

When I arrived at Leia's neighbor's house, I couldn't see how I could possibly make a living at anything in her town, so I thanked the woman profusely, packed up the kids' possessions, bought this three-story brick house with almost every penny I had, and "set up shop," as my mother would have said.

It was a good decision to leave Idaho. Leia, as usual, had not made a stellar reputation for herself. In fact, she had spent more than enough time in bars, and had had many boyfriends, most not married. Jacob and Sarah had been on the receiving end of kids' merciless teasing because of it. Heartbreaking.

"Come on in, Jacob, and I'll make you some of my Excellent Eggs Benedict with Cranky Crab."

He glanced up at me, skinny, pale, sad, and I ached so bad for that kid, I thought the pain would reel me backwards.

"And, I'll throw in some Boo Boo Blueberry French Toast on the side and cut them into Christmas trees."

That got a small smile out of him. I gave him a hug. "I love you, Jacob. You are a talented, kind person. Never forget that, buddy. I am so proud of you."

He hunched his shoulders. "Aunt Meredith, has my mom called at all? Or e-mailed you?"

Oh, how I had struggled when he and his sister, Sarah, had asked me these questions over the last months. Did I tell them the truth: No, she hadn't contacted me.

Or, did I lie to them to spare them hurt?

I opted for the truth. These children needed no more lies, no more deception, no more blows to their sense of reality. It was disrespectful to them and would only lead to more pain.

"No, honey, she has not."

I hugged him close when he wiped tears from his eyes with both hands, made a choking sound, then banged his fingers on the piano keys, before drifting into a well-known, depressing song.

He liked the Christmas tree blueberry French toast, though.

The police were at my door at 2:00 the next morning. They knew to ring the doorbell to my upstairs quarters only, so as not to awaken my guests. I hurried down the creaking steps and yanked open the front door in my pink robe.

"Hello, Sato, hello, Juan," I said to the officers, pushing my white streak off my face and searing Sarah with what I hoped reflected my truly tremendous anger at her.

"Good evening," Juan said. Juan is the size of a Mack truck. He secretly reads romance novels.

Sato is slender and enters, and wins, weight lifting competitions. He has six children, and his wife is a firefighter. He was two years ahead of me in high school. "She wears the pants in the house," Sato told me once, then stared up into the air with a smile on his face, "But, dang, she looks so *good* in them, so I let her."

"Hi, Meredith," Sato said. "We found Sarah downtown again behind the Santa Claus display. Her male friend ran off. Sarah did, too. She's fast if I do say so myself, but she made a wrong turn down the wrong alley, so we caught up with her."

I thought I was going to cry.

I motioned for everyone to come into the parlor and shut the front door. When we were in the parlor, I shut that door, too, so my guests wouldn't wake up.

I do not feel up to this job of parenting. I am overwhelmed and outgunned. I am lost.

Sarah scowled at me. She was wearing about eight layers of makeup, a mini skirt that barely covered her you know what, tights, and her snow boots. She had a jacket on but had not bothered to zip it, and as she had taken to wearing her shirts unbuttoned way too far down, I instinctively reached to yank her shirt up.

"Aunt Meredith!" she said, appalled. She slapped my hand away.

"Sarah, you pull that shirt up and cover yourself like a lady, or we will stand here and wait all night. You get your boobs back under your shirt *right this minute.*"

"I can do what I want! I told you I'm not going to be constrained by the rules of a Puritanical society anymore, I'm not going to be locked up in a box and do what everyone else in suburbia does, I'm not going to become a cultural zombie—"

"No one asked you to be a zombie," I said, semi-shouting. "We asked that you not sneak out at night and run into alleys with the police behind you."

"I wasn't sneaking. I was exercising my right to be an independent person, make my own decisions, and be who I want to be!"

"Gee, Sarah. We all want to be who we want to be, but hopefully that does not involve the police!"

It was at that moment that Sarah's face, up until now defiant and furious, crumbled. "I'm sick of this! Sick of my life. Sick of it here. Sick of everything."

My initial reaction was to feel sorry for her, but I bucked up. Letting someone wallow in self-pity never helps anyone. "Sarah, you are to apologize to the officers for being out late." I crossed my arms, stared meaningfully at Juan and Sato, and decided to get tough. This was one too many times to be brought home by police. "Is she staying here tonight or are you taking her to jail?"

Juan and Sato understood what I was saying immediately. Juan turned to Sato. "I think this is it. We can't have her continuing to break curfew." He cleared his throat. "We came by, Meredith, uh, as a courtesy. She needs to change into something more conservative, like a sweatshirt. We don't want her inviting problems in jail."

Sato nodded as Sarah's face went white.

"There's a couple of tough gals in there we picked up earlier tonight," Sato said, chest out. "One had the knife, remember? Sharp knife. And she's covered in tattoos. She's from Los Angeles. I think she's still drunk as a skunk. Man, she's got a temper. The other gal's pretty calm, but she was in for murder a few years ago. . . ."

"Can't we separate Sarah from them?" I asked, the solicitous aunt.

Sato and Juan regretfully shook their heads. "Probably not. The gals in the other cell are even worse."

Sarah was having trouble breathing, her breath coming in hiccupping gasps.

"We can't bend the rules for anyone, Meredith. Even if she's a minor," Juan said. "She was out late again, she shouldn't have been, now she has to pay the consequences."

"I understand. I'll get her sweatshirt. I'm sorry, gentlemen."

"No problem, Meredith. It's exhausting dealing with a difficult teenager," Sato said. "We'll take her on into the jail, let you rest. Come and get her tomorrow about two in the afternoon. Sarah, when we get to the jail, I'll have Larinda teach you some self-defense moves. They're not foolproof, but they'll help if she gets busy at the desk and one of the other women comes after you—"

"No! No!" Sarah cried. "Oh no! I don't want to go to jail, oh, please, Aunt Meredith, I won't sneak out at night again, I promise, please . . ."

We let her blather on, petrified down to her toes, for some time, with talk thrown in of "You've broken the law. . . . Your aunt can't control you, so we will. . . . No one's died in the jails here; you won't either. . . . Clench your fists up tight before you box your cellmate, it'll be a better hit. . . ." Then Sato glared at Sarah. Juan kept shaking his head back and forth. I tapped my foot and said, "She needs a lesson. . . ."

Sarah dissolved.

Sato sighed. "Last time, young lady, then we're taking you in. And if we pick you up on a Friday, you're not out 'til Monday, especially since it's the Christmas season and there's all those Christmas parties. We won't be able to get a judge to let you out."

A few minutes later I walked a teary, radically relieved ex-zombie up the stairs, her shoulders slumped, and insisted she take a shower.

When she came into my bedroom, in her pink bunny pajamas, no caked-on black makeup, she looked like a kid again.

When I saw the tears on her cheeks as she slept, I finally cried.

I can't handle my own life. It is truly bigger than me and my capabilities.

"I am enormous," Mary, my very pregnant employee, said cheerfully as she pushed open the swinging doors to our kitchen with used plates. "I am the size of a tank. I think I have five kids hiding in my stomach, and the gorgeous cowboy in the corner eating your Meredith's Sock It To You Pancakes wants to talk to you. Hee haw!"

My hand shook on the spatula. "No. He doesn't. You're kidding. And you are not the size of a tank."

"I'm not kidding." Mary waddled over to the fridge for a pitcher of fresh-squeezed orange juice. She is twenty years old, married, studying to be a teacher, and seven and a half months pregnant but looks sixteen months pregnant. "He asked for you. Said he needed to talk to you about buying proper cowboy hats since you know so much about them. By the way I do like the one you're wearing today. Green with jewels suits you. It's very holiday-ish."

Logan Taylor was in my dining room next to the Christmas tree I'd decorated with pink and white angels and pink lights. I was so nervous I cut through a strawberry and almost cut off my finger. I poured whipping cream in a bowl and half of it dripped down the cabinets. I flipped a pancake and it dropped to the floor because my hands were trembling. "I can't talk to him."

"Why not?" Martha asked. Martha is Mary's sister,

and she is always busy, busy, busy, whereas Mary will sit down and enjoy life now and then. Currently Martha was darting around the kitchen, refilling a bowl with powdered sugar, whipping up eggs, and arranging our Rockin' and Rollin' Chocolate Raspberry Stuffed Croissants.

"Because I don't want to talk to him." What was I supposed to say? I can't talk to him because he makes me sizzle in special secret spots?

"That's not a good reason, out you go. Everyone says he saved you at Barry Lynn's, so go be nice. You know how to be nice, right?" Mary shooed me out. "Don't be a chicken."

"He didn't save me and I'm not a chicken and I can be nice sometimes."

The sisters made clucky chicken noises at me, then got louder and louder as I refused to go. I started worrying that Logan could hear them so, nonchalantly, as if I didn't have a care in the world, I grabbed a glass pitcher, pushed through the swinging doors of the kitchen, and began to pour orange juice for my customers.

Many had stayed overnight. They all gushed. About the house ("charming"), their rooms ("decorated beautifully, so authentic to the period"), the breakfast. ("These pancakes make me want to sing," one woman told me. "Please don't," her companion said. "You'll ruin breakfast.") One man told me he felt like he was in a finely decorated nineteenth century brothel. "It almost feels . . . *seductive* in my room, I don't know why." I did not take offense.

Others were from town. Three of the priests from the cathedral were discussing professional football teams at the same table as two professors from the local college. One professor taught Elizabethan literature; the other was a hard-core scientist. They had a visiting professor with them today, a man named Chinaza, from Nigeria.

The Old Timers Still Kickin' Band, a group of four older gentlemen, including Norm and Howard, the World War II vets, plus their two friends, Charlie and Davis, were playing two games of backgammon. I'd never heard their band, but I'd heard they were good. When they saw me I heard Davis count out, "One, two, three," then they all yelled, "Merry Meredith!"

The guests jumped; the people from town laughed. That's my nickname, "Merry Meredith." I get that nickname because I make people laugh with my food. On Davis's seventy-fifth birthday, I put seventy-five candles on a huge stack of pancakes. On Charlie and Mabel's anniversary I made them a white cake in the shape of a mountain and smothered it in whipped cream because they'd met at the top of a snowy mountain. Though I take my cooking seriously, I believe that food should also be served up with humor. Hence, Merry Meredith. They all think they're hilarious.

And then there was Logan.

Leaning back in his chair, beige shirt, worn jeans, cowboy boots, smiling at me with those white teeth. His hair looked as if it had been lovingly ruffled by the wind, the sun had kissed his face, and the mountains around Telena had stamped him with a manly man look.

I felt sizzly all over, and instantly nervous, the breath swooshing from my body, and then I did something particularly special.

I dropped the pitcher. The noise was deafening, and glass splattered everywhere.

"Please sit down with me, Meredith."

"No, and what are you doing here anyhow?" I

stared up at Logan. He had gallantly leaped up, as had other customers, and Mary and Martha, to help me clean up the shattered mess.

"I'm here because I wanted to eat the best breakfast Telena has to offer, and I want to apologize."

Why did his voice have to be so low and manly and velvety? Why couldn't it be high and squeaky? I swear, each word rolled through my body like liquid chocolate. "What do you want to apologize for?" I snapped.

"I want to apologize for the other night."

"For interfering? For making me look weak?"

"I am not sorry for interfering, but I am sorry for how it made you feel. I really am."

"You're not sorry for interfering?"

He glanced away for a sec. "No, Meredith, I could no more sit back and watch that scene than I could tie my ankles up with a rope and hitch them to the saddle of a galloping horse, but I'm sorry how you ended up feeling about the whole thing. That, absolutely, was not my intention."

Men hardly ever apologize. No man I'd been with had apologized, even after saying such hurtful things, labeling me so harshly, I'd been left reeling. And here was Logan, apologizing because I had ended up feeling bad when he'd gallantly protected me.

I sniffled. I felt warm. I felt my heart crack, and then these darn tears came out of nowhere and filled my eyes.

"Enjoy your breakfast," I choked out then turned to leave. He blocked my exit. It did not escape me that I was now the center of attention.

"I would like to enjoy breakfast with you."

I couldn't. I'd probably cry on the man. I shook my head.

"Go ahead and sit down," Mary called out, waving her chicken wings.

"Yes, do, Meredith," Martha said, making a soft clucking chicken sound. "We can handle everything in the kitchen."

"No—"

"Sit, sit!" Chinaza called. One day I'd arranged blueberries in whipped cream cheese and made the outline of Nigeria for him. "You work hard too much. Please. I tired watching you."

"Yes, Meredith," Davis intoned. He owns much of the downtown property in Telena. "I'll control the boys here, and you have a seat. That man saved you at Barry Lynn's, least you can do is have breakfast with him."

"He did not save me, I do not need saving, I can save myself," I harrumphed. Sheesh! Knowing this banter was not going to cease, I grudgingly sat down at Logan's table, next to the Christmas tree with the pink and white angels. Maybe the angels could save me from this torture, or at least divert my attention from how truly *hot* this man was.

"They look pretty together," Charlie mused. He recites poetry beautifully, but he is part-deaf. When he was in the military the guns blew out part of his hearing.

"Yes, they are an attractive couple," Howard boomed. "She needs to lay down her battle arms and get married."

"No, she doesn't," Davis croaked out. "If she does I can't flirt with her anymore. I'm still holding out on that marriage proposal I offered her."

"She shouldn't get married. It'll lead to captivity," Ranna May called out. She is a former opera singer. Her husband owns a fly fishing store here in Telena. "Captivity, Meredith. Think: captivity."

"Good morning," Logan said to me.

I glared and willed the tears back in my eyes.

"How are you?"

I glared again. Go back in, tears! Why was I crying anyhow? *Because you're attracted to him and know you can't have him because of you know what.*

"I'm fine, too," Logan said, with a smile, a *handsome* and kind smile. "Thank you."

Third time: glare.

"In the morning I like to talk about the weather, what I'm going to do that day, what you're going to do that day, news features . . ."

"I am sure you have had plenty of experience talking to women at breakfast, Logan, but I don't have that much experience talking to men. Please excuse me if my abilities at morning chit chat are not at your level." For some truly blighted reason, his speaking to other women at breakfast ticked me off.

He leaned back in his chair. "Actually, Meredith, I don't have much experience at all talking to women at breakfast."

"No?" I raised an eyebrow.

"No. I was talking about you and I."

"There is no you and I. I'm sitting with you until I can make an escape back to my kitchen."

"We did not meet under the best of circumstances, and I'm sorry about that, too." We shared one of those long, heated glances until I looked away because my insides were way hotter than they should have been.

"I would like to take you horseback riding on my ranch."

Of all the things I thought he'd say, that was at the end.

"No, thank you." I leaned back in my chair. "I'm busy."

"Please."

"No."

He glanced out the window, then those green eyes pinned me back down. I had a momentary flash of being under that man's body, being kissed by him, with maple syrup pancakes floating around our heads. See what I mean about an odd sense of humor with food?

"You do ride?"

I scoffed. "Of course I ride." I'd spent years on horses growing up on our property outside Telena.

"It's a date then."

"No date." I leaned forward. "Logan, may I be clear? I'm not looking to spend more time with you."

"Well I'm looking to spend more time with a woman who wears red cowboy hats. Know anyone?"

"The woman who wears red cowgirl hats says no, she's sorry, but you're too much." Oh, now darn it! Why did I have to say that!

"Too much? What do you mean by that?"

I envisioned whipping myself with a string of garlic. "You're too much. Too much to handle. Too ferociously male, too take-controlly. I have enough . . ." I struggled with the wording here, "*stuff* going on in my life without adding a cowboy."

"That's a shame." He winked at me, but the rest of his serious expression didn't change. Why did I have the feeling this man was playing me? It was at that moment that Jacob launched into the well known notes of a popular love song. I cleared my throat.

I could tell that Logan was working hard not to laugh.

"So, I'll pick you up Monday at 1:00. We'll go out to my ranch, I'll have lunch ready for us, and we'll ride horses. How does that sound?"

"No." I loved riding horses, hadn't ridden in years. I imagined Logan on a horse. For some reason the horse had sausages for legs and a peppermint saddle.

"I have to get going, I have some work to do, but I'll look forward to seeing you."

"I said no. Aren't you listening?"

"I have the perfect horse for you. She's strong and fast."

"Hello?"

He picked up my hand, no kidding, and kissed it. My hand. Like a prince or something. "It's been a pleasure, thank you," he said, then he got up and left as I watched, stunned. Perplexed. Confused. Sizzling. A vision of lying on top of Logan while pink cookie hearts swirled around our heads entered my mind. . . .

Jacob's love song crescendoed. Logan laughed, deep and growly.

As soon as the door shut, my customers, Martha, and Mary applauded.

"Merry Meredith has a date!" one of the priests said, grinning. He gave me a thumbs up.

"Merry Meredith, don't be lured into captivity!" the ex-opera singer insisted.

"It doesn't mean she won't marry me!" Davis yelled, to laughter.

I buried my head in my arms.

I cannot handle my own life, that I know for sure.

Chapter 4

As I made my way back to the kitchen I stopped at Simon's table.

Simon comes in every morning. He is a small, fluttery man who always wears a worried expression on his face. His hands tremble; he's pale. Simon is polite, but he likes his routines to be exact. He sits at the same table, at the back of the dining room, near the window, every day. We reserve his table for him. His decaffeinated coffee is to be served with two squares of sugar, no more, and cream in a silver pitcher on the side. He has three pieces of toast, cut in triangles, lightly buttered, scrambled eggs, no cheese, and five apple slices. None of his food can touch other food on his plate. There is to be no pepper or hot sauce on the table; both make him nauseous. I am to serve him, no one else, no offense, please.

"Good morning, Simon, how are you?"

"I'm well, Meredith. I was so relieved to see that you weren't hurt when you dropped the pitcher." He pinched the bridge of his nose. "But the whole thing,

the noise, the confusion, worrying about you, it was
upsetting for me."

"I'm sorry, Simon." And, I was. I didn't know what
had happened to Simon in his life to make him so
nervous, so compulsive about things, but I had a lot of
compassion for the guy. "I'll be more careful in the
future."

"Please, Meredith. Please do. It was upsetting."

"Have a nice day, Simon."

"I don't think I can do that anymore. That was a
loud noise. Upsetting." His hands trembled. "I think I
will go and lie down so I can decompress."

Over the weekend, Jacob, Sarah, and I spent hours
decorating the bed and breakfast with garlands, wreaths,
and outdoor lights. I'd bought five Christmas trees.
One each for the entry, dining room, parlor, the landing on the second floor, and one for our living quarters.

Each tree had a theme. The pink angel tree was already decorated for the dining room. The entry tree's
theme was an old-fashioned Christmas, in keeping
with the house, so we popped popcorn and strung it,
strung cranberries, candy canes, old toys, strings of
lights that looked like candles, and raffia. The parlor
tree was Jacob's idea: it was a music tree. We wrapped
it in colored lights, and attached a lady's violin, a
flute, a few small drums, and sheet music tied in ribbon. The ornaments were all musical instruments.

The tree on the landing was the "Shiny Ornament
Tree," dubbed so by Sarah. Only huge, shiny, colorful
ornaments and white lights.

It was decorating the tree in our living space on the
third floor, a winter sun peeking through the French
doors, that brought on the tears.

"Let's get out the ornaments we brought from the other house," Sarah said, angry. "Then we can remember that our mother dumped us in favor of her boyfriend."

Jacob slumped on the couch.

"Or, hey," Sarah said. "Maybe we can remember all the Christmases where Mom either wasn't there or had another boyfriend lying around."

Jacob scrunched his shoulders in.

"She's not coming to visit us, is she, Aunt Meredith?" he asked.

My heart ached for the kids; my stomach burned with anger toward my sister. "I haven't heard from her."

Jacob buried his head. Sarah kicked the couch, three times. "I don't even like her, and I'm glad she's not coming, but I'm so mad at her!" She kicked the couch again. I hugged her, she tried to struggle away, I held her close, she struggled more, then gave up the fight and hugged me back. We both hugged Jacob. "I love you two so much," I said. *And I want to string your mother up by her toes on a tree deep, deep in the forest.*

We did not use the ornaments from the other house. We went and bought entirely new ornaments: bears in canoes, Santas on skis, Mrs. Claus in a tutu, upside-down elves, a confused Rudolph, singing reindeer, a snowman sunning himself on a chaise lounge, and two crosses. When we finished decorating the tree, we were actually laughing.

I dreamed of the accident again.

The clanging noise, the burning, acrid smells, the pitch darkness, my sister's giggle, that wrenching pain. I saw him running toward me; he was blurry. I

*saw his hands reach for me. The blackness enveloped
me, sucked me in. The last thing I saw was his eyes.*

"I wrote in my Grateful Journal that I'm glad I didn't
have to do the twister last night with my husband."
Katie blew her bangs out of her eyes. No wonder she
was so thin. Four kids and a husband who chased her
around the house. "We settled for the hurricane. So
much easier, and I could wear my trench coat. How
popular do you think weather games in bed are with
other women?"

"I hardly know what to say, Katie," I said. The hurricane? The twister? Dare I ask?

"I wouldn't know, Katie," Hannah said. Her T-shirt
said, "E=MC squared." "For some reason, members
of the opposite sex do not find me attractive. I do
think I would be good at the hurricane and the twister,
as long as there was some sort of mathematical equa-
tion I could attach to it." She pushed her glasses further up her nose. "There are no solid mathematical
equations for human emotions, though. It's so per-
plexing."

Vicki flicked her brown and gray ponytail back and
said, "I wrote in my Grateful Journal that I'm glad I
have the horses I have. Fast and afraid of nothing.
Plus I got another ranch hand. The man's gorgeous. If
all he does all day is walk back and forth in front of
my windows, he'll earn his salary."

"I wrote in my Grateful Journal that I am so
thrilled I've memorized another twenty-five prime
numbers," Hannah said. "And, I've decided to attend
a mathematics convention in Sacramento. All day,
every day, math. It'll be the trip of a lifetime."

There was another silence.

"Sometimes I don't understand you, Hannah," Katie said, dumbfounded.

We were interrupted by Barry Lynn, who stood on top of a chair and pointed at her Christmas tree in the corner. It was decorated with white lights and beer and wine glass ornaments. Already, there were loads of gifts and bikes. "Folks, only a few more weeks for my toy drive. Kids are in need. We need to give them a Christmas. Bring those gifts and bikes in or you'll get suspended from my bar."

We raised our beer glasses. The Three Wise Women and I had already dropped off four bikes and a pile of toys.

"So how is it being the director of the Telena Christmas Concert Series?" Vicki asked.

"I might lose my mind over it. It'll probably fall out of my head, land in my eggs. I'll whip it right up, and I won't even notice. We need people who can sing and dance and play instruments and be in skits. I'm signing you three up for a skit."

"Us? I haven't been in a skit since fourth grade," Vicki said. "I played a sheriff, and at the end of my solo I shot off my gun into the ceiling. My teacher, Mrs. Phillips, had told me, 'Remember, Vicki, end your solo with a bang.' I thought she meant for me to shoot off my gun. It got the audience's attention."

"Well, you're going onstage again," I said. "But no shooting of guns."

"What will our skit be about?" Hannah asked.

"You'll figure it out. I have faith in the Three Wise Women."

They gaped at me and then, slowly, Hannah nodded. "Are there any rules? Any formulas?"

"Rules?" I pondered that. "Well, it's a Christmas concert so your skit should have Christmas in it somehow. And keep it clean."

"I think I have an idea," Katie whispered, then giggled. She stared into space. She chuckled. She tapped her fingers. She laughed. "Ha! Ha ha! I've got it."

"Good."

"Put us down. We'll do it."

"Well, at least there will be one act," I said.

Katie laughed, huge and rollicking. "Yes indeedy. There will be an act. I'll invite the gals from my Bible study to come. They have a warped sense of humor, so they'll like it." She motioned for Vicki and Hannah to put their heads near hers, then started whispering.

They kept whispering. They giggled. They chuckled. They laughed.

"Hey!" I protested. "I'm sitting right here, ladies! Hello!"

Hannah hissed, "We need math in there to inspire our young people to become mathematicians, the greatest occupation."

"You're gonna love our Christmas skit, sugar bell," Vicki said. "We Three Wise Women know exactly what to do."

I had no plans to go horseback riding with Logan. None. I would say no when he arrived.

On Monday I watched the clock hit 11:30, then 12:00, then 12:30. I took a shower, washed my hair. Not for Logan, for myself, put on my cutest jeans and sweater, not for Logan, for myself, and added a bit of makeup, not for Logan, for myself.

By the time the doorbell rang, exactly at 1:00, I was happy that I looked nice, for myself, and ignored the trembling in my hands and how sizzly I felt in those special secret spots.

He smiled when I opened the door and handed me a beautiful Christmas bouquet tucked into a wicker basket with red roses, white lilies, baby's breath, and greens. "I'm hoping, Meredith, that you've changed your mind and will come horseback riding with me."

"No." I smelled the flowers, couldn't help it, tried not to bawl. I couldn't remember the last time I got flowers. . . .

"For three hours, total, that's it."

"No." I reminded myself that the hulking he-man with the sharp emerald eyes could cause me calamitous heartbreak. "You would have to carry me off by force before I would go horseback riding with you."

He stepped closer to me and, before I knew it, he had swung me up into his arms. I almost dropped my Christmas flowers! "Darn it! What are you doing?"

"I would like to take you horseback riding, Meredith, but I won't carry you off by force, so let's stand here and chat for a while. I'm comfortable. Are you?"

"Put me down." My voice sounded shrieky. "We're not going to chat, we're not going horseback riding, you can't give me Christmas flowers like this and sweep me off my feet. . . ." I stopped. How stupid could I have sounded?

"Then let's talk for a while."

"Talk? I'm in your arms. I can't talk, I can't even think!"

Logan grinned at me. I thought of cupcakes, I don't know why. Pink and blue ones. I wanted to lick the cupcakes.

Three older ladies, all neighbors, gaped at us from the end of my pathway. I heard one of them say, none too quiet because she is a loud person, "That's Logan Taylor. He saved Meredith the other night at Barry Lynn's. He's come for Christmas. He has nice hips, doesn't he?"

"Yes. Firm. Not too thin. Enough to grip," her companion added.

"My Sherman had nice hips. I miss his hips. I do not miss him. He was a cross between a lizard and the devil," the third lady said.

I didn't ponder that confusing statement for too long. "Please, Logan," I whispered, furious. "Put me down. The neighbors are going to talk. . . ."

"Young man, what are your intentions?" one of the ladies demanded.

"My intentions for today are to take Meredith horseback riding."

"Oh my stars and sex! Isn't that romantic!"

"Go, Meredith, go! Take it while you can; get it while you can get it!"

"I'll go and ride your horse." One of the ladies poked her cane in Logan's direction. "I'll ride you all night."

My mouth dropped open. Is that what would happen when I was older? I would still be thinking about . . . *that!*

"Meredith, if you don't say yes, I'll go in your place. I'm a she-lion."

The ladies continued to have their fun while I hissed, "Put me down, you giant giant. Let go of me, you obstinate boar."

"Meredith, we can stand here all day," Logan drawled. "Believe me, you don't weigh more than a shovel full of feathers, you should eat more, but I think it would be easier if you agreed to go horseback riding with me."

My face was inches from his. I saw the way his hair was ruffled by the wind, the slant of that full mouth, the humor in those eyes.

"Okay," I whispered, knowing, *knowing,* I was signing up my heart for brokenness. "I'll ride you this once." I squeezed my eyes shut. "I meant, I'll ride *with you* this once."

His eyes, no kidding, they twinkled again. His mouth tilted. He held me closer for a second, then gently put me on my feet.

"Thank you, ladies," he said, waving. "Meredith has agreed that a horseback ride is exactly what she wants to do this afternoon."

"How come Meredith gets all the fun! Excitement is wasted on the youth!"

"I'd still like to ride you, young man. I'd have to bring my cane. . . . Do you mind canes?"

"You can ride my horse any day. . . ."

I rolled my eyes and slammed into the house, stomping up to my bedroom to get a jacket and my gray cowgirl hat with a black ribbon. I pretended that I didn't care that the Christmas flowers Logan had brought me were so lush and beautiful and that he was lush and beautiful.

"You're on, macho cowboy, tell me more about yourself."

Logan moved his horse closer to mine, both horses panting, the two of us panting, too, after we'd galloped them across his property. It had been so much fun, I had laughed, and laughed again, for the first time in a long, long time.

"I'm a man from Montana." He grinned.

"And?"

"A businessman."

"Ah. You're mysterious."

"Not at all. I'll tell you everything if you want, but can I get away with saying that I'm a professional fly fisherman?"

"You could, but I already knew that. It was the glint you got in your eye when I asked you about your fishing rods at your cabin."

Logan had a new log cabin, about fifteen minutes outside of Telena, on a hill. I knew at night his view of the town lights would be pure magic. As it was, during the day, he had a full-on sweeping view of the town and the Elk Horn mountains.

The "log cabin" definition should not be misunderstood here. His home was sprawling, with a pitched roof and high ceilings. The logs were a golden color on the inside that seemed to glow. A modern kitchen had all the cool, new appliances; there was a breakfast nook, a great room, and a den. We'd had lunch in the breakfast nook, bought by Logan, from my favorite Greek restaurant, which was delicious.

Upstairs there were three bedrooms, with a master bedroom that faced west so, as Logan explained, "I can see all the sunsets I've been missing out on all my life because all I've done is work so far."

I about choked on that one. I had this *thing,* this incessant interest in and excitement about sunsets. Every night they were different, radically, utterly different, like a gift, and I wanted to see each and every one of them, too.

I scooted out of that bedroom fast, so fast that Logan laughed. I had imagined him, sleeping on that bed, naked, and for some reason there was a pile of talking lemon meringue cookies on the nightstand, a glorious sunset lighting up that room like gold and pink fire.

"Do you happen to like fly fishing, Meredith?" He was relaxed in his saddle; he'd obviously spent a lot of time on horses, like me.

Should I tell him? Would that link us too strongly, fly fishing pole to fly fishing pole?

"Have you ever been?" he asked.

We already loved charging horses over wide open spaces.

"It's a great experience. Beautiful," he said.

We loved sunsets. We did not like drunken sea urchins.

"I think you might like it."

We both wore cowboy boots.

"Logan," I said, turning toward him, "I *live* for fly fishing. I live for it."

Now, men should not get that excited about women who fly fish. It's a bit too carnal, but he could not stop that easy grin from spreading across his face. He looked up briefly to the sky as if saying, "God, thank you."

At the same time, I was almost quivering. *He loved fly fishing, too!*

Our horses neighed to each other. He didn't say anything for a second, and I knew he was in a state of fish-bliss, like me. The wind ruffled that blondish hair of his. He had the kind of face you get when you spend much of your life outside, which made him look like a man, not a pretty boy. "Tell me how you came to love fly fishing, Meredith."

Well, first off, *I loved it because I did not have to be with my sister.* Could I say that this early in the relationship? No, I would sound like an unforgiving, mean loon.

"I loved it because I had my mom and dad to myself." That was the utter truth. My sister didn't like it, so she and her temper tantrums and mood swings didn't come. "We'd get up early and take our drift boat down the Missouri or Smith Rivers."

"I've been on both rivers many times."

"All good fly fishermen and women have," I said, pushing my gray cowgirl hat back. Logan was a fly fishing dude. Of course he'd been on those rivers, and many more.

"What else did you love about it?"

"I loved being outside with my parents, being on the water, watching the wildlife, not seeing it from behind a glass window. I loved catching the fish, of course, the challenge, the techniques, but more than that I liked the peace. I liked being in natural beauty. I still do. My mother always said, 'Rivers are a gift, Meredith. Fly fishing is a gift. It is a gift that I always catch more fish than your father.'"

Logan laughed.

"And my father said that fly fishing is like having one foot into heaven. So, you see, loving fly fishing is in my genes."

Incredibly, Logan asked me questions after that, about my parents and my childhood in Telena, and hung on every word. I say, "incredibly," because in my experience men ask women one or two questions, as if they need to check it off their lists, then they launch off on themselves again, addicted to their own lives, their voice a song to their shriveled brains. He asked about my sister. "Can we talk about her another time?"

He nodded. "Sure."

He was a smart man. I had told him earlier that her kids were living with me, but I had the feeling that he already knew. Clearly there was a problem there, but he let it go.

"How did you come to love fly fishing?" I asked him.

"I had a coach named Bill Rotowsky who literally collared me into every sport my school offered. Football, basketball, track, wrestling. I think he saw my home life, how my mother and I struggled financially, saw my rebellious, anti-authority streak, and he came right for me. Sometimes, when I was younger, Mr. Rotowsky used to take me out fishing. His son, Caleb, who is still my best friend, always came, too. They would pick me up early in the morning, we'd drive to the river, and we'd fish all day. Mrs. Rotowsky always made a lunch, and snacks for us, and put everything in a wicker picnic basket. At the time, I didn't know what I was more excited about: fishing or what was inside that picnic basket. But the best thing about those fishing trips was that I felt I belonged. I was part of a family. I had a father figure in Mr. Rotowsky, a mother figure in Mrs. Rotowsky, and a brother in Caleb. That picnic basket was a microcosm of what family love looked like to me."

A wind picked up and blew by, and I huddled into my coat. I wanted to huddle into Logan's and hug him. It was hard to see a young, hurt, lonely kid in Logan now, but it was there, and it made me hurt. I thought of Jacob and Sarah, how lost they were, how lonely for a mother who had never acted like a mother.

"I'm sorry, Logan," I said. "I'm sorry that your childhood was . . . such a struggle, a challenge."

"I didn't tell you so you could feel sorry for me, Meredith; I told you because I wanted you to know about it. I wanted you to know what was behind my love of fly fishing. If I'd had a different childhood, with less bumps in it, less trauma, I wouldn't be where I am now. I wouldn't be the person I am now. I understand people better because of what I went through. I know what it's like to be poor. I know what it's like to be scared. I know how people can morph into someone they're not when they're struggling. I get it. The river, for me, was the great equalizer. It's you and nature and fish."

"Fly fishing isn't only about fly fishing, is it?" I said, and smiled at him.

He smiled back, and for a second I realized that my anger, such a constant for years since my accident, was gone. At least temporarily.

"You're right. Fly fishing is not only about fly fishing. But I still cannot truly explain how thrilling it is each and every time to actually hook one."

I laughed. "There's nothing like it, is there? *Nothing.*"

"Well, there is something like it, only it's better."

"Something is better than fly fishing?" I asked.

"Yes."

"What?"

"Falling in love."

I swallowed hard. Yes, that would be better. I sneaked a peek at Logan. He smiled back.

"Even though you look so macho and male and testosterone practically oozes out of you, I think you've got a romantic side, don't you?" I said.

"Now you know my secret."

"You hide it."

"Yep. I do. But I'm showing you it's there. Only you."

"Thanks, Logan, I'll take note of that."

"You do that."

I thought my heart would flip.

"Want to race?" he asked.

I did. I had to, or I would probably lean over and kiss that Montana man.

I kicked my heels, and our horses thundered off.

I won.

Chapter 5

That night, alone in bed, scrunched up in my yellow comforter, I admired the manger I'd set up on my dresser. I took it out every Christmas season, the day after Thanksgiving, as my parents had. My grandma, the first owner of the manger, always said to me, often with a whiskey tonic swirling in one hand and a cigar in the other, "Gifts are great, but don't forget the ultimate gift." Then she'd give Jesus a kiss.

The manger had seen better days, but then so had the barn where Jesus was born, so I figured it was authentic. There was fake hay, a pitched roof with a tilted star on it, the back wall painted blue. One of the wise men had no head. A lamb was missing a leg. A shepherd had lost an arm. The drummer boy's face was mostly gone, I don't know how that happened. But Jesus, Mary, and Joseph were in good shape.

I thought of my grandma then, long gone. Her thoughts on love? "Love big, sweetie. Love the right man. Love love." Then she'd kiss me and say, "And don't forget the bedroom. That's a man's favorite place to be."

I thought of Logan in my yellow bed. I groaned.

With those tantalizing images dancing through my head I thought about this impossible situation. Logan has a house here. He would be in and out of Telena. I live here full time, therefore I could not get involved with him, be rejected when he knew more about me, end up emotionally shredded, and then have to see him all the time and pretend everything was fine.

I couldn't do it.

I wrapped my arms around myself and rocked back and forth. The problem with getting older, as a woman, and losing all innocence and naïveté, is that you have lost all innocence and naïveté. You know things don't always work out. You know what's coming down the pike in terms of pain. You know that your heart could get pummeled.

And, you know when you meet a man, like Logan Taylor, whom you are connecting with on every level, that he's the one who's gonna do it to you.

He's the one who's going to send you under the covers, crying your eyes out for days, sniffling into tissues, your face a blotchy mess, as you contemplate joining a nunnery in rural Iowa.

I can't do it.

I won't do it.

I should have been able to do it. I felt that anger creep on in again.

"We have to get our numbers back up again for the concert," I told the board of the Telena Christmas Concert Series the next night. I had brought my No-Flour Freak Out Frozen Chocolate Pie.

"This is exquisite," Norm said. "A sensory slice of heaven."

"My goodness it tastes like romance!" Becky Nutt sighed.

"By cannons and guns," Howard said, "This is the best pie I've ever had."

"Here's what I'm thinking," I said, and leaned forward. "We need something new, something different . . ."

They nodded.

"We need a concert with energy, originality, spark. We need to make the audience laugh, sing, and most important remember what Christmas is all about. We've got a terrible economy here, and bringing people in from all over will add money to Telena's businesses, with all our profits going to the children's hospital wing."

"Can't do what Ava the Hun did last year," Barry Lynn said.

"She picked only a few people to be in the concert! Excluded so many people."

"That's right. People who had been in the concert for years were knocked out so she could have the perfect, boring choir up there."

"She hurt people's feelings by kicking them out."

I thought of Telena, the people I'd known as a kid, the ones I knew now. I thought of the mix of people who came into my bed and breakfast every day.

"I have it," I whispered, the idea forming in my head, gaining speed by the second. "I think I've got it . . . How does this sound . . ."

"I wrote in my Grateful Journal that I'm grateful my husband is going out of town for a week so I can get a break," Katie said. "He bought me a Mrs. Claus outfit with a red thong and short, ruffled skirt with white fur trim. The satin shirt has a V neck plunging to my waist and no back."

I brought a beer to my lips. "I hardly know what to say, Katie."

I noticed that the Christmas tree in Barry Lynn's bar now had many presents underneath it. Of course the sign, IF YOU DON'T GIVE TO MY TOY DRIVE YOU'LL BE SUSPENDED FROM MY BAR, helped, too.

"In my Grateful Journal I wrote down that when I'm herding cattle through a snowstorm I'm grateful that I've never gotten lost. God gave me a GPS system in my head." Vicki tapped her head.

"I'm grateful that God gave us math, and I finally received my new calculus textbook. I can't wait to start working on it! I'm saving it for Friday night," Hannah said. She pushed her brown curls back with both hands, she was so excited. "I'm sure my students will be thrilled, too. I get positively orgasmic off of math, equations, quantum physics . . ."

There was a dead silence. "I don't understand you sometimes, Hannah," Katie said, confused.

"What did you write in your Grateful Journal, Meredith?" Vicki asked.

"I wrote I'm grateful that . . ." What I was grateful for was that I had not flung myself into Logan's arms yet, stripped off his shirt, buttons flying, yanked off his belt, pulled off his pants, and jumped him. I could, so easily, take the pleasure for as long as it lasted and live off those memories the rest of my life. "I wrote that I'm grateful for you three." That was true; you have to be grateful for your girlfriends.

Vicki sniffled. Hannah held my hand.

"That's so sweet," Katie said, tearing up. "I don't know what I'd do without you three. All day long, with four noisy kids, then Mr. Creative Love Life comes home and my second shift begins, and I usually have part of a Bible study to finish. . . . Do other women like wearing vampire masks with their husbands to bed? Those plastic teeth are so uncomfortable."

Jacob had a day off school and he played his own haunting, emotional songs in the parlor while Martha, Mary, and I served breakfast to the overnight guests, no cranky ones, none too odd, and the regular crew of people from town who were in and out all morning.

It was when I was pouring coffee for the professors and their professor friend from Nigeria, Chinaza, that I heard him talk about how he loves to play the drums.

"Have you played for long?" I asked.

"Oh yes, since I was child. In our village, we all play drums."

"Does your family live in Nigeria still?" I asked.

His face fell. "Some. Too many gone. My aunt, though, she live in France, my father and his wife in Germany. I here."

We fell silent for a moment, and I was struck, as I often am, by others' pain. But then I had an idea. "Would you like to play the drums for the Telena Christmas Concerts?"

I could tell by his huge smile that his answer would be yes.

"I bring my village in Nigeria to here, to Montana, to my new friends, my new home." He patted my hand. "Yes, I play the drums for you. Thank you. Now I can give a gift."

I didn't spare the professors. "I hear you play the xylophone, Stan."

"Yep, I do. My grandfather taught me."

"Good. I'm signing you up to play in Telena's Christmas Concerts."

"Me? In a Christmas concert?"

"Yes, you. Start practicing. And, Terry, you have a low, deep voice. You're going to be my narrator."

Terry, with the low, deep voice looked so surprised, and so pleased. "Are you sure? The narrator! I've always wanted to be the narrator! Whoa ho! Thanks, Meredith!"

"No problem. Rehearsals start immediately."

Buoyed by my new drummer and company, I headed back to the kitchen. But I was stopped by Charlie, one of the Old Timers, who said, "By golly, if I were to die today and meet my maker and hear the choirs of angels singing, I would be happy, Meredith, because I've had your Kick Butt Crab Cocktail and it is scrumptious! Scrumptious."

I eyed the Old Timers.

They eyed me back. Davis counted off, one, two, three, and they all yelled, "Merry Meredith!"

"Very funny. Gentlemen, do you sing Christmas songs?"

I later peered out the window, up and down the snowy street. Who else had talent in this town who I could throw up on stage for this Christmas extravaganza? My high school friend, Marty Shan, had a dance studio, and everyone likes seeing little kids in costumes. . . . I would ask my artist friends, Claudia and Tim, if they could paint something holidayish, maybe we could transfer their work up to a screen during the concert. . . . The choirs from different churches, schools . . . Ranna May for sure . . .

"Do you think it's normal to crave avocados in your cereal when you're pregnant?" Mary asked. "Because I do. Do we have any avocados?"

* * *

"Good evening."

Logan. Right behind me.

I kept my eyes on the towering Christmas tree in the middle of the town square that would soon be lit with hundreds of colored lights. My body felt like melting into a warm puddle of caramel.

Currently, a group of kindergarteners on bleachers in front of the tree were singing Christmas songs for a large crowd of people. One of them was picking her nose with her middle finger and studying the contents so it looked like she was flipping the audience the bird; another was turned completely around wriggling his butt in time to the music; a third, Katie's daughter, kept exuberantly raising her red velvet dress up over her head, then down again, after displaying her underwear.

Her mother, Katie, stood beside me, "Oh gracious God, oh gracious God," she kept muttering. "Do something!" she hissed to her husband. He was a kind and dear man and tried to signal their daughter to stop flashing the audience.

It backfired. She brought the skirt way, way up and waved the skirt at her parents. "Lord Almighty," Katie breathed. "And she had to wear her brother's Spider-man underwear, didn't she?"

"Hello, Logan." My voice sounded squeaky. I tried to breathe, couldn't, then decided to pretend to be composed. "Logan."

"Meredith," he said. He was way too close, making me feel small compared to that giant chest. "Nice to see you again."

"You, too." Darn that squeak! But how could I talk when I was now envisioning Logan fly fishing next to me, with wedding cakes on silver platters gently sailing down the river around us? I shook my head. Wedding cakes! Where had that come from?

"Where are Sarah and Jacob?"

"They're at home. I invited them but . . ."

"They didn't want to come?"

I shook my head. No, Sarah didn't want to come because, she said, "The girls don't like me. Larissa drew a picture of me with all this black makeup over my eyes. Everybody laughed. She called me raccoon-hooker face." She'd pretended she didn't care, but she ran up the stairs lightning quick and slammed her door.

"Jacob, do you want to go to the tree lighting tonight?" I'd asked.

He'd pounded out Bach on the piano then said, "No. Did my mom call today?"

When I said no, he went back to a ferocious pounding of Bach, but I saw the tears.

Telena was in high Christmas gear. The main street of town had been decorated with garlands, with huge displays of red and green lights arching over the entire street. Trees were wrapped in white lights, and each lamppost was decorated with a huge wreath.

Logan suddenly laughed, and I knew he had spotted the girl who was flipping everyone the bird.

"How about dinner afterward?" he said.

"No." I felt that tension instantly between us.

"Why not?"

Why not? Because I was feeling way too much for this man, way too soon, and the situation was an impossible heartache speeding toward me that I needed to avoid. "I . . . uh . . . I need to get home . . . to wrap presents."

"To wrap presents," he said, long and low. "Ah. Well, with Christmas weeks away, it's a good idea to get right on it."

"Yes. It is."

"How about dinner, then I'll help you wrap the presents up?"

"No." I turned so I was facing him. I tried to speak quietly because the Three Wise Women, Katie, Hannah, and Vicki, were nosily eavesdropping. "Logan, I don't date. . . . I told you that. . . . I'm not in the . . . mood."

"All right, if you don't want to call it a date, let's call it dinner."

"That's not going to work—"

"So would everyone please welcome . . ." Norm, standing on stage, dramatically drew his words right on out, "our next director of the Telena Christmas Concert Series, Merry Meredith Ghirlandaio!"

Whew. For the first time in my life, I was glad my name was being announced over a loudspeaker. I scooted on stage, everyone clapping and shouting and cheering, and stood right in front of Katie's daughter. I subtly waved my hand down, and she dropped her dress to her knees, covering Spiderman. I knew Katie would thank me forever.

"Hello everyone, this year's concert is going to be spectacular. We have a few changes, but I think . . ."

I went on with my spiel, smiling, and at the end was given a red cowgirl hat with a Santa Claus on the brim from the mayor. "She knows how to wear 'em, doesn't she folks? Coolest cowgirl hats in Montana. We all know that, well, maybe not *everyone*. We have a new man in town, many of you know him, from Copper, Logan Taylor. Welcome to Logan! We're glad you're here! Folks, he was the one who saved Meredith at Barry Lynn's. A real gentleman."

I wanted to dissolve, disappear, hide.

Logan grinned at me as people slapped him on the shoulder, clapped, cheered.

The Christmas tree lit up, everyone oohed and aahed, and we were into, officially, the Christmas season.

And soon I was, unofficially, on a dinner date with Logan. I don't even know how he got me into the restaurant. The man's so persuasive I don't know why he bothers to use a fly when he fishes. I'll bet he can just as easily ask the fishies to jump up on shore, and they'd do it. . . .

"So you've never been married before, Meredith?"

I dropped the bell-shaped Christmas cookie to my plate and tried, once again, not to envision Logan kissing me outside his huge, decorated gingerbread house. Argh. I am so weird.

"No, I've never been married. I'm surprised no one told you that; you seem to know everything else. I wouldn't be surprised if you knew the circumference of my head, my grades in high school, and my favorite rock star."

He smiled in the dim light, the candles at our table flickering. "Okay. I was told you hadn't been married, but I was confirming it."

I picked up my coffee and tucked my white streak behind my ear. I love when coffee is served, as I do at my B and B, in thick white ceramic cups, and I love adding cream from cold silver pitchers. "Consider the fact confirmed. I'm still trying to figure out why I'm here, out at a restaurant with you, eating all sorts of delicate appetizers and miniature lemon meringue pies. You're smooth, Logan. How come I'm letting you push me around?"

"I'm not pushing you around. I simply convinced you that a dinner tonight would be a good start to the Christmas season. Ho ho ho."

I rolled my eyes.

"Have you ever wanted to get married?"

"No." I dragged my thoughts away from him and being married to him, waking up each morning, making strawberry crepes together, kissing, fly fishing dates, fires outside a tent while camping, kissing, canoeing, hugging, laughing, horseback riding, hanging out with the kids for movie nights, making love, kissing more . . . and then the pain came. Hard, fast, like it was splitting me in two, followed by the anger because I *couldn't* go there, because the choice to go there had been taken from me.

"No? Why not?"

"Because I'm good on my own. I'm too independent. I can drive a tractor, bale hay, break a horse, and shoot a gun. I run my own business, I have two kids with various problems, and directing this concert may drive me to drink copious amounts of scotch, but no, I do not need to throw a husband into that melting pot of terror." Yep. I am good on my own. Except for when I think the loneliness is going to kill me; then I'm not so good. Not so good, either, in the darkness of the night when my worries attack and there is no hand to hold.

"You *are* good on your own," Logan said.

Why did candlelight have to highlight all the sexy grooves of Logan's face?

"You're one heckuva woman, Meredith. Very capable and strong and smart. You remind me of a stallion, the Rocky Mountains, and lightning bolts. And pink cake."

"Pink cake?" *That was one of my favorites.* I resisted the urge to tap the heels of my cowboy boots together.

"Yes, it's my favorite. It's delicious, unforgettable, sweet, feminine . . . you."

"You're a flirt." I tried to sound stern as I attempted to take a sip of coffee. My hands shook. I put it down. There was a cookie shaped like holly. Maybe I'd eat it.

He laughed. "Meredith, if you knew me, even a little bit, you would know how wrong you are."

"You're not a flirt?"

He stared right at me. "No. I'm not. I have no idea how to flirt; I don't even try. If relating you to a cake sounded flirty, it wasn't my intention. I'm telling you the truth, cowboy girl."

"Something tells me that you have not needed to flirt in order to meet women in the past."

"Most of what I've done for the vast majority of my life is work. I don't flirt. Except with you. I'm trying to flirt."

I blushed. "You are?"

"Yep. Is it working?"

"Well . . . uh . . . when . . . yes . . . no . . . no, yes . . ." His flirting was flustering me.

"I'm not doing a very good job of flirting. You don't even know I'm doing it."

I used to be a tough woman! What happened to me? I could handle Logan! "Let me know next time before you start flirting. Put up a banner or something so I'm not caught off guard."

He grabbed a crayon sitting in a cup and then wrote on the paper tablecloth, "Meredith, I'm flirting with you."

I laughed. I couldn't help it.

He tried to draw a flower; the flower looked like it had been strangled by a black spider. "Nice flower. It looks like it was strangled by a black spider."

He drew black legs coming out from a black spot, then gave up. "I tried. So, no husband for you. Ever?"

"No. Yes. No. No husband." I sighed inwardly at my fumbling words. "What about you?"

"I have no desire for a husband."

We smiled into each other's eyes. "I didn't think that would be an issue."

I tried not to shiver, but I shivered anyhow. The man gave me the shivers. In a good way, and a sad, mind-shattering way, because I knew I would not let this relationship go anywhere. Not past tonight. Tonight would be it.

"Have you been married?" I asked. "Kids?" Already I did not like his ex-wife. Jealousy struck like a mad green elf.

"No, I've never been married. As for kids, I can assure you that if I had them, they would be with me now. Unfortunately, I don't have any children."

I was touched by the look on his face. He seemed genuinely, deeply saddened. "Do you want kids?"

He nodded. "I do. No question. Five is a good number. I want a family."

"So you're shopping for a wife." I wanted to challenge the Unknown Future Wife to a kickboxing match in which I would personally have her down on the floor in seconds begging for mercy.

"I wouldn't call it shopping, I hate shopping. Can't stand it. To me, hell would be a shopping mall where I'd have to endlessly try on clothes and buy stuff."

I pretended an interest in my coffee and Christmas cookies. Next to the bell were a reindeer, a wreath, and a Mrs. Claus.

"Why do you want to get married?" I hated that Future Wife!

"I want to live forever with my best friend."

"Well, that's very touching." I tried not to let my sarcasm ooze. "If I lived with my best friends I would be living with Vicki, Hannah, and Katie. Vicki would have us all roping calves, Hannah would have us at math parties, and Katie would wander around in bed-room costumes."

He laughed. "You're pretty darn funny, Meredith."

"Answer the question, he-man."

"I want to get married because I think that I can build a happy life with someone I love more than my own life. I want someone to talk to, laugh with, dream with, have children, and build a family, complete with grandkids. I want to ride horses with her on our ranch."

He grinned and I felt this wave of black sorrow swirl around me.

"I want to have dinner on the deck, breakfast with hot coffee together. I can make an outstanding cup of coffee by the way, Meredith. I want to travel the world so we can have experiences together. I don't want to be alone my whole life. Do you?"

No, I did not. But I also didn't want to live any-where near Logan and the Unknown Future Wife who I would kickbox and intensely dislike all the way down to my molars. "I don't feel alone. I'm close to my parents, I'm close to Jacob and Sarah, although Sarah thinks I'm an idiot, and I have friends. A man would add stress and mood swings."

"You don't even like to talk about marriage, do you?" he asked.

Not when it concerns you. "No. I'd rather dental floss a shark."

He laughed again, rich and seductive, but I knew that he didn't know he was rich and seductive. "Why?"

"Because it's not something that I'm going to do. I don't think I'd be happy married. It's too complicated, difficult . . . My life is too complicated, difficult. A mess." Oh, what a mess.

"Life is complicated. It's a mess. It's difficult

sometimes, tragic, heartbreaking, but even with all of that, I would rather go through the complications, the mess, the tragedy, with someone I loved, someone I could count on. Someone I could grab and hike to the top of a hill and have a picnic, even if we were both crying over something that had happened. One thing I am not is naïve, honey. I know marriage isn't perfect at all. I get it."

No, it couldn't be perfect. Life made sure of that.

I ate Mrs. Claus's head, then took in Logan's huge shoulders, that steady gaze, the unyielding strength, the funny flower. No, marriage wasn't perfect, but with Logan, well, it could reach toward perfection.

The skinny blonde bomb he would marry would be very lucky. He would probably be very unhappy with me when I kickboxed her.

I ate Mrs. Claus's feet. Then I ate her bottom.

Chapter 6

Late at night, after I made myself a cup of peppermint tea, I wandered into the parlor and stared up at
the music Christmas tree. In the corner, behind the
piano, I noticed that the wallpaper was coming up. I
put my cup of tea on an antique table, bent down, and
studied it.

It wasn't only one layer of wallpaper. As I peeled
one carefully away from the other, I counted six layers. Flowered, striped, paisley, it was all there. Each
wallpaper was different, each picked by a different
woman, in a different time. What was going on in
their lives at that time? Were they excited to be redec-
orating a room? Had they moved into this house will-
ingly? Was one a war bride? Was another married off
young and regretting it? Was one of the women pas-
sionately in love with her husband or did she fall in
love with someone else? What hardships did they en-
dure? Did they have children? Did they ever go
broke? Were they happy with the way their lives
turned out? What would they have changed?

All these thoughts, from wallpaper. I did not need the walls to talk; I needed the wallpaper to talk.

I heard the swishing of long skirts in the kitchen and walked back in with my tea cup. Nope. No one there. I laughed to myself and went to bed, but not before I called out, "You sure picked out nice wallpaper."

"The worst part is that no one will sit with me at lunch. No one."

I thought my body would split from pain, as I covered Jacob's small hands with mine across the kitchen table. Not even the Wowza Walnut Caramel Tarts I'd made for him were going to sweeten over this problem.

"Yeah, I'm having fun, too," Sarah said. "A bunch of girls at school, you know the popular ones"—she drew quotes in the air with her fingers—"they've told everyone that I'm a modern day Lolita, as if I'm after all their fathers or something. Why do they hate me?"

"I try to go slow to the cafeteria," Jacob said, "so most of the kids are almost done eating when I get there, and then I find a table with a few kids at it but I don't sit close to them in case they tell me to go away geek-head, but I sit sort of close so not everyone in the whole cafeteria knows I don't have any friends."

"I'm past even that," Sarah said, defiantly, but I saw the tears in her eyes. "Every time I walk past one of the 'popular girls,' they call me names, or run their shoulders into mine, or stop everything they're doing and glare at me."

I tried not to cry. Kids are so awful to each other sometimes.

"I sit in my classes and do the work and try to look busy at my desk when the teachers let kids talk,"

Jacob said. "Everybody talks to each other, but not to me. It's like I'm invisible. They treat me like I've got leprosy or something."

Later, after the three of us had pounded out our anger in a mad game of Scrabble, I gripped the sides of the counter and cried my eyes out.

How many other mothers who had lived here before me spent time crying in this kitchen for the kids they loved dearly whom they could not protect from the outside world?

All of them, I thought. All of them.

Our concert rehearsals were in the exact place where we would have the concerts, and because we had so, *so* little time, they were long rehearsals.

The first night I took the first set of acts and worked with those specific groups, including a huge chorus, which I'd cobbled together from various churches and schools, all ages.

The next night, I worked with the second set. The third night, we were altogether.

It was a disorganized, noisy, calamitous disaster.

"Well, Aunt Meredith, you and me are going to have the same problem when this is all over," Jacob told me, patting my arm. "No one's going to want to sit with you at lunch either."

"Yeah," Sarah said, cracking her gum. "You're definitely not going to be in the popular group. But hey, no one in our family is in the popular group."

I rolled my eyes, yanked up Sarah's too-low-cut shirt, then hugged my kids, before they scooted off.

Martha waved and made a beeline for me. She had agreed to handle the décor of the Community Center. The woman could take twine, duct tape, and tree branches and make something museum-worthy.

"Okay, Meredith," Martha said, consulting her clipboard. "We'll have a cross, natural-looking, tall, in the middle of the stage. We'll use white boxes, white gauze, white material, and cotton to form snow, sparkling white lights, shiny giant ornaments hanging from the ceiling, and tons of Christmas trees. . . . Oh, look who's here! Thanks for coming, Logan."

I whipped around and there he was.

The man who never left my mind, who made me tingle and tripped me up and left me hot and bothered.

"Meredith, Logan can do anything with a hammer and saw." She blushed. "You know what I mean. I talked to him at your place, and he's going to help with the set construction. You simply have to tell him what you're thinking about. He can do it with a saw! And he has a big drill!" She blushed further. "You know what I mean."

He was so hot. "Hello, hot—" I stopped myself, cleared my throat. "Hello, Logan."

He was wearing a black jacket, jeans, cowboy boots. He grinned at me.

I blushed.

He winked.

I blushed further.

I used to be tough! I didn't blush. *What was happening to me?*

He held out his hand to mine, to shake, as if we were meeting. I put my hand in his and hoped that he did not notice the tremble in it. See? This is what that man does to me.

He held on tight to my hand. It trembled. He winked again.

He knew it. By darn, he knew it.

I was so embarrassed I wanted to go out and ride a horse at full gallop.

To Oregon.

                              *   *   *

"So why are you here, Logan? In Telena? What
brought you home?" I tried to scoot away from him.
Everyone else had left the rehearsal, and he and I
were sitting at a table. He wanted to discuss the details of the stage, although I had the sneaking suspi-
cion he knew exactly what he wanted to do. I
assumed he would sit across from me.

Nope. The cowboy with the shoulders a thousand
angels could dance on sat right next to me. I scooted
again. I could smell him. He smelled like Montana
wind, mint, pine trees, and serene fly fishing rivers.

"I'm here because of Christmas."

"Christmas?"

"Yes." He drummed his fingers on the table. "I was
in a meeting, in Los Angeles, about this time last year.
We were acquiring another business. It was an engi-
neering firm, and they would complement the construction part of my business in California. Anyhow,
the meeting was long, started to get heated, and I was
wiped out. I'd been traveling almost constantly for
years, I had boxes stacked in my home, which I was
rarely in, I hadn't had a vacation in as long as I could
remember, and I slept about six hours a night.

"I remember looking around the room at all these
high powered, Type A people, whom I'd hired. They
were all like me. Driven, relentless, ambitious. Anyhow, it was 8:00 at night, and I broke the meeting up,
and everyone went home. I drove to the beach and
walked out on the pier. I remember thinking how
beautiful the ocean was, which got me thinking about
water, fishing, then Montana."

"And?"

He didn't say anything for a while, brushed a hand

through that thick hair, then focused those bright eyes on me. "And I realized that I had achieved what I needed to achieve."

"Which was?"

"Financial stability."

I nodded. I wanted financial stability myself. Dumping all the money I'd earned in New York into one business scared me to death.

"And I was ready to go home. You know I grew up poor, Meredith, and being poor, that feeling of desperation, of inadequacy, the fear and struggle, it never leaves you. Never. My mother worked all the time because my father, who was no *man* in any sense of the word, decided it would be better if he ran off and saw the world than stay home and take care of his wife and son. She worked for the mining companies in the office, then three nights a week as a waitress.

"I ran a paper route starting when I was nine, mowed lawns in the summer, and worked in the mines before I left for college. In the summers, I'd go back again and work in the mines. It was dangerous, hard work. I watched my mother struggle and decided at a very young age that I would never sit at the kitchen table counting out quarters for food, and crying when the car broke down, and worrying about how to pay a medical bill, and I haven't.

"Financially we were always right on the brink of going over a cliff. Once we went over the cliff when my mother got pneumonia, couldn't work, and we lost the house. I knew I didn't want to live like that. I had to make money. No other way around it." He rolled those huge shoulders. "A lot of people who have successful companies, who chase after money, had the same sort of childhood that I had. We can't, under any circumstances, go back to where we were. So we scramble to create what we didn't have, and desperately needed, and can't relax until we have it."

I nodded.

"But the price I have paid for that financial security is that I had no personal life to speak of. All I did was work. And yet, always, I have wanted my own family. My mother passed away when I was twenty-five. She was an only child, so there was no one else. After that night in Los Angeles, I thought about things for about six months, and every day I was more sure that I wanted to move back to Montana and find a life. I'm still going to work, but I've promoted people, restructured some, and will delegate more."

"How's the move gone?" I asked.

He leaned in, our shoulders together, and smiled that easy smile. "Better than I could have possibly imagined."

"But do you miss the excitement of your business, the deal making, the people?"

He shook his head. "I miss some of the people I work with who have been with me for years. We still talk, e-mail. They're threatening to come to Montana and move into my house and fish all day, but I've told them they can't because I need someone running the company. But the other parts of building a business? The travel, the intensity, the politics, working with people's difficult personalities, no, I don't. In fact, the longer I'm here, the more alive I feel. It's almost like I've been half dead these last years, buried under a crush of work."

"So you're here to stay."

He grinned at me. "Yes, Meredith, I'm here to stay. Coming back was the best thing I've ever done." His eyes swept my face, my top half, in a flirty, warm sort of way that brought every nerve end to screaming awareness. "I needed to meet someone with a white streak in her hair."

That night I dreamed of the accident.

In my dream I could see his eyes, but it was dark, and I had black in my head. I heard his voice, dimly, and watched him work on my body as if I was floating above it. I heard him yelling at me, and then, in my dream, I started to die.

I woke up with a start, sitting straight up in bed, breathing heavily.

The motorcyclist, I was told later, did CPR on me. Another motorist, a friend of my parents', rushed for a phone and called for an ambulance, which arrived within minutes, my parents following the ambulance. By then, the motorcyclist had stabilized me, and I was breathing again, though unconscious.

My parents told me later that they had thanked him, but were so panicked, so hysterical at seeing their daughter on the pavement awash in blood, they never asked his name.

"It is to my everlasting shame that I did not get that young man's name," my father had bemoaned.

"We searched the police reports, but they didn't have it, either," my mother had said. "He was your angel, Meredith. Your angel. At least you know you have one." My father had kissed me, then my mother. "We love you so much, Meredith. How about some tea and scones. You love scones."

"What she needs is some of my calzone!" my father had announced. "We're *all* lovers of my calzone!"

Now I stared out into the darkness toward the cathedral. The priests had put up the lighted deer all across the lawn and a huge cross was lit in the center to celebrate the miracle of Christ's birth.

I took a deep breath. I needed a miracle of my own this Christmas.

Chapter 7

I continued to find acts for the concert.

Maly, a Cambodian chef in town, built a magnificent gingerbread house every year for Christmas, which she displayed in the storefront window of her restaurant. She agreed to decorate one house a night, on stage, while the choir sang. We'd have a camera on her and project the images to a huge screen as she iced and decorated it, turning the gingerbread into a magical, fantastical, tasty Santa's house.

"Me you want at your Christmas show?" Maly asked, as we drank tea in her restaurant.

"I sure as heck do, Maly."

"I honored."

"We're honored."

We made chit chat for a while about the holidays, presents, et cetera, and then she said, her voice catching, "Meredith, my family, we come here in boats from Cambodia. First we stay in camp for one year. Hardly no food. My husband die, he sick. I put my three little sons in boat with me. First one sank. We rescued, back to camp. Second time, we in boat, we pay pirates no hurt us, boat no sink, and we come here. No war. No camp. No bombs. No scary police." She shook her head. I did not miss the tears. "We work hard. We have restaurant. Sons go to college, all doctors. Help others. Now we ask to make Christmas house in Christmas show in Montana. Funny, life. And sad, too. That life, right? Funny, sad, happy. Yes, I happy to make Christmas house. Meredith, I thank you."

"Thank you, Maly. Can't wait to see it."

"Ya, me too."

We held hands between our tea cups.

I found another act in my dining room when I sat down with Norm and Howard the next morning after everyone else was gone.

"I accidentally shot at my brother in World War II," Norm mused.

"You did?" I asked.

They both nodded.

"I spent one Christmas as a prisoner of war after the Battle of the Bulge, Meredith," Howard said. "All of us were packed in a cattle car, no windows, headed for a camp. We heard the engine of a plane, and then we were shelled. We all got down on the floor as the train kept moving."

"Later Howard and I compared dates and locations," Norm said. "I was a fighter pilot, and it was me who hit his cattle car. Of course I had no idea there were people in it, much less American POWs, or the order wouldn't have been made." Norm's face grew grave. "We were trying to disrupt the train lines."

"I became a guest of the Germans," Howard said. "It wasn't pleasant. See this scar? And this one? I got all of those, plus a bunch more on this old body, in the POW camp. By the time the Americans rescued me I was under a hundred pounds and ill. But I remember Christmas there." He smiled, though the smile was tinged with sadness.

"We sang Christmas carols. Some soldiers hummed, they were too hurt, too weak to sing. Other guys didn't sing at all; maybe they didn't want to remember where they weren't. A couple sang as loud as can be. Old Petey, a kid from Arkansas, he sang the loudest. He was nineteen, told me later that he sang loud so he could hear his uncle's voice in his own. The other loud singer was Dirk from Texas. He said he sang because he believed in hope, and Christmas is full of hope. A third guy, Paul, from Georgia, said he sang for Jesus and he sang because he was grateful. I said, 'Why are you grateful? Look where we are. No food. No clean water. We're prisoners.' He said, 'I sing because I'm still alive, thank you Jesus, that's why, and I'm proud of us. I'm proud of the American soldiers.' Then he hit me on the shoulder and said, 'Howard, I'm glad you're alive too, even though you snore like a cave man.' Me and Paul, Norm here, we're all still friends. We see him once a year. And every year he tells me, 'I'm grateful to be alive, and even more grateful you two are alive, thank you Jesus and Merry Christmas.' You get what I'm saying, Meredith?"

"I do, Norm, I do. And you and your brother are going to retell that story at the Christmas concert." I wiped the tears off my face.

"We are?"

"Yep. To 'Silent Night.' No arguing." I handed them a plate of pink divinity cookies.

Howard took five and winked at me. "When you're this old you stop worrying about what to eat and what not to eat."

Norm took six. "Delicious, Merry Meredith. My life got so much better after you moved back to Telena."

Hannah found me one more act, and that was a wrap. "Do you still need more people for the concert?"

"I do, if you have someone good."

"Ask Simon."

"Simon?" Simon, the nervous one, the one with trembling hands, five apple slices, and lots of obsessions?

"Yes, Simon. When he moved here I introduced myself to him. His name rang a bell so I looked him up on the Internet." Hannah looked pretty pleased with herself. "Math and music go hand in hand. Very similar."

"So who is he?"

Hannah hummed through one of my favorite classical songs. "That's who he is."

"Who?"

"He's Simon Baumgartner. Famous international violinist from Boston. Had a nervous breakdown. Quit playing violin and disappeared."

"And he's reappeared here in Telena," I mused. "Excellent. I think this concert might be what Santa ordered for him."

"I can hear math in his music."

I rolled my eyes at her. "You could hear math in the wind."

"Actually . . ."

* * *

The past week or so had flashed by in a crush of work. Four of my rooms were now filled with singles or couples, and all of the guests were cheerful and easy, which doesn't always happen. Now and then I'll get guests who are the next worst thing to a furious Frankenstein, and somehow it is my fault they've made a wreck of their lives.

One woman complained twice about my scrambled eggs. She said they were overcooked. Twice. No one ever complains about my eggs because they are spectacular. The third time she complained I cracked four eggs in a glass and slammed it down on her table. "Are those under cooked enough?" I asked.

One man was ticked off because his wife had left him. It wasn't difficult to see why. He ranted and raved to anyone who would listen about his lousy witch of a wife. Davis counted off and the Old Timers yelled, "Merry Meredith!" when I came out with a platter with raisins that spelled SHUT UP. The guy shut up.

The rest of my time was filled with B and B business, concert rehearsals, my glowering at my balance sheet, and my massive sense of responsibility to the town of Telena, which was struggling; Telena needed to have a successful Christmas concert series for its economic health. It made me feel ill.

Sarah told me, "You can't control me, Aunt Meredith. I have free will. You're not my mother you know. You're my aunt. I'm an adult, and I can make my own decisions, and you're not going to ruin my life." Jacob later said, "How old do you have to be before you can drop out of school forever, because I'm thinking about it."

I was burnt through, and I was hardly sleeping.

Except when I thought of Logan.

He plain ol' burned me up.

Soon it would end. Before things got out of control. I would break things off and that would be that.

When he found his Future Wife I would move to Antarctica so as not to kickbox her face in.

"We're going fishing."

"What, now?"

"Now." Logan smiled at me, then got serious. "The weather finally broke, nothing on the rods will freeze, and, honey, you're working yourself to death. I'm tired looking at you. Let me take you fishing for a few hours. I've already got lunch in the car; and I bought pink cake and beer. We're ready to go."

I poured him more coffee in my dining room. He was coming in three days a week for breakfast. Mary and Martha switched off waiting on him because he was, "The best tipper in Montana."

"I can't, I'm too busy." I put the coffeepot down. I desperately wanted to go. I was liquid, walking stress.

"Come on, honey," he said, so soft. "Let me help you. I want to help you."

I envisioned candy canes sticking out of his fishing vest.

I couldn't believe that I found myself nodding.

"So when did you decide to become a chef, Meredith?" Logan said as we stood in the freezing Missouri River wearing waders and fishing vests and holding the most precious objects of all: fly fishing rods. "Was there a defining moment? Something in your childhood?"

"I wanted to be an artist, but I had no artistic talent

at all. None. My father loved cooking Italian dinners, and my mother loved preparing English breakfasts. I joined in, and voila. A love of cooking was born. I think it was a combination of tomato sauce, garlic, scones, and croissants. I graduated from high school, went to college, finished in three years, then headed off to culinary school in New York and stayed." I dropped out a hundred details I didn't want, and couldn't bear, to share.

"And you loved it."

"Yes, I loved it. I could make food into art." And I love fly fishing. There is something magical, if shivery cold, about winter fly fishing.

"Your food looks like art, Meredith."

"Well, thank you." I blushed at his compliment, darn it. I blushed. "But I think food can also be humorous, too, that it should warm the heart, not just the stomach."

"Which is why when Ming's breakfast arrived, her sunny side up eggs and bacon formed a smile, and Torey Higadishi received three shot glasses of orange juice."

"One time Torey told me that he needed to see the sun three times a day to feel happy. So the orange juice is the sun from me."

Logan's eyes softened. "That is unbelievably kind, Meredith."

"I want people to feel noticed when they're at my B and B. I want them to laugh. I want them to enjoy their food in a place where they're comfortable and people know their names and what they like."

"I'll bet Sarah and Jacob appreciate that, too."

I thought of Sarah, struggling, lonely at school, furious, and Jacob, dealing with the same destructive emotions brought on by their mother, then felt that sharp swell of fury in my stomach again. "I think they

do. But it takes more than food to lighten the heart of
a kid in a bad place."

"Mind telling me about that situation? I'd like to
know. In many ways I can relate to both Sarah and
Jacob."

I cast again, hoped for a bite, then gave him the
story, trying to reign in my simmering anger.

"You gave up your life in New York to raise the
kids, Meredith. That was selfless, heroic."

"No, it wasn't. I hate to tell you the truth, but I
wasn't selfless about the whole thing. I wish I'd left
New York with a grin, a skip, and a jump, but I would
be lying to you." The river sparkled all around us, the
sky pure blue. "I liked my life there. I liked my job,
the excitement. But I was lonely sometimes." I
sucked in a breath. "I shouldn't have said that."

"Why not? It's honest."

Because it made me too vulnerable. "I was furious
with my sister; sometimes I still am. I had to change
my life once before when she . . ." I slammed my
mouth shut. Can't go there. "Anyhow, I came because
I love the kids dearly, and I didn't want to raise them
in New York."

"How are they doing?"

"They're . . ." I swallowed hard. "They're fine." I
swallowed again. "Actually, they're not doing . . .
well."

"You're worried, I know. Tell me about it." He
turned his full attention to me.

Worried? *Worried?* I was *panicked* about Sarah's
behavior, her attitude, the rebelliousness. I felt sick
about the poor kid being ostracized in school. She
had a mother who had abandoned her, and she was
being attacked in school. And Jacob? He was almost
completely closed up, depressed, played piano obsessively, and never smiled. It about killed me to think of

him eating alone at school, all the other kids ignoring him, or throwing rude remarks his way, his self-esteem shredded.

"I don't think I can talk about it. Give me a second, I'm . . . I don't know what to do . . . I'm trying . . . Sarah is . . . Jacob he . . ." I choked back tears, as I thought of those two sweet kids. "I can't believe I'm cry-cry-crying. . . ."

"It's okay, Meredith, cry all you want. Crying's good. You're worried about the kids. I understand. I would be, too. Tell me what's going on. Please. I want to hear it. Maybe I can help."

I don't know why, but as I made a lousy cast into the river, tears falling on my cheeks and running into my fishing vest, I took one more peek at those compassionate green eyes to make sure he truly wanted to hear this, and I burst like a human dam.

I sobbed my way through the story, my tears landing in the freezing river, and it ended with me crying in Logan's arms, our fishing poles held out, one arm linked around the other, fishing vest to fishing vest.

I do not know much about parenting, but this I get: The worry one feels about one's children who are hurting, lonely, lost, or doing dangerous things can bring even the strongest cowgirl-fly fisherwoman to her knees.

See now. Fly fishing isn't only about the fishing.

An interesting thing started to happen over the next few rehearsals.

A woman named Liberty Hall, an attorney in Telena, decided that each rehearsal should have, in the spirit of Christmas, a potluck, and organized everyone into bringing dinner, appetizers, holiday desserts, non-alcoholic drinks, et cetera.

So each night, we worked hard, ran rehearsal, then we had what many termed "their favorite part," and everybody ate together.

Liberty came up to me after dinner one night. "You know, Meredith, I have never been happier to live in Telena than I am now. I have gotten to know so many people, hear all their stories, people I never knew before, yet they've been my neighbors for years. I used to be lonely because I didn't know very many people outside of work." She smiled at me. "I'm not feeling so lonely anymore."

I heard the same story, one way or another, from at least ten other people.

If I needed proof that people loved being a part of the concert, I had only to listen to the laughter at dinner, see the hugs when we left, the new friendships.

Darned if I didn't want to click my cowboy boots together.

"He blew a duck whistle at me."

My evening out at Barry Lynn's bar with the Three Wise Women was off to a rolling start.

"What do you mean he blew a duck whistle at you?" Hannah asked. She was wearing a sweatshirt with a picture of Einstein.

"I mean," Katie said, "he dropped the kids off at his mom's, got stark naked, except for his hunting hat, stood at the top of the stairs, and blew a duck whistle at me. That was his way of calling me!"

"Do you mean," Vicki said, pulling on her ponytail, "that your husband blew a duck whistle at you requesting . . . intimate relations?"

"I'm saying that exactly!" Katie threw her hands up. "That's how he called me to him. Does he think that's exciting for me? Does he think it turns me on?"

We pondered that. A naked husband, at the top of the stairs, blowing a duck whistle at his wife so she would come up for "intimate relations."

"I hardly know what to say, Katie," I said, choking on my beer as I laughed.

"What's the statistical probability of a man doing that again," Hannah wondered, wiping the beer foam from her mouth. "What did you do?"

"I did what I wanted to do!" Katie harrumphed.

"And what was that?" I asked.

"I stomped into the garage, stripped, pulled my camouflage pants on, hooked the suspenders over my boobs, slammed a camouflage hat with feathers over my head, grabbed my hunting gun, and yelled, 'I'm coming for you, duck'!"

I spit beer right out of my mouth. "What did Mel do when you came upstairs pointing a gun at him?"

"Well, it wasn't *loaded,* Meredith," she said. "As soon as he saw me he quacked again, and we ran all over the house. He kept quacking. I kept yelling, 'Bang, bang! I got you, duck!'"

"And then?" Vicki prodded.

"Well, we ended up in the kitchen. The duck laid on the table, shot, but not actually shot, I laid down my rifle, and we quacked together on the table."

"On the kitchen table?" Hannah asked. I could tell she was intrigued.

"You showed that duck who's the boss," I said, laughing through my tears.

"I sure did. He was one lucky duck."

"I'm sure." I laughed. "Two lucky ducks."

"Quack, quack!" Vicki said.

"Okay, folks, here we go," I said to the mob of people at rehearsal. "We have one problem. We now have a Joseph, but we still need a Mary. Who for Mary?" I asked.

"I know," Shawnelle Williams piped up. She was my principal when I went to high school and was now principal at Sarah's school. "I know the perfect Mary." She paused for dramatic effect. "Sarah."

Barry Lynn said, "She's right. Your Sarah would be the perfect Mary. Tell her to get rid of all that makeup and the scary clothes, and we've got ourselves a mother. And, everyone, to avoid suspension, don't forget my toy drive!"

"She'd never agree," I said. Sarah as Mary? The I-Will-Do-As-I-Want-You-Can't-Stop-Me child? The girl whose boobs hung out of her shirt? The girl with the black makeup?

"Ask her," Barry Lynn said. "She's a rebel, Meredith, and we all know why. Heck, I've been a rebel all my life, and my childhood was a heck of a lot better than hers. Give her the opportunity to be someone else."

"Tell her we all want her to do it, that'll make her feel welcome, feel good about herself, get approval," Shelby Narrin said. Shelby's about twenty-five and was an annoying, complainy person until she started volunteering at our soup kitchen and realized it was about time to quit whining about her life.

"She'll rise to the occasion, you'll see, Meredith," Norm soothed. "It will be a blessed event, too."

Chapter 8

"There's a horse and wagon like thing outside our house, Aunt Meredith."

"A what, Jacob?"

He pointed out the parlor's window.

I scrambled over the couch, got my leg stuck in a cushion, twisted, and fell flat on my face.

Jacob helped me up. "You're kind of klutzy, Aunt Meredith."

"You're right, I am." I got myself rearranged and put together again, then stared out the window.

The driver and . . . oh my gosh . . . the driver and *Logan* waved back at me. I watched as Logan jumped out of the buggy and came toward the door.

"Is that the man you're going to dinner with?" Jacob asked.

"Uh. Yes." Logan had control of my mind, I was sure of it. He'd stopped by the B and B two days before and said, "Meredith, I'd like to take you out to an early dinner on Wednesday before rehearsal. I'll be by to get you at 5:00." I had nodded my head as if I was a robot.

"He's huge. He's like a giant."

I put my arm around Jacob's shoulders. "Come and meet him."

He shook his head. He was so, so shy.

Sarah pounded down the steps as the doorbell rang. "That's the date, right?"

I eyed her outfit, suggestive, inappropriate, and her makeup, suggestive, inappropriate.

"Don't argue with me now, Aunt Meredith. You've got a man at the door. First date in forever, right? You've been on a drought. A barren desert. No water at all."

I rolled my eyes as Sarah opened the door. "Hi. We haven't officially met. I'm the rebellious teenager. I have stressful problems and cause Aunt Meredith all sorts of worries. I know the police by name. They know me, too. My aunt thinks I dress like a—"

I clamped my hand over her mouth. "Hello, Logan. Come on in."

He shut the door behind him, and the entry seemed to shrink exponentially; even our old-fashioned Christmas tree with popcorn and cranberries seemed smaller.

"It's nice to see you again, Sarah," he said, his voice kind. He shook her hand. Sarah looked surprised at first and I thought she blushed, but then she turned to glare at me. I don't know why she glared at me except to say that she is an angry teenage girl and they glare for no reason.

"Jacob," he extended his hand to Jacob. "I've listened to you play the piano many times. You're a talented musician."

Jacob hung his head as he blushed.

"Chin up," I whispered. Jacob obediently put his

chin up. I was working with him to look people in the eye, stand tall. It was a constant battle. He'd simply been metaphorically hit too many times in his life.

"He's either playing piano or writing songs. He has more talent than anyone," Sarah said. "Man, that would be boring for me, though. I prefer sneaking out at night."

I rolled my eyes at her. Sarah rolled her eyes back, crossed her arms over her chest, and stuck out a hip.

Logan didn't say a word until Sarah glanced up at him.

"Sarah," he said. "Don't sneak out at night again. It's dangerous. You're a young woman, alone, and you will eventually attract someone dangerous to you, and then you will regret ever leaving this home. In fact, you will pray that you were back in it . . ." Logan had a few more pointed sentences for her then said, "Don't cause your aunt worry. She cares about you, she loves you, and she doesn't deserve it. You don't deserve it, either. You're obviously bright and articulate. Don't ruin your life with poor choices."

I thought Sarah was going to turn away in a huff, but I think Logan scared her too darn much to do that, standing there with those huge shoulders and that authoritarian air. Yep, I hid a smile. Logan intimidated her. Ha! Maybe I had a secret weapon.

When he was done, Sarah whispered, "Okay . . . okay . . . I hear you . . . I won't do it . . . okay . . ."

Then he turned to Jacob. "When did you start playing piano?"

"A long time ago," he said, his voice soft. "The ladies at the church let me come in and play. One of them gave me lessons. It gave me somewhere to go when . . ." He rolled his lips in tight.

"When our mom was out running around at night," Sarah said, back to sarcasm. "Or when she was out running around during the day. She'd leave for days at a time. I took care of him."

I wanted to slam my hands to my face, then jump on top of my cowgirl hat. *How could she have left them like that?*

"She did take care of me," Jacob said, pointing at Sarah. "I remember watching Sarah make me pancakes for my third birthday, and she made me a cake out of a mix and we put the pink icing on it together. She walked me to school, and she always packed my lunch with Pop-tarts and peanut butter and jelly, and she came to my parent-teacher conferences."

The innocent words of a child can pierce right through the heart, can't they?

"At Christmas Sarah always wraps up a bunch of presents for me," Jacob continued. "She makes most of them herself. She can do anything. Art. Painting. Embroidery stuff. Sewing."

As Jacob went on and on about the glories of his sister, the only time he was ever animated, I saw, once again, the fierce love those two had for one another. They had raised each other.

"You're a wonderful sister, Sarah. Kind and giving." Logan turned to Jacob. "You're going to play in the Christmas concert, aren't you?"

I had already told him that Jacob had refused.

"No." He looked down at his clasped hands. "If I played at the concert all the kids would see me."

"What would be wrong with that?"

"They already think I'm a nerd. They call me that and other names. They call me sissy and girly and wimp."

"What do you say back?" Logan asked.

He shrugged his shoulders. "Nothing. I tried at first but they made fun of me. It got worse."

There was a loaded silence, and I knew that Logan

was thinking this through. Maybe he could help here. The only thing I could think to do was to teach Jacob how to fight better, but the kid was a lover not a fighter, and that had not worked.

"Come with us to dinner, Jacob," Logan said. "Sarah, you can tell me more about the things you make, and school, and what you like to do besides sneak out at night which you're not going to do anymore."

She humpfed at him.

"Would you like to go to dinner with us?" I asked. I saw hope rise in Jacob's eyes, but he peeked up at Logan, trying to figure out if Logan really wanted him to go, or was faking it.

"I'd like you to come, Jacob," Logan said.

Jacob didn't need further encouragement. He ran to get his coat.

"Sarah," Logan said, "I want you to go, too, but you're going to have to take off that makeup and pull a sweater on."

"Gee whiz. That's a nice idea," I drawled, noting again Sarah's clothes, inappropriate, and makeup, inappropriate.

She opened her mouth to argue, then got a sulky expression on her face to which Logan said, "Sulky expressions don't work with me, and they'll also give you wrinkles. We're leaving in five minutes. Want to come or not?"

She did.

And, unbelievably, amazingly, the four of us had a wonderful time in a restaurant decked out in red, green, and gold for Christmas after an old-fashioned carriage ride.

In the middle of dinner, Sarah actually smiled at me with no makeup on her face and wearing a pretty purple sweater.

I wiped my tears with my napkin. I was touched. Logan had heard about a problem in my life and had taken action to help me. What a man.

Logan patted my knee under the table.

What a man.

My dishwasher blew, along with a rush of water. I called the plumber. He pulled the dishwasher out.

"Groan," I sighed.

"Yep, Meredith. This is definitely a groan sort of project. We'll be here tomorrow. I'll take the dishwasher out with me."

I peered into the hole left by the dishwasher. What was that? Was there a cutout in the wood? I tapped at it and it moved. I drew my finger around the edges. It was about twelve inches by twelve inches. I moved part of it, then another part, which seemed to be clinging to each other more from years of decay and water damage than by anything man-made. I pulled on an edge, and it opened like a door.

A hidden door.

I scrambled out and grabbed a flashlight, then scrambled back in. Inside the hole I saw it.

Shiny and tall.

It was a menorah. I held it up in wonder.

A hidden menorah.

If only this house would talk to me.

"I am the size of a dump truck," Mary said. "I feel like I have a St. Bernard strapped to my waist. Wait. I don't have a waist anymore. I can hardly see my feet. Do I have feet anymore? I had no idea skin could stretch this much. My boobs are so big I don't know what to do with them."

"Leave them where they are," Martha said, whizzing around the kitchen, as usual. She was whipping cream, rolling a cinnamon roll, and mixing eggs, seemingly all at once. "You'll need those suckers in a few weeks."

"I am a crazy pregnant woman, aren't I?" Mary asked. "I'll be a crazy mother, a terrible mother, and my baby will write papers in first grade about how crazy I am!"

She burst into tears.

Hormones. Those hormones.

"Can I walk you home, Meredith?" Logan asked.

We were both standing outside the Community Center at the end of a long rehearsal. Christmas carols were ringing incessantly in my head.

"If I said no, you'd do it anyhow, wouldn't you?"

"Probably." He grinned. "It's dark, it's late, I don't want you walking home by yourself."

We said good-bye to a few people. Logan was thanked by all, who were duly impressed with his stage building. We started up toward my house, the cathedral shining in the distance.

"Meredith, I've been thinking."

"You seem to do that way too much, Logan." I pushed my black cowgirl hat with silver trim down on my head.

"I'm thinking that you and I should officially begin dating. Both fly fishermen, both horseback riders, we love everything you cook, and we love our cowboy boots. We're a fine pair."

I felt like crying. I felt like raging. "Logan, listen," I said, as we passed by the lit up Christmas tree in the middle of the square, so calm and peaceful under a light snowfall. "I don't want . . ." I stared into those green eyes, steady on mine, serious, listening. "I don't want to date you."

"You don't?" He stopped and put his hands on his hips.

Oh yes, I do! Desperately! "No."

"Why not?"

"I don't have room in my life for you or anyone else." *But you could make room!* "My business is struggling, I have two kids living with me who are grieving and difficult, I don't even know how to be a mother, I have a concert to plan, and I'm not looking for a date."

He studied the sky for a second, as if pondering it for answers. "What about a boyfriend?"

That sounded yummy! "No, not a boyfriend . . ."

"A suitor, then?"

That sounded romantic! "No, not a suitor."

"Then I'll be your escort."

An escort! *That sounded kinky.* Immediately visions of a heart-shaped bed with heart-shaped chocolates piled up around it came to mind. "I don't need an escort. I can take care of myself." I started walking, his shoulder brushing mine.

"Meredith," his voice grew low, "give me a chance. Give us a chance."

Okay! Sure! You're on! "No. I don't deal in chance; I deal in reality. But, thank you." I so wanted to cry heaving, shaking sobs.

"Sometimes you have to jump, Meredith."

"What do you mean?"

"I mean, sometimes you have to jump and dare and trust."

"Trust?"

"Trust yourself. Trust me."

"I don't know you enough to trust you."

"I trust you."

"You do?" I asked.

"Yes, I do."

"But we've hardly been together at all."

"We've been together enough, Meredith. We're not teenagers. We've both seen the world, been through the good and the bad. We have experience with life, we know ourselves, and we know what we want."

I want you, Logan. To keep my tears hidden behind my eyes where they should be, I admired all the Christmas lights people had decorated their homes with. Lights around trees, bushes, house trim. Santa Clauses and sleighs and presents and a Rudolph with three legs.

"I know you sacrificed your life in New York for two kids. That was honorable and selfless. I know you're smart and competent because you're running your own business. I know you'll volunteer your time to help an entire town. I know you're funny, that you like to laugh, but you also have had sadness in your life that you seem to be dealing with still. I know you're a deep person, who's sincere and genuine, and I could spend a lifetime trying to figure out who you are, and there would still be mystery there, but I'm okay with it."

I shook my head. This man with the tough face, who towered over me, never ceased to amaze me. I had never met a man who honestly wanted to know anything more than the basics of a woman, starting with her bra size. That's as far as they went.

I put my hands to my eyes so I wouldn't spurt tears. "Do you always analyze people this closely, Logan?"

"Only ladies who wear fancy cowboy hats which, by the way, I like about you, too. I like the color, the style. Every day a new surprise hat. Meredith, I've got a deal for you. Call it a Christmas deal."

"I don't think I want to take your Christmas deal."

"Meredith, I told you that I would kiss you when you asked me to. I want you to ask me to kiss you."

Please kiss me, please! "I am not going to ask you to kiss me."

He took a step closer. "Please."

That sounds delicious! Terrific! Can we lie down? "I'm not going to do this."

"I have been wanting to kiss you since I saw you deck that jerk at Barry Lynn's. Something about a woman who has perfected her right hook gets to me, but you need to ask me to kiss you, like I promised."

You have gotten to me since the second I saw you. You have tugged at my heart until I couldn't breathe. We have this unbelievable sexual attraction and a friendship attraction and a talking attraction, not to mention fly fishing, and I can hardly think around you. "Have you been listening to me at all, Logan? I'm not looking to date. I'm not looking to kiss you or hug you or kiss your neck or do any hugging or getting close to your chest or your legs . . ." Oh, I squished my lips closed at that.

He chuckled. "One kiss, Meredith. Ask me. I dare you."

Take the dare! Could I? I could kiss him and remember it my whole life. I could enjoy the moment, this once. I took a deep breath. He took a step closer. He smelled like a Christmas tree, fishing on a warm day, a gold and pink sunset, and the mountains.

"Ask me, Meredith." He took off my black cowgirl hat. "I want to kiss you, honey." He took off his cowboy hat.

Was I his "honey"?

He hooked an arm around my waist, placed his warm hand on my cheek, and I was up against his strong body, inches away from that mouth, those green eyes soft and inviting and promising a kiss that would blow my cowgirl boots off.

"Okay, cowboy," I said, my voice trembling. "I'll take your Christmas deal. Kiss me."

He pulled me right on in, his lips on mine, soft and warm and demanding, and it was so glorious and passionate and wonderful I could not even think. I could not get enough of those yummy lips, and he could not get enough of mine, and the whole time my body was lit on fire for him, but I felt . . . safe, too, and secure . . . like he was there now and always would be.

Logan pulled back for a second, and I am embarrassed to say that I groaned, I so didn't want that kiss to end, and I leaned forward again, and the he-man took control, like a real man should. I linked my arms around his neck, to bring him closer, and because, exactly like in those sappy movies, my knees went to mush. Oh, mush! We were pressed tightly together, chest to knee, and I felt like I was making love to the man by my mouth.

He was the one who pulled away. I was lost in this sweet, boiling hot desire, where all I wanted was more, and I leaned against his chest, which was heaving, and my own breath was coming in embarrassing gasps, as if I was dying. Logan said, voice breathless, "Thank you for asking me to kiss you, Meredith. It's been a pleasure. Trust me on that one."

"Trust me," I stuttered out. "I think I can't stand yet, so don't let go."

He hugged me closer and murmured low in my ear, "Hon, letting go of you was never in the plan."

I took a deep breath. Letting go wasn't in your plan, yet. Not yet. But wait until you knew.

Wait until you knew. Then I would see you letting go hard and fast.

I scrunched up even tighter in my yellow comforter that night and cried my eyes out. Why do men make us ladies cry so much?

The next morning, as I was cutting up kiwis, strawberries, blueberries, and pineapple to form a Christmas wreath for a woman customer who was celebrating being free of cancer for five years on that very day, I thought about people.

How is it that you can be friends with someone, dating a person, having lunch with a member of your family you've known for years, and sometimes, or often, you don't feel close to that person, and then you meet someone and instantly it's like you've met your other half? You've met the person you've been supposed to meet your entire life, and your other relationships seem hollow now, soulless. You've met your heart and your future. Or your new very best friend. How is that?

How many women, living in this house, wearing corsets, long layers of undergarments, tight bodices, short twenties dresses, jaunty hats, poodle skirts, hippy shirts, conservative sweaters, or slinky negligees had had the same thoughts? Any of them? None?

I heard the distinct sound of wine glasses clinking together.

"I heard that," I called out.

I would definitely come back and haunt this house as a chef.

Chapter 9

I met with the Three Wise Women at Barry Lynn's bar, but only for a half hour because we all had to get to rehearsal.

"Get out those Grateful Journals, ladies," Vicki said to us. "I wrote that I'm grateful I was able to find my steers, Little Todd and Little Todd's Brother, when they escaped and headed to town. Last time they got near to town Little Todd's Brother followed snooty Ava. She about had a cow herself. What's in your Grateful Journal, Hannah?"

"I'm grateful for partial differential equations, variational calculus, and linear algebra."

"I need a drink," Vicki sighed. "What'd you write, Meredith?"

"I wrote that I'm grateful for Jacob and Sarah and for my antique claw foot tub. When I'm crying my eyes out in it, I know other women have cried in it over the years, too, and it makes me feel less alone."

"Crying alone isn't good," Hannah said. "Better to

cry with others. When I'm upset I focus on basic algebra. It's soothing."

"Sometimes I don't understand you, Hannah," Katie said, perplexed.

"What did you write, Katie?" I asked, not wanting to dwell.

Katie whipped her journal out and pushed her brown waves off her face. "I am grateful that when the paramedics came to our house last night because Mel pulled his back out when we tried the Korindike position, they didn't laugh when I said that making love made mash of my Mel's back."

Well, I'll be. Such alliteration.

"One of them said, 'What's the Korindike position?' and I showed them the photo and they all stared at it, and then they looked at me with these shocked expressions, and one of them said, 'Ma'am, you can actually get in that position?' and the other said, 'Don't you all have four kids?' and Mel, who was still lying on the kitchen table in pain said, 'So what? I'm not allowed to swing wild with my wife?' But I'm grateful that Mel is not permanently hurt. Still, the doctor said he needs to lie still and be careful. Hopefully I'll get a break." She closed her journal. "It gets so tedious swinging like a monkey from that rope in our bedroom in my Jane outfit."

There was silence for a bit.

"I hardly know what to say, Katie," I said.

"I know what to say," Katie huffed. "I'm sick of being exhausted in church on Sunday mornings after our Saturday night whoo-haw-haw, so now I'll be able to listen to the message without falling asleep, thank God."

Yes, thank God.

* * *

"Why do you keep pulling back from us, Meredith?"

I threw my hands up, layered in two pairs of mittens, then pulled on my white cowgirl hat with the silver medallion. "Do you ever, ever engage in small talk, Logan? Light exchanges? Banter? Do you know how to have a shallow conversation, because now and then I'd like to have one with you. A conversation about nothing. Chat. You always go right for the heart of everything. Your conversation is like an arrow."

He stopped by the grass in front of the cathedral, the lit-up golden deer behind him, the cross standing tall. "I like arrows. Bows, too. Next time you come to my ranch, say, tomorrow, we'll have bow and arrow practice. You'll love it. You're a very complex person. I like complex, but I wouldn't mind if you trusted me a little more. You're also difficult, Meredith. Very difficult."

"I am not!"

"Yep. You are. Dance with me."

"What? I'm not going to dance with you."

"Sure you are. Right here, in front of the cathedral. We can practice for later."

"Later? What do you mean?"

"Later." He brought me in close with one arm, my hand in his with the other. He started singing Christmas songs. "Jingle Bell Rock," "I Saw Momma Kissing Santa Claus," "Grandma Got Run Over By A Reindeer". . . I was laughing, and singing, too, the moon luminescent, the stars shining, the North Star beaming, and having the most beautiful time of my life.

Darn the man, darn Logan, who I hadn't known that long, who I knew I should stay clear of. I could feel myself falling in love, swirling around, tumbling straight in, like an elf jumping into a pile of fudge from a diving board.

Yes, I was falling in love with Logan.

He kissed me until I couldn't think a single thought.

All good Christmas tales come to an end. Mine came on a Thursday, about 1:00, when the snow was falling, light, quiet, pure, the kids in school, the guests out the door, the kitchen cleaned up.

I was drinking peppermint tea and eating a candy cane. I had about twenty minutes of break time before I had to work on stuff for the concert, but I'd had a vision of being on horseback with Logan, my arms wrapped around his waist, and we were being followed by white chocolate doves holding sprigs of thyme, and I was indulging it.

The phone rang. I shouldn't have answered it; I should have at least looked at caller ID. I did not.

"Hello?"

"Hello, sister," Leia said, quite cheery.

I felt myself go cold, everything in my body freezing up tight, as fear strangled my throat. Where was she, and was she coming to get the kids?

"Why are you calling, Leia?"

"How about, hi, how are you?"

"Why are you calling?" Please, please, don't say you're coming for the kids. Don't ruin what I have finally, finally started to heal. It had been months since she'd called, and that was best.

"I'm calling to say Merry Christmas."

"Merry Christmas. Good-bye."

"Wait!"

"Wait for what, Leia?"

"How are you?"

"I'm fine."

"Good. Ask me how I'm doing."

"I don't care how you're doing."

"Anthony and I are in Texas."

Relief rushed through me, sweet and quick.

"We're having a great time." She regaled me with the details of their "great time." I decided not to hang up because I needed to make sure she was not coming back to Telena.

"Anthony and I are still wildly in love, still together. It's bliss. It's perfect." She sighed. "I'm sorry that you won't ever know about this, Meredith. This love between a man and a woman."

Barring her saying something terrible about the kids, those words could not have hurt me more.

"I feel so guilty about that, Meredith," she said, her voice catching. I knew she'd feel terrible for about one minute; that was the extent of her ability to feel guilt. "It was an accident, though. I didn't mean for it to happen, but I know I forever ruined you for a man in your life. It would be impossible for a man to get past that; they want beauty, don't they?"

I clenched my teeth and scrunched up my eyes, as if I was bracing for a hit, a slug to the face. I heard the other crushing comments from men over the years zinging through my brain: "Deformed . . . gross . . . can't deal with it . . . crip . . . I am so not going there . . . not interested . . . I need a chick who is sexy all over, not just the face and hair . . . that'd be awkward and weird in bed. Eww." It was like I'd heard them yesterday. They had followed me over the years, like a black, mean cape. My stomach hurt, like a razor was scraping right across it.

"But you're a good mother," Leia added, cheery again. "I know that Jacob and Sarah are much better off with you than me. You can cook. You're a home-

body. You were always so proud of your cooking job
in New York but you're more domesticated than I am.
You're a mommy. I can't stand suburbia. Too boring
for me. I'm going to send them Christmas presents,
haven't had time yet, will you tell them Merry Christmas for me? I'll try to call again. Are you there?"

"I'm here." I so wanted to tell her off, to let my rip-
roaring anger out, target her, but I didn't. Not for her,
for the kids. I knew Leia, and if I made her mad
enough, to spite me, she would probably come and
get the kids and take them away.

"Good. Well. I guess that's it then. Anthony says
howdy hello. I say, after a while, crocodile. Bye, bye,
Meredith. Toodle-hee-hoo!"

I hung up and stared at that cross on the grounds of
the cathedral.

I could not let Leia have the kids back. I had meant
to take legal action for full custody, but I didn't think
the kids were ready for it, and I thought Leia would
fight back. But now I had to. No other way. I couldn't
risk her hurting them when she decided she wanted to
play mommy again and dragging them into her sordid
lifestyle.

I dropped the candy cane to the table as the accident flicked across my mind. The wet pavement, his
eyes, seeing the darkness fold in on me, the operation,
the rehabilitation, the months of nerve screaming
pain, some that was real, some that wasn't, depression
like I'd never felt, the fury, the shock and anxiety, seeing myself, my body, in a whole new light, then finally, *finally,* finding the light and going on with my
life after months and months because I chose to live,
because I could not choose to die.

My parents had cried over me, gotten me the best
doctors, the best care, never leaving my side . . . and
Leia had skipped on off, not missing a beat.

She had changed my whole life because of her ir-responsibility. I knew she was a lousy sister, a lousy mother; that anger had been in me forever. But a few of her words, despite my best efforts to deflect them, hit the mark.

They hit that mark hard, and all my insecurities and fears that I'd worked so hard to smash down came roaring at me like an emotional tsunami.

I smashed the candy cane with my cowboy boot.

Logan had no clue what hit in the next few days.

We went from dancing by the cathedral at night, chatting and laughing during rehearsals, and my making him the largest Funky Fly Fisherman's Omelet Telena has ever seen and the highest pile of Roarin' Raspberry French Toast because I wanted to hear him laugh, to my frozen coldness.

"What the hell's going on?" he asked, never one to mince words.

I denied there was anything going on. He accused me of avoiding him, dismissing him. "Don't lie to me, Meredith. Ever."

I didn't take his calls. I cooked him a normal breakfast when he came in, instead of turning his scrambled eggs into a river with parsley on the side for trees and fish made out of orange slices.

I wouldn't let him drive or walk me home after rehearsal. "Why can't I take you home? Damn it, Meredith, talk to me."

I knew I was being awful. I was trying, trying to get up the nerve to break up with him, but I couldn't, it killed me, and yet I knew I had to, so I pulled away, hoping the relationship would simply sever, break, he'd go away . . . although I had no solid plan, be-cause no solid plan can be made when you believe you are dying from a heart that is no longer beating the way it should.

I was blackly miserable, and I saw Logan's misery, his anger, and the raw hurt in those green eyes. I wanted to hug him close, hold him, cry on him.

"Meredith," he said, barging into my kitchen and bringing with him the scent of mountain air, honey, and a picnic basket on a drift boat.

Mary and Martha scurried out.

"We're going to talk about this."

"No, we're not. Not now. Please. Not now."

My eyes filled up with tears; my hands shook; I dropped a plastic bowl.

He wanted to argue. He was so stubborn.

"Please, Logan," my voice squeaked.

He ran a hand through his hair. "You are going to talk to me about this tonight, do you have that, Meredith? After rehearsal, we're going to talk. You are so difficult, but this time it isn't funny and it isn't amusing and I've had it. I don't play games. You're playing them, and we're done with that. I'm too old for that, and so are you."

No, this wasn't funny, or amusing; it certainly was no game.

It was gut shrieking awful.

"Get in the damn truck," Logan said to me as he roared up beside me outside of rehearsal. He slammed out of his truck, stomped through the snow, and grabbed my elbow. "Right now, Meredith. We agreed we'd talk after rehearsal. It's after rehearsal, so let's go."

Rehearsal for our Christmas concert had gone surprisingly well, despite the fact that I thought stress would strip away my ability to stand up, and despite the fact that during the potluck dinner, Logan sat right next to me, seething, his thigh hard against mine, and I couldn't even concentrate on my food because of his glare. Part of me wanted to swing myself around on his lap and kiss him; the other wanted to hold him tight and never let go.

"Logan," I croaked out. "How about later?"

"No, now."

I was manhandled into the truck and we were driving off in about three seconds. He drove to a quiet street near the downtown, deserted at this hour, except for the huge Christmas tree and the white lights wrapped around the other trees. He did not say a word, his jaw set, hands gripping the steering wheel, then he turned the truck off and turned toward me.

"What the hell is going on?"

How to end it?

"You have got to talk. This isn't fair to me."

What to even say?

"Is it something I said? Something I didn't say? Is there someone else?"

Oh, the very thought of someone else infuriated him, I could tell. I shook my head.

"Then what? What is it, Meredith?"

I looked up into those green, confused, ticked off, hurt eyes, and I burst into tears. "I'm sorry, Logan, oh, I'm so sorry . . ."

And I moved, and he moved, and we were in each other's arms, passionate and hot and overwhelming, and all I could think of was Logan, his lips, his tough, sweet face, the chest I leaned on when he lifted me up and straddled me across his lap, our breath mingled, a groan, a moan, bliss . . .

It was when my cowgirl hat was knocked to the floor of the truck, my jacket and sweater on top of it, my blue blouse unbuttoned, my bra unsnapped, his jacket on top of mine, his shirt almost off, our heat together creating more heat, it was when his hands stroked me from shoulder to breast to waist to hip, to thigh and lower that I wrenched away and scrambled off his lap.

"I can't do this," I breathed, reaching for my sweater with shaking hands and yanking it over my head. I heard my sister's voice. *"I forever ruined you for a man in your life. It would be impossible for a man to get past that; they want beauty, don't they?"*

I couldn't let him see me.

"What?" Logan panted back, those warm, skilled hands that had brought me to the brink of some fantastic ecstasy, slapped up to his head. "What are you *doing?"*

"I said I can't do this." I tried not to cry; I did. I cried anyhow.

"Why not?" I could hear the crushing anger ringing through the disbelief in his tone.

"I can't . . . I can't be on your lap like this. I can't kiss you."

"Dammit, Meredith!" Those green eyes flashed at me where seconds ago they'd been languid and aroused, yet so primitively fierce as he took control of this whole panting, velvety, *hot* encounter. "What are you talking about? Why can't you kiss me?"

I rolled my lips in tight and let my black hair cover my face, my white streak flashing in the darkness. "Because I can't."

I reached for my jacket and shoved my arms through before I was tempted to fling the rest of my clothes out the window and launch myself at him again. My heart wanted to stay. Stay in his embrace, stay in the passion, the heat, the comfort of his friendship, the trust I had for him.

"Answer me, Meredith." He brought a fist down on the dashboard, not in a scary way, but in an "I've had it" way. He leaned toward me and put a hand on the window behind my head. "I'm not asking you to make love to me, Meredith, for God's sakes, I sure as hell wouldn't do that in my truck, I respect you more than that, but what is this? You're passionate, you're cold, you're passionate again. Why do you keep pulling away from us?"

"Because there is no 'us'," I bit out, then clenched my teeth together, so I wouldn't sob like a drunken maniac on his chest. "There is no 'us', there is not going to be an 'us'."

"Why is there not going to be an 'us'?" He shook his head, the moonlight glinting on that hair I wanted to run my hands through. "Why is there no 'us' now? Why can't you at least trust this, trust what we have now?"

"Because I can't. I can't." I grabbed my purse and smashed my cowgirl hat on my head. "Please, Logan, let me go."

"No, I'm not letting you go." A pulse jumped in his temple, his face still flushed from all that passion. Mine was probably about as red as squished cherries. "I don't understand you; I don't understand what you're doing, where you're going here. What's wrong, Meredith? *What is wrong?*"

I was awkward, clumsy, as I tried to unlock the door, my hands shaking. I would probably be brought home by Officers Sato and Juan tonight. Wouldn't Sarah think that was hilarious?

I found no humor in it at all. The only thing I found was desolation. Bleak, stripped, raw desolation. I found the lock, I unlocked the door, he locked it, then placed a hand over the handle. Our faces were about six inches from each other.

"What's wrong, Logan, is the same thing I've been telling you. I don't want to get involved with you."

Oh, but how I did. "You suck me into this relationship, and then I have to pull away again. I'm pulling
away now."

He looked at me like I'd slapped him, his face
stony. "But why?"

I shook my head.

"No? You're going to say, sorry, Logan, not interested, that was fun, thanks for the romance, thanks for
your time, that's it? I'm done. We're done. You have
no *explanation?*"

I had an explanation, but I couldn't share it with
him. He would pity me, tell me it didn't matter, but it
would. I knew it would.

"After all the time we've spent together you can't
take one minute to be honest and tell me what it is
about me, about us, that you don't like? You can't tell
me why you see no future for us?"

That darn dam in my eyes broke again, and tears
seared my cheeks, sobs catching in my throat. I
wanted to bring my arms up around those shoulders
again and kiss him until I couldn't think.

Instead I dragged his hand away from the lock,
opened the door, and threw myself out of the car.

I started running, ignoring his command to stop, to
come back, to talk to him.

I ran up one street, knowing he was following me
in his truck. I cut down another, then ran up the steps
to the elementary school I'd attended and headed toward the grassy field, now covered in snow. I hoped
he wouldn't follow.

He did. He parked the car and started running after
me.

"You have got to be kidding, Meredith," he shouted,
still angry. "I am actually chasing you across a school-
yard so we can talk?"

I kept running. He caught up to me in about five seconds. I turned to push him away, lost my balance, grabbed his shoulders, and we ended up in the expected heap on the snowy ground, him on top of me, the stars shining, that North Star still so bright, and I pulled my leg away from him. He felt so good on top of me, so strong and comfortable. I bit down on my lip in total misery. I would never have this, never have him on me again.

We were both panting, but I was the one crying, hiccupping sounds emerging from my throat, other animal-like cries embarrassing me.

"Meredith," Logan's voice softened as my sobs became worse. "Honey, I don't like to see you this upset. I'm sorry, baby, I'm sorry." He turned over on his back and brought me with him. "Calm down, it's okay."

"You're . . . you're . . ." I gasped. "You're going to get wet."

"I don't care, honey, get your tears out. Cry, I'm right here. I'm not leaving you."

I shook my head, and he stroked a hand over my hair, another over my back, and murmured, "I don't understand what the problem is, I don't get it, I don't know why you're struggling with me, with us, but please calm down, honey, breathe, breathe in and out, here." He stroked my back, up and down, my head on his chest as I cried, all over that muscley chest of his, as he laid in the snow, next to the elementary school I'd attended, that North Star shining.

"I can't see you anymore." My voice was dull, but resolute. The tears were, for the time being, imprisoned inside me again. I'd forced them in, and I was once more in Logan's truck, although now we were parked outside my brick home, my Christmas lights twinkling.

Logan groaned, his knuckles white around the steering wheel. "You're not going to tell me why, are you?"

"We're not going to make it, Logan, so why continue?"

"We could make it. You're not allowing it." His jaw was clenched, his body rigid. We were both exhausted.

"We're different."

"Not at all. We have a passion together I've never had with anyone else. *With no one else.* We talk like we've been best friends our whole lives. We laugh. I respect you, I like you as a person. We love to fly fish, ride horses, be outside. I get along with Sarah and Jacob. But you can't trust, can you? You can't let go of your own independence. You don't need anyone, do you, Meredith? You can do everything on your own, run your life on your own, you don't need help of any sort, and you don't want to make any room in your life for me."

My own words, hundreds of times uttered, came back to haunt me: *"I can do it myself! I don't need help! I can do everything everyone else can!"*

I knew they weren't true. I needed Logan. I loved Logan. I wanted him in my life.

I had never felt so despairing in my entire life. Never. But I knew he wouldn't be attracted to me later. I knew I'd have to see him around town, probably for the rest of my life, and know exactly why he rejected me, and I would have to pretend that I didn't care that we were not together. I would see pity, and I could not stand that.

I climbed out of the truck, and this time he didn't try to stop me.

Chapter 10

"Logan's gone."

I froze, one hand clenched around my cell phone, my other clenched around a garlic press. "What?"

"Logan's gone, Meredith," Martha said. "I went down to the Community Center to do some decorating and I walked in and, wow, Meredith, *wow*. Logan must have been there all night. Liberty Hall said he left around 4:00 this afternoon and was catching a flight to California for work. He did everything, Meredith, everything. The stage is completely done. He finished building it out; the stairs rise in both directions. The balconies are finished. He finished building the boxes for all the Christmas trees to stand on, and then he and Paulo put all the Christmas trees on top, it looks beautiful. Meredith, are you there?"

He was gone. "Did . . . did he say when he would be back?"

"He said he would be gone for a while, that's what Liberty said. He said something had come up. Liberty said that he was polite and nice like always but she said he seemed upset, sort of angry, too. Did you two have a falling out?"

"What are you talking about?" I dropped the garlic press on the counter.

"Well, Meredith, everyone knows that you two have been seeing each other. It's a small town you know. People have been talking about how sweet it was that the two of you were dancing in front of the cathedral and how Logan always smiles at you, even when you're not looking at him, and how he comes in so often to have breakfast and the two of you end up sitting down together for coffee and laughing. We all think you're a fabulous match! If there's a wedding, can I do your flowers? I already have the dinner menu in my head. Mary's so excited, she wants to sit down with the three of us, have some orange mango tea, a few scones, like your mother would enjoy, maybe she can fly in for the planning?"

I couldn't speak. People knew? This shock was only secondary to the first one. The first one being: *Logan was gone.*

"I have to go, Martha." I hung up.

Dark, dark sadness settled over me, about as dark as the darkness was after the accident.

Two days after Logan left, Maly brought me an exquisite gingerbread house decorated with white icing. Tiny green candies formed a walk to the front door, which was surrounded by a string of red licorice. Mints covered the roof. "For you, Meredith. Because you seem so sad."

She set the house down, then gave me a hug as my eyes flooded. "He come back, I know it. He come back. You perfect wife for him."

* * *

"My friend, Meredith, please." Chinaza indicated the chair across from his in my dining room. I glanced around at the other diners; they were all fine for a few minutes.

"Thank you for making elegant swan in my coffee latte this morning. You are fine woman."

"You're welcome, Chinaza."

He leaned forward, his dark eyes sad, earnest, and took my hand in both of his. "Tell me."

"Tell you what, Chinaza?"

"Logan has broken your tender heart. Let us, you and I, talk about it. I will offer you my solace and friendship. Remember, hold true friends with both hands. I am your friend, Meredith. I will help you."

He knew, too. Did everyone know?

"Friend, Meredith, I am so sorry. Life is full of these challenges, isn't it?"

I nodded.

"Yes, we have a saying in Nigeria. 'However long the night, the dawn will break.' Your night will break, friend Meredith. I know you and Logan will be together again soon, I feel it."

"Good morning, Simon," I said, standing by his table after talking with Chinaza who had insisted on bringing me his favorite Nigerian dish for my dinner that night.

Simon dropped his hands in his lap and twisted his napkin. He had eaten his eggs; he had eaten three of five apple slices; he had drunk his decaffeinated coffee. "Good morning, Meredith."

"How was everything?"

"It was perfect. As usual. Your cooking skills are impeccable."

"Thank you."

"However, I feel that you're upset, which is bringing me some indigestion. My stomach is uneasy. Is there a problem?" His brow scrunched.

Don't cry! "I'm fine, thank you." Oh, Logan, how I miss you. I want you back. I want you here for the concert. I want you here so I can see you, be with you.

"Well, I wish my concert directing skills were as good as my cooking skills."

"I am positive that the Christmas Concert Series will be hugely successful."

"Thank you, Simon, but I don't know." I cleared my throat and tried not to feel too guilty about a sudden inspiration and perhaps a wee white lie. "It's not coming together right. We so need the concert to be a success, to attract people to Telena, what with the economy being so bad. We need to add some class, a high caliber performance. Simon, would you like to play your violin?"

Simon went pale. His shoulders slumped, his breathing became labored.

Of course I felt terrible. We needed him to play at the concert. What a gift his presence would be. On the other hand, wouldn't playing again help him, too? He was a world class talent. Surely he didn't want to hide forever?

"I can't do it. . . ." He closed his eyes, blew through his mouth. "I can . . . I can't . . . I could try . . . one song . . . perhaps . . . no no . . . I could try to be brave . . . A favorite Christmas carol."

"Great!" I leaned down and kissed his cheek. "Rehearsal is tonight!"

I quickly spun on my heel and darted toward the kitchen before he could say no.

For a moment, my gloom lifted.

Norm called out, "Well done, young woman. Well

done." Then Davis counted down and all the Old Timers yelled, "Merry Meredith!"

The next week passed in a painful, wrenching blur, and I cried for each and every reason.

I cried when I watched snowflakes drift down and when the bells of the cathedral rang. I cried sitting in front of the pink angel Christmas tree. I cried when carolers came to our door and when I wrapped Sarah's and Jacob's presents. I cried thinking of the chicken feathers I found underneath the house because someone must have kept chickens there years ago and I wondered if her life had a lot of tears in it. I cried when I decorated the trees at the Community Center with white lights.

I cried when Mary put my hand on her stomach and I felt the baby kick and she said, "Do you think I'm having quadruplets? That's how huge I feel. I will never be sexy again," and burst into tears. "I will be frumpy. A frumpy Mary mommy!"

I hid the tears from Sarah and Jacob, but they knew I was sad. Sarah said, "You know, Aunt Meredith, I have decided that Logan is pretty cool except when he keeps telling me to respect myself and that I'd better get good grades or I won't have a future. He's a dude."

So, as I figured other women in this house had done, I brushed off the tears and kept on keeping on. I had kids to raise, a business to run, a concert to put on, presents to wrap, carols to sing, eggnog to drink.

No time for tears. Buck up, Meredith, I told myself. Buck up and Merry stupid Christmas.

I thought I felt a pat on my back. I turned. No one was there, of course.

* * *

"Okay, everyone, we're running through this rehearsal one more time," I shouted. "Everyone in place . . . choirs on the wings. Mary and Joseph! There's Joseph, where's Mary?"

And that's when I had to stop and get all choked up and everyone else stopped and stared at who I was staring at, which was Sarah.

Sarah, the girl who used to dress like a streetwalker with black makeup was transformed. No low cut shirt, no tight pants, no rebellious, sulky expression on her face. No, this was the new Sarah, dressed as Mary would have dressed, complete with a simple cotton shift, her hair covered, sandals on her feet, and no makeup.

Who had gotten her to accept the role as Mary? Logan had. "No one's perfect, Sarah, but you would make the perfect Mary."

Joseph, a top athlete and academic at Sarah's high school, waved at me. "Mary and I are ready to have our baby!" he called out as everyone laughed. "We need our donkey, and we're off to Bethlehem to get ourselves checked into a five-star hotel!"

I glanced over at Jacob. He was at the piano, ready to play. Who had gotten him here? Logan.

Logan had encouraged him, told him his was a talent to be shared, that Christmas was a time of new beginnings, that it didn't matter if the kids at school called him "a piano geek," which Jacob said they would.

"You can get past that, Jacob," Logan said. "What you're not going to be able to get past is declining to play in the concert your aunt is directing even though I think you want to and your aunt needs you. Real men don't worry about what other people think, except for the people they love. Real men act with integrity and honesty and keep working hard, they keep going even when the people around them are trying to knock them down. Don't let anyone knock you down, son."

Jacob ran those talented fingers over the keyboard, then he looked up at me and grinned. I grinned back. I was so proud of him.

At that very second, Simon walked in with his violin. He was greeted by several people. I could tell he was scared to death. But he was there.

Christmas has many miracles.

If only my heart could breathe.

"Everyone says a terrible rehearsal is a sign of a stupendous opening night, right?" I tapped my cowboy boot. Dark green, silver details. Christmassy.

"Sure, Aunt Meredith," Sarah drawled in her pregnant Mary outfit. "One of the kid angels refuses to wear her halo and wants to wear her devil mask instead. Those teenagers playing 'Jingle Bell Rock' have dyed their hair pink. The choirs are off-key and sound like hyenas. Anybody know when to come up on stage?"

"Meredith," Martha said. "The prop with Rudolph collapsed, Lee can't find the extra microphones, Juan wants to know where the elf costumes are, and the cradle for the baby Jesus has mysteriously disappeared."

I ran my hands through my hair. Think, Meredith, think.

I strode to the middle of the stage that Logan built. I stared out at the milling, chatting, jolly people who had all made new jolly friends and felt so jolly living in jolly Telena.

"People!" I yelled. They kept up their jolliness. I pulled a microphone toward me, "Mrs. Claus is going to start throwing meringue cookies if you don't listen!"

I knew that would do it.

"Here's what we gotta do, right now . . ."

The next morning Mary said to me, "I am going to explode."

"Mary, please," I told her, exhausted from another nightmare last night, the car accident in glowing, Technicolor, 3-D detail, as if I was watching it from a tree. "Please, I have told you to go home, you shouldn't even be working, I told you I would pay you to stay home."

She patted my arm. "I want to be here, though. I like you, Meredith, and I want to be here for you in your time of need. You're my friend."

Martha kept bustling around the kitchen, busy, busy, busy.

"Please go home," I told Mary. "I'm tired looking at you. You're humongous."

"I told you, I am going to explode."

"Meredith."

I whipped around in the darkness outside the Community Center, then sagged with relief.

Logan.

He was back.

The relief was replaced by anguish and roaring pain. I wanted to fling myself on him and wrap my legs around his waist.

"Hello, Logan." I was the last to leave and, after running through the program twice, I thought maybe, maybe, we were ready for tomorrow night. "You're back."

Logan took a few steps closer, walking through the shadows, and I felt my breath catch. The angels should not have blessed this man with such wondrously sexy looks. It was almost sinful.

"Yes, I'm back."

Don't cry, Meredith! Buck up! "Is everything okay?"

He scoffed, then crossed his arms, that cowboy hat low on his brow. He looked like he'd lost weight, in fact, he didn't seem that . . . *well,* he was pale under the tan, his face drawn. "What, specifically, are you referring to? My business? My life? You?"

"You left abruptly, and I thought there might be a problem." In the distance I could see the tip of the town Christmas tree, bright, shiny, colorful. That made me want to cry, too.

"With my business, there are no problems. With my life, with you, there is a problem. It's a big problem."

He was not going to let this, to let us, go. I don't know why I thought he ever would. I hadn't known him long, but I knew him. I knew the depths of this man, how he felt, how he lived. I sure loved him.

Yep, *I sure loved him.* I wanted to reach out, hug him close to me, strip off that beige jacket, flick off that cowboy hat, and follow him down onto his bed with the perfect view of the pink and gold sunsets. Ah, these womanly emotions, they can wrangle you into nothin'.

"The problem, Meredith, is that I am never going to be able to forget you."

I tried to breathe in and out like a normal person.

"I went to California to work, to check on my business down there, and I could not," he snapped his mouth shut, and looked away, "I could not get you out of my head for a single damn second and you know

what? I don't think I'll ever be able to get you out of
my head, and here you are, in Telena, breaking off our
relationship, breaking off us, and I have no idea in
hell why you did it. *None.*"

"Logan, I—"

"You what?" He glowered down at me, that frustration, that raw hurt emanating from him. "You want to
throw out what we have? You are driving me up the
wall. No woman has ever hit me in the heart like you
have, but you want to go back to your bed and breakfast and hide, Meredith, from me."

"I don't think you understand—"

"I *understand,* Meredith, that you keep pushing me
away, but you don't have the courage to be honest
about why. What's between us is normal, it's natural,
and I adore you and your cowboy hats so why are you
cutting me out of your life?"

I felt hot tears spring to my eyes and I blinked
quick, told myself to suck it up, be a strong cowgirl,
and deal with the blow I knew was coming. This
would be it. I knew he would not want to see me after
this. I knew that. I heard the voices of those other men
and my sister in my head, that black cape of pain settling on my shoulders.

I couldn't bear it. I ran a hand through the white
streak in my hair, pushed all my black hair back, then
wrapped my arms around his shoulders, pulling him
in tight. I wanted one last hug.

He hesitated for a minute. I knew he was fighting
with himself, but then those strong arms were around
me again, tight and loving. "I have never met anyone
as troublesome and as difficult as you, Meredith."

Within a minute, though, he was pulling away,
hands on his hips, inhaling deeply. "Okay, I can't do
this, Meredith, I can't get thrown into all the passion
between us only to have you walk, or run, away from

me. Is it me? Are you afraid of getting hurt? I will
never hurt you. Are you still afraid I want some short
fling? I can assure you that's not what I want."

Those tears dropped out on their own accord. I
probably resembled a menopausal porcupine. What
had happened to my tough girl demeanor? My
strength and fortitude? What happened to the woman
who could break a horse? Who could belt a drunken
sea urchin? Where was she?

"Meredith, tell me now. I thought things were
going great, I can hardly resist you, but if the feeling
isn't mutual, tell me, and I will go away this time. I
will. It'll kill me, but I will."

"No, Logan, it's not that." I adored him, too. So
much. "It's that. . . . I don't think you're going to like
me after I tell you . . . something."

"Babe, I will like you. I don't care what you tell
me, I will like you. I will never stop liking you. You
are the most likable person I've met . . . What is it?"

"I . . ." I hated this. I hated this moment. So, I blub-
bered some more and tried to get control.

"Aw now, honey, honey," he pulled me close, and I
clung to him. I knew after I told Logan about my leg
he would pretend it didn't matter; that was the kind of
man he was. But I knew it would matter. It had mattered to everyone else. He would not want to sleep
with me. He would not want to be with me. He would
not want to ride horses and fly fish and eat my strawberry crepes anymore. He would make his excuses,
and he would be gone, and these last holiday weeks,
which had been so . . . magical, so fun and warm and
happy . . . gone. All gone.

"I have to tell you that . . ." I about choked, the top
of my head under his chin. "I . . . Logan, I . . . I
haven't wanted to get close to you . . . physically be-

cause . . . because Logan, I don't have . . . I have a
right leg, but I only, my left leg was amputated below
the knee." I closed my eyes and more tears slipped
through. "I wear a prosthesis. I was in a car accident
when I was younger. . . ."

Harsh, screaming images of that night flashed
through my mind.

"I know."

"What?" I pulled away to stare into those green
eyes. "You know?"

"Yes, I know."

I wanted to conk myself in the head. Of course he
knew. It was a small town. Who was I fooling? *You
were fooling yourself.* Yes, I was. I didn't want him to
know, so I hoped he didn't. "Someone told you. A lot
of people told you, didn't they?"

"No, honey. No one told me. They kept your privacy. The reason I know"—he cupped my face with
one warm, strong hand—"the reason I know is because I was there with you the night of the accident."

I tried to form a word, but couldn't.

"I was the one who put a tourniquet on your leg
with my T-shirt. I ripped your sweatshirt in half and
gave you CPR. I stabilized you until the paramedics
and your parents came."

I held tight to his shoulders so I wouldn't collapse.
"That was you?"

"Yes, it was. When I saw you in Barry Lynn's, I
recognized the white streak in your hair. You were
critically hurt that night, and I didn't think you would
remember me, plus it was a long time ago. I didn't tell
you before this, Meredith, because I didn't want it to
be something odd, something heavy between us. I
didn't want you to feel obligated to me. I wanted us to
be built on us, not that event, or any other misplaced

emotions surrounding that tragedy. I'm sorry. Maybe I should have told you before."

"I . . . I . . ." I was shocked.

"Sit down, Meredith. Let's talk." I collapsed on a bench, and we talked about the accident, my sister's reaction, my medical trauma, and how he left for California the day after the accident for work but called the hospital to get a report on me. "I felt terrible for you. Just terrible, and I worried about you. You have no idea how often I've thought of you over the years and wished you well, hoped that you were happy."

When the nerve-blowing shock of sitting next to the man who had literally saved my life waned so I could think again, we got back to my leg.

"My prosthesis doesn't bother you, Logan?"

He looked utterly confused and more than slightly ticked off. "Why in hell would it bother me, Meredith?"

"Because I have a prosthesis, because I'm not whole. . . ."

"You've got to be joking." He did not say those words too nicely.

"No, I'm not—"

"You're not that self-pitying are you? You can't possibly believe that?"

I closed my eyes. Had I been self-pitying? Had I let my resentment of the loss of my leg, the anger I felt toward my sister, mottle my thinking that badly? Had I allowed the accident to take more than part of my leg, but also a huge chunk of my self-esteem, my joy, who I am as a woman? Had the anger taken me from me? *Yes,* I thought instantly, *yes, it has.*

"I do . . . I have . . . Other men . . ."

"Meredith, I am not 'other men'," Logan semi-shouted. "I have never been 'other men'. I will never be 'other men'. Has this been why you've pushed me away? Why you can't commit, why you can't be . . ." He struggled to find the word. "Is this why we can't be together?"

"Yes. I don't want you to see me . . . I'd feel exposed . . . I feel ugly . . . I don't like to be naked with that . . . I always wear pants . . . *Doesn't it bother you?*"

Now that steamed him to the boiling point. "After all the time we've spent together, do you think I'm that damn shallow? Do you think I'm the kind of man who would let something like that *bother* me?"

I bit my lip.

"You did, didn't you? Haven't I shown you that I'm more of a man than that? Why would you think I would break up with you once I found out?"

Why would I think that? Because I didn't like that part of myself. *Well, of course you don't,* I thought, of course you would rather have your leg back. Anyone would. And yet, your leg is only one small part of yourself. It isn't your compassion, or your kindness to others, or your smarts, or your ability to shoot targets in the center, fly fish, or hug Sarah and Jacob. It's a sad thing. It's done. You're still here, aren't you? You're still alive, right, at Christmastime, in Telena, with Logan?

"I . . . I didn't . . . I judged you unfairly, Logan, I did. I assumed you would react a certain way, based on my past, how I let others make me feel, how stupid men made me feel, and based on how I feel about myself. And I was wrong."

"You certainly were!" he roared, a bull now who was not happy. "One hundred percent wrong."

For a long time we locked gazes, his furious, mine apologetic. I knew I still looked like a menopausal porcupine.

He stood and turned around, those shoulders huge and solid, and I heard him swear, and mutter something about me being "an impossibly difficult woman," but by the time he turned around, hands on those yummy hips, I knew we'd crossed a threshold. He sighed. "Damn, but I thought I was going to lose it in California, alone, lonely, wanting you by me. Is there anything else, sugar, that's going to keep you from kissing me for the rest of my life?"

For the rest of his life? Dare I hope? I shook my head.

"Nothing?"

"As long as you promise never to give up your cowboy boots, I think we'll be good." The menopausal porcupine smiled through her tears.

He pulled me into his hug and this time, with that Christmas tree glowing in the distance, the North Star extra bright, I gave Logan Taylor a big smackeroo right on the lips.

"I love you, Meredith," he murmured. "I love you so much."

My life had not turned out as I had planned. I had lost part of a leg. I had spent months grieving, had to relearn to walk, and was in mind-smashing pain because my sister drove drunk. After that I had had to leave New York and my career to take care of her kids, who had brought me pain and joy, but much more joy than pain, and I had faith there would be more joy to come. Plus, I loved those kids with my whole happy heart.

Everything had worked out near perfectly, barring the loss of my leg. It wasn't the plan, but it was a near-perfect plan.

"I love you, too, Logan. And thank you for saving me that night at Barry Lynn's."

He laughed, and that laughter flew up and around

us, swirling around, like Santa's magic, sparkly and bright.

"Thank you for saving my life years ago, too, cowboy." Then I did what any tough Montana cowgirl/fly fisherwoman would do: I went toe to toe with him with our cowboy boots and didn't stop those happy tears slipping down my face, mixing with his, as I kissed those luscious lips.

I had a sudden, yummy vision of me and Logan kissing in front of his giant gingerbread house.

Chapter 11

For the concert I wore a black, satiny, sparkly dress that displayed a bit of cleavage (for Logan). The dress dropped to a few inches below my knees. I wore black cowboy boots with sparkle and my red cowgirl hat with the Santa Claus from the mayor. My prosthesis showed, and I felt fine about it.

It was time for me to stop hiding. I was me, Meredith Ghirlandaio. I'd lost part of my leg. I still had my heart. Still had my arms, my white streak, and my frazzled brain. More importantly, I had Sarah and Jacob, Logan, my parents, and my friends. Logan said I looked like the bionic woman, exposed. I kissed him. He kissed me back, and Simon whipped out his violin and played part of a passionate love song.

I'd learned a lot these last weeks. From Norm, Howard, Chinaza, and Maly I'd learned about enduring hardship and still embracing life. From Simon I'd learned to be brave again. From Logan I'd learned how to love and trust, and to continue my independence while depending on him for who we were together.

From my sister I had learned who I did not want to be. Maybe we learn as much from others about how *not* to treat people as we do about how to be good, kind, and compassionate. I also learned I had to let go of the anger I had for Leia and the impact she'd had on my life. I had to stop wishing I could lasso her around the waist and drag her to Florida and leave her in a swamp with chomping alligators. That had to stop. Not for her, for me. My anger was hurting me. And, it had hurt my relationship with Logan. That was never, ever going to get in the way again.

So I wore a shimmery black dress and my cowboy boots up on stage, smiled hugely, and said, "Good evening, everyone! Merry Christmas to all of you!"

The concert began with the pink-haired teenagers rockin' the house with "Jingle Bell Rock" with their own special slant, and we were off. The lights came down, and the full choir, wearing white robes and carrying candles, swayed down the center aisle singing upbeat Christmas carols. We put the words on two huge screens, and the audience stood and sang with them. Jacob came out next and softly played "O Little Town of Bethlehem," while his new friend, Tuck Daniels, who held the hand of his sister, Marky, a specially-abled child, wondered aloud why we celebrated Christmas.

A ringing solo by Ranna May, the former opera star, of "Let There Be Peace on Earth," came next. While Tim and Claudia painted a lone, decorated Christmas tree on a snowy hill, their work projected on the screen, the choir belted out, "Rocking Around the Christmas Tree." We had a duet backed up by the choir with "Go Tell It on the Mountain," and a gospel number that brought the house down. The Wise Women Christmas skit could sometimes hardly be heard through the laughter. I can only explain it by saying it was about Christmas, single women, hot flashes, men, push up bras, tummy tuckers, math, birthing cows, runaway horses, Santa, and dating.

Maly and one of her sons iced and decorated an exquisite gingerbread house, their work also projected up on the screens. The Old Timers Still Kickin' Band came out and sang, in their shepherds outfits, "O Come All Ye Faithful." A children's choir sang two songs about Santa with Stan on his xylophone, with a bunch of little girls in red tutus and Santa hats dancing around. There were no devil masks. Norm and Howard spoke about their wartime experience, how the soldiers sang Christmas songs, and how their friend Paul said, "I'm grateful to be alive, and even more grateful you two are alive, thank you Jesus and Merry Christmas." You could not hear a peep when they were talking. The Old Timers sang "Silent Night," all lights off, each man holding a candle.

Chinaza played his drums after telling a short story of his life in Nigeria, Jacob played "What Child Is This," and we launched into the story of baby Jesus with Terry narrating and Tuck throwing in more questions about what Christmas is all about. We ended that scene in total silence with one spotlight right on Joseph and Mary/Sarah/Rebel Child as they held Jesus, the cross glowing behind them.

Finally, Simon played his violin. Two Christmas songs. "I'm going to be brave, Meredith." I heard the quick intake of breath as the audience gasped, almost in unison, "Oh my gosh, it's Simon Baumgartner!" At the end, Simon beamed, his relief a palpable, breathable thing. It had been a battle for him to get back on stage. Battle won.

We ended with everyone up on stage, in the balconies, candles lit, three more Christmas songs, including "Joy to the World" with Santa Claus (Logan) waving his way down the aisle, tossing candy, followed by a bunch of kids dressed like elves, and bam.

We were done.

Long, long, *long* standing ovation. The best part? After the concert I saw a whole bunch of girls surrounding Sarah, laughing and chatting, and a bunch of boys wrestling and talking with Jacob. Both of their faces were so joyful, so happy. I knew we had a new start.

As I locked up the Community Center well after midnight, Logan pulled me close. "You are the most incredible person I have ever met in my life."

"Thank you, Santa."

We were booked solid starting the next morning and had to add three shows.

We hadn't bargained for Mary's baby to be born on Christmas Eve. The sweetheart was two weeks too early. But babies have tiny minds of their own; this one was ready, so out it came.

The only problem? The mother, Mary.

Mary, despite my insistence that she go home and rest, did not. So, when she felt those universal pains that all mothers recognize, she ignored them and kept working around the bed and breakfast.

Me, Logan, Jacob, Sarah in her Mary outfit, Joseph (her new friend) in his outfit, the shepherds (the Old Timers), the Three Wise Women (still laughing about their skit), Martha, and the drummer man from Nigeria, Chinaza, arrived home for pecan pie and eggnog to celebrate Christmas Eve together.

When we found Mary, in the kitchen, on all fours, we knew we would soon be joined by one more. The paramedics were called and rushed in, but could not transport her because she was too far along. Her husband sprinted in, saw she was in pain, went pasty white all over, and raced to the bathroom. He came back in, hugged her, cried, went pasty white, raced for the bathroom.

"He's not very good at being pregnant," Mary panted. "It makes him feel sick."

Logan propped her up. The Wise Women and I encouraged her, breathed with her, and held the baby when she arrived, squawking. The shepherds stayed in the other room with Sarah, Jacob, Chinaza, and Joseph.

"Next time I'm going to make it to the hospital," Mary panted, "but thank heavens I didn't have to ride in on a donkey or give birth in a barn, amidst lambs and hay. That Mary was an incredible person."

That she was.

The sweet baby's name was Noelle.

"Merry Christmas," Logan murmured against my mouth before he kissed me on Christmas Day.

"Merry Christmas to you."

I gave him his gift. It was a wicker picnic basket filled with food. I'd made him turkey sandwiches carved into salmon shapes, two salads, and plate-sized chocolate chip cookies. He knew it stood for family.

His eyes shone with tears, and he had to sit down. He patted the couch beside him and hugged me close. I saw him wipe his eyes but I pretended I didn't. The big, emotional grizzly bear was a lot more emotional than he let on.

He handed me a pink box. Inside there was a pink cake. On top of the pink cake there was a jewelry box. A jewelry box for a ring. Inside the jewelry box was a gorgeous sparkler with smaller sparklers surrounding the mongo sparkler.

"Meredith, honey, I want you to marry me."

I could tell he was nervous about my reaction, which I thought was so infinitely sweet.

"I want you to be my wife, I want to be your husband, forever, and if you say yes—" He paused and that ol' grizzly bear got more emotional. He blinked fast, brushed his eyes with his hand. "If you say yes, it can be a long engagement, a short one, whatever you want. There's no rush. None. I wanted you to know, however, that I'm not looking for a date, or a girlfriend, I'm in this for life. I'm in this for you, for us."

I grinned up at him. "Me too, honey. For life. For us." I kissed him. He made me sizzle in special secret spots, and I envisioned us inside a pink cake on a pink bed. "I love you."

"I love you, too, Meredith. More than my own life, I love you."

I swear I could hear the sound of ladies applauding with white gloves on. I looked around. Nope. No one.

I would so haunt this house with my cooking.

Barry Lynn's toy drive was an enormous success. No one got suspended.

That night I dreamed of the accident again.

The car flipped, but this time it landed softly, no noise, amidst snowy Christmas trees, all lit up with colorful lights and shiny ornaments. Logan pulled me out of the car and hugged me close. He opened up a pink box, and it grew and grew and we stepped into it. Inside there were fly fishing rods and pink cake. When we opened the door again, we were fishing on a river.

Epilogue

Six months later

"Did everyone bring their Grateful Journals?" Vicki asked, after we were all settled on our stools at Barry Lynn's, the bar that has been around for over a hundred years and has the bullet holes to prove it.

I pulled mine out of my bag. "I've got mine. I am grateful that my sister let me adopt Sarah and Jacob." It had taken two aggressive attorneys who Logan had insisted on paying for, but the kids were now legally mine. Abandonment does not sit well with the courts. The brave testimony of two kids who no longer wished to live with their mother because of various sordid reasons also helped our case.

I stopped talking as the Three Wise Women clapped and hooted and hugged me.

"I am grateful that I am not angry anymore."

The Three Wise Women clapped and hooted.

"And I am grateful that Logan and I will be getting married by the river and I will have the four most wonderful boot-kicking bridesmaids in the world, you

Three Wise Women, plus Sarah, standing right by me."

Oh, how they clapped and hooted and hugged and made a big, teary, emotional fuss.

"I will give you a cow for your wedding present," Vicki said, wiping her eyes.

"I will give you a new china tea set," Hannah said, blowing her nose.

"Not a math book?" I asked.

"Of course not, Meredith. This is about you and your wedding and what you would like, not what I would like. You have a fondness for tea, therefore a delicate, hand-painted tea set is needed."

"You're getting married, Meredith!" Katie yelled, bopping in her seat with excitement. "I am so happy! I know exactly what I'm going to get you and Logan! Two pirate outfits! You'll feel wicked sexy in them. Wicked sexy! My pastor's wife, Cheryl, recommended them to me. They come with swords, eye patches, and one parrot."

I was going to say, "Katie, I hardly know what to say," but instead I growled, pirate style and said, "Argggh! Bring 'em on board, lassie!"

"A Very Maui Christmas"

MARY CARTER

Chapter 1

Good things come in small packages, but so does anthrax. This occurred to Tara Lane during her weekly phone call with her little sister, Nadine. At five-foot-three inches, Nadine was certainly a little package. And, she was using her sweet voice with Tara, at least on the surface. But Tara knew better. Nadine's message was laced with a poison they had all learned to dread, one Tara had catalogued as "Unresolved Issues." Alone, it was harmful, but not deadly. However, combine "Unresolved Issues" with "The Holiday Season," and suddenly, you were dealing with a combustible situation, possibly a lethal one. Or, maybe, just maybe, Tara was being a tad too melodramatic. After all, Nadine was simply upset with Tara for cursing during last year's Christmas dinner, and she didn't want her to do it again.

So why didn't she just come out and say that? Because then she would miss out on an opportunity to play professor. Thus, Nadine's current lecture: "Substitute-Swear Words for when Children are in the

Room 101, the Holiday Edition." Tara wished she could sit in the back of the room and slink into obscurity. Unfortunately, she seemed to be the only one taking the class.

"Like you could say—'Get the elf out,' " Nadine prompted.

Nadine had a point, and even before the lecture had begun, Tara had sworn to herself that she was going to be on her best behavior this year, no matter how crazy her family drove her. But between work and the impending holidays, Tara was stressed to the max (like she used to say in high school; geez, wasn't there a time when everything was, like, to the max?) and if she could squeeze a tiny drop of pleasure out of riling Nadine up, she figured it was worth the price she would eventually have to pay. After all, Tara had to put up with Nadine's shenanigans every year, and she did it with grace if she did say so herself.

"Get the elf out," Tara repeated. She said it slowly and clearly, like a foreigner in a survival English course.

"Exactly," Nadine said with a sigh of relief. "Or 'elf off' or—'elf you,' or you know—whatever variation shoots out of your mouth." Nadine sighed again; this time Tara registered slight disgust in her sister's gentle voice. "Of course," Nadine continued, "you could give me the biggest Christmas gift ever, and not say it at all, not in any form. But I suppose that's asking too much."

"Get the elf out," Tara said with a little more gusto.

"Perfect."

"Elf you."

"You got it."

"Elf you and the reindeer you rode in on."

"Too far."

"Should I 'rein' it in, 'deer'?"

"Tara."

"Okay, okay—but seriously—I have a question." Nadine's silence was Tara's cue to go on. "Get him out of what?" Tara said, throwing her hand over her mouth to stifle her laughter.

"Excuse me?"

"What are we getting the elf out of? Is the little guy stuck somewhere? Don't tell me it's the chimney."

"Tara," Nadine said, dragging her name out into infinity. Uh-oh, Tara knew that tone all too well. Definitely time to stop elf-ing with her. And, yes, Tara knew she had nobody to blame but herself. As she knew, it was just last year, while visiting Nadine, that Tara had dropped the F-bomb on Christmas Eve. Her niece, Tiara, named after Tara—only with an extra *i* because she was slightly more precious—glommed onto the colorful new word and not only repeated it, but began singing it with gusto, to the tune of "Jingle Bells." She was only a year old at the time. Tara thought this proved her niece was some kind of genius, but Nadine couldn't get over her humiliation enough to see it that way. Especially when Tiara said it to the Santa at the mall.

Santa: "Have you been a good girl, Tiara?"

Tiara: "F*&k you."

Once again Tara tried to point out how impressive it was that Tiara was using it correctly. Once again, Nadine did not see it that way.

And she was never going to let her forget it. But does she mention the fight that preceded the foul word's shooting out of Tara's mouth? Does she say one word about calling Tara *"almost middle-aged"* in front of the entire family? *Almost middle-aged, single, childish, and childless,* were Nadine's exact words. It was impossible to argue with single and childless;

they were just facts. Childish—yes, sometimes Tara did act a bit childish. She preferred to think of herself as carefree. But "almost middle-aged" stung Tara to the core. And slightly terrified her. Which was exactly what Nadine was trying to accomplish. Her twenty-six-year-old, married-mother-of-one sister was trying to terrify her into getting married and having children. Tara was thirty years old. Almost middle-aged. Tara was totally confused about what middle age was even considered nowadays, what with vitamins, and medical breakthroughs, and anti-wrinkle creams, and lasers, and scrubs, and injections, and dermabrasion, and MILFs and Cougars, and *Desperate Housewives*. Still, the prospect was terrifying.

Nadine's suggested remedy, marriage and children, was no less daunting.

Time and time again, Tara had explained to Nadine how difficult it was to date in New York City. Nadine would point out that she could move. Then Tara would tell her how much she loved her job. Nadine would ask her if her job tucked her in at night or sang to her, or made her feel like the most beautiful woman in the whole wide world.

And then Tara would tell her to elf off.

It was a pattern they were stuck in, a never-ending loop. And not only was Nadine doing it again this year, she'd ramped up her game. She was on the pulpit yet again, this time preaching, of all things, Internet dating. Nadine, who was a virgin when she married her high school sweetheart at eighteen. And even that, Tara always suspected, was just because Nadine had let her then boyfriend (now husband) Phil honk her boobs at the Sadie Hawkins dance.

While Nadine prattled on, Tara glanced at her bookshelf and calmed herself by staring Zen-like at her favorite book of all time, *Great Expectations*. She absolutely loved it, and used it to motivate herself whenever she was down. If little orphan Pip could claw his way out of despair, then so could she. It was fitting then, that this latest challenge was rearing its ugly sibling head during the holiday season. After all, her favorite book opened on Christmas Eve. And just because her little story opened in her studio apartment on the Upper West Side of Manhattan, and her favorite little orphan's tale began in a village churchyard, didn't take away her feelings of kinship; Pip was still her rock. Even if he was only seven—way under middle age—in fact, it just proved how connected they all were. Struggle, pain, and hope, were universal, timeless, and bonding.

True, Tara was speaking to her sister, and not an escaped convict (although a case could be made), nor was her sister trying to cajole her into cutting off her shackles (although a case could be made), but being the subject of another matchmaking plot was just as hideous. Tara cradled the phone between her shoulder and neck, tapped her fingertips together, and pondered how to deal with this latest upset. *What would Pip do?* she asked herself.

Squeak, was the only answer that came to mind.

It was beginning to dawn on Tara that expectations came with expiration dates. Now that she was thirty, when it came to her love life, certain people had expectations of their own. Namely, that she would start lowering hers. "You're too picky" was a refrain she'd been hearing a lot lately.

"Did you get my Christmas gift?" Tara heard Nadine ask. This was the subject she'd been dreading; she'd rather listen to the lecture again than venture onto this land mine.

"Yes," Tara said. She didn't want to upset her sister anymore, so she forced herself to use an upbeat tone and wandered into the kitchen. There, she took her frustrations out on the poor, fat tomato sitting on the cutting board. She stabbed at it with gusto and watched slimy red juice ooze out of its fleshy, lonely heart.

"And?" Nadine said.

"Not interested," Tara said. So much for not upsetting Nadine. The words escaped from her mouth before she could sound her internal alarm. She dumped the sliced-up tomato into a bowl and rinsed off the cutting board. Silence. Nadine was probably counting to ten.

"So you're not even going to look?" Nadine said. "Because you have more or less three weeks. And if you just happen to find someone you like—as long as you get a thorough background check—he is more than welcome to spend Christmas here with us."

Oh. My. God. Tara sucked in a mouthful of air and tried to hold it. She failed, and choked. Not only did Nadine expect her to go on a first date, she was assuming Tara would like the candidate enough to go on a second date. In Tara's experience this was like trying to catch not one, but two shooting stars in the sky. Furthermore, on the off chance Tara should happen to catch two shooting stars in the sky, Nadine's brilliant plan was for Tara to immediately invite her new two-date man to spend Christmas with her and her family in Montana. Priceless. It confirmed once and for all what Tara had always suspected. Nadine was certifiably insane.

"What a marvelous idea," Tara said. Nadine started rattling off the list of things she had to do to get ready for the holidays. As she listened, Tara glanced at her one Christmas decoration, a miniature live pine tree on the windowsill. It was too frail to hold any ornaments, but came with a base wrapped in gold foil and topped with a fat red bow. Tara suddenly saw herself arriving at her sister's house with the tree and pretending it was her date. She could even dress it in a tuxedo. "This is Bob," she would say. "We're in love." She stifled a laugh as she imagined Christmas tree Bob sitting in one of Nadine's massive dining room chairs, barely poking his little ferny head above the table.

Nadine suddenly stopped talking. "What's so funny?" she demanded.

"Nothing," Tara said. She took the knife and mimed cutting her throat. Then she dropped it in the sink and walked over to her office, a cramped space between the front door and the refrigerator. She sat down at her new Apple computer, an early Christmas gift to herself. She clicked on the Web site minimized at the bottom of the screen, and watched as a photo of a ridiculously gorgeous, smiling couple came to life on her screen.

Soul Mate Central

Nadine had gifted her with a six-month subscription. This, after Tara explicitly told her she was done with dating. She was going to resign herself to the fact that no one was ever going to match her "Must Have" list, which truth be told had whittled down to a "Would Like to Have" list, then had further disintegrated into a proclamation: "I Will Not Date Serial Killers."

No need to go into any of this with Nadine.

Tara clicked on the member log-in box and typed her screen name into the space provided. Sexy Sous-Chef. She winced at the name, but every rendition of Tara had already been taken. She didn't know who all the other "Tara"s were out there, but she hoped for their sakes, they were having better luck than she was. "Since I have you to thank for this, I thought I might read you some profiles and get your take on them," Tara said.

"Wonderful," Nadine said. She sounded so happy. Tara almost felt guilty. "I want to see their pictures too. Should I pull up the site?" Tara didn't need to have the Web cam turned on to picture her sister perfectly. She was probably sitting in her den, an immaculate yellow space where television was banned, and books reigned supreme. She would be curled up in the velvet orange- and white-striped chair she'd re-upholstered herself. Her tiny feet, housed in lavender slippers, were tucked behind her. Her delicate hands would be wrapped around a ceramic mug of peppermint herbal tea. And although she'd be listening to every word Tara said, her eyes would be gazing out onto their acres and acres of snow-drenched land, under that big, blue Montana sky. At least that's how Tara liked to picture it. Like *The Waltons*. Or *Little House on the Prairie*. They even trekked out into the woods every year to cut down the perfect Christmas tree. It was ideal. Tara loved their ranch, too, and would have been thrilled to spend more time there if not for the fact that during the holiday season, her normally semi-sane little sister morphed into a Holiday Hitler.

Tara used to enjoy Christmas. The idea of it anyway. The simple things made her happy. The tree at Rockefeller Center, the windows at Saks, the ice skaters in the park. Twinkling lights, shiny presents with fat bows, the promise of a snow fall on Christmas Eve, carolers belting out cheery songs, little sleep-deprived children hopped up on sugar and Santa. Who didn't love all that? Keep it simple, enjoy the small treats, that was Tara's philosophy.

But let's face it, there was another side to Christmas, a dark side. The money, the stress, the worry, the travel, the members of your family you'd never even say hello to on the street if you weren't related, and when it came to Nadine—the planning, the to-do lists, the assignments. Yes, when it came to Christmas, Tara was an impartial observer, but Nadine was a doer.

This year's "mass Christmas letter" and "dinner duty details letter" had yet to arrive, but they would, oh, they certainly would, and until then, Tara would be seen tiptoeing around her mailbox like it was a minefield. Internet dating was starting to seem like a pleasant distraction. Tara turned her attention back to the computer screen.

"Forget what the men look like for now," Tara said. "Let's just concentrate on their glowing personalities."

"Good idea," Nadine said. "Looks aren't the most important thing anyway. I mean look at Phil. He's not exactly the strapping man I first married." An image of Phil, tall, skinny, hairy, rose to Tara's mind.

"Right," Tara said. She clicked open the first dating profile. "First of all, I had no idea New York was overflowing with so many bald men who own slightly used catamarans and practice 'On Deck Yoga.' " Nadine's laughter filled Tara's ears. Tara laughed along with her.

"You like sailing," Nadine said.

"Don't you think the tops of their naked little heads get cold in the wind?" Tara said. Nadine laughed again. This was what it was all about, making her sister laugh. When Tara was in high school and Nadine was still in elementary, Tara used to make her laugh so hard Nadine would actually pee her pants. Ah, those were the days. There was no greater pleasure in life than making someone else wet themselves. And despite their many differences, Tara and Nadine shared the same wicked sense of humor.

"Don't be so critical," Nadine said. "Bald men can be scxy."

"I don't care. I don't want bald men practicing yoga on their sailboats. I don't want to Internet date. I don't want to date at all. I have Pete and Henry."

"Your bartender and your doorman do not count as boyfriends," Nadine said.

"They do in New York."

"Read more," Nadine said. "I only have about five minutes before Tiara wakes up from her nap." Tara clicked on the next profile and stared at the man before her. Tara wasn't a cruel person, but she did wish Nadine could get a load of this one. If Eeyore from *Winnie-the-Pooh* mated with an obsessive-compulsive basset hound, this is what their love child would grow up to look like.

"I have been told I have a sparkling personality. I have so many intrests it would be impossible to list even one of them." Tara paused for emphasis. "And apparently, spelling isn't one of his 'intrests'," she said, "for he spelled it i-n-t-r-e-s-t-s." Nadine laughed.

"Loser," she cried. "More." Tara sat up straight, smiled in anticipation, and clicked on the next one.

"I enjoy a good conversation, even if it is about nothing at all." They howled in unison.

"He thinks he's Seinfeld," Nadine said.

"They're all Seinfeld," Tara said. "Without the talent, money, or sense of humor." She went on to the next. "Relationships are great, all of them take a little work, but hopefully not TOO much work."

"Never been married," Nadine said.

"Show me a couple who has fun doing nothing,

and I'll show you true love," Tara continued, her mood rising with each quote.

"Lazy and cheap!" Nadine yelled. "And he's definitely been married." A wicked smile spread across Tara's face as she geared up for the last few. She'd saved the best for last.

"Being an avid comic book reader, I'm seeking the gal who can put the Wonder back in Woman," Tara read. Nadine shrieked with laughter. Tara wiped away happy tears.

"Okay that's enough," Nadine said. "I should have knitted you a scarf."

"Wait," Tara said. "There's one more." She was laughing so hard, it took forever to spit it out. "I have a fondness for the squirrels in Thompson Square Park," Tara shrieked. It was the funniest thing she'd ever heard. She was afraid *she* was going to pee her pants this time. She looked around for a paper bag. If she wasn't careful, she was going to hyperventilate. It took her a full minute to realize she was the only one laughing. "Come on," Tara said. "That is hysterical."

"He didn't say he fondles the squirrels," Nadine said. "He said he's fond of them. He's an animal lover." Silence swept in like a winter wind. "I'm sorry you hated your Christmas gift."

"I don't hate it," Tara said. "Honest. I'm just having fun."

"You're all alone. How fun is that?"

"Elf you," Tara said. She was joking, but apparently Nadine didn't see it that way. There was a click, then the hollow rebuke of a dial tone. Tara called back. It went directly to voice mail. "I love you," Tara said. "And I'm not alone. I have you, and Tiara, and Mom, and Dad, and the formerly-strapping Phil." Tara made kissing noises into the phone and hung up.

She tried to tell herself it was going to be okay, but she knew it was far from over. Nadine was going to milk this until Tara found the love of her life on Soul Mate Central and brought her new gift to Montana to be opened and inspected by the Lane Clan and the formerly strapping Phil. Oh, it was just like Nadine to stir up trouble during the holidays. Ho, ho, horrific, as usual.

Chapter 2

Later that evening, riding the downtown Number 1 train to work, Tara couldn't help but wonder if Nadine was right. Was she too picky? Was it time to let go of her expectations and just see what happened? Her last relationship had ended spectacularly. It had been Broadway-worthy really. He threw a huge fit at her place of work, a little French restaurant named La Fleur. All because she canceled a date with him at the last minute. True, it was New Year's Eve, but she had no choice. The owners of La Fleur had family in from France, and if she hadn't agreed to work that evening, she feared she'd never rise out of the ranks of sous-chef. She was shocked she wasn't fired anyway, after Gary Manning stormed into the restaurant a few minutes after midnight and erupted like Mount Vesuvius. Very anticlimactic. Her only saving grace was that the French visitors absolutely loved their front row seats to *American Men Misbehaving*. It wasn't the only time Gary had thrown a fit, but it was his public debut. He was a lawyer, who, when angry would actually stomp his feet, and if he lost a case, they wouldn't make love for days. It was two months of fun followed by six of hell. She vowed the next man she dated would be different. Easygoing. Laid back. Not the type she would meet working in the restaurant business, or in Manhattan at all for that matter. Nevertheless, she had her work. Even more exciting, she was about to become head chef at La Fleur, a position she'd been coveting for six years. It was the best Christmas gift a girl could ask for.

La Fleur. It had been love at first sight. The cutest little French restaurant in all of Manhattan. It was owned by Yvette and Stephan, a wealthy French couple. Wedged in between Union Square and Gramercy Park, it quickly became a mainstay for tourists and locals alike. Fruits, vegetables, and flowers were plucked fresh every day from the Union Square Farmers Market; eggs and meats were exclusively purchased from a private farm upstate; and truffles, oils, and attitudes were imported directly from Paris.

Fresh and direct herself from the Culinary Institute of America, Tara had wined, dined, and stalked Yvette and Stephan until they hired her. She visited the little gem no less than a hundred times before they even acknowledged her presence. She courted them like lovers, looking her best whenever she came in, alternating friends (who weren't on diets) to go with her, tasting everything on the menu, complimenting them nonstop, finishing everything on her plate, and appropriately moaning over every new creation they put in front of her. Psychology books will tell you that people love it when you say their names. Well Tara knew that chefs (and lovers) loved it when you said "mmm-mmm," and "yummmmm," or, "Oh my God." Tara said them all, often. She gained fifteen pounds during the courtship, but it was worth it. She was hired. And, happily, after sweating her butt off in the kitchen, she quickly slimmed down to her pre-courtship weight.

She paid her dues in other ways. Despite having attended a highly reputable culinary institute where French cooking was king, she soon learned that according to Y&S (as Yvette and Stephan were known), everything she had learned there was wrong. They were all too happy to school her in the "real ways of the French." S was a tall man with a protruding Santa Claus belly. Y was tall and skinny. Every time Y made a crack about Americans being fat, Tara managed not to point out that S looked like he had swallowed a baby whale. Besides, he was the one who seemed to be rooting for her, spending numerous hours tutoring her until she got every one of their signature sauces just right. She knew she'd been paid the highest compliment the day S tasted her Steak au Poivre sauce, closed his eyes, and said: "I'd barely know you aren't French. Not Parisian of course, but you'd pass for provincial." It was good enough for her.

The menu changed daily, and sometimes S would get a notion that he was going to decide what everyone was eating that evening, and if they didn't like it, they could "crawl on their distasteful bellies to the yellow arches." Like an actor who wouldn't dare mention the Scottish play in a theatre, he would never, ever, utter the unimaginable word "McDonald's." New Yorkers, despite their reputations for being bossy, impatient, and cold, were all too happy to be bullied by S. No one ever turned a meal away. Tara was learning from a genius.

And then Y&S decided they'd taken enough of a bite out of the Big Apple, and that they longed "for the sanity of Paris." But instead of appointing her head chef, they imported a representative from France. Alain Costeau. Yes, like Jacques Cousteau, but no relation except for the fact that he treated Tara as if she were twenty thousand leagues under his sea. Alain hated all things American and that included sous-chef Tara Lane. He didn't even half-smile like Y&S had eventually learned to do. And since Y&S smiled on opposite sides of their faces, on the rare occasion husband and wife stood together, they almost made a whole smile between them. But not Alain. Smiling would have interfered with his head-shaking, cursing, and pot-slamming. But all that was about to change. Tara had been given a Christmas miracle. Y&S had decided they missed crazy America after all, and so they were going to open a restaurant in the "Heart of the country." Las Vegas.

And Alain was going to run it. Tara was finally promoted to head chef. She couldn't have been more proud if she'd been knighted by the Queen. And the best bit of all, she only had to put up with Alain's cranky French ass for another few days.

"You're early," Alain said when Tara walked in. He slammed the copper pot in his hand. Early, according to Alain, was just as much of an offense as being late. Tara took a deep breath and smiled. She put on her apron, washed her hands, and hummed, "It's Beginning to Look A Lot Like Christmas."

"I'm early for a reason," Tara said. "I'm going to decorate for Christmas." Alain's jaw dropped.

"Christmas?" he said, as if he'd never heard the word. "Decorations?"

"Nothing over the top," Tara said. "A string of white lights outside, a few poinsettias—"

"No," Alain said. "We don't do this." It was true, they'd never decorated for any holiday. They were equal opportunity Scrooges. Once Tara had brought a tiny pumpkin in for Halloween, but before she could carve it Alain used it to make a puree for a soup. But Alain was leaving, he was leaving, he was leaving! She got to make decisions now; she was the head chef, and she was going to tastefully decorate La Fleur for Christmas.

"You won't even be here for Christmas," Tara pointed out. "You'll be in Vegas baby, remember?" Alain banged the copper pot, then picked up a silver sautéing pan and gave that a whack as well.

"I am 'ere now," he said, slathering on his accent like an overindulgent pat of butter. "And there will be no Christmas flooers."

"Flooers?" Tara said. Alain slammed the pot again.

"Ze stupid red flooers!"

"Oh. Flowers," Tara said. No flowers in "La Fleur," she thought. She waited for the familiar feeling of defeat and anger to drag her under. To her surprise, it didn't come. Instead, she smiled. Alain frowned, then turned away. Tara wanted to whoop with joy, sing Christmas carols at the top of her lungs. That's when it hit her. She should celebrate. She would celebrate. She would throw a good-bye party that really would be a kiss-my-ass party in disguise! It would look like the party was for Alain, but it would really be for her.

She tried to contact Y&S. After all, they should chip in. She kept reaching their voice mail. She thought it was strange they weren't answering; they should be in Vegas now, setting up shop. She turned to the other employees. Since it was a small restaurant there were only three servers, a hostess, and a busboy. None of them wanted to chip in. They all used Christmas as their excuse, but Tara suspected that like her, they didn't think Alain deserved a going away party. She was tempted to tell them it was actually a party for her, but she didn't want them to think their new head chef was too big for her chef's hat. Instead, she used good old-fashioned guilt. They eventually coughed up ten dollars each. Not exactly the budget of the stars, but it was enough to buy a cheap bucket of flooers.

She waited until the next day, when Alain wasn't due until much later, to decorate. In addition to the BON VEGAS-AGE! banner, there were twinkling white lights, poinsettias, and early New Year's noise accoutrements. Noise blowers, hats, and the cheapest champagne she could find, except for one bottle of Dom, which she was saving for an after-party of one. She picked up the nearest pot and banged it on the counter. Alain's last day had arrived.

At Tara's urging, they hid in the walk-in refrigerator. Three slim, brunette waitresses, a jittery busboy from Ecuador, a tall African American hostess-slash-model, and Tara. They all had pots to bang, and cheap champagne to spray the minute Alain entered the walk-in to pick up his meat. Life was coming full circle, and it was a beautiful thing.

"He's late," Sahara, the hostess-slash-model pointed out. They were all shivering, and Sahara's nipples were poking out of her low cut dress. Tara didn't want to be known as the boss who gave them frostbite.

"Sorry," Tara said. "Let's get out of here." It was just like Alain to be late on his last day. Sahara marched over to the freezer door and pulled. It didn't budge. Tino, the busboy, stepped up with a smile and flexed his bicep. He put his hand on Tara's shoulder and gently pushed her out of the way. He flexed the muscles in his arm again as he pulled on the handle.

"It's locked," he said. All heads turned to Tara.

"It can't be," Tara said. "It only locks from the kitchen side." Tara tried the door next. She could feel the glares from her employees, and they were colder

than the sub-degree temperatures. Yep, it was definitely locked, and there was only one person who
could have locked it.

"I told you he'd hate a party," one of the brunettes
whined. Tara pounded on the door. Soon, everyone
joined in. They threw their bodies into it. When they
heard the click of the door unlocking, it was too late
to move back. It swung open with a groan and sent
them all hurling toward the newly mopped kitchen
floor face first. Their cheap champagne bottles
dropped, rolled, burst, and drizzled across the floor,
and the pots they'd been holding landed with disappointing pings and thuds. Alain towered over Tara.
She looked at him through champagne-soaked bangs
and tried to figure out what was different about him.
When she realized what it was, she opened her mouth
in a silent scream. He was smiling.

"Zurprize," he said. He had a string of her little
white lights bunched in one hand and a large poinsettia in the other. Tara lurched out of the way as he
dropped them on her. Enraged, she looked up to find
him holding her prized bottle of Dom.

"No," she screamed. It was too little too late. He
popped the cork. It rocketed to the ceiling and champagne burst out of the top. He upended the bottle over
Tara's head. Furious, she fought the urge to lick it off
as it ran down her face. It was so expensive! Alain
laughed, held his iPhone out, and snapped her picture.
Tara pulled herself upright, slipping as she did, on the
wet floor. She'd never been so furious and so humiliated.

"We did this for you," she said. She pointed her
index finger at Alain's long, thin, nose. "You, you,
you, you—French asshole!" She heard gasps behind
her. Nobody had ever stood up to Alain, let alone
called him names. (Except for the ones they called

him behind his back, which everybody knows don't
really count.) Tara didn't care. Years of culinary abuse
had taken their toll. "You're the biggest baby I've ever
met in my entire life. You're an ungrateful snob.
You're mean, you're rude, and—your sauces are flat!"
That one hit its target. Alain sucked in air and bel-
lowed like a wounded animal. His hands flew up to
his mouth. Tara ducked in case he was going to swing
one of his pots at her head. Instead, he dropped his
hands to his hips, shook his head like he pitied her,
and smiled again. Holy Christmas, that made three in
a row. Dread flooded her.

"Did you not get the mammo?" Alain asked.
Mammo? Tara absentmindedly touched her breast.
Could he see a lump through her apron? She was too
young for a mammogram. Especially since they had
raised the age to fifty, which was still causing raging
debates—

"Memo," Sahara whispered in her ear.

"What memo?" Tara asked. Alain shook his head
and made a tsk-tsk-tsk sound.

"Y&S went to Vegas ahead of me. Zey discovered
zey like to gamble. Zey gambled ze restaurant. Zey
lost."

"Zey did?" Tara said.

Alain's frown deepened. "Zey did!" he shouted.
"Zey lost ze restaurant. So zis French asshole, zis
biggest baby, is back!" He leaned in and stared at her.
His blond hair was full of static, flying away from his
angular face as if he were coming in on a trapeze. His
light blue eyes flashed with anger. "I am back," he
said, "for ze rest of my life." He straightened himself
out. Smiled again. "And you can call me ze Donald,"
he said. He waited for her to ask why. She didn't. She
already knew. He said it anyway. "Because you are
fired!" Tara looked around for support. Sahara hur-

ried off to the hostess desk, Tino began sweeping up, and the brunettes flew to the tiny back patio to share a single cigarette. Tara squared her shoulders, picked up her poinsettia, lights, and near-empty bottle of Dom.

"Elf you," she said. He raised his right eyebrow quizzically and just stared at her. Definitely not as satisfying. She lifted her head, and waltzed out, resisting the urge to grab tablecloths and yank the place settings off the two-seaters as she exited. She waited until she was standing out on Irving Street to bust into tears. There was only one place on earth she wanted to be now, only one person who could help put a little bit of order back into her world. Thank God for her bartender-boyfriend.

Chapter 3

Pete Hillerman was the world's best bartender-boyfriend. He was sexy, courteous, and funny. Some said he made the best cocktail in town; others said he was the best cocktail in town. Tara took a seat at the bar, trying to hold back her tears for his strong shoulders and understanding eyes. A tall, busty redhead appeared in front of her and plunked down a coaster.

"What can I get you?" she said with a slight, ambiguous accent.

"Pete," Tara said. "You can get me Pete." A loud cry went up from the other end of the bar. Tara looked over to see a young girl, hunched over and sobbing.

"Pete's gone," the redhead said.

"Gone," the sobbing girl echoed. "Gone, gone, gone."

"Gone where?" Tara asked. Just her luck. He was probably skiing in Vermont, or visiting his grandmother in Florida.

"Hollywood," the redhead said.

"What?" Tara asked.

"He moved to LA," the sobbing girl said. "Some wench told him he was wasting his talent in New York and should go to Hollywood. So he did. He landed the lead in a new pilot." Tara froze. A month ago she'd come into the bar after a horrific fight with Alain. Pete listened to her go on for hours, even gave her a couple free drinks. She remembered being grateful, slightly tipsy. She had felt guilty she'd hogged the whole conversation, so she asked him about himself.

"I came here to be an actor," he said. He wiped down the counter and removed a couple of empty beer bottles. "Look at me now," he said, holding them up. Tara knew what it was like to fight for your dream. Pete, of all people. He was so gorgeous and funny. He should be a star. He was loved by all the Upper West Side women. Tara stood on the legs of her barstool.

"You should move to LA!" she cried.

"You think?"

"I don't think, handsome, I know."

"I don't know."

"I'm telling you—they'll eat you up out there! Do you know how sexy you are? Do you? I swear to God, Pete—you have to move to LA! You'll be a movie star!"

Tara put her elbows on the bar and rested her head in her hands. He listened to her? He actually listened to her?

"If I ever find that bitch I'm going to kill her!" the girl at the end of the bar screamed.

"What can I get you?" the redhead repeated.

"Did he leave anything behind the bar for me?" Tara asked.

"Like what?"

"Like a letter? Or a small gift?" A freaking plane

ticket to LA? Tara stood on the rails of her barstool
and tried to peer behind the counter. "Does anything
back there say 'Tara' on it?"

"Or Melody?" the girl said, also standing on her
barstool.

"Sit down, ladies," the redhead said. "He's gone.
He's never coming back. And there are no 'Dear Tara'
or 'Dear Melody' or any other letters back here. Now
what do you want to drink?"

"Cyanide," Tara said. The redhead glared.

"I'll buy," Melody said.

"Forget it," Tara said. "I'm going home to my
doorman." Melody put her head down on the bar and
resumed sobbing.

Men never listened to her. Leave it to Pete to actually follow her drunken advice. Move to LA. Well,
she'd done a good deed. He had the lead in a pilot. So
what if she was out a boyfriend? Oh, who was she
kidding? It was awful. The thought of meeting a new
bartender she liked just as much, taking the time to let
him get to know her, what drink she ordered depending on what mood she was in, knowing when to make
her laugh, when to compliment her, when to offer real
advice, and when to tell her she looked absolutely
gorgeous, exhausted her. How many times was she
going to have to go through this? At least she still had
Henry.

Henry Roulston was never going to abandon her.
He'd been a doorman at her building longer than she'd
been alive. He never took sick days. He always
smiled. His uniform was always pressed, the door was
always wide open, and he always had a cheery comment to throw at her. Always, such a comforting word
at such a trying time.

"I was wondering," he'd say. "Did you poach anything today?" Henry could converse on a wide range

of subjects. With Tara, he usually stuck to cooking. He confessed to watching cooking shows in his free time. He'd been encouraging Tara to sign up for *Top Chef.* Weekly, he'd inform her on the latest episode. "The secret ingredient last night was boar," he'd say. "Now what would you have done with that?"

"Hmm," Tara would say. "Roast it over a flaming pit and serve it with a mango-chutney." It didn't matter what her response was, Henry would clap his hands in delight, then rub his stomach. Finally, he'd pat her on the back as if thanking her for being such a good sport. Just thinking of his kindness infused Tara with hope. Who cared if Pete flaked off to LA? Henry was her true love, the one man she'd always be able to count on.

"Good evening, Tara," he said. "Did you sauté anything this evening?" Tara torpedoed herself into Henry's arms. He was stiff at first. But when her tears started, he let go of the door and hugged her back. Then gently, he pulled away, and handed her a handkerchief.

"A handkerchief," Tara said. "A real handkerchief." Henry went over to the concierge desk and picked up a large yellow envelope. He handed it to her. Nadine's mass Christmas letter. Of all times to get this. Tara dabbed at her eyes with the handkerchief.

"What's wrong, darling?" Henry asked. Darling. He called her darling. Tara cried harder.

"Do you know how hard it is to get even a cheap Kleenex off a man these days?" Tara said. "But you. You gave me a real handkerchief, Pete."

"Henry."

"What?"

"You called me Pete. I'm Henry."

"I'm so sorry. Pete's my boyfriend."

"The bartender across the street?"

"You know him?"

"He's your boyfriend?" Now why did Henry sound dubious?

"He was," Tara said. "But he's up and left me for a pilot!" Henry made a tsk-tsk-tsk sound and shook his head.

"What airline?" Henry asked.

"What?"

"American? Jet Blue? United?"

"A television pilot."

"Oh," Henry said. "Good for him!" He clapped his hands in the air. And held his fist out to Tara for a bump. Instead, she poked it with her finger. For the first time ever, she had ill feelings toward her doorman-boyfriend.

"But bad for me," Tara said. "I was sacked today, and all I wanted was a pomegranate martini and some sympathy!"

"You were sacked?" Henry said. "Fired?"

"Can you believe it?" Tara said. "Tonight was supposed to be the best night of my life. I was going to become head chef. Then Alain locked me in the walk-in refrigerator, and when I finally escaped he announced he wasn't going to Vegas because Y&S lost it gambling and I was a goner!" Tara really had to hand it to Henry. He looked horrified. His mouth flew open in protest. He clutched his heart as if it were breaking for her. Good old Henry. "I know," Tara said. "Can you believe it? Can you believe how much my life sucks?"

Henry didn't answer. Eyes wide open, hand still clutching his heart, Henry lurched forward. Before Tara could catch him, he went down like a sawed tree.

In his lifetime, Henry Roulston had opened the door 14,600,000 times, give or take. He'd fathered three daughters with three different wives. He knew every secret of every person who lived within a ten-block radius. He was a diehard Yankees fan. Every morning without fail he bought his coffee at the deli on the corner. Light and sweet, that was how he took it. That was how he lived too. He was loved by all, and would be missed by many. And the last words he would ever hear were Tara Lane shouting, "Can you believe how much my life sucks?"

Henry's funeral was lovely. He had so many people who loved him. The place was packed. Tara wore a little black dress and clutched the handkerchief Henry had given her. She let herself have a good cry. All the people in attendance were so kind. They kept shaking Tara's hand and saying how much they felt for her loss. They understood! They understood how much a person could touch your soul—

Henry's daughters, all three of them, were marching toward Tara. The look on their faces immediately halted her tears.

"Who are you?" the closest one said.

"I'm Tara," she answered, holding out her hand. None of them went to shake it.

"Were you sleeping with him?" one hissed.

"What?" Tara said. "No."

"Because you won't get a dime."

"I don't want a dime."

"Then what are you doing?"

"What do you mean?"

"You're crying 'why me' so loudly nobody could hear the service!"

"I'm so sorry," Tara said. "I lived in his building. I was the last person to talk to him." This seemed to soften the women a bit. Their shoulders relaxed. The smallest one reached over and touched Tara with cold hands.

"What was he talking about?" she asked. "Was he poking fun at the Mets?" Tara tipped her head to the side.

"No," she confessed. "He was listening to me complain about my life." The guilt had been weighing her down. It felt good to confess. Henry would have forgiven her, but now she needed forgiveness from his daughters. She clutched the smallest one's hand. "I'm so ashamed," she said. "The last words your father heard was me yelling 'My life sucks!'" Tara started crying all over again. The daughter yanked her hand back.

"Please go," she said.

"But I thought I'd come back to the house with you," Tara said. "And sauté something for Henry." The three women stared at her.

"I see," Tara said. She blew her nose into her handkerchief.

"Is that Dad's handkerchief?" one of the daughters asked.

It was all innocent and cheery looking on the outside. A padded yellow envelope with a decorative holly border and Santa stamps. Tara held it by the corner as if it were a dead mouse and dangled it over her trash can, daring herself to let go. The trash can, operated by foot pedal, shouted at her like a ravenous, open-mouthed metallic monster. *Feed me! Feed me your sister's letter. I'll gobble it up for you!*

"Dearest Friends and Family," Tara said to the dark, inner depths of the can. For that's how Nadine started all her annual "spread the joy" letters. Dearest Friends and Family. Note how "friends" came first. "I wish I could write you all individually," Tara continued. "Wouldn't I love to have that kind of time." Listening to herself make fun of her sister, to a garbage can, brought a slight measure of guilt to Tara, and she retracted her foot. The lid slammed shut with a reproachful bang.

Tara turned to the cabinet behind her, and took out the bottle of Baileys left over from last year, and took a swig straight out of the bottle. Slightly fortified, Tara brought the letter over to the window and opened it.

> *Dearest Friends and Family,*
> *I'm so sorry I cannot write to each of you individually. Wouldn't I love to have that kind of time! Those of you with toddlers will understand what I mean!*

Those of you without have no inkling whatsoever what it's like to be pressed for time—

> *Here at our ranch under the wide-open sky, it's beginning to look a lot like Christmas! Tiara, our little angel, literally, turned two on Halloween. If you missed the pictures of her in her angel costume, please follow the family album link at the bottom of this letter. We also have posted photos on Facebook, MySpace, Bebo, and our personal family Web site, Theluckiestfamilyintheworld.com. Now we're making snow angels in our front yard, and eagerly awaiting Santa. . . .*

Tara started skimming the letter.

—Phil's blood pressure—
—Pilates—
—Volunteering at the shelter—
—Our little miracle on—

Tara was about to skip the second page when she spotted something that stopped her dead.

> *We are pregnant! Although it is very early yet, we just had to share the news. Phil and I are thrilled to be expecting another baby. We don't care if it's a boy or a girl, as long as it is healthy and as happy as the rest of us. Phil is also predicting our little bundle will grow up to be a politician since we believe he or she was conceived during a particularly heated Wolf Blitzer episode on CNN—*

Tara started skimming again.

> *—My mother and father will be celebrating their fortieth wedding anniversary next Spring—*

Our mother and father. She acts like she's an only child.

> *—My sister Tara is still living in the Big Apple—*

Oh no—

> *—And has been promoted to Top Chef at La Fleur, the little French restaurant where she's been chopping away for the past nine years—*

Head chef—six years—

—and even though she's all Sex in the City *about her life, we are still wishing she'd meet her ideal match—*

No. No, no, no, no, no.

—So if you know any handsome, single—

She is not—

—eligible men who want a fiercely indepen- dent New York woman who can cook up a storm—

Oh, but she is.

—E-mail us their pictures and profiles, and we will send you the link to a new section of our Web site— "A Man for My Sister"—

"No!" Tara said out loud.

—Please note that my sister is very, very picky. Bald men, sailors, and animal lovers need not apply.

A personal letter followed.

Dear Tara,
Instructions for your contribution to Christ- mas dinner are included. We drew names and dishes, so bear in mind the dish you are making has nothing to do with your wonderful culinary skills. You won—the salad! Hurrah! Go crazy.

Just not too crazy. Remember the mashed potato incident last year? You really should have remembered Uncle Ted's proclivity to gassiness. Also, since you missed the summer auditions, we have assigned you the role of Innkeeper/ Cleaning Lady in this year's production of "We Will Find You a Room." We thought it was appropriate in the recession that the workers at the inn all do double duty this year, ha ha! And lastly, if you are bringing a date (fingers and toes crossed!), please provide us with a copy of the background check ASAP.

- *DO NOT mix the dressing in with the salad.*
- *Onions, if you must add them, should be on the side.*
- *Please respect our low-carb guests and put the croutons on the side as well.*
- *It is my belief that Uncle Ted is lactose intolerant. Please put the cheese on the side unless it is goat's cheese, in which case you can mix it in, just don't tell anyone what it is, as some people may be slightly anti-goat.*
- *Nuts are an obvious no-no.*
- *Personally, I'm a mixed greens fan, or "spring mix." Iceberg is too boring, and pure arugula too elitist. Please aim for the mainstream.*
- *Remember how Aunt Janie julienned the carrots into little snowflakes last year? Feel free to steal that, it was a big hit!!!!!!!!!!*

This time Tara dropped the letter in the trash without a second thought and grabbed her purse. She had to get out of the apartment. It was either that or kill herself.

Chapter 4

Central Park was her savior. She loved everything about it. Every season offered its own goodies, and winter was no exception. You could walk around and take in the beauty of a recent snowfall. You could ice skate at Wolman Rink. Stop and listen to carolers or the crazies, both with voices raised in equal fervor. You could take in the wares being sold just outside the park, nibble on roasted peanuts and make the squirrels go nuts with jealousy, watch the horse-drawn carriages go by. That's exactly what Tara was doing, watching the horse-drawn carriages and taking deep, calming breaths, when she was approached by a slim boy with a clipboard.

"Sign a petition! Put an end to horse-drawn carriages in Central Park! Switch to fuel efficient car tours instead!" he said in one breath. Tara stared at him. "The horses are mistreated," he added, as if she were personally mistreating them.

"They are?" Tara asked. "How?"

"They're kept in cramped stables with no pasture

in which to run." Tara knew the argument of course,
but she also knew a few of the carriage drivers. They
were good people who cared about horses. And
horses had been in Central Park for over a hundred
years. Everybody liked to feel useful, even horses.
Especially horses, probably. Until they learned how to
send text messages, what else were they going to do
with their days? Could these clipboard people guarantee the horses would go somewhere and have a better life if they weren't working at the park? Were they
going to personally follow up with each horse and
make sure it was living a good life? What if the horses
got bored and depressed and felt as if no one wanted
or needed them for anything anymore? What if they
liked taking tourists for a ride? What if it made them
feel special? She for one knew exactly how it felt to
be out of a job, unwanted, unloved, hardly missed.
She wouldn't wish that on anyone. That was the problem with do-gooders. Sometimes, they just weren't
doing anybody any good. *Give them better benefits,
clipboard boy, but let them keep their jobs!* What
would the park be without the horses? She just couldn't
imagine it without them.

"I'm all for trying to get a pasture for them," Tara
said. "But not 'putting them out to pasture.' " The kid
shook his head. "They're beautiful," Tara said. "And
magical. And they make me happy."

"It's animal cruelty," the boy said. "If you're not
part of the solution, you're part of the problem."

"Come back to me with a pasture petition, and
we'll be all set," Tara said. "Until then, let me enjoy
my day, okay?" He slunk away with a shake of his
head. What happened to the fight in her, she wondered. Because she'd been him once. Young, idealistic, full of hope and clipboards. "May I?" Tara asked a
carriage driver as she walked up to his horse.

"Aye," the driver said with a nod of his head. It was a magnificent white horse, with a red halter. He was eating from a bucket of grain and looked up as she approached. She touched the sides of his long, soft face, and kissed his nose. He smelled clean, and happy. He snorted, and grain blew out of both sides of his mouth. Tara laughed.

"I hope you get a pasture for Christmas," she whispered. "In the meantime, thanks for making me happy."

"If you like these beauties, you should check out the reindeer," the driver said. For a moment, Tara thought he was messing with her.

"Huh?" she said.

"Brought 'em from a farm in Wisconsin," the driver said, pointing. "Twelve reindeer and Santa. Although I don't know if Santa is from Wisconsin," he added with a laugh and a wink. "If so we should be giving him milk and cheese!" Tara laughed along with him. Twelve reindeer from Wisconsin. This she had to see for herself.

The line to see the reindeer was a mile long. Tara didn't care. She had nothing but time. And she absolutely loved reindeer. As a child she used to lie awake and worry about them on Christmas Eve the way some people worried about Santa getting stuck in the chimney. *Are they tired from flying? Are they cold? Are they lost? Is Rudolph lighting the way? Did that elf ever become a dentist?* (Sometimes random, non-related-to-reindeer thoughts crept in.) *Where do they go to the bathroom?* She never heard her dad complaining about cleaning reindeer poo off the roof, and he complained about everything.

In front of her stood a little boy and his mother. She was loaded down with shopping bags; he was bundled into a snowsuit that looked two sizes too small for him. But despite his restricted movement, he was bouncing like Tigger.

"Does Santa's sleigh have a jeeps?" he asked his mother. She didn't answer, so he asked her four more times.

"That doesn't make any sense, Carl," his mother said. "A sleigh is a sleigh and a jeep is a jeep. Santa doesn't drive, he flies."

"No," Carl said. "A jeeps. So he doesn't get lost." His mother looked lost. Tara leaned forward.

"I think he means a GPS," she offered. The boy and his mother both looked at her as if they wanted her to get lost. Tara tried to smile, that should lighten things up a bit. The boy's mother spun him around, stuck her hand in her coat pocket, and pulled out a half-eaten soft pretzel. When he opened his mouth to ask another question, she stuffed the pretzel into it. So much for being friendly, Tara thought. At least she was almost there.

She glanced at the poster announcing the reindeer. WINTER-ESCAPE TRAVELS. TROPICAL GETAWAYS! Tara hoped they never switched to using the acronym, WET, as it wouldn't exactly inspire one to fly anywhere with them. Underneath the company logo was a picture of Santa's sleigh flying toward paradise. Tara wondered if you'd have to pay an extra twenty dollars for your luggage on Santa's sleigh. She suddenly wished she were going somewhere else, anywhere else.

Just as it was her turn to see the reindeer, a light snow began to fall. Gingerly, she stepped up to the small fenced-in area where the deer stood, chewing and staring. They didn't seem at all stressed about their upcoming world tour. They were magnificent looking animals with proud, tall antlers. Tara could hardly believe they were real. She banked to the left, where the tallest stood brazenly close to the fence. Obviously, the extrovert of the group. She imagined him with a lampshade on his head. *Did you see how close I got to those humans?* He'd brag later. *Like I could totally smell them!* Tara stepped up softly, so as not to scare him. He stared at her with big brown eyes. She loved him.

"You're my reindeer boyfriend," Tara said.

"It's okay," a woman in overalls said. "You can pet him." Tara reached out to touch his soft face, just as she had with the horse. Suddenly, the little boy with the pretzel was back. He cut in front of her, took the last bite of the pretzel out of his mouth, and shoved it at the reindeer.

"I don't think salt is good for—" Tara started to say. She reached forward to prevent the reindeer from eating the pretzel. The boy's mother yanked him out of the way. Then, Tara felt a sharp pain in her wrist. Her first thought was that the kid had been hiding a Swiss Army knife in his pretzel and had stabbed her. What kind of a sentence would they give a five-year-old? *You have been sentenced to five years of hard Lego work my man.* Even after she saw what was really happening, Tara didn't believe it. The reindeer's mouth was clenched around her wrist; his sharp teeth were sunk deep into her skin. No matter what, she wasn't signing any petitions for this guy; he was definitely getting adequate dental care. "That is not a pretzel!" Tara cried.

"Oh my God," the little boy screamed. "He's eating her." It surprised her, how worried the little boy sounded for her, and she suddenly felt a rush of love for the kid. "Why doesn't he like my pretzel? Why is he eating *her?*" the boy whined. He kicked the fence with his tiny snow boot and pointed a gloved hand at her. "My pretzel tastes way better than you!" he screamed. And like that, the love was gone.

"Help," Tara said. The reindeer's mouth remained stubbornly clenched around her wrist. Tara was terrified that any quick move would cause further damage. Where was the woman in the overalls? Tara wildly looked around. Several people were staring in horror, but like her, seemed frozen with fear. "Bad reindeer," Tara said. "Bad, bad, reindeer." His teeth pushed in a little bit further. Tara began to scream.

After six hours in the ER, Tara's wrist was cleaned, stitched, and bandaged. She was also given a shot, and assured the reindeer was up to date on all of his. The woman in overalls had been absolutely hysterical that if word of the attack got out, the publicity would bring great harm to Alfred. Alfred. Dumbest name for a reindeer Tara had ever heard. Blitzen was his stage name. Tara agreed not to make a fuss as long as the woman agreed to retire Blitzen/Alfred from contact with the public. A representative of the travel agency had nervously followed Tara to the hospital and was sitting in the emergency waiting room. Tara was about to tell him to go home when the doctor started asking her strange questions.

Was she depressed? Had she suffered any big losses recently? Were the holidays getting her down? Oh yes. Yes, yes, yes, she said. How nice to have a doctor care about her. How did he know? Was it that obvious? He threw another nervous glance at her wrist.

"I'd like to send you upstairs for an evaluation," the doctor said.

"Upstairs?"

"Yes. We have a wonderful staff of psychiatrists—"

"Oh, no," Tara said. "I don't need an evaluation. I mean—I don't know if I'd completely pass it or anything, but I'm not suicidal. I really was bitten by a reindeer." The doctor made a note in his chart.

"Named Blitzen?" the doctor asked.

"Well—Alfred, really. Blitzen is his stage name."

"I see," the doctor said. "And where was Santa when this reindeer bit you?" Tara glared at him.

"Santa wasn't with them," she said. "Just Mrs. Claus in overalls." He made another note in his chart. "Look," Tara said. "It was a promotional event. In Central Park. They're from a farm in Wisconsin. A carriage driver told me about them. He said we should be giving Santa cheese." This little tidbit didn't seem to win the doctor over. He made another note in his chart.

"I can't believe they still allow horse-drawn carriages in Central Park," the doctor said.

"I know," Tara said. "I for one long to see fuel efficient cars instead."

"Do you have anyone who can validate your reindeer story?" the doctor asked. "Besides Santa?" Tara called in the representative of the travel agency. He spoke quietly with the doctor. The doctor looked between them for a few minutes. "She sure has been a good sport," the doctor said. "I was starting to think I had a real whacko on my hands."

"I can see that," the travel representative said, looking her up and down.

"I think the least you could do is give the woman a free trip," the doctor added. Had it not been for the wedding ring on the doctor's finger, and the fact that

he'd come close to having her committed, she would
have married him right then and there.

> *Dearest Friends and Family,*
> *I wish I could write to each of you individu-*
> *ally. How I'd love that kind of time! But here's a*
> *quick update, in a snapshot. I lost my bartender-*
> *boyfriend and my doorman-boyfriend on the*
> *same day. One elf-ed off to Hollywood; the*
> *other practically died in my arms. (If I had*
> *known he was going down, I like to think I*
> *would've tried to catch him.) The highlight of*
> *my week was being bitten by a reindeer named*
> *Alfred slash Blitzen from Wisconsin. But yes,*
> *Tara, there is a Santa Claus! Winter Escape*
> *Travels (or WET, as I like to call them) is send-*
> *ing me on a twelve-day all expense paid trip to*
> *Maui. I am very sorry I will not be there to*
> *dumb-down the salad or play the Innkeeper/*
> *Cleaning Lady in "We Will Find You A Room."*
> > *Love,*
> > *Tara*

Tara reclined her seat in first class, and smiled. She
was free. The only thing remotely Christmassy in her
bag was the little red bikini she planned on wearing
the entire twelve days. Twelve days to forget about
everything. Maybe she'd even have a little island
fling. That would show Nadine. And since, by definition, flings were supposed to be brief, she would even
practice lowering her standards. As long as he was
hot.

Chapter 5

Tara looked out the window of the plane as it made its descent into Maui. The sun was bright and welcoming. She could already smell the ocean, and suntan lotion, and the tropical drinks. Any guilt she felt over abandoning her family at Christmas evaporated the moment she felt the Hawaiian air caress her skin. She practically skipped into the airport. She hadn't checked any luggage, so she was able to go straight to the car rental service. There were only a few people in line ahead of her.

"Tara." It was a woman's voice. Tara looked around, despite the fact that the woman couldn't possibly be talking to her. "Tara!" The voice came from behind her. Tara whirled around. There stood her sister.

"Nadine?" Tara felt her mouth drop open, and she knew she should shut it, but her jaw was on lockdown. Nadine squealed. Then, she threw a red and green lei around Tara's neck. "Surprise!" she said. She hugged her fiercely. Tara pulled back in time to see her mother and father running toward her. Tara didn't want to admit it, but she felt slightly embarrassed watching them bounce. Unlike their slim daughters, Nancy and George Lane carried a little extra weight, which was fine, really, at their age they should just enjoy all things in life, but, seriously, they shouldn't be running in public. Power walking at the mall maybe, but not running in public.

"Mele Kalikimaka!" her mother shouted. She threw her arms up in the air and waved them excitedly. The fleshy backs of her arms continued to wiggle long after her mother stopped moving them.

"That means Merry Christmas in Maui," her father said. Besides a Christmas lei, he had a camera, and sunglasses hanging off his neck, a laminated map in his hand, and a pencil stuck behind each ear. Tara's brother-in-law Phil was the last to appear, with Tiara on his hip. She had chocolate smeared on her face, and drool dripping down her chin. They were all wearing red and green leis. Nancy pulled a jumbo bottle of sunscreen out of her purse and shook it at Tara. But before her mother had a chance to open it and slather Tara against her will, an airport cart beeped and pulled up alongside them. It was piled with suitcases.

"What the—" Tara started to say.

"Tara," Nadine warned.

"Elf is all that?" Tara finished, glancing guiltily at Tiara. Tiara stuck her entire hand in her mouth and smiled.

"I brought all our Christmas decorations," Nadine said. She jumped up and down and clapped her hands. "Surprise!"

"Why?" Tara said. "What are you doing here?" Tara tried at the last minute to make her voice sound friendly and happy, but from the look on her sister's face, she knew she'd utterly failed. Nadine put her hands on her hips and waggled her finger at Tara.

"We couldn't let you spend Christmas alone," she said. "Not after your"—she glanced at Tara's bandaged wrist—"incident."

"It was just a little nibble," Tara said. "From a reindeer." Looks were exchanged all around. Even Tiara looked at her with pity.

"We believe you, dear," her mother said. "But we couldn't let you have that big bungalow all to yourself."

"How do you know it's big?" Tara asked.

"I looked it up online," Nadine said. "It was obvious after that horrendous Christmas letter you sent out that you needed your family but were too proud to ask."

"I'm not proud," Tara said. "I have never been proud."

"Let's go," her father said. "I have a map."

"Everyone grab as many suitcases as you can," Nadine said. Nadine heaved what looked like the smallest of the litter off the cart and gestured for the rest of them to dig in. Tara glanced at the car rental counter. Everyone else grabbed suitcases and started to move. Tara stayed in place.

"Come on," Nadine said. Tara pointed at the car rental. She was going to get something shiny, fast, and red. To match her bikini.

"No need," Nadine said. "Dad got a family van. You can sit in the back with Tiara. I'm sure you'll want to spend as much time with your niece as you can." It was then, as she struggled with three suitcases filled with Christmas decorations, and trudged toward the family van, that Tara realized she should have packed more than her little red bikini. Heat, she realized. She should have packed some heat.

*   *   *

Tara's head was throbbing. Her father was driving while trying to read the map in one hand and flossing his teeth with the other. Every once in a while the van would drift past the center line; then her father would pull to the right, causing Tara to slide and slam into the passenger side door. The rest of them were too busy singing "Jingle Bells" to be appropriately alarmed. When the singing finally stopped, Nadine started reading her list of "Maui Christmas Events" out loud. There seemed to be something festive going on every single night of the week, and Nadine was acting as if they were going to go to all of the events. Tara was trying to think. Her family was here. Her family had crashed her vacation. Didn't she have a right to be a teensy, tiny bit pissed? Tara stuck her head out the window, hoping the island air would calm her down.

"Tara," Nadine said, over Tiara who was strapped in her car seat between them. "Would you rather go Snorkeling with Santa or Parasailing with Santa?"

"It's so hard to choose," Tara said. "I had no idea Santa was so athletic." She didn't bother to disguise her sarcasm. A fight was coming, and it might as well be now.

"I know," Nadine said. "I suppose if we cut out of snorkeling early enough we could just make the parasailing session."

"I was kidding," Tara said. "I'm not sure I'm going to any of those things." The chatter in the car suddenly stopped. Her father slowed down and glanced nervously at Tara through the rearview mirror. Dental floss hung from his tooth. Even Phil, who, sitting in the very last seat of the van, had been eerily silent so far, let out a nervous chuckle. His pink buttoned shirt was opened far enough for Tara to see his chest. If she didn't know better, she would have asked him why he was wearing a sweater. She should buy him hot wax for Christmas.

"I'm with you," Phil said. He laughed even harder, but stopped when Nadine glared at him.

"Santa, Santa, Santa," Tiara sang.

"See," Tara said. She put her hand on Tiara's little head and gave it a rub. "You have a captive audience right here. You and Tiara can do everything on your list." She kissed her niece's soft little head, and inhaled. She loved the scent of baby shampoo.

Nadine threw down her list. "We're here for you, you know," she said.

"I appreciate that," Tara said through clenched teeth. "That doesn't mean we have to spend every second together, does it?"

"I don't believe this," Nadine said. "You're trying to get rid of us already."

"No one is trying to get rid of anyone," their father said.

"Who wants a macaroon?" their mother said.

"I mean, it's not like I knew you were coming," Tara said. "Did it ever occur to you I might have plans already?"

"Well, why didn't you just say so?" Nadine said. "There's room on the list to accommodate everyone. What would you like us to do?"

"Let's talk about it later," Tara said. She was going to go straight to the bungalow, change into her bikini, and hit the beach. Then get several tropical drinks. Take a swim. She was not going to start planning Christmas activities.

"I can't believe you," Nadine said.

"Excuse me?"

"I knew you were going to act like this. Didn't I
tell you, Phil? Didn't I tell you she was going to be
stubborn?" Tara and Nadine looked at Phil. He pulled
his baseball cap over his eyes.

"I'm on vacation," Tara said. "I'm here to relax. I
do not consider running all over the island searching
for Santa, relaxing."

"Santa," Tiara said. "Santa, Santa, Santa."

"What could be more relaxing than snorkeling or
parasailing?"

"Did it ever occur to you that I'm here as a single
woman?" Tara said. She tried to keep her voice down,
but she could feel everyone listening to her.

"So now you're in the market?" Nadine said.

"What?" Tara said.

"I thought you were done with dating."

"Oh," Tara said. "You mean 'on the market'."

"That's what I said," Nadine said.

"No, you didn't. You said 'in the market.' I was
like—what does shopping have to do with my sex
life?" Nadine clapped her hands over Tiara's ears.

"Tara!" she said.

"Girls," Nancy said. "These macaroons are stale.
But you should have one anyway. They were on sale."

"Who said anything about dating?" Tara said, waving the stale macaroon out of her way. "Maybe I'm
just going to have a little fling."

"Fling," Tiara said. "Fling, fling, fling."

Nadine snorted. "You couldn't have a fling if your
life depended on it."

"What does that mean?"

"You're way too picky. By the time the man passed
all your criteria, your fling would be flung."

Just ahead, a beat-up pickup truck was pulled over
to the side of the road. A man in Hawaiian shorts was
changing a flat tire. A golden retriever watched from

the back of the truck, running the small expanse of the cab and wagging his tail. Tara's eyes trailed to the bumper sticker on the truck. It read:

NO SHIRT, NO SHOES, BUT I'LL SERVICE YOU

Seething from Nadine's comment, Tara studied the man changing the tire. Just then, he stood, and stretched. He was tall, tan, and muscular. He had a full head of brown hair. He ruffled the dog's head. Even her mother was staring at him, the macaroon she had been about to bite into frozen in place in front of her lips. He looked like a bum. A hot, tan, beach bum.

"Pull over," Tara told her father.

"What for?"

"Just do it," Tara said. "It's an emergency." Her father swung the van over like a man having an epileptic fit. The tires screeched. They came to a stop just in front of the pickup truck.

"What are you doing?" Nadine asked.

Tara jumped out of the van. "Lowering my standards," Tara said. She headed straight for the gorgeous, stranded stranger.

Chapter 6

The man leaned lazily against the back of his truck and watched as Tara approached. Then, he smiled at her. She smiled back, as giddy and nervous as a teenager. The closer she came, the better looking he got. Oh, please don't be married, she thought. Or a serial killer. A hand clenched around her wrist. The bad one. She screamed. Nadine had a hold of her bad wrist; her mother clutched onto the good.

"Let go," Tara said to Nadine. "That's the bad one."

"What are you doing?" Nadine hissed. Tara glanced at the handsome beach bum. His smile was even wider now. He was thoroughly enjoying the little drama playing out before him.

"I'm helping a stranger in distress," she said. Their mother leaned around them; if Tara wasn't mistaken, she was actually checking him out. Tara's eyes fell to the muscles rippling in his arms, and then lingered on his six-pack abs. She'd never dated a man with a six-pack; she'd have considered herself lucky to find one with just a couple of cans. Half the time her dates looked as if they'd swallowed a six-pack. The man folded his arms across his chest and grinned. The dog barked.

"It could be a trick," her mother said. Disturbingly, her mother's gaze also seemed to be lingering on the man's abs.

"What could be a trick?" Tara said.

"The flat tire," her mother said. "He could be staging it to lure young girls to the side of the road."

Nadine put her hands on her hips. "Exactly," she said. "Exactly."

"Ted Bundy used the same approach," her mother continued. "And he was very good-looking too." The three women glanced at the stranger again. He gave them a nod, and another wolfish grin. *I'd definitely lower my standards for him,* Tara thought. *Maybe even take "Won't date a serial killer" off the list.* She looked at his handiwork. He had the old tire off, but he didn't seem to be in any hurry to put the new one on. Tara took out her cell phone and stepped even closer.

"Can I call someone for you?" she said. "Or maybe we could give you a ride somewhere?"

"Tara," Nadine hissed. "I have a child in the car."

"No, thanks," the man said. He spread his arms against the back of the truck as if he had all the time in the world. "I'm late for work." He whistled, and the dog jumped out of the truck with a Frisbee in his mouth.

"If you're late for work—isn't that all the more reason to accept help?" Tara said.

"Not on the island, it's not," he said. "Here, a flat tire is the perfect excuse to be late for work. I figure this buys me at least two hours. We're going to fling the disc around—"

Fling, Tara thought. *He said fling.* It was a sign.

"Maybe get a beer and a burger." He looked at Nadine and winked at their mother. "Besides," he said. "I wouldn't go with the likes of you. That's how Theresa Bundy lured her victims."

Their mother fell for it. "Who is Theresa Bundy?" she asked.

"Ted Bundy's sister," he said, moving closer and lowering his voice to a near whisper. "She was the real mastermind behind all the murders. Sexy broad too. Just like the three of you. Always on the prowl for dudes in distress."

Their mother looked horrified. Tara laughed. "He's messing with you, Mother," she said.

"Mother?" the man said, feigning shock. "That's just not possible. You're way too young to be their mother." Nancy Lane shook her head and laughed.

"Well, dude in distress," Tara said. "We tried." He winked at her, whistled at the dog again, and walked toward the beach. He looked back at Tara as if he knew she was looking at his ass. She quickly averted her eyes. Then she looked again, just to prove to herself that she wasn't looking at his ass, but she wasn't going to not look at his ass just because he thought she was looking at it. Plus, she had to admit, it was nice to look at.

Unfortunately, Nadine caught her in the act. "Unbelievable," she said on their way back to the van. "East Coast prude turns into West Coast slut." Nancy's head shot up. She looked at the girls, and as they watched, their mother's cheeks turned bright red. "Not you, Mother," Nadine said. "Tara. Tara's the slut."

"Language," Tara said. "I have a niece in the van."

*   *   *

A series of winding roads along the coast finally brought them to the bungalow. Tara felt a twinge of guilt as she took in the sweet yellow house. It was definitely too big for one person. Flowers dotted the yard, and a large palm tree stood guard next to a small patio laden with beach chairs.

"It's adorable," Nadine said. "And since it's only one story, it will be easy to string the Christmas lights, Phil." Phil stared at the palm tree as if he wanted to hang himself from it. Nadine hopped out of the van and immediately started taking out the luggage. She was the first one to the front door. "Throw me the key," she said to Tara.

"I don't have the key," Tara said. "A handyman is supposed to be here." They all looked around, even though it was evident there was no one in sight. Nadine tried the door anyway, to no avail.

"Maybe there's a key hidden somewhere," Nadine said. "Phil, you check around back; Mom, you check under all the flower pots—"

"Enough," Tara said. "I'm sure he'll be here any minute."

Twenty minutes passed. It was getting hot. Everyone crowded under the palm tree, vying for shade.

"Call him again," Nadine said.

"I've called four times," Tara said. "It's still busy. I can't even get voice mail. Why don't you guys go get some lunch, or go grocery shopping, or go to the beach. I'll wait here."

"We could all go," Nadine said. "We'll just leave a note for him to call you."

"I don't want to miss him," Tara said. "Besides, no use loading all the luggage back in the van." That did the trick. A few minutes later Tara stood underneath the palm tree and waved them all good-bye. She smiled to herself. Alone at last. Even if she was locked out. She stretched out on the soft, sweet-smelling grass and waited.

She awoke with a start. Her arms stung. They were bright red. Despite her mother's toting it around in bulk, she'd forgotten all about sunscreen. She sat up and looked at her phone. He was an hour late. She tried his voice mail again.

"I'm here," a male voice said.

"Finally," Tara said. "My name is—"

"Not! Gotcha. Actually I'm gone. Not gone for good, but same diff' to you, right? You know what to do at the beep!" Tara hung up. That wasn't nice. Now she was furious. She called back. An automated voice told her the voice mailbox was full. She should call the travel agency and give them a piece of her mind. They were supposed to be pampering her. This was not acceptable. She should be in her bikini right now, lying on the beach. She would be, she realized, if she wasn't babysitting Nadine's luggage. She was going to have to find a coconut and break the window. She was searching for one when she heard the rumble of a vehicle.

His golden fur looked way too thick for the hot Hawaiian sun. His tail wagged, his large pink tongue lolled out, and from the way he was panting, he'd definitely enjoyed his two-hour break. She had to hand it to him. Sending the golden dog in first was genius. Tara squatted and welcomed the ambassador into her arms. He licked her face. His owner's voice preceded his body.

"Sorry we're late, I got a flat tire—" The voice stopped dead as he looked up at Tara. He definitely looked as if he had enjoyed his little break as well. He looked even more tan, and totally relaxed. His blue eyes twinkled.

"Oh, you poor thing," Tara said. She put her hands up to her mouth in mock distress. "A flat? And nobody stopped to help you?" The man looked at his dog and rolled his eyes.

"Just a couple of crazy New Yorkers who thought I was a serial killer," he said.

"I was the only crazy New Yorker. And by the way, the only one who didn't think you were a serial killer."

"Makes sense. You probably develop a high tolerance in that city." He pulled a set of keys out of his shorts and jingled them.

"And just how do you know where I'm from?" Tara demanded.

"Either you're the crazy New Yorker who scammed a free trip because she was"—he put his hands up to make air quotes—" 'bitten by a reindeer,' or you're in the wrong place."

"I was bitten by a reindeer, and I didn't scam anyone," Tara said. "I didn't even ask for the trip. WET offered it to me."

"All I'm saying is someone getting something for nothing shouldn't be complaining." He turned his back to her and walked to the door.

"You're the one who faked a flat tire and made us wait two hours so you could go play," Tara said. "You are despicable." He held open the door and waited. "At least your dog has manners," Tara said, as she shook his paw for like the fourteenth time.

"He'd skip out on you to run the beach in a heartbeat," the man said. "And he's only doing that because you smell like beef jerky." Tara opened her mouth to retaliate, but then remembered. There was a stick of beef jerky in her pocket. They'd been handing them out at JFK airport as some kind of promotional thing. How did this guy know? The question must have shown on his face for he laughed and pointed at her crotch. "Sticking out of your pocket," he said.

"Oh." She took it out. "He can have it," she said.

"No, thanks. We don't eat junk."

"I don't either," Tara said. "I'm a chef." Now why did she go and say that? This man didn't need to know anything about her. So what if he thought she was the type of woman who regularly stuck beef jerky in her pants?

"And I didn't fake the flat tire, I just took advantage of it."

"I got sunburned waiting for you," Tara said. He glanced at her arms, then his eyes trailed up and down her body. Tara felt a rush of desire, which made her furious with him.

"You coming in?" he asked. "Cuz if you're looking for an upgrade, afraid we don't have any rabid reindeers around these parts."

"Excuse me?"

The man held up his hands. "I ain't against it," he said in a way that let Tara know he was throwing the "ain't" in for show. "I dig chicks who want a free ride. Just saying—you and I—we're the same."

"We are not the same," Tara said, plowing past him. She couldn't believe he knew about the reindeer. Who else knew? Did they *all* think she was some kind of scam artist? "That reindeer really—"

She stopped talking the minute she saw the place. It was beautiful. Billowy white curtains against the back wall blew gently out, as if welcoming her in. The oak floors shone from a recent polish; the pillows on the wicker furniture looked recently fluffed. Photographs of the beach lined the wall. A bouquet of roses and a tin of macadamia nuts sat on the coffee table. It was perfect. Tara couldn't wait to change into her bikini. She turned to the not-so-handyman.

"Thank you," she said. "I'm sure you and your dog want to get back to your Frisbee game."

"We're in no hurry," he said.

"Well I am," Tara said. "You made me wait for over an hour; now I'm burned and tired. Just give me the keys, and you can go." So much for having a fling with him. No way would she have a fling with some-one who made her wait two hours while he played hooky. So what if he was gorgeous? He was a child. She came to have a fling with a man. Nadine was going to gloat, that was for sure, but that couldn't be helped. Tara was glad she had standards, even for a fling.

She wanted to enjoy her moment of serenity before her family came back and broke the spell. She wanted to change into her little red bikini and prance around the bungalow. She was alive, she was in a relatively good mood, and she had a very short window to be alone. But the man ignored her request to depart. He was tromping through the bungalow flipping light switches and water taps, saying something about the garbage and recycling days. Tara headed back outside to get her suitcase. She was startled to see he had al-ready brought in all of their suitcases. They were neatly lined up against the wall.

"You're welcome," he said.

"I was going to say thank you," Tara said.

"Sure you were." This time Tara looked at the dog and rolled her eyes. He bounded over to her and rubbed against her leg.

"Lucky dog," she thought she heard the man say, but when her head snapped up, his back was to her, and he was opening a closet door.

"I want to see the kitchen," Tara said. She wasn't

going to cook while she was here; she was on vacation. Still, it was part of her, and she had to check it
out. When she saw what a modest kitchen it was, she
almost wept with relief. If it had been a gourmet
kitchen, she would have felt compelled to cook.

"It's not much," the man said.

"It's perfect," Tara said, leaning against the counter
with a sigh. "Average, small, perfect." The man
looked as if he had a dozen dirty retorts on the tip of
his tongue, and Tara got the distinct impression he
was thinking about her breasts, but for once he kept
his mouth shut. She held out her hand for the keys.
But instead of handing them to her, he shook her
hand. A tingle went up Tara's spine as their palms
touched. She yanked her hand away.

"I haven't gone over everything," he said. Tara
turned and ripped a paper towel from the dispenser
behind her. It had little pineapples on it.

"Why don't you write it down," she said. She made
a beeline for her suitcase. He followed.

"You know, it's a myth that women are better lis-
teners," he said. She grabbed the key, and her suitcase, then ran into the nearest bedroom to change.
She heard the front door slam, and a truck roar to life.
What a relief. She didn't need to put up with the play-
boy slash Peter Pan man on her vacation. Let him
charm some other island visitor. Surely there were
plenty of men to have a fling with, even if he was incredibly good-looking and had a nice dog. Right now,
all she needed was her little red bikini. She slipped
out of her jeans, her shirt, her bra, her panties. A palm
tree near the bedroom window provided the perfect
privacy shade. That's when she spotted the Santa hat
on the bedroom pillow. What in the world? She
laughed, then put it on. Next she turned on the clock
radio next to the bed and flipped through stations

until she found "It's Beginning to Look A Lot Like Christmas." She turned it up. Maybe the way to get along with Nadine this season was to beat her at her own game. She would overflow with the Christmas spirit!

Where was her bikini? She'd flipped through all the items in her little carry-on twice, but couldn't find it. She moved on to the zippered compartments as panic began to crawl its way up her arm. She knew it wasn't in the zippered compartments. It should've been on the bottom of the suitcase; it was the first thing she packed. Or was it the last? She would calmly take everything out of her suitcase, one by one. It had to be there.

It wasn't. Was it in her beach bag? It has to be, she told herself, as she marched into the living room. There, gathered by the wicker sofa was her entire family and the not-so-handyman. He was going over the instructions Tara wouldn't listen to, and Nadine was happily writing them down. For a few seconds, Tara actually forgot she was wearing nothing but her wrist bandage and a Santa hat. Nadine's piercing scream brought it all hurtling back. So did the dog's fur, rubbing against her naked calf. Horrified, Tara locked eyes with the not-so-handyman. He looked almost as stunned as she felt. She ran back into the bedroom, praying no one was watching her ass as she ran.

She threw on a sundress and held her head high as she walked back into the living room. The man was holding court with her entire family, especially Nadine. What was going on here? Everything about her dream getaway was getting away from her fast.

"Tara," Nadine said with a big smile. "I'd like you to meet Darren Skies."

"Really?" Tara said. "Skies? As in 'bright blue'?"

"Really?" Darren said, looking her up and down. "Lane? As in 'Right down Santa Claus'?" Tara didn't respond. Had he meant that to sound dirty? It sounded awfully dirty. It kind of made her like him. Except Nadine liked him. Which made her hate him.

"Sing," Tiara said. "Sing Santa Claus!" Tiara started jumping up and down. Nadine picked her up, swung her around, and began belting, "Here comes Santa Claus." Darren joined in next, giving Tara a leering glance on "Right down Santa Claus Lane." He had meant it as a dirty joke. But nobody else seemed to get that. They were happily singing carols with the pervert. Tara folded her arms, shook her head, and watched everyone with disgust. She hadn't even realized Darren was standing next to her until he leaned over and whispered, "You were much more fun in your birthday suit and Santa hat."

Chapter 7

"Let's go swimming," Nadine said when the caroling was over. "Darren, would you like to join us?"
Darren looked at his wrist, as if he was wearing a watch. He wasn't.

"I have an appointment in a half hour," he said. "So I'd love to!"

"Unbelievable," Tara muttered.

"You're coming too, Tara," Nadine said.

"Can't," Tara said. "I left my bathing suit at home. I'm off to buy another one." She was going to get another little red bikini if it killed her. Something was going to go right on this trip.

"I have an extra suit, dear," her mother said. "I always bring two."

"That's okay, Mom. I'm just going to buy one—" Tara felt a small hand wrap around her finger. She looked down to see Tiara staring up at her, all eyes, teeth, and drool.

"Swim!" she said. "Swim with me!"

"As soon as—" Tiara's lips began to tremble, as if she could sense an excuse coming.

"I'll swim," Tara said. "I'll swim with you."

The sand shone so bright it looked like a shimmering blanket of snow. In the distance the ocean's frothy waves lapped the shore and filled Tara's head with a joyous rush. Now this was life. God, it felt so good to be here. Her earlier cares melted away. She squeezed Tiara's hand as they made their way down the beach, looking for the perfect spot. As Tara's toes sunk into the warm sand, she almost forgot what she looked like until a passerby smiled and said, "Your granddaughter is adorable." Tara gasped, and looked down at her body. It was covered in a hideous swim dress from the sixties. It was layered with so many flowers Tara was worried she was going to attract bees. It flattened her chest and accentuated her ass. To make matters worse, her mother had slapped a giant straw hat on her head, and zinc oxide on her nose before she could duck. The only reason she'd kept them on was the wish to become invisible. It didn't help that Darren looked like he'd just stepped out of a magazine. He was walking in between her mother and Nadine, and, apparently, the conversation was just hilarious, for there was an awful lot of laughing going on.

Tara noticed that Darren seemed to be making a concerted effort not to look at her, and when he did, he could barely conceal his laughter. Tara gritted her teeth, and reminded herself that she was here to spend quality time with her niece. Swimming.

Tiara's interest in swimming lasted about three seconds, until a wave rolled in and kissed her little toes, then she shrieked, ran back to her towel, and decided the sand was much more interesting. Darren was throwing a Frisbee with her father and Phil. She wanted to play too; why did the men think they were the only ones who could enjoy flipping a disc around? But she wasn't going to participate in her hideous swim dress. Her mother, she noticed, was wearing a nice, black one piece. Nadine and Tiara had matching blue bikinis. The only person who looked worse than Tara was her father. He was wearing SpongeBob swim shorts. Tara spotted a notebook in Nadine's hand. TO DO was written clearly across the top. Tara flopped down on her towel and pretended to sleep. Soon, she felt a shadow hover over her.

"We have to plan Christmas dinner," Nadine said. "Since it's only the five adults, we'll have to reassign roles. We also have to start on the decorations and the invitations—"

"Invitations?" Tara said. "It's just us. I assume we're all invited."

"I just thought you might like to invite a guest," Nadine said. She glanced over at Darren.

"He wouldn't be a guest," Tara said. "He would be a pest."

"I thought you liked him. I thought he was fling material." Nadine plopped back onto her own towel.

"I changed my mind."

"I knew it," Nadine said. Tara didn't know it was possible to do a seated victory dance but Nadine's little ass wriggled in the sand as her arms pumped the air.

"I didn't say I wasn't going to have a fling," Tara said. "Just not with him." Nadine glanced over at Darren. He was standing next to Phil. Phil was pale, and skinny, and hairy. Darren was toned, and tan, and smooth.

"I'm so lucky," Nadine said. Tara wondered if she was being facetious. "Still," Nadine said. "As far as fling material goes . . ." Her eyes lingered over Darren. Nadine was right. Tara hated when Nadine was right.

"I'm sure there are a dozen more just like him," Tara said.

"Yeah right," Nadine said. "Well, looks like you'll just have to focus all your pent up sexual energy on holiday planning like I do." Tara flipped over and stared at Nadine. Nadine was sitting up, hunched over her to-do list. "What do you say we make a gingerbread beach house with palm trees?" Nadine said.

"Is everything okay with you and Phil?" Tara asked. Nadine didn't look at her, or stop writing. Her hand shook and zipped across the page.

"Why would you even ask that?" Nadine said. She dotted a couple of *i*'s like she was ice fishing with a rusty pick. "We're married. We have a beautiful child and another one on the way. We're in paradise." Tara didn't get to pursue it any further. A Frisbee landed on her stomach. Then a pile of golden fur slammed on top of her. Sand rained in her eyes. Tara squeezed them shut.

"Sorry about that," she heard Darren say from above. "What are you doing?"

"What do you think I'm doing?" Tara said. "Can you tell your dog I'm not a sofa?"

"Wasn't talking to you," Darren said.

"I'm planning our Christmas dinner," Nadine said.

"Forget that," Darren said. "Why don't you just come to the local luau?" Tara no longer cared that she had sand in her eyes or a giant dog across her body.

"Yes," Tara cried. "Yes." She didn't have to be looking at Nadine to know what her face looked like. Diabolical.

"We're going to cook our own Christmas dinner," Nadine said. "It's a family tradition."

"Suit yourself," Darren said. "But the luau is a lot of fun." He started singing. "Piggies roasting on an open spit, warm air nipping at your nose—" Tara started giggling. Darren plopped next to her and continued singing. "Although it's been said many times, many ways—luau Christmas, where you always get lei'd." Tara wanted to roll on top of him and get the luau started. Propriety, and a large dog stopped her from doing so.

"Maybe we should break from tradition this year," Tara said.

"A rebel," Darren whispered in her ear. "I like that."

"Not happening," Nadine said. Tara opened her eyes, rubbed sand out of them, and heaved the dog off her body. Tara glanced at Phil who was making a sand castle with Tiara. He was on all fours digging furiously, sending sand flying in all directions. He looked as if he were digging an escape tunnel.

"Why don't we put it to a vote?" Tara said.

"What?" Nadine said.

"Traditional Christmas dinner or luau? We should vote."

Nadine's foot started tapping. "Fine," she said. "We'll put it to a vote."

Darren's hand shot up. "I vote luau," he said.

In the end, so did everyone else. They even acquiesced when Nadine insisted she was voting for two. Phil suggested they let the baby kick once for yes and two for no, but since the baby wasn't more than a tiny speck, this was vetoed with a glare. Nadine and the speck voted for the traditional family dinner. Their parents pretended to weigh the decision carefully, then voted for the luau, as if it were a toss up. *Well played, Mom and Dad,* Tara thought. *Well played.*

Phil, on the other hand, didn't even try to hide his joy. He whooped. He shouted. He chanted, "Luau, luau, luau," until Tiara joined in. Seconds later, he was teaching her to hula dance. On the outside, Nadine appeared to be fine. She even said she was fine. But Tara knew better. Her eyes were wide, her mouth pulled taut. Her skin was stretched so tight across her face, she looked as if she'd had an instant lift. As she looked at her sister, Tara knew her little victory was about to cost her big time. *Oh, silent night,* Tara thought. *Oh, holy night.* Nadine was about to declare Yuletide war.

Fifteen minutes later, and she would have been gone. They might have caught her at home instead, where she would have washed the zinc oxide off her nose and thrown on a nice sundress. Instead, Tara was bent over, picking up her towel, showing off the swimsuit's ass ruffles, when she heard a woman's voice.

"Are you the lady who was bitten by Rudolph?"

"She is, she is," Nadine cried. Tara stood, and whipped around. A camera flashed in her face.

"I'm from *Maui Mornings.*" A very perky girl with long dark hair was standing in front of her. She held out her hand. Reluctantly, Tara shook it. "You're like famous around here," the girl said.

"I am?" Tara said. For a minute she wondered how they knew about her. Had one of the locals visited New York, stopped in at La Fleur, and came home crowing about her culinary skills? Would they ask her to cook at the luau? It was incredibly flattering. Still, why had she let her mother convince her to wear this hideous swim dress? She should be in her little red bikini. Her nose should be sans-oxide. Her head should not be covered with a tiki hut of a hat.

"You're like as famous as that woman who sued McDonald's for having coffee that was too hot," the girl said.

"Oh," Tara said. Right. The reindeer. Darren chuckled. Tara glared at him. What was he doing hanging around them anyway? The girl continued to snap pictures.

"Can't you take pictures of me later?" Tara cried. "You can come over to my bungalow. I'll answer all your questions."

"We don't really have any questions," the girl said. "People just want to see what you look like."

"But I don't normally look like this," Tara said.

"It's true," Darren said. "You should see her in the nude."

"Excuse me?" Tara said.

"I'm sorry," Darren said. "She had a Santa hat on." The girl snapped another picture.

"Write whatever you want," Tara said. "It's not my fault I was bitten by a reindeer and offered a free trip. I only took it so my family could have some fun." She gestured to her chubby parents, her pale, hairy brother-in-law, her anal retentive sister. "This is what Christmas is all about," she said. "Family."

"And to think," Nadine said. "She didn't even know we were coming."

"What was that?" the girl asked.

"Of course I knew—"

"It was my idea," Nadine said. "We surprised her at the airport."

"It's a good thing too," her mother said, oblivious

to Nadine's plot to ruin her. "She would have been all alone in that big bungalow." Suddenly the girl was scribbling down everything they said.

"I thought you just wanted pictures," Tara said. She grabbed Tiara and hoisted her up on her hip. "Get a picture of this little cutie," she said.

"Is this your daughter?" the girl asked.

"God no," Nadine said. "Tara doesn't want kids."

"I never said that," Tara said.

"Well, in order to have kids she'd have to find a man first," Nadine said. "And since bald men and animal lovers are out—"

"You don't like animals?" Darren asked.

"Of course I like animals," Tara said. "I love your dog. Come here dog. Here doggie." The golden retriever remained at Darren's side. Darren chuckled again. It was such a sexy laugh, and Tara was furious with herself that his laugh made her absolutely zing with pleasure.

"Childless woman wins free vacation and tries to shirk Christmas!" Nadine shouted. Her hands gestured in a wide sweep in front of her. The girl chewed on the end of her pen and glanced up at the sky as if Nadine's headline were being pulled by a plane. Darren stepped up.

"Listen," he said. "Why don't you just forget about those pictures and the quote. Come over to the bungalow later. Get more of a family feel." The girl glanced over at their father's SpongeBob swim shorts.

"Our readers want the truth," the girl said. A minute ago they just wanted pictures. Tara wanted to strangle her.

"It's Christmas," Darren said. "Nobody wants the truth."

"Sorry. I got what I wanted."

Nadine, who had already organized all their beach

material, started walking away. "Let's go," she said. "Now that we don't have a Christmas dinner to plan, we've plenty of time to devote to the gingerbread bungalow."

"If you do this for me," Darren said. "I'll give you an exclusive peek at this year's village. It's going to be a doozy." He looked over at Tara, then leaned over and whispered something into the girl's ear. Her mouth flew open.

"Really?" she asked Tara. Tara frowned. She glanced at Darren. He gave her a slow smile. Tara's heart tripped. She didn't care what Darren told the girl. As long as it convinced the *Maui Mornings* girl not to print the picture of Tara in her hideous swim dress, she would go along with it.

"Absolutely," Tara said.

"See you at the bungalow," the girl said.

True to her word, a few hours later, the girl arrived at the bungalow and re-took the photos. Tara had changed into a sundress and washed the oxide off her nose. Before she left, the girl promised only to print the good ones. It was then, as they gathered on the patio, that Darren told Tara how he'd convinced the reporter to drop the hideous pictures. Nadine was ecstatic over his revelation. At first.

"You have a Christmas village?" she said. "Really? Really?" Phil looked startled. He hadn't been jealous of Darren's good looks, but if the guy was a Christmas nut just like Nadine, then he was going to pose a real threat. Even Tara felt slightly jealous as she watched her sister stare adoringly at Darren.

" 'The Island Pole'," Darren said. "It's a huge hit every year. I've kind of got a cult following." Nadine's smile faded slightly.

"The Island Pole?" she said.

"I go all out," Darren said. "Lights, displays, characters, the works. You should see my electric bill."

"Tiara will go nuts over a Christmas village," Nadine said. She clapped her hands.

"Um—she can't go," Darren said.

"What?"

"It's rated R." Phil visibly relaxed. Nadine did not.

"Excuse me?"

"It's just for adults," Darren said. Despite the horrified look on Nadine's face, a smile remained on his. Once again, Tara was glad nobody knew what his smile did to her.

"It's a pornographic Christmas village?" Nadine said.

"I wouldn't go that far. More—R-rated."

"An R-rated Christmas village?" Nadine spit out every word as if she could barely contain the sounds in her mouth. She folded her arms and stared at Darren as if she could incinerate him with a single look.

"What does this have to do with me?" Tara said.

"You my dear," Darren said, grabbing her around the waist, "are going to be our guest star."

"Do tell," Tara said.

"The rabid reindeer exhibit," Darren said. "And don't worry. You can wear your little red bikini."

"Not on your life," Tara said. "Not on your laid-back little life."

Chapter 8

Nadine was sketching the blueprint to her ginger-bread bungalow, her parents were on a walk, Phil was on his cell phone, and Tiara was taking a nap. Tara was contemplating finding a tiki bar. Darren was almost to his truck.

"You should come to the beach tomorrow," he called back over his shoulder. "Check out the Santa Sand Sculpture contest."

"Santa Sand Sculpture contest?" Nadine said. Her eyes were kaleidoscopes spinning and widening and bouncing color across the patio. "What's that?"

"It's a sand castle building contest," Darren said. "Except it has to be a Christmas theme." Tara shot Darren a warning look. He caught it. But instead of dropping the subject, he just grinned. "It's too bad you can't participate," he told Nadine. "It's a great way to get in the Christmas spirit."

"I think we could clear our schedule," Nadine said.

"No," Tara said. Darren leaned against his truck and smiled at Tara.

"Neither of us have a chance of winning," he said. "You even have local architects who compete."

"Winning isn't everything," Nadine said. "It sounds fun."

"Oh it is. Tons of fun. But we could make it a little more interesting by placing a little wager of our own."

"No," Tara said. "Absolutely not."

"Yes," Nadine said. "Absolutely yes."

"Would Santa approve of gambling?" Tara said.

"Lighten up," Nadine said.

"Great," Darren said. "Me against you two. We can get some local boys to judge."

"You're on," Nadine said.

"No," Tara said. She grabbed Nadine by the shoulders and looked her in the eye. "We're going snorkeling with Santa," she said. Nadine wavered. *Take that, Darren,* Tara thought. *You can't outwit me when it comes to Nadine.* "And parasailing," Tara added. Nadine turned to Darren.

"Sorry," she said. "We have other plans." *Point, match, game.*

"Too bad," Darren said. "If you won, I was going to make the Island Pole rated G this year." *Oh, Christmas crackers.* Tara didn't even have to look at Nadine to know the verdict. Some people were led astray by sin; others got their jollies by hearing the words "rated G." Besides, she could see Nadine jumping up and down out of her peripheral vision.

"Yes!" Nadine shouted. "You are on."

"If I win, Island Pole stays R-rated, and Tara agrees to guest star in the reindeer exhibit," Darren said.

"Deal!" Nadine held out her hand to seal it with a handshake. His golden dog stepped up and gave her his paw. Darren laughed.

"It's official," he said with a nod to his dog.

"No," Tara said. "I won't do it." Nadine whirled around and pointed her index finger at Tara.

"You owe me," she said.

"How do you figure?"

"You stole my Christmas dinner," Nadine said. Tara shook her head. "Please," Nadine begged. "We can do this. I'm really good at Christmas themes." Tara dropped her head. Nadine jumped up and down. "You're on," she said for a third time. Nadine patted Tara on the back, then squeezed her so hard it hurt. "Practice starts at six A.M.," she said. "Bring your own bucket."

Tara's dismay over getting up so early was diminished by the spectacular sunrise. She and Nadine had the beach to themselves. They stood in silent awe and watched the red and orange ball slowly peek over the horizon. Tara didn't get to enjoy it for long. Nadine roped off a section of the beach like it was a crime scene. She took a blueprint out of her bag and unrolled it.

"When did you have time to do that?" Tara asked. "Were you up all night?"

"You'll thank me later," she said. "What we have here is our own Christmas village. G-rated."

Tara peeked at the drawing and groaned. "We can't build all that out of sand," she said.

"Oh ye of little faith," Nadine said. "Now get your ass down and start digging." It was useless, but Tara stabbed at the sand anyway. Nadine was having fun, that was all that mattered. Of course when she was standing at a reindeer exhibit at the Island Pole, Tara knew she might not feel so generous toward her sister. It didn't matter, even if they lost, she wasn't going to

let Darren bully her into volunteering. He was trying
to capitalize on her. The nerve. Why were the sexy
ones so much trouble? He didn't even try to hide who
he really was. He just laid it all out there, in a cavalier
take it or leave it way. As if he didn't care what other
people thought of him.

That was it. That's what made him so sexy. Besides
the body, and the hair, and those eyes, and lips. He
didn't care what other people thought of him. Tara
wished she were more like him. All those years suf-
fering under Alain and Y&S, tiptoeing around them,
complimenting them even when she had better ideas
for their dishes. Did she once dare to speak up? No.
She whipped up concoctions at home all the time that
she knew were to die for. But she was too much of a
wimp to whip them up at the restaurant. If it were
Darren he probably would have just done it. Rebelled.
They probably would have fired her. Which they did
anyway. And she never even had a chance to see how
her recipes would have been received.

"I'm so jealous," Nadine said. "He's totally gorgeous." Startled, Tara looked up. As far as she could
tell, Nadine was making a little snowman, but it was
hard to tell. So far, Tara had dug a small hole, and Nadine had made a round ball.

"Who?"

Nadine hit Tara with her yellow plastic shovel.
"Who?" she mocked. "God, you are so, so lucky."

"Is that supposed to be a snowman?"

"What else?"

"You only made two balls. Aren't you supposed to
have three?"

"The way you two look at each other. It's electric."

Tara poured water into her hole. She dove two fingers into it. "Santa's swamp," she said.

"God, I love the beginning of a relationship. Sexual tension. Heart pounding. A single look between you that says—'If we were alone right now our clothes would disintegrate from the heat we're generating.' "

"Nadine," Tara said. "Is everything okay with you and Phil?" Nadine jabbed her shovel at Tara.

"You are sleeping with him," she said. "Do you understand me? You are going to sleep with that man. If you don't—you'll regret it the rest of your life." Tara stared at the tiny ball Nadine was making now.

"Is that another snowman?"

"What is your problem?" Nadine said. "It's a freaking elf."

Two hours into the practice they were both exhausted. Their North Pole was in need of an "Extreme Makeover Castle Edition."

"He said the judges would be local boys, didn't he?" Nadine asked Tara. Tara nodded.

"New plan," Nadine said, throwing down her shovel.

They went shopping. Tara bought a little red bikini. Nadine bought a green one. They wore them with matching heels, carried mistletoe, and flirted with the three male judges. It was working like a charm; the local boys were flirting right back. And although they couldn't see what he was doing because he'd erected a mini-tent over his sculpture, Darren was definitely distracted as well. Every so often his head would pop out, and he'd look at the sad little village they were constructing, then look suspiciously at the judges who at times appeared to be literally drooling, then linger on Tara's body, then pop back into his tent with a semi-scowl. The dog, meanwhile, was happy to sit in-between the two stations, his tail every once in a while threatening to take out a deformed sand-elf.

"I've been thinking about the restaurant," Tara said. "I should've taken more chances." The sand-chimney on Santa's house sagged and then toppled over. One of the judges took their picture. Nadine and Tara flashed seductive smiles at the camera.

"We are so going to win," Nadine said without moving her lips or breaking her smile.

"Totally," Tara said back. They glanced over at their parents who were playing at the edge of the ocean with Tiara. Phil was behind them, a cell phone surgically attached to his ear.

"Who is he talking to at this hour of the morning?" Nadine said. Tara was wondering the same thing.

"It has to be innocent," Tara said. "He's talking right in front of Mom and Dad."

"Of course it's innocent. Why wouldn't it be—" Nadine cut herself off. "You mean an affair?" she said, as if she'd never considered the possibility. "You think Phil is having an affair?" The judges stopped laughing and stared at Tara. Darren popped his head out. Even the dog's tail froze mid-whap.

"I didn't say that," Tara said. "I didn't say that."

"You hinted at it," Nadine said. "He's not a cheater. My husband is not a cheater."

"I didn't say he was."

"Then say it. Say 'Phil is not a cheater.' "

"Phil is not a cheater."

"Thank you."

"But he isn't exactly being good to you."

"I'm finished!" Darren said, emerging from the tent. He patted the dog on the head, brushed sand off his hands, and winked at Tara.

"I'm going to talk to him," Nadine said. "I'm going to tell him you've noticed."

"What? No! Don't do that."

Nadine pointed her shovel at Tara. "That's exactly what I'm going to do." She stood up.

"Now? You're going to do it now?"

"While the phone is fresh in his ear," Nadine said.

"But they're going to judge us now," Tara said. She turned to the judges and smiled. "Go ahead," she said.

"Ours sucks," Nadine said.

"Stick out your chest," Tara whispered. Nadine, despite being otherwise occupied, complied. The judges whistled.

"You ladies are looking good," one said. "Looking good."

"Yeah," another agreed. "Look like winners to me."

"Win, win, win," the third said. Nadine giggled nervously as he stared at her. "If I were your husband, I would throw that phone into the ocean, baby." He mimed doing just that. "Into the ocean!" Nadine laughed some more, and her face turned as red as Tara's suit. Darren clapped his hands.

"Look at this baby," he said. He whipped the makeshift tent off his sculpture. Everyone's eyes first went up it, then down it, then up it again. A sculpture of a naked woman lay in the sand. She was wearing only a Santa cap. Several of the judges looked at the naked sculpture, then at Tara, then back at the naked sculpture. Cameras started flashing; the judges whooped and fist-bumped Darren. Nadine pointed at the naked sand-woman.

"That is not very Christmas-like," she said.

"Yeah," one of the judges agreed. "Santa's been baaad." The judges grabbed Darren's arm and raised it in victory. Nadine kicked the roof of their North Pole.

Darren hugged Tara to his body. They were both sweaty and sticky with sand. Tara's face flooded first from desire, then from embarrassment. She pulled away. "I'll pick you up tomorrow," Darren said. "Rehearsals start early."

"Rehearsals?" Tara yelled after him. "What do you mean by rehearsals?" But he and his dog were already gone.

Chapter 9

As they neared Darren's house, homemade road signs began appearing at the side of the road with arrows pointing the way to: THE ISLAND POLE. RATED R. Darren's house was the last one on a dead-end drive.

"When the village opens, cars will be lined up for miles," Darren said, gesturing out the window. He beamed like a proud parent.

"Don't you have families who bring their kids despite the warning?" Tara asked.

"That used to happen," Darren said. "But it's a walk-through village, not a drive through. They park in the field." Darren pointed to the large empty plot of land next to his house. "We have a guy checking ID at the gate. It sucks to make a family turn around and go home, but it has to be done. We give 'em candy canes and send them on their way."

"That's horrible," Tara said.

"Not at all," Darren said. "The rest of the block goes crazy with light displays too. I was the one who kicked it off," he said with a wink.

"It's nice to have a legacy," Tara said. She was trying to be facetious, but he seemed to take it as a compliment.

"Definitely," Darren said. "But I was the one to persuade the rest of the block to be kid-friendly."

"Imagine that," Tara said. "Kid-friendly on Christmas."

"It's perfect," Darren said. "No one is disappointed. The families with kids can still walk up and down the street and enjoy the amateurs." Tara laughed.

"God, I love that sound," Darren said.

"What?"

"Your laugh. It's magical."

"My laugh? You like my laugh?" His laugh made her want to rip off his clothes and suction herself to his muscular stomach. She kept this to herself. "Thanks," she said instead.

"Don't thank me," Darren said. "Just keep doing it." He looked at her long and hard. Tara looked away, and brushed his comment off with a laugh. She closed her eyes and marveled at the sensations in her body. She never knew her back could mimic a grand piano, that one look from the right guy, and concertos would play up and down her spine. Everybody should have at least one secret to take to his or her grave, and this one would definitely be hers. Nobody's ego deserved that much of a boost.

Darren's house was wrapped in so many Christmas lights, she couldn't tell exactly what it looked like. She guessed it was similar to the bungalow she was staying in. A giant palm tree in the front yard was also adorned with lights. Tara bet it was something to see when it was all lit up. Next to the palm tree was a blow-up snowman.

"Three balls," Tara said, thinking of Nadine's de-

formed sand-snowman. "That's good." So far she didn't
see what was R-rated—

She stepped closer to Frosty. He was holding
something in his mittens. "Is that a joint?" Tara said.
In his other hand Frosty had a can of Budweiser. Tara
laughed, but shook her head. "Ridiculous," she said.

"But it made you laugh," Darren said. "Magical."

"I'm laughing at a grown man acting like a frat
boy," Tara said.

Darren shrugged, the grin never leaving his face.
"Look down," he said. Tara looked at the ground.
Condom wrappers and crushed beer cans littered the
ground. A bra was flung over Frosty's head.

"Nadine would go mental," Tara said. "I can't tell
you how bad I want to clean this up." Darren came up
behind her. He wrapped his arms around her, and
kissed her neck. She turned to face him, and he kissed
her full on. She forgot all about the dirty snowman.

"That was just for Frosty," Darren said when he finally pulled away. "He likes to watch." Tara swatted
Darren.

"This is just wrong," Tara said, looking at Frosty.
"Wrong, wrong, wrong."

"Then you're definitely not going to want to see
the rest of it," Darren said, taking her hand. "But I'm
going to show it to you anyway."

Darren's expansive backyard was indeed a Christmas village. One look at it, and Tara knew he deserved a hideous electric bill. It was Frosty times
twelve. Since most of the exhibits used real people,
Darren narrated the scene. "That's where hookers will
sit on Santa's lap. The elves read *Penthouse* and
smoke Marlboro Reds." He pointed to a model train.
"That will run continuously," he said. He started up
the train. When the whistle blew, a miniature Santa

popped out of the caboose, bent over, and showed
them his caboose.

"How did you get toys to do that?" Tara asked.

"I have friends in low places," Darren said. "Come
on, I'll show you your exhibit." Tara followed Darren
to the very back where a small patch of grass was
penned off with a small wooden fence. In the middle
of the pen stood a giant electronic reindeer. Darren
pushed a button on its neck. The reindeer reared back.
His eyes turned red. Smoke shot out of his nose. Then
he opened his mouth and revealed giant fangs. Darren
stuck his wrist into the open mouth and screamed.
Tara stared, dumbfounded.

"That's all you have to do," Darren said. "Just
reenact the attack. They're going to love it." He
jumped the fence, then rolled down a banner hanging
in front of it.

When Reindeers ATTACK

"I quit," Tara said. Darren just smiled. He pulled a
folded-up newspaper article out of his back pocket
and handed it to her.

"Maui Mornings," he said. "Hot off the press."

"That wench," Tara said, staring at her picture in
the newspaper. "She promised." But there Tara stood,
hands on hips, in her hideous swim dress. She didn't
even have to ask, "Does this suit make me look fat?"
because the answer was yes. The hat and zinc oxide
didn't help. She looked exactly like the type of
woman who would sue McDonald's for hot coffee or
scream that an innocent reindeer had tried to bite her
just to finagle a free trip. There was a second picture
in the article. It was Darren standing next to the me-
chanical reindeer. As usual, he was grinning ear-to-
ear. He looked gorgeous.

"Read it," Darren said, tapping the first paragraph.

LOCAL CHRISTMAS VILLAGE HOOKS UP WITH REINDEER
LADY. ISLAND POLE, RATED R. DONATIONS TO BE GIVEN
TO ISLAND ORPHANAGE.

Underneath was yet another picture, of a dozen smiling children who Tara could only assume were the local orphans.

"That's ridiculous," Tara said. "They aren't even allowed into the village."

"True," Darren said. "But besides giving them a large donation, I am taking them out for an afternoon on a glass bottom boat."

"You have a glass bottom boat?"

"I have a second job," Darren said. "I'm a glass bottom boat guide."

"Of course you are," Tara said.

"You should come sometime," Darren said. Tara didn't answer. She was still obsessing over the picture.

"She promised," Tara wailed.

Darren pointed to Tara's slathered white nose. "She thought this was reminiscent of Rudolph," Darren said. "You can't really blame her. It is Christmas." Tara looked around the perverted village and then shook her head at Darren.

"Ho, ho, ho," she said. Darren pointed to the **When Santa's Away, Mrs. Claus Will PLAY** exhibit.

"That's what she says," he said.

Tara spent the rest of the day helping put Christmas lights where Christmas lights shouldn't go. Still, as other volunteers showed up, and silly perverted Christmas songs played through the village, Tara had to grudgingly admit she was having fun. After several hours of hard Christmas labor, she felt Darren's hand on the small of her back. Another musical scale played up and down her spine, and when she turned around, she was half-hoping he was holding mistletoe.

"I just ordered pizza for the gang," he said. "But why don't you come in and have a drink with me. Take a little break." She didn't argue. She wanted to check out his place.

To her surprise, his home was neat and orderly. Bookshelves lined the wall. A blue marble globe sat on one side of a shelf, a telescope on the other. Tara imagined the two of them stargazing on the beach late at night. *There's the Big Dipper; there's the Little Dipper; what's that star? I don't know, so from now own, it will be our star.* Kiss, kiss, knock over telescope, fall onto beach, make love under your new star, how could you not fall in love with a man with a telescope? His furniture was masculine yet classy: a solid suede sofa, a sturdy coffee table, and a leather reclining chair. *A few throw pillows would give them a welcoming feel,* Tara thought as she took them in. She caught herself imagining her stuff mixed up with his stuff. They had similar tastes, and she was pretty sure her stuff and his stuff, their *combined stuff,* would get on like a house on fire. Whereas some people worried whether or not they would like their new love's friends, Tara always worried whether or not she would like their stuff. If you didn't like someone's friend, you just had to make an excuse whenever he was around. *I'm so sorry I can't play beer pong with you and Buck tonight, but I have a sore wrist.*

But not liking someone's stuff was much trickier. If things progressed, you would have to sit on that beer-stained Barcalounger, look at the *Aliens versus*

Predators poster, or listen to, say, that hideous cuckoo clock chime for the rest of its natural life. And Murphy's Law said the Barcalounger, *Aliens,* and cuckoo were going to outlive you by at least a thousand years. And forget about subtly trying to destroy or replace his things. You would pay for it. Every fight you had from then on would be subtly laced with—*You smashed my cuckoo clock with a ball-peen hammer, and no matter what I said, I'm never going to forgive you, never.* If she and Darren were live-in lovers, they wouldn't have that problem. She had yet to see a single thing she wanted to smash with a hammer.

She did, however, have a strange urge to touch his things, run her hands over them, as if she could soak up the sounds and scents of his life simply through her fingertips. Speaking of scent, his place smelled fresh, like lavender. And coconuts. Everywhere she went it smelled like coconuts. He had a nice flat screen television, but there was no video game system hanging off it. It was the anti-Island Pole. This was the place of a guy she wanted to date. Or fling. *He's not boyfriend material,* she reminded herself. *Even if he does have a telescope.* His kitchen was small, a typical galley with just enough room for a stove, fridge, and sink.

"Not a kitchen you can cook in," Darren said. He sounded disappointed.

"You're wrong," Tara said. "I can whip up a gourmet meal anywhere."

"Really?"

"Of course. You should see the things I've done with hot plates." She stopped as he burst out in laughter.

"Sorry," he said, gesturing out the back window. "When you work the Island Pole enough, everything starts to sound perverted." Tara didn't hear what he said. She was stuck on "work the Island Pole." She made a conscious effort not to look at his groin.

"Anyway," she said. "You can cook in here."

"Too bad I already ordered pizza," Darren said. He opened the fridge and took out a bottle of champagne. "But I have this," he said.

"Let them eat pizza," Tara said. "Take me to the nearest grocery store." They stood, grinning at each other. It felt so good to flirt. Darren took his truck keys out of his pocket and tossed them in the air.

"Let's go," he said.

She decided to make tilapia with mandarin oranges, garlic, and cilantro. She would also whip up a homemade cocktail sauce for peel-and-eat shrimp, and spicy green beans. Finally, broiled red potatoes and fresh bread with butter would round out the meal. Darren gave her a glass of champagne, and after being banned from helping her, left her alone to cook. He even put a Bing Crosby Christmas CD on. Tara was in heaven. She hadn't cooked in several days, and it felt good. She tried not to think about the fact that she no longer had a job back home. Once in a while Darren would pop back in and watch her work. He'd fill up her champagne glass or ask again if she needed help. He'd stand and inhale the scents of her cooking and once whispered, "My God." Then he looked out the window at the volunteers. They were chugging beer and munching on pizza. "Those poor bastards," he said with a shake of his head. "If they only knew what we had going on in here."

A warmth spread through Tara, and it took everything she had not to ask "What exactly do we have going on in here?" She told herself to just enjoy the moment. She loved the feeling of being watched as she cooked, admired for doing what she loved best. She had her hair piled on top of her head, and when a strand fell loose, Darren was there in a flash. In one gentle move he tucked the loose strand behind her ear, and before pulling away, kissed her softly on the neck. "Hey." he said when he pulled back. "You're not wearing your bandage."

"I'm all better now," Tara said.

Darren gently lifted her wrist to his mouth and kissed it. A shiver ran through Tara, head to toe. "No," he said. "Now you're all better."

He set his dining table with red place mats and gold-rimmed china plates. It was her turn to watch him. His dog followed him everywhere he went. It was adorable. "I don't even know your dog's name," she said. The dog trotted over and stuck his nose in Tara's crotch. She laughed and gently pushed him away. "Guess he's not too insulted," she said. "But I want to know it anyway."

"Dog."

"You're kidding."

"Nope."

"Your dog's name is Dog?"

"Yep."

"Very creative."

"Simple," he said. "Just like I like my life." Tara looked around the apartment again. Santa and hookers outside, Bing Crosby and Tolstoy inside. She didn't care what he said. She figured he was anything but simple. Dinner was amazing. As they ate, Darren wanted to hear about her work at La Fleur. Tara regaled him with tales of Y&S and Alain, stopping short of mentioning the bit about being fired. She hadn't even told Nadine. She wanted to pretend it wasn't happening. She didn't want her exotic vacation ruined by reality. A loud whoop rose from out-

side. Tara glanced out the window. She couldn't exactly see what was going on, but it looked like Santa
was getting a lap dance. Darren chuckled. Tara shook
her head.

"What?" he said.

"I just don't get it," Tara admitted. "Why are you
so anti-Christmas?" Darren set down his fork, took a
sip of his wine, and stared into Tara's eyes.

"You really want to know?" he said.

"I really do," Tara said.

"Follow me." They got up from the table and went
to the back window. Tara tried to ignore how close his
body was to hers, as he lifted his arm and pointed out
a woman standing in the middle of the yard. "Sheila,"
he said. "Forty-five. Four kids. Husband was a no
good accountant with girlfriends all over the globe.
Left them on Christmas. Before I started up the village she couldn't bring herself to celebrate the holiday. Now her kids get a Christmas, and she gets a
little stress relief." He pointed to a man. "John. Girlfriend left him at the altar. Allen. Goes broke buying
gifts for everyone, always thinking they'll be disappointed. Had a heart attack last year. Did you know
Christmas is the deadliest day of the year?"

"It is not," Tara said. Darren held up his hand as if
he were in court.

"Cross my heart," he said. "More people die on
Christmas than any other day of the year."

"My God," Tara said.

"Don't worry," Darren said. "Not around here they
don't. And you know why? Because we're no longer
allowing ourselves to freak out. I mean really—what
happened to Christmas? Isn't it supposed to be time
for family? Relaxing? The United States of Advertis-
ing, that's what happened to Christmas. You can't

even get through Halloween without the stores stocking Santa on the shelf."

"Tell me about it," Tara said.

"I'm just trying to bring a little joy," Darren said. Tara looked at a man playing an elf. He was strutting around with an enormous, strategically placed candy cane.

"What's his story?" Tara asked. She pointed to the elf.

"Oh, he's just nuts," Darren said. Tara laughed. They turned to each other, enjoying a shared sense of humor. Soon they stopped laughing, and just stared.

"So what's your story?" she asked.

"I should get you home," Darren said. "You've had a long day."

"I won't argue," Tara said. "Although don't think I didn't notice how you're ignoring my question." She went to clean up the dishes. Darren quickly put his hands on her, and took away the dish she held.

"Don't even think about it," he said. "Now get in the truck." Dog barked and wagged his tail. "Now that's the reaction I want to see," Darren joked. Tara punched him on the shoulder. He grabbed her hand. Soon, they were holding hands.

"I could stay," Tara said.

"Not tonight," Darren said. Tara tried to pretend she wasn't miffed. She thought he liked her. She was willing. She was on vacation. Men didn't just turn down sex. Especially men like Darren. He wasn't interested. She walked quickly to the door and opened it. He closed it. She didn't turn around, but she could feel him behind her. "Hey," he said softly. "Did I upset you?"

"No," she said. "It's okay. I get it. You're just not that into me." Darren put his hands on her shoulders and turned her to face him.

"I am so totally into you," he said. "Believe me."

"Then why?"

"I have a backyard full of horny elves and bad Santas," Darren said. "That's not exactly how I envisioned our first time."

"So you've . . . envisioned us?"

"Oh yeah," Darren said. "Have you?" *Oh yeah. And you have no idea how much my stuff would like your stuff.* Tara's answer was a smile. He smiled back. "I promise," he said. "Soon." He leaned in and kissed her cheek.

"Just remember I'm on vacation," Tara said. "We only have so much time." Darren nodded, but Tara couldn't help but notice the frown line that appeared on his forehead. And although she didn't want to admit it, she wanted him to say something back. Something that would make her feel better. She was already fantasizing about the two of them, and unless you moved in and had children with your flings, she was taking her thoughts a little too far. She was going to have to get a grip. He was a fling. Nothing more. He would never be anything more.

Chapter 10

Tara didn't think bringing Nadine with her to the opening of the Island Pole was a good idea, but Nadine insisted. Their parents were taking a late night stroll, and Phil was instructed to make Christmas cookies with Tiara.

"Did you know Christmas is the deadliest day of the year?" Tara said as Nadine drove. "Stress relief is very important this time of year." Nadine didn't take the bait. She wanted to change the village to G-rated and that was that. As Darren predicted, there was a long line of cars waiting to get into the village. Nadine drummed her fingers on the steering wheel.

"You're going to have to get out and make a run for it," she said.

"What?"

Nadine unlocked the passenger door. "It's going to take me too long to park."

"So what's your plan?" Tara asked. Nadine laid it out for her. She told Tara that instead of doing the "act," she should talk to the people about the magic of

Christmas, the gentle side of reindeer. Tara balked. Nadine held her ground.

"You have the power, Tara. Don't forget that." Nadine leaned over, opened the door, and kicked her out of the car.

"Reindeer," Tara said to the people walking by, "are actually gentle beings." She was still wearing her jogging suit, refusing to don her bikini. "You know Dasher and Dancer, and Prancer, and Vixen—"

She thought her voice was pretty good, but the people walking by didn't linger long. They looked slightly disgusted. When the reindeer opened its mouth to show teeth, she would shake her head. "It was one rogue reindeer," she said. "We can't paint them all with the same sordid brush. Alfred-slash-Blitzen was a diva. If male reindeers can be divas. Whatever— he had an ego. He was the Mel Gibson of reindeer. Really, most of them are hardworking and humble." Darren popped up in front of her.

"What the hell are you doing?" he asked.

"I'm behaving like an adult," Tara said. "Sharing messages of peace."

"You're boring everyone to death," Darren said.

"I'm teaching them the true meaning of Christmas," Tara said.

"Why don't you just make them laugh?" Darren said.

"Darren—"

"Just try it. Once. I promise, if you don't like it, you can go back to—whatever it was you were doing." Darren stood back, crossed his arms against his chest and waited.

Oh heck. It couldn't hurt. Tara took off her tracksuit and stood in her red bikini. She could feel Darren's eyes all over her, but she didn't dare look at him. She donned her Santa hat and slipped on red high heels. She wanted to try this once, get it over with before Nadine came through. When the reindeer opened its mouth, she stuck her hand in and gave a little scream. Darren nodded his encouragement. An elderly couple passing by stopped and laughed. Tara looked at the couple.

"Help," she yelled. "He's eating me." They laughed harder. "New Yorkers!" she said. "As long as your own wrist is reindeer-free you just don't care, do you?" People started to stop and linger. "Lawsuit!" she yelled. "Lawsuit!" The crowd roared. She cursed. She howled in pain. "Bad reindeer! Bad reindeer!" The crowd quickly multiplied, and their laughter was downright infectious. "I want to go to Hawaii!" Tara wailed. From-the-gut, pee-your-pants laughter rippled from her fans.

"Tara!" Nadine materialized in front of her, hands on hips, eyes flashing. Tara removed her hand, stuck it back in the reindeer again, and screamed. "You should be ashamed of yourself," Nadine said.

"Elf you!" Tara said. The crowd roared. Tara motioned to Nadine with her index finger. Nadine stepped up so Tara could lean over and whisper in her ear. "They like me," she said. "They really like me."

"No," Darren said. Tara turned to see Darren, who was watching her from behind a Christmas tree decorated with dildos. "They love you," he said.

The next night, Tara threw herself into her role like she was an actress on Broadway. She drew an even bigger crowd. Afterward, she and Darren lingered long after everyone else had gone home, sat in the middle of the village with glasses of wine, and replayed the comments and reactions of the locals. They laughed until Tara's stomach was literally aching. Darren kept the lights on for a while, so the two of them could enjoy their glitter. The following evening Darren didn't drive her home until the sun started to rise. Tara dreamed of her time alone with Darren, relishing the thought more than the excitement of performing her act. With the village all to themselves, and no hookers hanging around Santa, it was almost . . . Christmas-like.

The first night they kept their hands to themselves. On the second night, during a lull in their laughter, their fingers touched. Soon, they were holding hands. Next, he caressed her cheek, and trailed his finger along the length of her jaw. Finally, his hand reached around and rubbed her back. But when she leaned in for a proper kiss, he pulled back. But instead of making her want to give up, it drove her crazy, made her want him even more, which given how she'd been feeling since she first spotted him by the side of the road, seemed hardly possible. She appreciated a man with restraint, but time was evaporating.

"You're going to the Island Pole again?" Nadine said. "But we're all going on a family trip—Snorkeling with Santa, then off to the Hyatt to hear the Caroling Seniors."

"I hate to miss that," Tara said. "But you're the one who volunteered me. I can't just quit."

"I only volunteered you for one night."

"But I can spend my days and mornings with you guys," Tara said.

"You're exhausted in the mornings, and grumpy during the day," Nadine said. "You never wanted us here at all," she added.

"Don't say that," Tara said. "I'm happy you're here."

"You didn't even invite us," Nadine said. "You weren't going to spend Christmas with us at all. You came here to be alone and get laid!" Tara glanced at her parents who were helping Tiara put icing on the Christmas cookies. Guilt flooded her. Especially since it was true. She had wanted to be alone. She didn't want to go snorkeling with Santa. She didn't want to make Christmas cookies. She didn't want to hear Christmas carols sung by senior citizens. She'd had a hard year; she was out a job, and a doorman, and a bartender; she had no men to look forward to except ones who had a fondness for the squirrels in Thompson Square Park, and until she had to go back and face all of that, she just wanted to have fun.

"Ah, give her a break," Phil said. "Everyone likes to celebrate the holidays a little differently." Nadine gave him a look that would instantly freeze boiling water.

"Why don't you go with her then," Nadine said. "I'm sure the Island Pole would be right up your current alley." Tara started to protest.

"I'd love to go," Phil said. He headed out to the car.

"Nadine," Tara said.

"Go," Nadine said. "Just go."

Phil was having way too much fun for Tara's liking. She could hear his laughter all the way across the yard. Tara leaned over the little fence of her enclosure and tried to spy on him. She accidentally stepped on a tiny lightbulb. All color drained out of her reindeer, and he went slack, mid-roar. Darren popped up immediately. Tara hadn't even realized he was nearby, but obviously he'd been watching her.

"There are replacement bulbs in my living room

closet," he said. "I'd get them but I want to watch you walk away."

"Ha ha," Tara said. "I need a break anyway." Tara shook her ass at him as she walked away, eliciting a sexy laugh. She took her time in the house, took off her heels, and rubbed her feet. She watched throngs of people wind through the village. They looked a lot more relaxed than the shoppers in the mall, or the families standing in line with their children to see Santa. Maybe Darren had a point; maybe it was healthy to have an outlet like this to release all the Christmas stress. Wasn't this the time of year when there were the highest number of suicides? This was certainly a better alternative, a little comedy, the *Saturday Night Live* of Christmas. In the spirit of things she poured herself a glass of eggnog from the pitcher in his fridge and took her time making her way to his closet.

The lights were sitting on the top shelf, clearly visible. But when she tried to pull them out, every item on the shelf came tumbling down. She put the lights aside, and began putting the items back: a folded jacket, a Frisbee, a dog toy, a book, and a Christmas present. It was wrapped in shiny gold paper, and topped with a red bow. It was a medium-sized box. She examined the tag. It had Darren's name on it. If he didn't get it out soon, he would forget that he had it. Since he didn't have a Christmas tree inside, she put the gift under a large potted plant. That would have to do for a tree. He'd probably forgotten he'd put it away in the closet. She smiled to herself. She liked playing Santa.

"God, that was fun," Phil said. Everyone else had gone home, and Tara wanted her usual evening alone with Darren, but she was stuck. It was obvious from the way Phil was weaving through the yard that he'd had too much eggnog. Tara had only taken one sip, so she would have to be the designated driver.

"I'll drive him home and drive back," Darren said. He pulled Tara into his embrace with one arm and held something over her head with the other. Mistletoe. Tara leaned in and kissed him. Darren pulled back and laughed.

"What's so funny?" Tara said. Darren dangled the candy cane in his hand.

"Fooled you," he said.

"No, you didn't," she said. "I knew all along." She kissed him again.

"I'm going to run in, get my keys, and get him home," Darren said. "You and Dog can relax in the living room, watch a little telly."

"No problem," Tara said. She and Dog followed Darren into the house. She flopped on a chair, threw her head back, and opened her legs slightly. Darren stared.

"Close your legs," he said. "Or I'm not going to be able to drive." She laughed, took her time closing them. This was definitely going to be the night. Darren jingled his keys and headed back out. After a few steps he stopped cold. Something in his demeanor made Tara sit straight up. It was as if all the sexual chemistry in the room had been suddenly sucked out. He was staring at the present under the plant.

"Where did you get that?" he said. It didn't sound like his voice. It was strained, far away.

"In your closet," Tara said. "When I came in for the lights." Darren whirled around and stared at her. She stood up. "I thought you forgot about it," she said.

"You thought wrong," he said.

"I'm sorry." She wanted to defend herself, yell at him, tell him she didn't do anything wrong. But the look on his face told her it wouldn't do any good whatsoever. Was it a present from an ex-girlfriend? Wife? She realized she knew very little about the man. That was the problem with flings. You just didn't know who you were flinging with. It was a horrible idea. Dog whined and sat next to his master. She threw her arms open in frustration. "Should I go?" she said, fully expecting him to say no, to go back to flirting with her.

"I think that would be best," he said.

Tara and Nadine sat on the patio, each lost in her own misery. "He was laughing when he came home," Nadine said. "I don't remember the last time I heard him laugh like that." Nadine had a nonalcoholic strawberry daiquiri; Tara had a pitcher of eggnog. Nadine bemoaned the fact that she couldn't partake of any spirits, but made the best of it by putting a candy cane in her drink. She said it was surprisingly good. Maybe that's all you needed in life sometimes, a "surprising element." They stopped drinking long enough to watch their parents skip out of the house, hand in hand.

"Good night girls," their father said. "Don't wait up." Her parents giggled like children, and kissed.

"Disgusting," Nadine said.

"Unfair," Tara said.

"What's wrong with Phil?" Nadine cried. "Why does he hate me?" Tara put her hand on her sister's shoulder.

"He doesn't hate you," she said. "He's just . . ."

"What?"

"I don't know," Tara admitted. "I don't know what's

wrong with any of them. If Santa existed, I'd want answers, starting with—'What the hell is wrong with men?' "

"Amen," Nadine said. She glanced at Tara's half-empty pitcher. "You're sure slinging those back," she said.

"I'm drinking for two," Tara answered.

"Will you talk to Phil for me?" Nadine said.

"What would I say?"

"I don't know—be subtle—but—you know, find out if he's cheating on me, or planning on leaving me."

"I think you need to have that conversation with him."

"I can't. It's Christmas! If he says he's leaving me it will ruin Christmas for me forever."

Then you could cheer yourself up by going to the Island Pole every year, Tara thought but didn't say. "Wouldn't it be the same if the bad news came from me?" she said instead.

"I would expect you to lie to me until the holidays are over."

"I see."

"Let's go pop popcorn. I have strings to make."

"Yes, ma'am."

"Is that sarcasm I hear in your voice?"

"No."

"Because it's your fault we're here," Nadine said.

"Excuse me?"

Nadine stood up and threw her arms out. "Look at this," she said. "It's balmy. Beautiful. Warm. No snow in sight. Our parents are necking like teenagers. We aren't even making our own Christmas dinner and that"—Nadine pointed accusingly—"is a palm tree!"

Tara stood up. "Try it like this," she said. Tara took on a positive tone. "Look at this! It's balmy. Beautiful.

Warm. No snow in sight." She stopped. "All right the
parents thing is a little bit creepy. But not having to
make dinner—it's a Christmas miracle. And that"—
Tara pointed—"is a palm tree!"

"It doesn't feel like Christmas."

"You didn't have to come."

"And spend Christmas without you?"

"Nadine—did it ever occur to you I didn't want to
celebrate Christmas this year?" Nadine slapped her
hands over her ears.

"Don't say that."

"Why? Santa will hear me?"

"Don't make fun."

"Not everybody loves Christmas."

"Well, get over it. It's not just about you."

"I just wish we could relax—just for one year. This
vacation was supposed to be about relaxing. Not
about making popcorn strings until our fingers are
bleeding."

"That was one year, and that's because you weren't
stringing them right."

"There's not a right and wrong way to string popcorn!"

"Then why were your fingers bleeding?"

"I just think you need to lighten up."

"And you need to step up."

"Fine."

"Fine."

"You get a limited amount of Christmases on this
earth."

"I know that."

"Do you, Nadine?"

"How many Christmas cards did you send out?"

"Did you not hear? The planet is going green."

"So you're telling me the only reason you didn't

send out Christmas cards is because you're going green?"

"I'm just putting it out there. You can deduce whatever you want."

"You really are a New Yorker."

"What's that supposed to mean?"

"It means you have an attitude. I'm sorry—but it had to be said."

"Because I don't send out Christmas cards? Manhattan is the center of Christmas! Rockefeller Center, the Rockettes, ice skating—the windows at Saks, chestnuts roasting on every freaking corner!"

Nadine pointed a slim finger at Tara. "And where are you?"

Tara looked guiltily around paradise, which in Nadine's world was not akin with Christmas, then slipped down into her chair. Tara looked sad and unused, like a mother who'd lost her children.

"I was fired," Tara said.

"What?" Nadine's tone immediately softened. She sat down. "What happened?"

"Y&S lost the restaurant in Vegas. Alain is staying on as head chef. I told him he was the biggest French baby I'd ever met and that his sauces were flat. So he fired me."

"Oh my God. I am so, so sorry." Nadine started laughing.

"You find that funny?"

"You called him a big, French baby?" Tara laughed too.

"I certainly did," she said. "But it was 'Your sauces are flat' that sent him round the bend."

"Did he slam a pot?"

"Are you kidding me? He was a one-man demonic orchestra." They laughed again.

"You know," Tara said. "It was worth it. Just to see the look on his face." Nadine reached out and took Tara's hand.

"Why didn't you tell me?"

"I didn't want to spoil your Christmas," Tara said. After a moment they started to laugh. Nadine wiped tears from her eyes. Tara squeezed her hand. "Come on," she said. "Let's go make popcorn."

"You don't make popcorn, you pop it," Nadine answered. But she bounced out of her chair and headed for the kitchen.

If he'd acted normal the next day, Tara probably would have let it drop. She was no stranger to moody men. He didn't like her touching his present, he pouted and canceled fling-sex, end of story. She wouldn't have brought it up; she wouldn't have pressed, or snooped, or even cared. Much. Sure she would have wondered who sent him the present, why he kept it but didn't open it, and what was inside. Normal curiosity—but not worth pursuing. But Darren was the one who stirred her like-to-know into a need-to-know. He completely ignored her the next evening at the Island Pole. It hit her, as he passed by without so much as a hello, that she was spending her vacation sticking her hand into an electronic reindeer's mouth and faux-screaming, just for a few laughs from the locals and the possibility of a fling. Oh, and the orphans, she remembered, she was also doing it for the orphans.

"We're going on a family outing," Tara announced.

"You're organizing an outing?" Nadine said. "This I have to hear."

"We're going on a glass bottom boat trip."

"That's actually not a bad idea," Phil said.

"Is there a Christmas theme?" Nadine asked.

"Let's hope not," Phil said. Nadine glared at him. He stared back at her. Tara made a mental note of it; normally Phil looked away first. Nadine stroked her flat stomach. Tara wondered, fleetingly, if everything was all right with the baby. She immediately shut the thought out, she didn't want to jinx anything.

"Boat," Tiara said. "Boat!" Tara picked Tiara up and twirled her around the living room.

"Boat," Tara agreed.

"Santa's boat," Tiara said.

"You are your mother," Tara said. She looked around. "Speaking of mothers," she said. "Where is ours?" Nadine and Tara stared at their parents' door, which was still firmly shut at nine A.M. "What time did they get in?" Tara asked. Nadine shrugged. A loud noise came from the patio. They looked out to see their parents, hand-in-hand, trying to right the chair they had just knocked over.

"All night?" Nadine said. "They stayed out all night?"

"Are they drunk?" Tara said.

"Good for them," Phil said. Their parents looked up, saw they were being watched, and froze in place.

"They know we can still see them, right?" Tara said.

"Get a room," Nadine yelled.

"Get a room," Tiara echoed.

Tara didn't tell anyone that Darren worked on the glass bottom boat. She also didn't warn Darren that they were coming. But hadn't he invited her not so long ago? It was a glorious day for a boat ride. The air smelled like suntan lotion and fish, and pineapples, and of course, coconuts.

"Dog," Tiara said, pointing. Sure enough, Dog was sitting at the helm of the boat, greeting tourists.

"That's right," Darren said. "His name is 'Dog.' " He shot Tara a smug look. At least he was acknowledging her.

"Yes," Tara said. "It's great to have a name that two-year-olds can remember."

"Are you coming aboard or are you just here to sink me?" Darren asked. This time he sounded a little hurt.

"We're coming aboard," Nadine said, forging ahead. It was a medium-sized boat with a six-foot pane of glass set in the bottom. The passengers formed a circle around it, and stared down, even though they'd yet to move. Darren laughed.

"They all do that," he said. He was a perfect tour guide, handsome and relaxed, and not shy with the microphone. As they eased out into the ocean he mentioned the treats they might see, and he didn't disappoint. A glittering array of colorful specimens swam beneath them. Passengers oohed and aahed, and pointed. Tara's favorite were the neon fish, blues and yellows so bright and vibrant, she thought they couldn't possibly be real, and the giant turtles, gliding gracefully through the water, their wrinkled faces and tough shells persisting from prehistoric times. Nadine and Tiara were equally enthralled with the stingrays. Dog was the only one of them who wasn't impressed; he was curled up in the corner, and tried to lick an ant that was crawling up the side of the boat.

When they reached a point far enough out in the ocean, Darren let the boat idle. He stood at the helm, gazing outward. Tara broke away from the crowd, but when she approached, he didn't even turn and look in her direction. Tara started back to the group. Suddenly she felt his hands wrap around her waist, and he swung her into him. His hip was strong and hard against hers, and his hands felt protective and warm against her back. She wanted to stay like that forever.

"Wait," he whispered. "They're coming." At first she thought he was joking.

"Who's coming?" He put his finger over her mouth. She resisted the urge to kiss it. Or suck on it. That wouldn't be very proper. Suddenly his finger was gone, and he was pointing. At first all she saw were little gray mounds bobbing in and out of the water. "Dolphins," she cried. "Dolphins!" She dropped to her knees and leaned over the side of the boat. Darren knelt beside her. The dolphins were only a few feet away, watching them. Tara counted four of them. The other passengers had heard her squeals and gathered behind her. The dolphins put on a show, leaping into the air, flipping, and diving back beneath the water.

"Oh my God," Tara said. "Oh my God."

"Hold out your hand," Darren said, slipping a small fish into it. Tara held out her hand, and within seconds a dolphin teetered before her, cooed, and then took the fish right from her hand. Impulsively, Tara leaned forward and kissed the dolphin. Behind her, Tiara squealed.

"You kissed him," Nadine said. "You got your fling!" The sisters laughed between them, as only sisters could laugh.

"Your fling?" Darren said. Was he hurt? They were just getting along again. Tara turned to him. Suddenly, he kissed her.

"What was that for?" she asked.

"Why should the dolphins have all the fun?" he answered. She laughed, and he kissed her again. "I'm sorry about the other night," he said softly.

"Me too," she said. He had a faraway look on his face. "Was the present from an ex-girlfriend?" she asked without thinking. To her surprise he put his hands on her waist and pulled her closer.

"Flings," he said, "are supposed to be fun. No serious talk."

"So you still want to have a fling?"

"I promise you," Darren said. "I'm going to fling your brains out."

Chapter 11

The next day Tara announced that Darren was taking her on a romantic day trip. Nadine was not thrilled.

"The Road to Hana!" she said. "I want to go on the Road to Hana." Tara felt slightly guilty. She'd heard the Road to Hana offered jaw-dropping landscapes and soaring waterfalls. It was going to be a day filled with exploring hidden caves, private swimming holes, and hopefully each other. It was definitely not going to be a family trip.

"Do you even know what the Road to Hana is?" Tara asked. The trip involved driving for hours up a long and winding road that wove high into the mountains. Six hundred curves, and fifty-four bridges. Tara couldn't wait.

"I'm up for an adventure," Nadine said.

"The winding roads would probably make you nauseous," Tara said.

"Why would they?"

"Because you're pregnant."

"Oh," Nadine said. "Right."

"Besides, I think you and Phil should take a note from Mom and Dad's book and have a little private family fun. Ask Mom and Dad to watch Tiara for the day."

"You're right," Nadine said. "Maybe we'll go on the Road to Hana too."

"Go wherever you want," Tara said. "But if you see us, just pretend like you don't know us."

"Are you going to wear anything but that bikini this whole trip?"

"No."

Darren was a good driver. That wasn't why Tara was so nervous sitting next to him. His cologne smelled good. After a few minutes of being driven crazy by it, she asked him what it was.

"Oh, that's not me," Darren said, scratching Dog behind the ears. "It's Dog." Dog, who was sitting between them in the truck, swung his head toward her, and stared longingly into her eyes. He was even drooling a little. Tara leaned in and sniffed him. Sure enough, Dog was wearing cologne. "He knocked my bottle over this morning," Darren said. "I think he's in love." Tara laughed, and Dog barked. Tara relaxed, and gazed out at the green fields spread before her. Wildflowers flared so bright in the sun, they looked as if their tips had been set on fire. The ocean below them was framed by enormous ragged boulders. It truly was paradise. The road before them was just starting to wind and rise. "It's about to get really steep," Darren warned. "But before we go any further, I know a little spot." He pulled to the side of the road, and parked. "We have to walk from here," he said. "Are you down with that?"

"Oh yeah," Tara said. "I'm down with that."

They entered a patch of woods. The shade was soothing on Tara's hot skin. It smelled like cedar and the ocean. Parrots soared high above, conversing with each other through coded chirps and caws. It reminded her of the other day when she and Nadine had their picture taken with parrots. They were perched on their heads, their arms, and their hands. She loved Hawaii. She couldn't imagine allowing the pigeons in Central Park to do that.

It wasn't long until their path led them to a private swimming hole fueled by a towering waterfall. Tara's head buzzed from the sheer power of it. There wasn't another soul in sight. Dog was apparently immune to the awesome beauty, for he simply slipped past them and dove into the water. Tara took off her towel and flip-flops and followed. Soon thereafter, Darren dove in too. The water was warm, and felt like a gentle caress. Tara emerged, and the first face she saw, only a half-inch from hers, was Dog's.

"You're cute," she said. "But not who I was hoping to see." Suddenly she felt arms wrap around her from behind. Darren's mouth brushed her ear.

"Who were you hoping to see?" She answered by turning around and kissing him. Soon their kisses varied from soft and trailing, to insistent and hurried. Their wet hands groped and slipped down each other's bodies. Time disappeared, and Tara fully understood why they called Hawaii "The land that time forgot." The waterfall sealed them in like a privacy curtain. A multicolored parrot screeched good-bye from a branch above them, then darted across the sky. Dog grew tired of his swim and curled up on the shore where he respectfully turned away from them. Without breaking the kiss, Darren swam Tara closer to the falls. Before she knew what was happening, they were under them, water rushing over their bodies. Darren tried to keep the kiss going, but Tara started to sputter. He swam her a little further, so that they were behind the falls, encompassed within the wall of rushing water.

"Were you trying to drown me?" she joked.

Darren laughed. "Only so I could give you mouth to mouth," he said. He leaned in to practice the technique. They kissed for a long time. Then Darren pulled back, smoothed her hair, and wiped water out of her eyes. He kissed her eyelids, her cheeks, her neck.

"This is amazing," Tara said.

"You're amazing," Darren said softly. He moved in again, and this time their kiss took on more fervor, a gentle urgency that kept pace with the fever of the waterfall. Darren lifted Tara onto a large flat rock behind them, and, even though there was barely enough room for the both of them, he laid her down, then gently climbed on top of her. Their hands began exploring and caressing each other. Just as their passion was reaching the point where Tara didn't want to turn back, Darren pulled away.

"I didn't bring condoms," he said.

"Talk that love talk," Tara said.

Darren laughed. "I want you so bad," he said. "I was just thinking that our first time should be in a bed with roses and room service. But now that we're here, and I see how beautiful you look—how incredible it is here—"

"Shh," Tara said. She kissed him again. "I can wait," she said. She pulled back, looked at her wrist as if she were wearing a watch and lunged at him again. "Are you ready now?" She asked. She tickled his neck with her tongue. He tasted like salt and something a little spicy.

Darren groaned. "I've been ready," he said. "But not now. I'm getting too hot and bothered—time for Plan B."

"What's Plan B?"

Darren slid off the rock, and grabbed her ankle.

"Don't you dare," she said. He laughed and pulled her in with him. She sunk slightly, then emerged sputtering. He immediately splashed her, sending a wall of water her way. She splashed back. Dog barked from the shore, then jumped in again. They played for what seemed like ages. Tara felt joyful, like a child again. When they finally crawled out, wrapped themselves in towels, and headed back for the truck, it hit her. This was the most fun she'd ever had in her entire life.

They stopped at a little food stand and bought strawberries, and mango, and kiwis. Then Darren bought the island's famous banana bread. It was a soft, sweet bite of heaven. Tara was just thinking that her impulse to feed him a strawberry was juvenile when he reached over and popped one in her mouth. His fingers trailed her lips, and when he kissed her, his tasted like sugar. "What's so funny?" he asked when she laughed.

"I feel giddy and silly," she said. *Like a teenager in love,* she thought. Then they started up the road with Christmas carols playing on the radio, Dog, worn out, between them, half his body lying on Tara's lap. New York felt so far away, as did the restaurant, the stress, the fake Manhattan boyfriends. This was a great vacation. But soon it would all be a distant memory. She'd be back in her studio apartment, avoiding Nadine's questions about how her last date went care of Soul Mate Central, and looking for a job. Maybe she and

Darren would e-mail or talk on the phone for a while, but how long would that last? She couldn't imagine the two of them living in Manhattan; he was the type that needed a lot of space, and very little stress. Her city wouldn't offer him either. And as much as she complained about it, she couldn't quite imagine giving up Manhattan. Even for paradise.

"What are you thinking about?" Darren asked. Tara bit her lip, willing herself not to cry. It had been so long since a man wanted to know what she was thinking about. The sarcastic "what were you thinking?" that she heard from Alain all the time didn't count.

"I'm thinking how different my life is in Manhattan," Tara said.

"I couldn't even imagine."

"Have you ever been?"

"When I was a kid," Darren said. "With my mom." His hands tightened slightly on the steering wheel, his voice deepened.

"Did you have a good time?"

"We did." Again, his tone of voice implied he didn't want to talk about it any further. Talking about the mother definitely went against fling rules. Although he'd already met her entire crazy family, but not as her boyfriend—

He wasn't her boyfriend. He was an island fling. She was going to have to keep reminding herself. If he was her boyfriend, no way would she let him squiggle out of this conversation. But if he didn't want to talk about a memory, he didn't have to. So she wouldn't ask any further. A car was coming in the opposite direction. The tight curve of the road was barely big enough for one. Darren expertly pulled over a half inch, and the other car did the same. They passed with barely a breath between them.

"I'm impressed," she said. She couldn't imagine her father being able to maneuver the van so gracefully. The thought of him trying to floss and take these curves at the same time brought a smile to her face. "My parents are having a really good time on this trip," she said.

"That's great," Darren said.

Tara groaned. "And horrid. They're way too amorous for our comfort."

Darren laughed. He took her hand. "It's the island air," he said with a wink.

"Why don't you have a girlfriend?" she heard herself ask. What was she doing? Breaking all fling rules, that's what. But didn't she have a right to know? For all she knew he did have a girlfriend and she was away for Christmas.

"Why don't you have a boyfriend?" he asked.

"Because I live in New York," she answered.

"Maybe you should move," he said. He was still holding her hand. He was kidding right? Then again, he didn't say maybe you should move here—just maybe you should move. For all she knew he meant New Jersey. Maybe you should move to New Jersey.

"Maybe," she said, trying to sound nonchalant. "I can go anywhere as long as people there like to eat."

He laughed again. It filled her with a wonderful, happy feeling. She loved his laugh. She loved making him laugh.

"My legs are starting to go numb," she said. Darren whistled and Dog shot straight up.

"Sorry," Darren said, looking over at her legs. "But you can't blame the guy."

They sprawled out near Charles Lindberg's grave, and ate the lunch Tara had prepared. Darren made appreciative noises, way too appreciative. Tara prayed he would stop, for his adoration was turning her on. So she changed the subject, and talked of Lindberg's adventurous life, and the tragedy that befell him. The lesson, Tara realized, was to live your life to the fullest. Against all odds, despite all adversity. After lunch Tara was full and sleepy. They stretched out on the grass. In New York she'd be exhausted after running around the city, but this was a different type of tired—between swimming and the sun, she was tired in a floaty, happy sort of way. She fell asleep against Darren's chest. When she woke who knows how long later, he had placed a hat over her face and his shirt over her body so she wouldn't get burned. *You're very protective for a fling,* she wanted to say, but she didn't want him to take it the wrong way.

"This is the life," Tara said instead. "So peaceful. Seems so simple."

"It is so simple," Darren said.

"Not in my world," Tara said.

"It's a matter of choice," Darren said. Although it was in a gentle way, he pushed her off of him and sat up. He reached for Dog and wrapped his arms around him. "That's why it's just me and Dog," he said. "Me, Dog, my truck, my odd little jobs. Once a year the Island Pole. That's my life. Peace, baby, peace." Something about the way he was talking set off a silent alarm in Tara. He was pulling away. They hadn't even made love yet, and he was already pulling away. Why did men do this? Why were they moaning into your ear one minute and sailing out to sea the next? And what did she expect? He was a fling, a fling, a fling, a fling. Who, despite having them littered all over his yard, hadn't even thought to bring condoms. Apparently, he'd never been a Boy Scout. Suddenly, her floaty feeling came in for a crash landing.

"Do you plan on living the rest of your life this way?" she asked. The change in his eyes was immediate. Guarded.

"Something wrong with my life?" he asked.

"I can't be the judge of that," Tara said. "But we can't all shirk our responsibilities. I mean, there are days I'd love to give up—I could move here, open some little island hut, and sell gourmet meals to tourists on the go." Now why had she said that? She was being mean and spiteful; she could feel the negative energy flow through her. She was acting childish, just like Nadine. She'd picked up a beach bum after all, so why was she now trying to convert him? It's not like he was coming home with her. It's not like the fling would mean anything.

"Why don't you?" Darren said.

"Why don't I what?"

"Move here, open an island hut, sell gourmet meals to tourists."

"You're making fun."

"I certainly am not." He leaned over and kissed her on the nose. "I've tasted your gourmet meals. I think they'd be a hit." She couldn't believe it. He was acting like the mature one. She was throwing a slight fit, over nothing, and he had the nerve to rise above her. She stood up.

"You're breaking the rules of the fling you know," Tara said. Darren remained sitting.

"Excuse me?"

"You don't talk about your future and moving in together when you're having a fling."

"I wasn't talking about our future; I was talking about your future."

"Which just happens to involve moving here and setting up shop?"

"You could move to any island and set up shop,"

Darren said. He sounded logical and calm. It inflamed Tara beyond words.

"So you don't care one way or the other?" she said.

"Why would I?" This time there was a defiant catch to his voice. He stared at her, as if engaging in a contest to see who would blink first. She wished they weren't in a fight because she was dying to crawl on top of him and consummate the fling. God, he was sexy. He wasn't a pushover either. Had she misjudged him? Just when she decided she was totally the one at fault, and was about to apologize, he stood in a huff.

"I should've known from the minute you started that serial killer stuff that you were trouble."

"That wasn't me—that was my mother and my sister—"

"Same crazy gene pool." Darren swiped the empty picnic basket off the ground and started tossing the remnants of their lunch into it.

"Oh yeah? Well at least I don't keep wrapped presents around for years," Tara said. That did it. He turned and stared. She looked away first. Then, without another word, Darren headed for the truck. The descent to civilization was long, winding, and silent, anything but civilized. Even Dog didn't sit on her lap. Darren dropped her off at the bungalow.

"I'll see you at the Island Pole—"

"Forget it," he said. "I'm replacing you." She couldn't believe how much his words stung. She wanted to say something to turn it all around. She should apologize. They should run to the nearest store and get condoms. Was this her fault? Didn't he know that all day in the sun without sex could turn a woman a little crazy? They were supposed to be having fun. Earlier she'd had the best afternoon of her life. It couldn't end like this. It couldn't. Was this really all because of a Christmas present?

"Fine," Tara said. Her voice echoed through her head, hollow and sad.

"Fine," Darren said.

"I'm still coming to the luau though," Tara said. "I refuse to make twelve different kinds of mashed potatoes just to satisfy Nadine."

"The table is all yours," Darren said.

"So I guess the fling is over," Tara said. "I guess we've officially been flung."

"For once," Darren said. "We agree." A thin layer of red Hawaiian dust lifted into the air as he spun out of the driveway. Only Dog looked longingly back at her.

Chapter 12

Tara glided through the warm water. Next to her, Nadine gesticulated wildly to Tiara every time a fish swam by. Tara would have thought Tiara was too young to snorkel, but she was taking to it like—

A fish to water.

Tara laughed at the cliché. This was the life. She didn't need Darren. She was snorkeling with Santa. Unfortunately, Tiara could not have cared less about the fish passing by her little face. The fat man in the red dive suit was all Tiara was pointing at. Tara wondered if it would mess with her mind, Santa and his twelve swimmers instead of twelve reindeer. Strange to think that all of this, this trip, this life, her brief love affair, all came about because of a reindeer.

Darren was replacing her at the Island Pole. It was a relief actually, to no longer be a part of that anti-Christmas display. Even if it was a blast. Even if he did have a point about Christmas, how stressful it could be. At least they were still going to the luau. Would Darren show up? Did he have anyone to spend

Christmas Day with? Would he open his present, whoever it was from? Not that she cared.

At least their parents were still having fun. So far they didn't seem to be looking at anything but each other through their enormous goggles. What was their secret? Phil, on the other hand, was swimming like he was shackled. Poor Nadine, she was right, he was definitely not a happy camper. Nadine waved her arms at Tara, signaling they were going ashore. Sounded good to her; she'd spent precious little time on her tan. She spun around and slammed into another swimmer. Her goggles and mouthpiece slid up her face, and she struggled to right herself. The other swimmer popped up with her. It took Tara forever to finagle the goggles over her head and wipe water out of her eyes.

"Are you okay?" a male voice asked.

"Sorry about that," Tara said. Finally, her eyes cleared. Darren treaded water in front of her. He didn't seem surprised to see her, and he was looking at her with genuine concern. "Are you following me?" Tara said.

"What?" Darren said.

"You're—snorkel stalking me!"

"I'm snorkel stalking you?"

"How did you know I was here?"

"Gee—I don't know—maybe I microchipped you."

"Are you here to apologize?" Oh, please be here to apologize, she thought. She didn't want the fling to end. She was also dying to go back to the Island Pole. How could she not like it? Every evening had been filled with laughter. And Darren. Every evening had been filled with Darren.

"No," Darren said. "I'm not here to apologize." Suddenly, another swimmer popped up next to Darren. Tara was taken aback by the size of the woman's chest. In fact she was surprised the woman could swim at all. With those jugs it looked as if she would simply float. Then the woman removed her goggles, and Tara was devastated to see that she had a face that might actually encourage people to glance away from her chest.

"What happened to you?" the woman asked Darren. Then she flashed Tara a huge smile. Tara wanted to bite her.

"Just got caught in traffic," Darren said. The woman continued to smile as Tara and Darren glared at each other.

"Aren't you going to introduce us?" the woman asked.

"No," Darren said. Then he put his hand on the busty beauty's shoulder and steered her away.

"Did you see that bimbo he was with?" Tara said.

"There's something wrong with that man," Nadine said.

"Thank you."

"I mean who makes a Christmas village that won't allow children?"

"And who dates a bimbo over me, right?"

"Something must have happened to warp that man's mind," Nadine said.

"Thank you."

"I'm still talking about the village." Everyone was laid out in the condo, exhausted, full, and slightly sunburned. For once their parents were acting like normal people and barely looking at or talking to each other. Tara and Nadine were sitting on the patio watching the sun set. Nadine lifted her index finger and shook it at Tara. "I bet it has something to do with that Christmas present you found," she said. Nadine had that tone in her voice. The one that organized birthday parties, baby showers, and Christmas dinners for twelve-hundred. Tara shrugged.

"It doesn't matter," Tara said. "It's over."

"I think he's a good soul," Nadine said. "He just needs a little guardian angel to guide him."

"Nadine."

"We need to find out what's in that Christmas present."

"We need to forget about it," Tara said. "No," she revised. "We are going to forget about it. We have forgotten about it."

Nadine and Tara crouched in Darren's front yard. The darkness was starting to settle, the Christmas lights glowed, and a happy din rose from the revelers.

"It sounds like a huge party," Nadine said.

"I told you," Tara said. "It's like this every night."

"Heathens," Nadine said, craning her neck to see if she could get a look around the corner of the house.

"It's not that bad," Tara said. "I'll show you."

"Should we sneak into the house before or after?" Nadine said.

"I told you—we're not doing that. We'll tour the village, and then we're going home. I am not breaking into Darren's Christmas present."

The last time Nadine had only stayed at the Island Pole long enough to see Tara. This time she was given the full tour. They saw Santa frolicking with bikini-clad women, elves making naughty toys, and carolers singing Christmas songs with a twist. Tara was hoping the **When Reindeers ATTACK** exhibit would be closed. Instead, she'd indeed been replaced. By the snorkeling bimbo. Tara grabbed Nadine's arm.

"It's Big Boobs," she hissed into her ear. Nadine watched as the busty blonde put her wrist into the reindeer's mouth and screamed. Nadine let out a genuine laugh.

"Is that supposed to be you?" she said. "Oh God, that's funny."

"It is not funny," Tara said. She also let out a small laugh, then tried to reign it in, then laughed again. Soon she and Nadine were giggling like schoolgirls.

"Where is that man?" Nadine said. "I'm going to give him a piece of my mind."

"Excuse me," Tara said to her replacement. "Do you know where Darren is?"

"He's away somewhere," the bimbo said. She took her hand out of the reindeer's mouth, then stuck it back in and commenced screaming.

"She's very professional," Nadine said.

"It's actually the other wrist," Tara told the bimbo.

They stood in Darren's living room.

"This isn't right," Tara said.

"Look," Nadine said. "I'm a pregnant woman. Nobody would blame me for coming in to use the restroom."

"So go use it."

"And if I happen to accidentally open the door to the closet instead of the bathroom—" Nadine marched over and yanked open the closet door. The present was right where Tara first found it. Nadine dropped to the floor and began removing items from her purse like a cat burglar preparing to pop open a safe. She pulled out a pair of scissors, tape, and a pair of black gloves.

"Aren't you overdoing it a little bit?" Tara said as Nadine donned the gloves.

"They can get fingerprints off anything nowadays," Nadine said.

"And are your fingerprints in an FBI database?" Tara asked. "For what? Public displays of excessive Christmas spirit?"

"Just shut up and keep watch," Nadine said. "Is anyone coming?"

"Just a couple of elves," Tara said. Nadine glared at her. "Just do it," Tara said.

"Okay—operation open present underway." Nadine reached up, and took down the gift, then gingerly set it on the floor. She turned it over and examined every nook and cranny. Then she removed a large magnifying glass from her purse and held the present up to her enlarged eye.

"All right, Susie Sleuth," Tara said. "Hurry up." Nadine took out a letter opener. Effortlessly she sliced open the present. Tara knelt down next to her sister and peered at the contents of the gift.

"A baseball mitt?" she said as Nadine held it up.

"This wouldn't even fit my hand," Nadine said. "It's a child's mitt." A piece of paper flew out of the mitt and fluttered to the ground. "Pick it up," Nadine hissed. "Pick it up." It was a letter. "Read it," Nadine barked. "Operation read it!" Tara took a minute to pinch her sister, and then implemented Operation Read It.

> *My Dearest Darren,*
> *You are my world. I wish I could be there to hold you forever, but since I can't, let this glove wrap you in my love and warmth whenever you wear it. And don't even think of dropping out of baseball, because you are going to hit many home runs this year. I close my eyes and think of all the "catches" you will make with this glove, and all that you will accomplish in your life. You*

*are my brave, strong boy. I know you will be
sad, but you can do this. Do it for me. Be happy
for me. Live your best life for me. Merry Christmas, my darling. I know this will be difficult,
your first Christmas without me. Be brave. I
want you to be happy, and I promise you, I will
be with you always and forever, and may you
catch the whole world in your hands.*

    Merry Christmas now and forever,
        All my love,
        Your Mom (for always and forever)

Tears dripped down Tara's cheeks. Nadine was crying too, and making little gasps after each sentence.
They read it again.

"He's never read this," Nadine said. "He never
even opened it."

"We shouldn't have either," Tara said. "I can't believe we've done this."

"Are you freaking kidding me?" Nadine said. "We
were guided to open this."

"Guided?"

"By his mother," Nadine whisper-yelled, pointing
at the ceiling. "She wanted us to find this so we can
get Blockhead to finally open it and stop perverting
Christmas!" Nadine was practically glowing, a fever-
ish twinkle sparked out of her tear-filled eyes. "Did
he grow up without a father too?"

"I don't know."

"She doesn't mention him. I'll bet he did. He was
an orphan."

"Like Pip," Tara said.

"What?"

"Nothing. Hurry and wrap it back up."

"We have to do something."

"We will. Just—wrap it." A door slammed behind

them. It sounded like a gunshot. Tara and Nadine whipped their heads around. The bimbo stood in the doorway. Her giant boobs glowed in the aftermath of the Christmas lights.

"You could light Santa's sleigh with those babies," Tara whispered to Nadine.

"What are you doing?" the woman asked.

"Just looking for the bathroom," Nadine called out. "I'm pregnant."

"Oh," the blonde said. She pointed. "It's down the hall."

"Thank you," Nadine said.

"Do you mind if I use it first," the blonde continued. "I'm on duty."

"Go right ahead," Nadine said.

"Thank you, thank you, thank you." She wiggled her way past them and down the hall. Tara tried not to stare at her perfect ass.

"She's living up to the stereotype," Nadine said with a sad shake of her head.

"Shut up and wrap," Tara said.

Tara and Nadine, who couldn't imagine what it would be like to be orphaned so young, went home and loved on their parents until they broke free and locked themselves in their room. At Tara's suggestion, Nadine and Phil went for a walk on the beach. Tara prayed they would be able to work things out. They didn't hold hands on the way out, and Tara tried not to worry about what that meant. She felt guilty for allowing Nadine to open Darren's present, but she also felt as if she knew him better now. So much for his bravado about stress relief and making people laugh. He didn't like Christmas because of a childhood wound. Not that Tara could blame him. She couldn't imagine losing anyone, let alone a mother at that time of year. Maybe Nadine was right. Maybe they were being guided to help him. But how? What could they do about it? She decided to send him a text.

> I'm sorry. I heard you were away.
> Is everything okay?

Her hands were sweating when she pushed SEND. Would he answer? Where was he? She even missed Dog. It was almost Christmas Eve. It was all going so fast. She heard a bang on the wall and jumped clear off the couch. Horrified, she stared at the shut door from whence it came. From behind the wall came the unmistakable sound of a mattress creaking followed by the headboard banging into the wall. Tara ran out to the patio to escape. Who would have known her parents would be the only ones ending up getting their island freak on?

She found herself back at the Island Pole. She wouldn't dare tell Nadine but she missed the fun. From the side of the house she watched the people laugh. She stared at her phone. There was no reply from Darren. She couldn't believe how much she missed him. Her blond replacement was leaving her post and headed to the house.

"Hello," Tara called out.

"Oh hey," the blonde said. "I'm just taking a break. This job is so hard." Tara laughed until she saw that the woman was serious.

"I can finish your shift if you want," Tara said.

"Really?"

"I am the originator of the role."

"Huh?"

"Never mind. I'd be happy to do it."

"You're on, sister. I have a hot date."

A lead ball dropped in Tara's stomach. "Oh," she said. "With Darren?"

"Darren?" the blonde squealed. "I've tried with that one—it's a lost cause!"

"Why is that?"

"Because he's not the dating type—he's the relationship type." Joy spread through Tara. Just then a text message beeped through.

No apologies necessary. See you at the luau?

It was a sign. And this time, she wasn't going to mess it up.

Chapter 13

It was Nadine who suggested the trip to Haleakala volcano on the east side of Maui. Tara was dying to tell Nadine what she'd heard about Darren, but she was making a conscious effort to think about someone other than herself. She also wanted to find out how Nadine and Phil's stroll on the beach went, and vowed not to talk about herself until she found out. The volcano was located in the Haleakala National Park, a beautiful trip away from the ocean up to the heights of the clouds, where hiking and the breathtaking sights of the volcano awaited them. Again, Tara couldn't help but notice that Phil and Nadine weren't holding hands, or looking lovingly into each other's eyes like their parents were. Tiara was fussy too, and Tara felt an ever growing burden to be cheery. She knew the real reason she was in such a good mood was that it had been crossing her mind in recent hours that if Darren wasn't the fling type, and had been willing to get involved with her, then he must really like her. And his abrupt change toward her was further proof of this. Not that she knew the solution. She still lived in New York, and he lived here. They arrived at the park, piled out of the car, and headed for the crater.

Joe Versus the Volcano, Tara thought as they skirted the edges. First, their parents disappeared. Being used to it, and too tired from hiking to care anyway, nobody sent out a search party. Then, the fight started. Tara was following around after Tiara, who was toddling after a bug, when Nadine and Phil started bickering. So much for a reconciliation. The next thing she knew, Phil was scooping Tiara up and whisking her away.

"You deal with your sister," he said to Tara. "I for one am dropping out of Christmas this year."

"You can't drop out of Christmas," Nadine yelled. "There's no dropping out of Christmas!"

"Watch me," Phil said.

"What about your daughter? She wants Christmas!"

"She's two, Nadine. She wants to follow a bug around a volcano." Tara thought he had a point there, but she wisely kept her mouth shut. Phil started to walk away with Tiara.

"I'm not pregnant," Nadine yelled. Phil stopped dead. Slowly, he turned around.

"Were you ever?" he asked. Nadine slowly shook her head no.

"I didn't think so," he said.

"You knew?"

"I suspected."

"Why didn't you say anything?"

"Why were you lying to me?"

"Because I was trying to save us."

"By making up a baby?"

"It was crazy, I know. But you've been so distant

lately, so cold. I thought if you thought I was having a baby, you would stay."

"What do you mean? Where did you think I was going?"

"To live with your girlfriend, maybe?"

"My what?"

"Come on, Phil. Just tell me. Are you having an affair?"

"Are you serious? Is that what you really think?"

"I don't know what to think anymore. For all I know you're screwing an elf at the mall!"

Phil threw up his arms and shook his head. "I am not screwing an elf at the mall," he said. "Or anyone else."

"Then, what? Why have you been acting so weird?"

"It's you, okay?"

"What about me?"

"Your endless events, and decorating, and planning dinners, and sending Christmas cards, and stringing lights, and buying presents, and making Christmas cookies, and stringing Christmas popcorn, and rehearsing plays, and taking Christmas pictures, and playing Bing Crosby until I want to puke, and the list goes on and on and on."

"But—it's Christmas!"

"I know. I know it's Christmas. But it's too much and, the truth is, I've grown to hate it. And once a year—from about Halloween to New Year's, I hate you!" Nadine gasped. "I'm sorry, honey," Phil said. "But Tara's right. You're a Holiday Hitler."

Tara froze. She prayed for the volcano to erupt, wrap her in boiling lava, and nuke her like a microwaved burrito. But it remained still, and silent. But not as still and silent as Nadine. Phil must have seen it too, for he finally stopped talking. "I'm sorry, honey," he said. "I just—just once—wanted us to have a nice, relaxing holiday." But Nadine wasn't listening. She was walking away. Headed straight for the mouth of the volcano.

Tara followed her sister, hoping to steer her away from the edge. If anyone was going to plummet to her death, it should be her. When she caught up with Nadine, she saw that she was crying.

"You—you called me a Holiday Hitler?"

"Once," Tara said. "I called you that once. I'm so sorry."

"When?"

"It doesn't matter—"

"When?"

"Uh. That year that all the Christmas cards had to feature Santa with a child on his lap, the uh, presents had to be wrapped in green paper with red bows or you said they wouldn't be opened, and uh—we were forced to wear a Christmas-themed sweater at the dinner table, or, or, we couldn't eat." Nadine nodded solemnly. Then, she crumpled over.

"I'm a horrible person!" Nadine cried.

"You're not a horrible person." Tara wrapped her arms around her sister. "In fact I was glad I got a chance to wear that sweater." Nadine stopped her with a look.

"I told him I was pregnant," Nadine said.

"People do crazy things when they're stressed." Tara rubbed Nadine's back. "We all know you mean well," she said.

"That's why you came here for Christmas," Nadine sobbed. "You were running away from me."

"No," Tara said. "I was being selfish. You're the one who gave up all your plans and traditions to spend it with me. That doesn't sound like a horrible person, now does it?"

"Well, I've learned my lesson," Nadine said. "I hate Christmas. Christmas sucks!" Some Japanese tourists stopped to take their picture. Nadine gave them the finger. Tara quickly hid Nadine's hand in hers and waved to the group with a big, fake, smile.

"You have to hang on to your joy no matter what," Tara said. "You have a right to enjoy Christmas. You have to keep it alive for all of us, like Darren's mom tried to keep it alive for him."

"But it didn't work," Nadine said. "He never even opened the gift! He turned into a Christmas pervert. Life sucks. Christmas sucks!"

"All right, all right," Tara said, putting her arm around her sister and steering her home. "Let's go get a drink. And no more nonalcoholic stuff for you."

"Can I still drink for two?" Nadine sniffed.

"Absolutely," Tara said. "Absolutely."

"I didn't mean to destroy all her Christmas spirit," Phil said. He paced back and forth on the patio. "She's in there telling Tiara there's no Santa Claus!"

"Tiara will forget all about it," Tara said. "I have an idea."

"I love her," Phil said. "I just—sometimes she's so—"

"I know, I know."

"But this anti-Christmas Nadine is a thousand times worse."

"Who would have known," Tara said. Nadine was in the process of removing every Christmas decoration from the condo. The radio wasn't allowed to play carols; the tree was stripped of lights and popcorn; she was threatening to find and unwrap all gifts. She was even talking of skipping the luau, and ordering a pizza on Christmas. It was only when she said—

"And I'm going to the Island Pole tonight, and I'm going to laugh my ass off!" that Tara knew what she had to do.

Luckily, with Darren gone, it was easy enough to persuade the other volunteers. She laid it on thick, telling them a small woman's sanity was at stake. "Just once," she said. "Just one time—it's Christmas Eve—please." They finally agreed. They would have to shut the Island Pole down for a few hours in order to clean it up. Meanwhile, they would send volunteers around to announce that this evening the village would be G-rated, and all the children on the island were welcome. Tonight, it would be the "North Pole," and there wouldn't be a whiskey bottle or red lacey bra in sight. One of the volunteers said her child sang in a chorus, and they were quickly booked for the evening. To Tara's surprise, all the "actors" were for it. Even the Santas, who everyone agreed had the most fun, were for it. When they were done, and the lights came on, and the children started to sing, and all the elves were keeping their hands out of their pants, even Tara had a tear in her eye. The lights glowed, the children held candles and sang like angels, and Tara felt something very much like joy.

They blindfolded Nadine and brought her through. Word had spread quickly, and the line to get in was four times as long as Tara had ever seen it. This time the laughter that ran through the village was mixed with a sense of wonderment. This was stress relief too, Tara thought. She just wished Darren were here to see it. Would he be angry? Nadine and Phil held hands as they immersed themselves in Tiara's amazement. The sparkle was back in Nadine's eyes. Things were going to be all right.

"Thank you," Phil said to Tara. He leaned down and kissed Nadine.

"Thank you," Nadine whispered.

"You're welcome," Tara said. *"Mele kalikimaka."*

"Now for *your* surprise," Phil said. He turned to Nadine. "Tell her your plan, Nadine."

"Not another plan," Tara groaned. Then she remembered, they were trying to make Nadine feel better. "Yea," Tara said with forced enthusiam. "Another plan." Nadine laughed.

"I think you're going to like this one." Tara listened as Nadine explained her idea. When she was finished, Tara's eyes were filled with tears. "Do you like it?" Nadine said.

"No," Tara said. "I love it."

"Do you mean that?" Nadine asked. Tara crossed her heart. Nadine wrapped her sister in a hug.

"We'd better hurry," Phil said, "Darren is on his way."

Darren and Dog stood at the threshold of the village. Tara ran toward them, and before he could say a word, she threw herself into Darren's arms and kissed him. He kissed her back without hesitating, and it wasn't until Dog barked that they pulled away. Tara took Darren's hand, and they walked among the visitors, reveling in the glitter, the song, the laughter. Finally, they reached Santa.

"I'm not sitting on his lap," Darren said as Tara stood waiting.

"He has something for you," Tara said. Darren looked at Santa, who was for the first time in a decade not smoking a cigar; instead, he was holding a medium-sized box wrapped in gold paper and topped with a red bow. Darren stared at it. "Go on," Tara said. "You can do it."

Darren took the gift, and looked at Tara. "I don't know if I—" Tara walked up, and put her hand on top of his.

"It's time," she said. "It's time." Darren nodded and moved slightly away from the crowd. Tara respectfully turned away as he opened it.

"A mitt," she heard him say. "It's a mitt." Tara turned to him. Tears welled in the corners of his eyes as he held the glove to his heart.

"There's a letter," Tara said softly. She held it out to him.

"I can't," Darren said. "Will you?" Slowly, softly, Tara read the letter. Darren put the glove on. It only covered the tips of his fingers. He pulled Tara into his arms. "Thank you," he said. Dog nuzzled Tara's ankles.

"You're making Dog jealous," Tara said.

"You mean Nick," Darren said. "I'm calling him Nick."

"As in Saint Nick?"

"No," Darren said. "You're the saint. He's just Nick."

"Believe me," Tara said. "I'm no saint."

"That's okay," Darren whispered into her ear. "Sinners are still welcome here too."

When everyone had gone home, and the last of the Christmas lights went quiet, Tara and Darren lay underneath the large palm tree in the backyard, and held each other. "So," he said. "Now that we've cleaned this village up, I don't suppose I'm allowed to take advantage of you." His lips brushed her neck, his hands slid up her waist. Seconds later, Frosty was once again covered in a lacey red bra. Darren pulled

condoms out of his pocket. "You did not buy red condoms," Tara said.

"Where's your Christmas spirit?" Darren said. She
laughed. He smothered her mouth with kisses. Then
finally, with Frosty watching, they flung themselves
to their hearts' content.

The table overflowed with food. Red and green leis
adorned everyone's neck. Champagne and music
poured out with abandon. Their parents danced the
hula. Nadine and Phil kissed without mistletoe. Nadine looked more relaxed than Tara had ever seen her.
It was as if they were all under a spell. Later, on the
beach, as the sun was setting, Darren pulled her close
to him. "Stay," he whispered. Dog obediently sat at
his side. Darren laughed. "I wasn't talking to you,
Nicky boy," he said.

Epilogue

One year later

    Dear Friends and Family,
    I wish I could write you all individually. Wouldn't I love to have that kind of time! We are spending Christmas in Maui again this year with my sister Tara. We're happy to announce that our darling Tiara is runner-up in Little Miss Visiting Hula. Phil and I will be renewing our marriage vows at this year's Christmas luau.
    Now on to some exciting news. As you read in my autumn newsletter, Tara and Darren have been splitting their time between the Big Apple and the Big Coconut, as Tara likes to call Maui. But my dear sister has finally chosen her forever fruit, for Tara's restaurant will be opening in Maui on January second. And even though we know she's going to be wildly successful dishing up her creative culinary concoctions, we're all still hoping that Santa will bring us an engagement this year. . . .

Tara put the letter down and just laughed. "She hasn't totally changed," she said. "But I wouldn't want her to." Darren had a sneaky smile on his face. "What? Why are you smiling?" Darren didn't answer. Instead, he held out a Christmas present. It was the size of a small book. It was wrapped in golden paper and topped with a red bow. Tara opened it.

"Great Expectations!" she said. "Oh my God—is this a first edition?" The book looked old and worn.

"Not exactly," Darren said. "Go on." Tara opened the book. It had been hollowed out. In the center sat a small, velvet box. Tears in her eyes, Tara looked at Darren.

"You know this goes against all rules of our fling," Tara said.

"It's been a year," Darren said. "Will you please stop calling this a fling?"

"Okay," Tara said. "I'll upgrade us."

"Great," Darren said. "Now open it."

Gently, she opened the box and stared.

"It's a dog bone," she said.

"Well, give it to him," Darren said. Tara rolled her eyes, but took the bone and knelt down to give it to Nick. His collar was sparkling. A diamond ring dangled from his nametag.

"You're a weirdo," Tara said. She removed the ring and stood up.

"Is that a yes?" She smiled, handed Darren the ring, and held out her hand. He slipped it on her finger.

"Now this is a Christmas to remember," she said as she stared down at it.

"Just wait until you see what I have in mind for New Year's," Darren said. Tara leaned in for a kiss. Darren pulled back. "Where's your mistletoe?" he demanded.

"Right here," Tara said, pointing to her heart. "Right here." And this time, when she leaned in for a kiss, there was no stopping her.

"A Cedar Key Christmas"

TERRI DuLONG

For Shawn, my Christmas gift of December 16, 1966
All my love

ACKNOWLEDGMENTS

I'm grateful to all of the people in Cedar Key for continuing to inspire me with a sense of place.

Heartfelt thanks to Bonnie Lee Thomas, the Yarn Works gals in Gainsville, the Tuesday Morning Book Club in Quincy, Washington, all of my Facebook fans, and every single reader that sends support and encouragement. It means everything to me!

Wishing you a blessed and joyful holiday season!

Chapter 1

"Orli," I hollered, racing through the house like a category three hurricane. "Have you seen my knitting bag?"

Lifting up toss pillows from the sofa and kneeling down to peek under chairs, I turned around to the sound of my daughter's voice.

"In the golf cart," she stated.

My knitting bag was in the golf cart? Oh, Lord, that's right . . . I'd placed it there that morning so I wouldn't forget where it was.

I threw my eleven-year-old daughter a grateful smile. "Thanks, honey. I'm running late for the knitting group at Spinning Forward. Carrie should be here any second," I said, racing toward my room to grab a sweater, with Orli close on my heels.

"But, Mom," she pleaded. "I wanted to tell you . . ."

"Not now, sweetie. I just don't have the time."

Coming back into the family room I saw that Carrie had arrived. A high school senior, she was very reliable staying with my daughter on the few occasions

I needed a sitter. "Hey, Carrie," I said in greeting. "I'll be back by nine. With only a week left till the Christmas sale at school, we have to get the knitted dishcloths finished."

"But, Mama," Orli said, clutching her twenty pound Maine coon cat and following me to the door. "I told you I had something I have to tell you."

I leaned over to kiss her cheek and give Clovelly a pat between his ears. "Oh, right," I said, inching toward the door as I recalled Orli mentioning something about this after supper. Although I was willing to listen while I cleared the table, filled the dishwasher, and folded a load of towels that had sat in the dryer for two days, Orli wanted my full and undivided attention . . . something I hadn't been able to give her for a few months.

When the economy went south, I'd been forced to take on more hours waitressing at Cook's Café, and recently I'd begun cleaning for two extra clients. Being a single mom wasn't easy, but I wouldn't trade it for anything. Despite my parents' objections and even some interference from Grant, Orli's father, from the moment I found out I was pregnant, I knew the route that I would take . . . and it wouldn't be abortion, adoption, or marriage. When the test strip showed a plus sign and a doctor confirmed my pregnancy in May, I only had a few weeks left to finish my first year as a journalism major at Emerson College in Boston—which is what I did. And then I came home to Cedar Key, Florida, to build a life for my daughter and myself.

"Honey, I'll be home from knitting by nine. It's Friday night, and you'll still be up, so we can talk then, okay? I really have to get to the knit shop. You know how important it is that we finish those dishcloths for the kids to buy."

My daughter's arms went around me in a tight embrace, and I heard her say, "Okay, I love you."

"Bye," I hollered to Carrie as I raced down the steps to the golf cart parked in the driveway. "Love you too," I told Orli and said a silent thank you for the best daughter in the world.

Jumping into the golf cart, I put the key in the ignition, glanced at the battery indicator, and groaned. "Oh, shit!" I'd forgotten to charge the battery. Thank God it was only a short walk down Second Street to the yarn shop.

I walked in to find the ladies busy at work. Monica looked up. "Oh, Josie, we weren't sure you were coming. I'm glad you could make it."

I took a seat beside Polly on the sofa. "Sorry I'm late. I was interviewing with another possible client for cleaning and got way behind in everything."

"Not a problem," Miss Dora said. "Would you like some tea?"

"No. Thanks anyway." I reached into my bag and removed the brightly colored lace pattern dishcloth I was working on.

Every year, a few weeks before Christmas, Cedar Key School held a Christmas sale for the children to purchase inexpensive gifts for their family members. The new items were either donated by community residents or were purchased with money that had been donated. Small, but meaningful gifts that the children could purchase for a minimal price. Our knitting group always donated hand-knitted items, and this year it was dishcloths for the mothers.

"You're taking on another cleaning job?" Miss Dora questioned. "My goodness, do you have any time for yourself to relax?"

I sighed as I concentrated on my yarn overs and slipping stitches. "Not at the moment, and lately I'm feeling like I'm on a road to nowhere. All the hours and hard work I put in working for other people, yet financially I can't seem to get ahead. For the first time in eleven years that college degree that I tossed away is looking mighty good."

"Well, I know it's a touchy subject with you, Josie, but . . . you know that if you asked your mama for some help, she'd be more than happy to do so."

"You're right," I snapped. "It *is* a touchy subject, Miss Polly."

"So," Polly said, clearing her throat as her needles clicked away. "Did y'all hear about the latest upheaval with Mr. Al's house?"

I now recalled that Orli had mentioned Mr. Al's name earlier when she said she needed to talk to me.

"No. What's going on now?" I felt a tad of remorse for being abrupt with Polly, but my mother's success and her disappointment in me wasn't a subject I enjoyed discussing.

Albert Casey was in his early seventies, and I'd known him from the time I was a child. Never married, a fisherman, and not overly sociable, Mr. Al—as he was known to the locals—had lived with his mother until her death a few years before. He remained in the same house after she died, but became not only a recluse but very eccentric. Over the years his front yard filled up with a broken boat, pieces of plywood, fishing nets, an old-fashioned wringer washing machine—anything and everything that never made its way to the dump. For the most part, locals were used to it. Mr. Al didn't bother anybody and besides, much of it was hidden by the huge oak trees surrounding his property. But every now and again, somebody would complain and attempt to get something done. Over time, it was forgotten and nothing changed.

"Well, it seems a *group* has now gotten together, and they've put it on the agenda for a City Commission meeting in January."

This sounded serious. Mr. Al's debris had never turned legal before.

"You've got to be kidding," Dora said. "Gosh, why can't people just leave that poor soul alone? He doesn't cause any trouble. That's just how Cedar Key is—we have million dollar homes and we have trailers." She let out a giggle. "I think that's why people say we're a funky island."

I laughed. Dora was right. Like me, she'd been born and raised here. But Miss Dora was in that older segment. She was in her early seventies like Mr. Al and had never left the island. Many of the younger generations either left for college and only returned for visits or didn't return permanently until they retired. Of course, some of those in my early-thirties age group had stayed on after high school.

Grace looked up from her needles. "You know, that's just it. If somebody marches to the tune of a different drummer, people feel the need to make that person conform. I'll never understand that. Whatever happened to a live and let live attitude?"

I could certainly relate to that; I remembered the pressure put on me by both Grant and my parents to marry. It just made no sense to me. Yes, I loved him as one loves during their first serious romance, but Grant was graduating from Harvard Business School a few weeks after I found out I was pregnant and had plans to continue on for his master's degree. What purpose would it have served for him to drop out to rent an apartment and support a wife and baby? None. And after many hours of discussion, Grant finally came to agree with my decision under certain conditions—that he would be completely involved in Orli's life right from the beginning; that he would support her financially and emotionally; that we would work out amicable and realistic visitation based on her age. I agreed to all of it, and, eleven years later, with Grant living north of Boston, despite our deviation from the norm, it worked well for us.

"Well, if it isn't enough that the City Commission is going to review the complaints," Polly related, "Mr. Al's nephew is coming down to get involved. Heard he booked a room at the Faraway Inn."

"What?" I said, dropping my knitting in my lap. I recalled Ben Sudbury from his summer visits to the island when we were teens. He was about three years older than I was and never failed to let us *kids* know how bored he was spending an entire summer on an island off the coast of Florida. His mother, Miss Annie, kept her sense of family closeness and responsibility after she left Cedar Key to attend college in New York. When she married a physician a few years after graduating and settled in Manhattan, Annie Sudbury still returned to her roots every chance she got—which was something that her only child showed no interest in when he moved out of his parents' home for college.

"You mean to tell me that Mr. Wonderful is actually going to bother coming down here to visit his uncle? He hasn't been here for ten years, since his mother's funeral. Why the heck is he coming now?" Yeah, okay, so I might not have the best relationship with my mother, but I sure wouldn't go ten years without being in touch. Family *was* family, after all.

Polly cleared her throat before speaking, not making eye contact with any of us. "I'm afraid he's coming down to put Mr. Al in a nursing home and put the house up for sale," she said softly.

"What?" our four voices chorused, as we all began talking at once.

"Well, that's just downright silly," Dora said. "Al's about my age, and we're certainly not nursing home material."

"Mr. Al might be considered a bit odd," Grace added, "but whenever he's dropped by my coffee shop, I've never seen signs of mental instability or thought he was a safety risk living on his own."

"That's right," Monica chimed in. "Adam told me just last week that he bumped into Mr. Al walking downtown with his dog. Seems they had a very enjoyable conversation about world events."

I gripped my knitting needles tighter as the unfairness of the situation hit me. "Right. Put Mr. Al in a nursing home, and you may as well take away the air he breathes. After all the years he spent out there on the water fishing for his livelihood, there's no way he could be cooped up in a two by four room on the mainland."

We debated the subject for the next two hours as we continued to knit away on the Christmas dishcloths, but by the time 9:00 arrived we were no closer to a solution that would help Mr. Al.

Walking home along the quiet downtown area, I let out a deep sigh. Not for the first time, I felt fortunate to have been born and raised on Cedar Key and even more fortunate to now have the opportunity to raise my own daughter here.

I stopped for a few moments along First Street to gaze up at a million glittering stars. There was no light pollution on the island, and it was such a gift to be able to glance up and see the beauty of the night sky.

When I walked in my front door I was disappointed

to hear Carrie inform me that Orli just couldn't keep her eyes open beyond 8:15 and had gone to bed. I'd been looking forward to spending some quality time with my daughter—something we hadn't done in a while. A ripple of guilt surged through me as I realized that I was the cause of this.

With Christmas around the corner and money tighter than usual, I'd been working a lot of extra hours lately. I knew my parents or Grant would provide the iPod and various other items Orli had on her list this year, but I wanted to be the one to give her what she wanted.

After I paid Carrie and thanked her, fatigue began setting in. I tiptoed into my daughter's room and saw her sleeping soundly, Clovelly curled up at her side. Leaning over, I kissed the top of her head and whispered, "Good night, baby. I love you."

Shutting off lights around the house and preparing for bed, I vowed to do better over the weekend spending time with my eleven-year-old.

Chapter 2

I awoke to the aroma of toast and bacon. Rolling over in bed, I was shocked to see the digital clock read 8:35. It had been ages since I'd slept beyond 6:30. Stretching my arms above my head, I let out a loud yawn. Orli wasn't allowed to turn on the stove without my being awake, but she was a pro at using the toaster, microwave, and coffee maker. I got up and followed the scent of Maxwell House to the kitchen.

There was my daughter sitting at the table, munching on toast and bacon, a book propped against the sugar bowl. I smiled at how grown-up she looked, and that's when it hit me that her twelfth birthday was three days after Christmas. God! I'd been so busy I hadn't given it a thought.

Walking over, I placed a kiss on the top of her head. "Good morning, sweetie, and thanks for making the coffee. But why'd you let me sleep so late?"

"Because I know you've been working a lot, and you're tired."

I smiled as I reached for a mug and poured myself

a steaming cup of dark brown liquid—nice and strong, just the way I liked it.

"How'd I get so lucky by getting the best daughter in the whole entire world?" I asked and joined her at the table.

Without missing a beat, she replied, "Because I have the best mom in the whole entire world."

My smile broadened. We'd been reciting this exchange from the time Orli began talking. I made no secret of it—she was my best friend, my buddy, my everything. I had a relationship with her that I never seemed to be able to manage with my own mother.

As if reading my mind, Orli said, "Oh, Grandma called last night while you were at the yarn shop."

"And?" My mother was a drama queen and always had some catastrophe going on. In reality, she's a romance writer. Yes, really. Over the years I've gotten used to people either gushing over this fact or being bewildered by it. Actually, she's quite successful across the country, and the name *Shelby Sullivan* is fairly well-known among women readers. She began writing the month she took me home from the hospital, and by the time I was four-years-old, she'd secured a contract with a New York publisher, and the rest is history.

"She wanted to remind you to make sure that I'm appropriately dressed to go for lunch and shopping with her in Gainesville this afternoon."

I shook my head and then gulped some coffee before letting out a deep sigh. "Darn, I was all set to send you off wearing a polka dot bikini, hip boots, and a tiara."

Orli giggled. "Sometimes I get the feeling that Grandma thinks you're still my age."

"Hmm, either that or she just can't resist controlling every situation like she does in her novels." I got up to refill my coffee cup. "Okay, enough about Grandma. I'll have you at her house by twelve noon. Tell me what it was you wanted to talk about yesterday."

An expression of concern crossed my daughter's face.

"Well . . . it's about Mr. Al," she said. "Some of the kids at school are being mean to him. When we walk past his house on our way home, they throw trash and junk over his fence into the yard, and then they yell 'here's some more stuff for the Cedar Key dump,' and that's not right. He came out yesterday yelling and screaming at them, said he was gonna call the cops if they didn't stop, so Danny yelled back that it wouldn't matter because pretty soon Mr. Al would be in a nursing home and his house would be gone. Is that true, Mom? Did you hear anything about that?"

From the moment my daughter was born, I made a promise that I would raise her much differently from the way it had been with my mother and me. Orli and I would be able to tell each other anything, and we'd always be open and honest.

"As a matter of fact, Miss Polly mentioned this at the yarn shop last night."

"So it's true?"

"I don't know about that. All I know is that some people have complained about the condition of Mr. Al's property, and his nephew is supposed to be coming down here to see about putting him in a nursing home. Even though Mr. Al is a little odd, he's of sound mind, and I don't see how it's possible to force somebody to sell his home and go to a nursing home."

"And what would happen to Pal?" my daughter asked, distress now covering her face.

Pal had been a stray that adopted Mr. Al. The dog had showed up at his back door a few weeks after Al's mother passed away.

"Hmm, I'm not sure, honey."

"Well, this just isn't fair," Orli stated. "Mr. Al doesn't bother anybody. He's lived here all his life, and he'd be so lost without his dog."

I nodded and had to agree.

"So," my daughter said with emphasis as she stood up to begin clearing her breakfast plates from the table, "I'll just have to figure out something we can do to stop this."

"Orli, sometimes things happen that we just don't have any control over. This might be one of those times."

She turned around from the dishwasher to face me. "You've always told me nobody makes anything happen for us. We have to do it ourselves. You said it might not always be easy. Okay. So now I have to figure out a way that Mr. Al can keep his house and not go to a nursing home."

It became abundantly clear to me that not only had my daughter been listening to me over twelve years, but maybe she'd been *listening* a little too closely.

At precisely twelve noon we pulled up in front of my parents' house. The home where I'd grown up was situated on the west end of the island. The huge, two-story, brick house sat by itself on a point overlooking the water. Surrounded by a wrought iron fence with fenials and two acres of oak and cedar trees, the house and property were impressive any time of the year, but during the Christmas season, they became spectacular. Large, red velvet bows were spaced six inches apart around the perimeter of the fence. Life-size statues of Santa, his sleigh, and reindeer stood just inside on the right, along with an animated winter village scene, complete with an electric train chugging its way through the village blowing smoke and tooting a horn. On the left, a four-foot-high nativity scene displayed Mary, Joseph, baby Jesus, and the wisemen, along with various realistic-looking donkeys, sheep, and camels.

My mother had begun this tradition when I was in first grade and felt it was her special way of saying Merry Christmas to the island. But it didn't take long, thanks to word of mouth, for families to start coming from the mainland to see what was spectacular during the day become magical at dark with a myriad of Christmas lights twinkling on the house and property.

Leaning over, I pushed the intercom button to gain entrance.

"Yes? Can I help you?" Miss Delilah's voice floated out to us.

"It's us," I told my mother's housekeeper.

"Ah, very good, Miss Josie," she said, as the tall, decorative, iron gate slid open.

I maneuvered my golf cart along the path bordered by patches of bright red hibiscus, pink azaleas, and cassia trees in full bloom of yellow flowers leading to the circular driveway. Flanking the steps of the wide veranda were huge ceramic pots of blood red poinsettias.

I recalled the year I spent in Boston at college and how when November arrived, my northern classmates looked at me with pity. One certainly couldn't get the true *feeling* of Christmas, they thought, in a southern climate, where some years the temperature hovered at eighty. I quickly discovered that Floridians seemed to

go above and beyond when it came to decorating, as if
to prove that snow, ice, and cold weren't what defined
the season as *festive.*

"All of it looks great again," Orli said, as we got
out of the golf cart and headed up the front steps.

I nodded and realized we hadn't been to my parents'
house since the decorations had been completed—no
doubt I'd probably hear about that.

"Girls," my mother said, opening the door wide.
"How nice to *finally* see you."

One point for me.

"Hi, Grandma," Orli told her, while being pulled
into an embrace. "I know, and I'm sorry. I've been
pretty busy with school stuff lately. I've missed you
and Grandpa, and I'm really looking forward to
spending a lot of time with you when we start vacation in a few weeks."

My daughter—ever the diplomat, attempting to
keep peace between my mother and me.

"That will be nice. Come see the tree and decorations," she told us, leading the way from the foyer into
the large family room with a view of the Gulf.

"Oh, Mom, it's gorgeous," I said, stepping over the
threshold and taking in the eight-foot-tall cedar tree
whose top branch touched the ceiling and held a
blinking star. I never failed to wonder how year after
year my mother managed to find a tree with such perfection, a cedar tree grown right on the island. The
branches fell in symmetry, displaying a thick gold
garland, red and white beads, treasured glass ornaments, and Victorian ribbon and bows. Even in day-
light my mother kept the white fairy lights turned on,
creating a cozy atmosphere.

"I think it gets prettier every year," Orli told her,
walking over to inspect various decorations.

I had to give my mother credit. She could easily

hire somebody to do all of the work, but she wouldn't think of it. For as long as I could remember, she would finish her final manuscript for the year in mid-October, and come November first she considered herself on holiday from anything book-related until January 8. Her time was devoted to decorating, baking, cooking, shopping, and gift wrapping.

"A winter wonderland," I said, my gaze going to a table filled with the Dickens Collection Village. Another circular table near the window was covered with a gold tablecloth and held an assortment of decorative nutcrackers that my mother had purchased on trips to Europe. The mantel above the fireplace was draped with thick, green boughs of spruce, and red candles were placed strategically around the room. All of it done in exquisite taste and style. I *did* love Christmas—it had always been my favorite holiday and even more so the year I gave birth to my daughter.

My warm mood was broken when I heard my mother say, "Lord, Josie, couldn't you have dressed a little better on a Saturday?"

I glanced down at my faded cropped pants, stained sweatshirt, and worn Reeboks that probably should have been tossed in the trash months ago. With no makeup on and my pixie-style short hair needing a shampoo, I knew I was the complete opposite of my mother who stood there perfectly made up, her auburn chin-length hair sporting a perky cut. She was wearing a pair of black Liz Clairborne slacks and a red cashmere pullover. I had to give my mother credit in this department too—she was one of those women who always looked good and certainly didn't look a few years shy of sixty. But instead of complimenting her, I let my anger kick in. "Oh, well, excuse me! I was told to be sure *my daughter* was dressed appropriately. I didn't think it was necessary to be clad in designer clothes to drive her over here. Besides, I have two cleaning jobs this afternoon."

"Oh, Josie, you're working again today?" was my mother's response.

"Well, yeah, some of us have been hit pretty hard with this economy, and Christmas is just around the corner."

My mother adjusted an ornament on the tree. "I hate to say it again, but . . ."

"Then don't," I retorted.

"You were a journalism major in college just like I was," she said, ignoring my request. "So much potential. You could have married Grant and had a much different life—probably could have returned to finish your degree after Orli was born, worked part-time as a reporter, and . . ."

"Mom, *please!* Enough. We've been through this a million times. That was twelve years ago—let go of it. It was my choice and my life, not *yours*. And I've never regretted that choice for a second."

I saw the raised eyebrows on Orli's face as she threw me a smile. She'd witnessed this conversation so many times, she probably knew it verbatim.

Walking toward her, I pulled her into a tight embrace. "Have fun at lunch and shopping," I told her.

She nodded and kissed my cheek. "I love you, Mama."

"Love you too, sweetie."

"You'll drive her home after shopping?" I directed at my mother.

"Oh, Josie, honestly. No, I'm going to leave her stranded in Gainesville. Of course I'll drive her home, but it might not be till around seven."

"That's fine. Bye," I said and headed out to the golf cart.

I gripped the steering wheel as I drove away. God,

that woman could be frustrating. Just because she graduated college, worked as a reporter for two years at the *St. Petersburg Times* until she met my father when she interviewed a group of professors at USF, married him in a huge church ceremony with most of Cedar Key in attendance, produced a daughter a year later, and went on to become a bestselling author—it didn't mean that I wasn't entitled to my own life. Dammit. I was thirty-one years old, had a wonderful daughter, lived on a beautiful island, had lots of friends, and I was *happy*. Wasn't I?

Chapter 3

The ringing telephone jolted me awake. I glanced at the clock on the mantel—6:30. God, I'd been sleeping for two hours.

Reaching for the phone next to me I heard Mallory's voice.

"Josie, did I wake you up?"

Mallory had been my best friend since before we were even born—well, that's the story that our mothers told us. They had been best friends since childhood and ended up being pregnant at the same time and caused some amusing jokes on the island when they took it a step further and gave birth to daughters born five hours apart.

"Nah," I said, rubbing my eyes and stretching. "Well, actually, yes, I was sleeping, but I really needed to get up. I can't believe it's six-thirty."

"Sugar, with all those hours you've been working it's a wonder you haven't turned into Rip Van Winkle."

I smiled as I got up and headed to the kitchen to make a pot of coffee. During all the upheaval of my pregnancy, quitting college, not getting married, and deciding to raise Orli on my own, it was Mallory who had stood by me 110 percent. Without a doubt, she was the best girlfriend a woman could have, leading me sometimes to question if perhaps we had bonded in utero by osmosis.

"Orli's gone to Gainesville with my mother for the day, and I did a couple extra cleaning jobs this afternoon. I was sitting on the sofa reading the newspaper—and the next thing I knew, the phone was ringing."

"Well, you needed that sleep. Hey, listen, the reason I'm calling—did you get your tree yet?"

Christmas tree? I hated to admit that just the thought of decorating one this year brought on even more fatigue.

"Ah, no . . . not yet. Why?"

"Because Troy went to get ours and ended up bringing two of them home—said he couldn't choose which one he liked best. I think he actually thought I was going to decorate both of them, but I quickly put that thought out of his mind. I swear, he's worse than a kid when it comes to Christmas."

I laughed. Mallory had really hit the jackpot with Troy. He had moved to the island with his family when we were freshmen in high school. His parents ran one of the restaurants in Cedar Key where Troy was employed as a chef. Because of Mallory and Troy, I had to adjust my thinking on love at first sight. The August after we graduated high school I went off to college in Boston, and Mallory became Mrs. Troy Wilson. Five years later, after two miscarriages and a lot of disappointment, their son Carter was born.

"So," Mallory continued, "since you don't have a tree yet, would it be okay to drop this one off at your house?"

I smiled while pouring water into the coffee maker. Mallory thought she was pulling a fast one on me, but she should know better. I recalled the week before when I'd complained about the price of the Christmas trees in front of Wal-Mart. Typical of the island. This wasn't a case of a husband who would like two trees, but rather a friend helping a friend.

"Hmm, well, I hate to see you get stuck decorating another tree," I told her. "So sure, you can bring it here, but I can't guarantee when I'll find the time to get it decorated."

"Oh, thanks, and I'd be more than happy to come by and help you and Orli get it decorated when you're free."

Right, I thought, *and just when might that be?*

But instead, I said, "Okay, I'll let you know."

"Great, then I'll have Troy swing by with it tomorrow morning."

We hung up and I poured myself a cup of coffee. It was then that I realized I'd neglected to put the chicken into the oven to have ready when Orli got home. Damn. It was going on 7:00 now, and she'd be here any minute. As I was scouring through the fridge I heard the front door open.

"Mama," she called. "We're back."

Damn again. My mother had come in with her?

I turned around as they both walked into the kitchen.

"Hey," I said. "Have a good time?"

"We did," Orli told me, coming over to kiss my cheek. "The mall is decorated so beautifully for Christmas."

I saw my mother's eyes dart around the kitchen as

she placed some bags on the counter. I might have been a disappointment when it came to my education but she could never fault me for my domestic abilities. No matter how busy I was working outside of my home, I had always maintained a clean and spotless place for Orli and me to live.

"Got you some bags of holiday coffee at Starbucks. Thought you might like that. I think one is spice and the other pumpkin or something like that."

I unfolded the top of a bag and inhaled the wonderful aromas of cinnamon and nutmeg. "Thanks, Mom, and yeah, I'll enjoy these."

My mother opened a Dillards bag and pulled out a shoe box. "Here," she said, handing it to me. "And for God's sake, please throw those things on your feet away immediately."

I opened the box to see a pair of pure white Reebox staring up at me. Yes, I did need new sneakers, but Christ I felt like a ten-year-old depending on my mother to purchase them for me.

When I neglected to remove them from the box, I heard the frosty edge to my mother's voice.

"Not the right size? Or you just don't want them because *I* got them for you?"

Biting my lower lip, I let out a sigh and forced a smile to my face while removing one of the sneakers. "Nope, perfect. Size 7. Thanks, Mom, that was really nice of you."

Brushing off imaginary lint from her slacks, she said, "Okay, well, I need to get going. Your father will be sending the Levy County Sheriff's Department out looking for me pretty soon." Her gaze went toward my stove. "Nothing for supper?"

"Chicken in the oven, and I just have to cook up some rice and a veggie."

My mother nodded, heading to the front door,

when she paused in the family room looking around. "No tree yet?"

"Tomorrow. Troy picked one up for me, and he's bringing it by tomorrow morning."

"Oh, good," my mother replied, and she was gone.

Orli and I looked at each other and giggled.

"Omelets and hotdogs?" I questioned.

"Sounds like a plan to me," my daughter said.

Monday morning at Cook's Café is usually busy because of tourists enjoying a final breakfast on the island before heading home. I was covering the outside dining area and had every table filled. Running inside to pick up another order, I heard somebody yell, "Miss, hey, Miss, what do I have to do to get some service here?" Christ, an unhappy and impatient customer—not what I needed on a Monday morning.

I turned in the direction of the male voice and was surprised to see an exceptionally good-looking guy with such a nasty attitude. With thick, curly dark hair and olive skin, he was dressed casually in polo shirt and khaki slacks. Good-looking, yes—but the frown on his face detracted from his good looks.

I held up an index finger, hollered back "one minute," and kept going to pick up my order. Grabbing silverware and napkins, I realized the customer looked a little familiar, and that's when it hit me. *No,* I thought, *Ben Sudbury? Mr. Al's nephew?* If it was him, I didn't recall his ever looking that good when he used to vacation here as a teen.

After I unloaded my tray for the party of four, I walked over to his table. He had his head bent reading the *Wall Street Journal.*

"Can I help you?" I asked, using my sweet waitress voice.

"Well, since I've been sitting here for close to an hour, I guess you can. Finally."

Not only was he nasty, he was a liar. There's *no* way he'd been sitting there any longer than twenty minutes.

With my pad of paper in one hand and pencil poised in the air, I remained silent and glared at him. Damn. Up close he was even better looking. The years had most definitely been kind to Ben Sudbury.

When he got the hint that I wasn't about to verbally spar with him, he said, "Right. Ham and cheese omelet, home fries, and bacon. Oh, and do you think it would be possible to get a cup of coffee now? God only knows how long the food will take."

Two thoughts went through my head—he was a cardiac surgeon's dream, and it seemed pretty apparent he had no clue who I was and didn't remember me.

"Well, now," I replied with an edge to my tone. "You're right. If those hens out back are being stingy this morning, yup, that omelet could be a long time coming."

I spun around to walk inside and get the coffeepot. Who the heck did that guy think he was? It seemed to me that he'd done the entire island a favor by never liking it here and staying away. Cedar Key was known for its friendly people, and he was far from friendly.

Walking back to his table, I began pouring coffee into the mug. My silence matched his.

When I went inside to pick up another order, Ida Mae signaled to me from the back of the restaurant.

She grinned and leaned close. "Hey," she said. "That's sure a good-looking fellow you're waiting on out there . . . and he's alone."

Ida Mae was the owner of Cook's, in her late six-ties, and considered the matchmaker of the island. She adored romance and was one of my mother's biggest readers.

"Hmm, he can stay alone as far as I'm concerned. Do you know who he is?"

Ida Mae adjusted her glasses and walked closer to the front window, then shook her head. "No. Who?"

"Ben Sudbury. Mr. Al's nephew."

That was all it took.

Romance was replaced with indignation.

"Well, how dare that miserable excuse for a family member come to *my* establishment. I oughtta tell Hal to burn his order."

I shook my head and grinned. Yup, for some peo-ple family was more important than business.

"Should I ask him to leave?" It sure would make my day to boot him off the premises.

Ida Mae sniffed. "Right, and he'd be on that fancy cell phone of his with a lawyer before we had time to clear the table. No, I don't need a discrimination suit thrown at me. But . . . I couldn't blame ya if you were a little clumsy this morning pouring that coffee."

I laughed as I heard the bell telling me his order was ready.

Setting the plates in front of my nemesis, I felt his eyes on me.

"Will there be anything else?" I asked in the cold-est tone I could muster.

His head tilted to the side as his stare intensified. Then he surprised the heck out of me by smiling. Okay, I have to admit—he had a killer smile. The up-turning of his mouth transformed a good-looking face to drop-dead handsome.

Waving a finger at me, he said, "Now I know who

you are. I thought you looked familiar. Little Josie Sullivan, right?"

The intensity of his stare deepened as his eyes scanned all five feet seven inches of me and I wasn't sure if the flush creeping up my neck was caused from rushing around waiting tables or from what his stare indicated.

"But . . . you're sure not so *little* anymore," he said, clearly enjoying the fact that he was making me feel uncomfortable.

Now I wished that I'd worn jeans this morning rather than my white shorts that were probably a tad *too* short.

"Not sure you'll remember me, but I'm Ben Sudbury. I used to come here during summer vacations to visit my grandmother and uncle, Al Casey."

"I remember you," was all I said. I also remembered somebody mentioning he worked as an editor for a publishing house in Manhattan.

"Hey, did anybody ever tell you that you sure do resemble Winona Ryder? You know, that cute actress?"

"More times than I'd care to remember, and for somebody who complained so much about the poor service here . . . your food is getting cold." I started to walk away and then turned around to face him again. "Oh, and by the way, I know exactly *why* you're back here on the island and just so you know—you're not going to be welcomed here at all. Cedar Key people don't take kindly to treating your family members like wayward dogs that get sent to the pound."

The frown returned to his face, and anger laced his words. "Really? Well, I certainly don't think that's any of your business or anybody else's. And I can see that a degree from some fancy college in Boston sure did you a lot of good, huh? I wasn't aware they required college degrees to waitress tables nowadays."

I seriously wanted to toss the pot of coffee I was holding into his smug face, but instead I flung around, inhaled a deep breath, and marched back inside the restaurant.

Chapter 4

I stood beside Mallory and watched one group of children leave the school gym as another group headed in.

"This is a nice thing we do every year for the kids, isn't it?" I said to her.

"Yup, a lot of these kids don't even have the money to shop at Wal-Mart for family members. They know they can come here and get some nice gifts pretty cheap."

I glanced down at the table holding our knitted dishcloths. We'd managed to make one hundred and fifty between all of us in the knitting group, and we were selling them for fifty cents. The money that the school made was put toward a school picnic at the end of the year.

A little girl who looked to be about five or six stood in the middle of the room, her head turning slowly from one table to the next as if she was trying to decide what to buy. We were having a cold snap on the island that week but I noticed that, unlike many of the other kids who wore jeans and sweatshirts, she had on shorts and a T-shirt. Her pale blond hair hung to her shoulders, and she had the resigned look of a kid who already knows that life isn't always easy.

"Who's that?" I asked Mallory. "She doesn't look familiar to me."

"Oh," she said, and I heard sadness in her tone.

"That's Penny—Penelope, actually, but Carter told me she likes to be called Penny. She's in his class. She moved here with her mom in October. I'm not really sure why they chose Cedar Key. They don't have any family here, and they live in the government housing on G Street. According to Carter, her mother is pretty sick. Like seriously ill, and I guess last week Penny's grandmother arrived to live with them and help out. It's really sad."

I nodded as I watched the little girl wander to one of the tables across the hall. Yeah, it *was* sad. It always bothered me that some people had so much and others so very little and also how tragedy seemed to be a frequent visitor to some, while others floated through life as if on a magic rainbow with an abundance of joy and love.

"Probably good that they did move here though," I said. "Cedar Key takes care of people." And the town did—if one of the clammers got sick and had no health insurance, the Eagles or one of the other organizations would get together and hold a benefit dance, dinner, or some event to bring in money and help out. And these events were always well-attended, because people cared.

"Hi, Miss Mallory, how much are the dishcloths?"

"Hey, Chelsea, fifty cents each."

"Oh, good, then I'll buy four. My dad gave me five dollars this morning. Now I have gifts for my mother, my two grandmothers, and my aunt. And I'll still have money left to get something for him and my brothers."

"You're a savvy shopper," I told her, and she laughed.

"Oh, there's Orli," Mallory said, pointing across the hall.

"Yeah, I guess she'll make her way over here. I was surprised this morning. She asked me for ten dollars for the sale—that seems like a lot to spend here, and she doesn't normally ask for a specific amount."

"Maybe she wanted to have the extra for when you go to Wal-Mart."

"Hmm, could be."

Over the next half hour we sold quite a few dishcloths. Our shift was up in fifteen minutes, and I was rearranging the pile we had left on the table when I glanced up and saw the little girl, Penny, standing there.

"Hi," Mallory said. "How're you, Penny?"

"I'm good."

"This is my friend, Miss Josie. I'm not sure you know her daughter, Orli. She's a few classes ahead of you."

"Nice to meet you," I told her.

It was then that I noticed Penny was empty-handed. For all of her wandering around, it looked like she hadn't purchased anything.

"Thinking of buying some dishcloths?" I asked.

"I'm not sure. How much are they?"

"Fifty cents each," Mallory told her.

"Oh," was all that Penny said.

Mallory and I exchanged a look.

"Did you want to buy one for your mother?" Mallory asked her.

"Yeah, she'd like that. They're really pretty, but . . ."

"Well, you know," I said. "You're very lucky that you waited until almost the end to come to our table."

Penny's face took on a curious expression. "Really? Why?"

"Well, because," Mallory continued, "at the end of the sale, we reduce our prices. How much do you have?"

Penny opened her tightly clenched fist to reveal one quarter.

"Aha," I said. "If you'd like to get a dishcloth for your mother, you really are in luck, because just before you walked over we cut the price to twenty-five cents."

This actually brought a smile to the child's face. "Really?" she said again.

"Yup. Choose which one you'd like."

Her hand hovered above one, then another, as she worked her way amongst the dishcloths that remained. Finally she took her hand away from the table and stepped back.

"Something wrong?" Mallory asked her.

"Yeah, my grandmother is living with us now. I can't get a Christmas gift for my mom because Grandma wouldn't have anything to open."

"Oh," I said. "But we didn't tell you the best part of our sale—if you buy one dishcloth, you get the second one free."

Unadulterated joy spread across Penny's face as she looked at me and then at Mallory. "Really?" she said and giggled.

"Absolutely," both Mallory and I told her at the same time.

"Oh, wow," Penny said. "Then I'd like this for my mom and this one for Grandma. Oh, and here's my money," she said, proudly passing me the quarter.

"Thank you," I told her. "You're a good shopper."

She clutched the two dishcloths to her chest. "Thank you both and Merry Christmas," she said, as she skipped her way out of the gym.

Mallory and I looked at each other, smiled, and raised two palms in the air for a high five.

"I already know that they're on the list to get some gifts delivered to the house for Penny and also Christmas dinner."

I nodded. "And who says there's no Santa Claus?"

I glanced at Orli across the supper table. Normally babbling away, sharing her school day with me, she was unusually quiet tonight. I wondered if she might be coming down with the flu that was going around.

"Feeling okay?" I asked.

"Yup," she replied, as she pushed meatloaf around her plate.

"Then what's up?"

"Nothing."

"Did you get your gifts today at school?"

"No. I didn't see anything I liked, but Grandma said I could go to Wal-Mart with her this weekend."

I thought it was odd that Orli hadn't been able to find something at school, but I dropped the subject.

It wasn't until dishes were finished, homework was done, and Orli was sitting on the sofa in her pajamas reading a book that she decided to converse with me.

"Dad called me today on my cell phone."

"Oh," was all I said, as I continued to work on the sweater I was knitting. When Grant had suggested getting her the phone during the summer, I hadn't been crazy about the idea. I honestly didn't see the need for an eleven-year-old to have one. But he explained it was difficult sometimes to reach Orli because of all the activities she was involved in and assured me he would pay for the phone and the monthly bill. Not wanting to be the person who decreased their communication, I had agreed.

"How's he doing?" I asked when she remained silent. Grant and I had had minor disagreements over the years concerning our daughter, but for the most part we concurred when it came to important issues.

"He's okay. He told me he has some time off work right now until after the first of the year."

"That's nice," I said, while I concentrated on my knitting pattern.

"Yeah, and he was kinda wondering if . . . ah . . . maybe . . ."

I glanced up. This sounded important. "If what?"

"Well, he's planning to go to Paris for the week over Christmas . . . and he knows this year I'm supposed to be here with you, but . . . he wondered if maybe you could change your mind."

By the way Orli was twirling a strand of hair around her finger I knew the poor kid was nervous about her father's request. Damn him. He had our daughter last Christmas, and then he has the nerve to broach this subject with her before he discusses it with me? I could feel my anger building, but made the supreme effort to remain calm.

"What would you like to do?" I asked.

"I'd love to go to Paris . . . just not this year for Christmas. I was looking forward to being here with you this year."

I nodded. Settled. "Then that's what you should do. It's your choice, Orli."

"Really?" The concern that I'd seen on her face all evening was replaced with her usual brightness.

"Really. Would you like to call him to tell him your choice or do you want me to?"

"Well . . . I *do* feel bad that he'll be alone, but I spent last year with him. Would you call him?"

"Absolutely. I'll try to reach him later."

After she'd gone to bed I dialed Grant's cell phone number. He picked up on the second ring.

"Hey, Josie. Had a feeling you'd be calling me."

"Did ya now?"

"I overstepped my bounds, didn't I?"

"Ah, you could say that."

"I'm sorry. . . . It was wrong of me not to speak with you first. It won't happen again."

"I hope not, Grant, because if she was a different kind of kid, she could be playing both of us against each other. Important issues will be coming up during her teen years. We have to both be on the same page."

"I know that. It's just that I'm leaving for Paris on the nineteenth, and I thought how great it would be if I could spend Christmas there with Orli. I was being selfish." He paused for a second. "She doesn't want to go, does she?"

"It isn't that she doesn't *want* to go, Grant. I'm sure she'd love to go. You should know by now she's a loyal kid, and she hates disappointing anybody. But she's also honest. She said she felt bad that you'd be alone, but she wanted to be here this year with me."

"That's fair. Hey, where'd we get such a great, mature kid?"

I laughed. "Beats the hell out of me."

"So how're *you* doing? Are you managing all right financially?"

"Yup, fine. I've managed to pick up some more cleaning jobs. So yup, I'm doing fine." There was no way I'd let Grant know how difficult it was becoming. Nor would I share with him my recent thoughts that perhaps I'd made a major mistake by not getting my college degree.

"Anybody important in your life?"

I smiled. This was a question that we'd tossed back and forth to each other over eleven years. Although Grant had had a couple serious relationships, they ended up going nowhere. Which I found bewildering. A good-looking Harvard grad, with a great job, financial security, a terrific sense of humor and yet—he remained single.

I gave him my usual answer. "Only Orli."

His laughter came across the line. "Okay, well, I apologize for this incident, and I promise it won't happen again. Tell Orli I love her, and I'll call her over the weekend."

"Will do," I said, hanging up the phone.

Chapter 5

I had just put the last load of laundry into the washer when the doorbell rang. Opening the front door, I was surprised to find Al Casey standing on my porch shifting from one foot to the other in a nervous fashion. I could count on one hand the number of times he'd paid me a visit.

"Mr. Al," I said, pushing the screen door open. "Come on in. How're you doing? Haven't seen you in a while."

"Yeah, yeah, I know," he replied, following me to the kitchen at the back of the house.

"How about a cup of afternoon coffee? I know I could use a break from housecleaning." I began spooning coffee into the paper filter. "Have a seat."

"Thank you, Miss Josie. That's mighty kind of you, and coffee sure sounds good."

Filling the glass carafe with water, I wondered what had brought about this visit.

As if reading my mind, he said, "I guess you're wonderin' why I've come by."

I joined him at the table and smiled. "You mean it's not because I'm such a pleasure to be with and great company?"

"Oh, well, yes . . . that too," he replied, obviously flustered.

"I was only joking with you, Mr. Al. What can I do for you?"

Despite the coolness of the afternoon, he removed a pristine white handkerchief from the pocket of his jeans and mopped his forehead, which I saw had beads of perspiration.

"Well, uh . . . I suppose you heard all the scuttle-butt around town. About a group that's gonna be going before the City Commission. Guess they wanna take my house and my property and do away with me. Even that highbred nephew of mine is in on it."

I got up, poured coffee into two mugs and sat back down across from Mr. Al.

"Yes," I told him. "I've heard all about it, and I think it's terrible. You can bet I'll be at that City Commission meeting standing up for you. And I happen to know there'll be many other locals right along with me."

Al took a sip of his coffee and then let out a deep sigh. "That sure is kind of all of ya, but I'm not sure it'll do any good."

"What do you mean? You own that house and property—free and clear. Nobody can just boot you off your own land."

"Oh, nowadays, who knows what's possible? I know my front yard looks a mess, and I'm afraid I let the outside of the house get away from me. But since my mama's been gone, I guess I've kinda lost interest in everything. You know . . . there was a time when I truly welcomed each new day. Up before the sun, I'd head downtown to Cook's, get me a good breakfast, and I'd be at the City Marina easin' my Boston Whaler out into the Gulf for a day of fishin'. Fishin'—that was my livelihood, ya know."

I nodded and took another sip of coffee while I listened. There was no doubt poor Mr. Al was both lonely and depressed.

"And then, in 1994 they ban net fishin'. Said it was harmful to the environment, and we were depleting the volume of fish. I don't know nothin' about that—all I know's, they took away my livin'."

"But Mr. Al, the government sent people to the island to instruct anyone who wanted to learn clam farming. And now, Cedar Key has become the number one place in the country for farm-raised clams."

Waving his hand toward me in agitation, he said, "I didn't wanna be a clam farmer. I was a fisherman. Fifth generation of fishin' those waters out there. And nothin' was gonna change that. I just thank the good Lord that I've had enough money to get by, and I never did have to do clam farmin'."

Mr. Al wasn't the only one on the island who felt this way, so I wasn't surprised at his attitude.

"So they take away my work, then my sister Annie passes on and a couple years ago my mama joins her in heaven. And now it's just me that's left. Well, except for that whippersnapper nephew of mine. But I swear he don't have an ounce a Cedar Key blood in him. Poor Annie must be turning over in her grave."

"Have you seen Ben since he got here?"

"Oh, yeah, he stopped by to *talk* to me. Talk? He didn't wanna talk—all he wanted to do was *tell* me what *he* thought should be done. Said I should put the house up for sale. Said I'd be much more comfortable in one a them old people places. Hell—excuse my language—I'm not *old!*"

"No, you're not," I said, reaching across the table

to pat his hand. A hand that was still large and strong, with dots of brown spots. A hand that had hauled untold amounts of fish into his boat over so many years.

Mr. Al sniffed and brought his handkerchief to his eyes.

"Well, now," he said, clearing his throat. "I didn't come here to complain to you. I came to ask a favor."

"A favor?"

He nodded. "Yup. You and your mama both— you've always been real nice to me. And now, that little girl of yours—you sure raised her right. She's got a kind heart, she does, and I admire that. Oh, I remember when you came back to the island from college. All the talk and gossip. But don't you ever pay attention to any of that. Because that daughter of yours— she's proof that you did the right thing."

I now felt moisture in my own eyes. I'd had no idea Mr. Al felt this way.

"So that's why I figured I could ask you my favor and you'd understand."

"What is it that you need?"

"Well, the one thing that really bothers me if I have to go live someplace else is that Pal won't be able to come with me. He's a great dog, but that won't matter, because those places—they don't allow dogs. And he's my best friend. Best friends look out for each other and that's what I aim to do. So I was wonderin' . . . if I have to go to one a those places . . . do you think maybe . . . you could take Pal for me and let him live here with you?"

I guess his request was probably about the last thing I expected, and, when I remained silent, he said, "He wouldn't be no trouble. Really he wouldn't. He's a good dog. Doesn't wander off, comes when he's called, sleeps on the floor beside my bed every night. He sure does love chicken though." Mr. Al chuckled.

"So when you're cookin' a chicken, you'll see that Pal will hang around the kitchen. And maybe—you could give him a couple pieces when you're done eating. He sure would love that."

God, I didn't know what to say. I certainly never expected a request like this from Mr. Al. And a dog? What on earth would Clovelly think about that?

But in a heartbeat, I said, "Yes, yes, of course we would take Pal for you," as I squeezed his hand. "You wouldn't have to worry about that. Orli and I would give him a good home."

"I know you would. That's why I wanted to ask you."

"But Mr. Al, you're not *going* anywhere. We're all behind you on this. Really!"

He got up from the table, took the last sip of his coffee, and placed the mug in the sink. When he turned around to look at me, he had the look of a defeated man. A man who's lost all of his loved ones and all that had ever been important to him. His white beard matched the halo of bushy white hair surrounding his head. Medium height, Mr. Al carried an extra ten pounds but that had always made him look jolly. Today I noticed his normally tan skin was paler, and, now that I looked closer, I could swear those ten pounds were no longer there.

"Well," he said, heading toward the front door. "I do thank ya for that, but I'm not sure anybody can do anything."

I patted him on the back. "Now I don't want you worrying, understand? We'll get this all straightened out."

"Oh," he said, reaching for the screen door and stepping onto the porch. "That nephew of mine— guess he didn't come just to *talk* to me. He sure had a lot of questions about you."

"Me?" I said, dumbfounded.

"Yeah. If I didn't know better—I'd say he was sweet on you. You have a good day, Miss Josie, and thanks for everything."

Mr. Al headed down the street leaving me standing in my doorway feeling more confused than I had in ages.

"Sweet on you? That was all he said?" Mallory questioned.

I continued folding towels at the kitchen table and nodded. "Yup. That was it, and I was so flabbergasted, I didn't say anything."

"From the exchange you had with Ben Sudbury at Cook's last week, I find it difficult to think he might be interested in you—in a romantic way."

"He's a jerk, so he'd better not be interested in me in *any* way. Be right back," I said, heading out of the kitchen to place the towels in the linen closet.

I poured myself another cup of coffee and joined Mallory at the table. "There's poor Mr. Al about to be sent out to sea on an iceberg—and that selfish nephew of his is doing nothing to stop that from happening."

"I know. I spoke to Troy about it. Isn't there anything we can do?"

"Except for going to the City Commission meeting next month and attesting to the fact that Mr. Al is definitely safe living alone and not confused? I just don't know what the heck we could do."

"Well . . . I did have one thought." Mallory paused. "Now don't go biting my head off, but . . . I was wondering . . . maybe you could get with Ben. See if you could talk some reason into him. Make him understand that forcing Mr. Al to go to a nursing home is the worst thing he could do."

"Me? Are you crazy? I can't stand that guy. He's arrogant, mean-spirited, and has a holier-than-thou attitude. No thanks. I'll pass on that."

"Just a thought," Mallory mumbled as I got up to answer the phone.

"Josie, sweetie," I heard my mother say.

"Hey, Mom. What's up?"

"Well, honey, you'll never guess who I bumped into downtown today." Without waiting for me to answer, she said, "Ben Sudbury. Gosh, I haven't seen him in years. He certainly did turn out to be *quite* the good-looking guy. And so . . . I invited him here for dinner Saturday evening, and I wanted to be sure that you and Orli were free so you could join us."

"You *what?*" I said in a volume that caused Mallory to look at me with raised eyebrows.

"I said, I bumped into Ben . . ."

"I *heard* what you said, Mom. But why on earth would you invite him to dinner? You don't even know each other."

"Well, now that's not entirely true. I knew Ben as a kid when he'd come here for the summers. And Ben's in the book industry—you knew that. We know a lot of the same people, so I thought it might be nice to have him over. What's wrong with that?"

"Mom, do you know why he's here? He's here to put poor Mr. Al in a nursing home, sell the family house, and then he'll be on his merry way back to the Big Apple. I don't want anything to do with a self-centered jerk like him. Sorry. So no, we're not coming."

I could tell by the way my mother said "Oh?" that she wasn't aware of any of this, so I proceeded to bring her up to speed.

"Hmm," she said. "I did know about the complaints related to Mr. Al's property, but I didn't think

Ben was involved. I thought he was just here to visit his uncle."

"Far from it."

"Well, I'm not canceling the dinner. It wouldn't be right. Besides, maybe I'll discuss the subject with him."

"Whatever," was my only reply.

"So you're going to dinner at your mom's house with Ben Sudbury there?" Mallory questioned when I hung up the phone.

"Not on your life."

"You shouldn't be so hasty declining. Remember, you get a lot more flies with honey than you do with vinegar."

"Well, I've never been overly attracted to honey—it wreaks havoc with my blood sugars. Not to mention all the calories."

Chapter 6

Once again I found myself racing around the house looking for a misplaced item. Unfortunately, Orli was spending the night at Carla's and not able to help search.

Rushing into the kitchen I glanced at the clock above the fridge. Damn—7:10. I was already ten minutes late for my mother's dinner. Mallory had ended up convincing me I should go—that maybe I could persuade Ben to drop the idea of selling Mr. Al's house and sticking him in a nursing home. I seriously doubted that I had the ability to do this, but figured it was worth a shot.

There was the small shopping bag I'd been searching for. Hidden from view on the chair behind the table. Scooping up the bag, I ran into the living room, grabbed keys for the golf cart, a jacket, my handbag, and I was on my way.

Lights were blazing inside and out as I pulled into my parents' circular driveway. Before I even had a chance to get out of the golf cart, my mother had swung open the front door and stepped out onto the porch.

"Good Lord, Josie!" she hissed. "Can't you ever be on time for anything?"

I mumbled an apology and handed her the small shopping bag. "The yarn you wanted me to pick up for you at Monica's shop."

Mention yarn, and my mother gets all warm and fuzzy—just like any addicted knitter.

"Oh, thank you," she gushed. "I needed these extra skeins to finish off the afghan I'm making for the charity bazaar. Well, come on, come on. Ben's already here having a drink with your dad."

My mother ushered me into the family room where I heard my father laughing at something Ben had apparently said. It was then that I realized I'd committed another fashion faux pas and would most likely hear about it later from my mother.

Both my dad and Ben had on sport jackets. No tie, but open-collar dress shirts. My mother looked elegant and festive wearing an ankle-length skirt and silk blouse, both in a shade of green that closely resembled holiday pine trees. No, I wasn't wearing my usual jeans and sweatshirt, but perhaps a dress would have been more appropriate than the simple black slacks and pullover sweater that I'd chosen.

"Josie," my father said, getting up to give me a hug. "A glass of white wine? And you know Ben, so no need for an introduction. He's just been telling me some humorous anecdotes from the summers he spent here as a kid."

Ben had never struck me as the humorous type, but I only nodded and smiled.

We made small talk over the wine, then Delilah announced that dinner was ready, and we trooped into the dining room. The table was beautifully set with a vase of blood red roses in the center, flanked by green pillar Christmas candles.

"Josie," my mother directed. "If you'll sit here and Ben, right across from her will be fine."

My father took the seat beside me, and I wished that she had placed Ben there instead. I wasn't very keen on having him stare across the table at me through an entire dinner.

Delilah brought out the first course, pumpkin soup, which the four of us raved about. Without a doubt, most women on the island were the best cooks I knew. Recipes were handed down and fiercely guarded from one generation to the next. Delilah shared a lot of those great recipes in my mother's kitchen, much to our culinary delight.

Over the main course of lamb, roasted potatoes, and squash casserole the conversation flowed mostly between my mother and Ben who were discussing the publishing business, recent trends in the industry, and people they knew.

By the time Delilah brought out her scrumptious blueberry cobbler, I thought perhaps I'd been a bit harsh in my initial assessment of Ben. Two things struck me. One, he was quite personable conversing with my mother—not at all like the demanding and irritating customer I'd waited on at Cook's. And two, he was even better looking than I had thought he was. A third thing had struck me as well. I noticed that he kept throwing glances my way throughout dinner, but I was unwilling to make eye contact with him. Instead I focused on my food or directed my eyes toward my parents.

"And so," I heard my mother say. "What on earth is this nonsense I'm hearing about you wanting to sell Mr. Al's house and put him in a nursing home?"

Her statement succeeded in forcing my attention to

Ben, and I stared across the table, waiting for his answer.

"Well," he said, directing his glance away from me.
Actually, he looked uncomfortable as he shifted in his
chair, fingered his napkin, and cleared his throat. "I
got a call from an old buddy of mine here on the island. He explained that my uncle's house was an eyesore and . . ."

"An eyesore?" I interjected. I couldn't hold back
any longer. "Since when did having property that
could be judged an eyesore become cause to force
somebody out of his home and into a nursing home?"

Deep mahogany eyes glared at me. "Hey, look, I
don't want to fight with you about this. Although
Uncle Al's property is a mess, of course that's *not* the
only reason I feel it's time for him to be in a facility.
I'm told he's been acting odd since my grandmother
died. Hardly ever goes out, doesn't mingle with his
old friends anymore . . . He's become unsafe living
there alone."

"And you know this *how?*" I questioned. According to Mr. Al, Ben had only visited him once since arriving on the island to force the idea of a nursing
home.

Ben remained silent, keeping his gaze on the half-
eaten dessert on his plate.

"Yeah, right! You have no answer because you did-
n't even take the time to try to get to know Mr. Al.
Your uncle is depressed—plain and simple. You
would be too if the two people you loved most in the
world were gone, along with some friends you'd
known since childhood. Mr. Al is lost and depressed,
not to mention lonely."

I noticed my parents made no attempt to get into
the conversation. Both sat quietly listening to Ben
and me spar back and forth.

Before Ben could toss a retort at me, I said, "And another thing—you can't just force somebody out of his own home. So what's your plan? Going to go to court to try to get your uncle declared incompetent? Well, you can bet that half the town will be there in Mr. Al's defense. I can guarantee that!"

Ben's head shot up as a defiant expression crossed his face. "You're making me out to be an ogre and I don't think . . ."

My anger notched up a level. "That's exactly what you are," I said, interrupting him. "You might have spent summers here, but you're not one of *us*. Always acting like we were beneath you, you couldn't wait till you were no longer forced to come here. And once you left for good, you never looked back. So now— here you are, arriving in all your glory to put things right. Except you're wrong about your uncle." I stood up and flung my napkin onto the table. "You're nothing but an egotistical, arrogant jerk, and I'm sure poor Miss Annie is turning over in her grave knowing what a rotten person her son turned out to be."

I leaned over to kiss my father's cheek. "Sorry, Daddy, but I can't stay here a minute longer."

Walking into the foyer to get my jacket, I heard my mother holler, "Josephine Shelby Sullivan, get back here right now and apologize. Where are your manners?"

If I hadn't been ticked off enough, leave it to my mother to compound the situation by using my full name—a name I *detested* and changed to Josie at age six, the day I began first grade. After three months of my refusing to answer to Josephine, my mother finally acquiesced and it was *Josie* forevermore.

"My manners? Probably where the sun don't shine," I yelled back, before slamming the door on my exit.

* * *

The following day I was cleaning Orli's room, trying to release the anger I still felt toward Ben Sudbury from the night before. We'd have snow in Florida in July before I ever gave him an apology. My mother— different story. I knew before the day was over that I'd have to call and make amends for walking out on her dinner party.

"Damn," I yelled out loud as I pushed the vacuum around Orli's carpet. My anger had increased my strength, and I'd managed to shove her basketball under the bed.

Reluctantly I got down on all fours to pull it out and couldn't believe what I was seeing. Lifting the dust ruffle higher to get a better look, I said, "What the hell?"

Flat down on my stomach, I inched my way further under the bed to discover five one-gallon cans of paint. *What the heck was Orli doing hiding paint under her bed? She certainly wasn't planning to give me this for Christmas, was she?*

Staring at the paint, totally confused, I recalled a few weeks ago she *had* mentioned something about wanting her room repainted. But typical for me lately, with never enough time for my daughter, I'd forgotten to resume the subject with her.

Crawling out, I sat there leaning back against the side of the bed. Sometimes I felt like such a failure as a mother, and, yup, this was one of those times. That wasn't much for a kid to ask for—to get her bedroom repainted. And yet, I'd let her request slide right out of my mind, too busy with work and all the other demands of being a single mom.

Guilt now began to rear its ugly head—if Orli had her dad living in the same house, chances were that he would have gotten the paint job done in a weekend.

Before I even realized it, I felt the tears sliding down my cheeks. I was tired, I was worn out, and for the first time in twelve years, I was willing to admit that maybe I'd made some mistakes. Raising Orli on my own, however, was not one of them. My most damaging error had been not completing my college degree. Education was everything. I knew that, and yet I allowed it to slip through my fingers. Too stubborn and independent to accept help from my mother that would have enabled me to return to college after my daughter was born. Education was the key that opened untold doors, and I'd foolishly tossed it away.

I stood up and swiped at my eyes. Reaching for a tissue from the box on the bedside table, I blew my nose and headed into the kitchen to brew a fresh pot of coffee. Not one to stay maudlin for long, I scooped coffee into the filter as a plan began forming in my mind.

Maybe, just maybe, if I accepted some help from my mother I'd be able to start attending classes at the university in Gainesville. Watching the water pour into the carafe, it suddenly occurred to me that I had no earthly idea what I might want to major in.

Yes, twelve years ago I'd been a journalism major, but that didn't appeal to me at all now. Besides, I needed something practical—a career that would provide enough financially for Orli and me. And a career that wouldn't require my working an additional job.

But what could that be? What did I want to be when I grew up?

"Well, Josie Sullivan," I said out loud, "you're thirty-one years old; it's about damn time you figured that question out."

Chapter 7

I made Orli's favorite for supper, tuna casserole, and planned to discuss the paint situation with her when we were finished. Again this evening, she'd been quiet while we ate.

"I spoke to Grandma this afternoon," I told her, as I filled the dishpan with hot water and Palmolive Liquid. "She's planning to make her annual Christmas gingerbread men on Saturday and thought you might like to go over and help."

"Yeah, that would be fun. I'll go. Oh, *this* Saturday? I'm not sure I can."

I couldn't recall seeing any event for Orli on the calendar that hung in our kitchen. That calendar was our Bible—Orli had inherited her sense of organization from me, which had been passed down from my mother. Any event going on, any doctor appointment or meeting was faithfully jotted down by one of us.

"Really? Why not? I didn't see anything on the calendar for this Saturday."

"No . . . ah . . . um . . . I forgot to write it down."

When she volunteered no further information, I said, "Well, what kind of plans do you have?"

"Um . . . it's like a surprise. Something I'm doing with Carla. We're doing it together. Saturday afternoon."

"Oh," was all I said as I continued to wash dishes. It *was* that time of year, after all. Homes were filled with Christmas surprises, so I dropped the subject. "After we finish up here, I'd like to talk to you about something. Homework all done?"

"Yup, I finished it before supper."

"Good. I'll make some hot chocolate, and we can have some of those yummy pumpkin cookies I picked up at Grace's coffee shop this afternoon."

Major discussions in our house almost always took place at the kitchen table. It had been that way when I was growing up, and I continued to follow the same pattern.

Orli dipped her spoon into the hot chocolate and proceeded to lick off the whipped cream. "So what's up?" she asked.

"Well . . . I was cleaning your room this morning and . . ."

"Oh, I know, I promised not to clutter my desk so much, but that's the project Carla and I are working on for school."

"No, no, the desk is fine. I happened to knock your basketball under the bed with the vacuum and . . ."

Orli's eyes widened. "Oh, ah . . . I was going to tell you about that, Mom. Really I was."

"The cans of paint?"

She nodded, looking down at the uneaten cookies on her plate.

"Well, I feel it's really my fault."

"*Your* fault? For what?" she asked, looking puzzled.

"You've been trying to talk to me for weeks about all sorts of things. It's no excuse, I know, but I've been so darn busy working extra hours, but you know what . . . finding that paint could have been the best thing to happen. I've decided it's time to make some changes in my life, and, as soon as I figure out exactly what I'm doing, you'll be the first one I share it with. Now—about repainting your room."

Orli raised her eyebrows and began giggling. "Mom, what on earth are you *talking* about? I do think you've been working too much—you need a vacation."

Now I was confused. "I found the gallons of paint under your bed. You mentioned to me weeks ago that you'd like to have your bedroom repainted." When she remained silent, I said, "Isn't that why the paint is there?"

She shook her head slowly back and forth. "No, it's not for my bedroom."

God, this was becoming worse than pulling teeth. My kid was normally so forthcoming; I couldn't figure out why she was clamming up.

"Okay, what's going on? What's this all about?"

She hesitated for a second and then said, "It's for Mr. Al."

"Mr. Al?" I repeated, still not catching on.

Orli nodded. "Yeah . . . well, see . . . I figured the main reason he might be sent to that nursing home was because of the way his house and property looked. And so . . . I recruited a bunch of kids at school to help me."

"To help you *what?*"

"To help me paint Mr. Al's house and clean up all the junk on his property. Then that way, nobody could use that as an excuse to make him sell and leave the island. He doesn't wanna leave, Mom. Me and Carla . . . we've been going there every day to talk to him, and he's so sad. But he just didn't know what he could do, so I told him not to worry. That I'd figure something out . . . and I did."

"And a little child shall lead them." The verse from scripture floated into my head. This is what the cans of paint were all about? Orli had been secretly meeting with Mr. Al, determined to find a solution to his problem? And I had been so busy, so uninvolved that I'd had no clue my daughter had gone to such lengths.

"Where'd ya get the paint? *How* did you get the paint?" My mind was swirling with a million questions.

"Well, we got it downtown, at the Marina Hardware. Mr. Bob didn't have a lot of choices—actually he only had pink and white left. Mr. Al said he'd love to have a pink house, but thought it might be better if we chose white."

I shook my head and smiled.

"And the money to pay for it . . . well . . . Remember the money you gave me to buy Christmas gifts at school? I didn't think you'd mind my not buying you a gift this year, but I'm making you something in knitting class. Miss Monica said I'm doing a really good job with it too. So I used that money and then I had saved money from my birthday. Carla also chipped in, and, once we got the other kids on board, they all donated whatever they could."

I let out a deep sigh. Here were children doing something that not one adult had thought, or taken the time, to do. But instantly I knew what *I* was going to do.

I jumped up and headed for the phone.

Orli's face wrinkled up like she was on the verge of

tears. "Are you mad, Mom? Are you mad because I did this?"

I pulled my daughter into a tight embrace as I clicked the automatic dial for Mallory.

"Mad? Gosh, no! I've always been proud of you, but I don't think I've ever been as proud as I am right this moment."

She smiled up at me as I heard Mallory say hello.

"Mallory, my BFF, you and I have some work to do."

"We do? And when I hear that *best friends forever* phrase you use, I'm not sure I'm gonna like this."

I laughed as I stroked the top of Orli's head leaning against my chest. "You know poor Mr. Al's dilemma? I think we have it solved. *All* due to the ingenuity of my daughter and her friends."

I proceeded to explain everything to Mallory.

"That's amazing," she said. "To think the kids would be the ones who might prevent Al Casey from going to a nursing home."

"That's right. Now . . . you know the phone tree that we use for emergencies on the island? We're utilizing it now. I'm calling the troops together. You call everybody from A to K, and I'll do the rest. Tell them we're having a meeting tomorrow evening, seven sharp, upstairs in the library. And tell them it's not voluntary—I wanna see this whole town turn out. So they'd better all be there."

And they were. I was surprised to arrive at the library to see it was standing-room-only. Chatter filled the air with an energy that was palpable. Mallory came rushing over.

"Isn't this great?"

"It certainly is," I said, catching her excitement. "Okay, let me get this meeting started."

To signal for quiet, I began clapping my hands loudly. Within a few seconds a hush came over the room, and everyone was staring at me.

I cleared my throat. "Okay, people. First of all, thank you so much for coming, but then, I knew you would. People on Cedar Key have taken care of their own for generations—and we're not about to stop now."

A multitude of heads nodded in agreement, and I continued. "As Mallory and I explained on the phone, we're here to do something about preventing Mr. Al from going to a nursing home. All of us know he's in his right mind, he's not unsafe to live alone, and the major reason any of this got started is the condition of his house and property. It's been like this for a few years. I'm not saying that's right, but I think those of us here have just gotten used to seeing it that way. As we know, a few residents have banded together with complaints, and they want something done."

"Used to be, a man's home was his castle," Mr. James hollered from the back of the room.

The thought of Mr. Al's dilapidated house and property being referred to as a castle made me smile. "Yes, well." I went on. "That may be true, however, we have to admit all of it could use a sprucing up, and it took some of the children in this town to see the problem and attempt to find a solution." I went on to explain what the children ·had done, pooling their money to purchase paint and coming up with a plan.

One of the mothers seated in the front row said, "So that's why my Jeremy wanted extra allowance money the past few weeks. I just bet he's been giving all of it toward the paint."

"I'm sure you're right," I told her. "And obviously the kids can't do a job like this alone, but if all the adults in this room pitch in to help in some way—I think that together we can accomplish what we need to. If Mr. Al's place is looking good, there'd be no reason for the complainers to go to the City Commission next month."

Miss Dora stood from her seat in the middle of the room. "And I have to say, shame on all of us for not seeing such a simple solution. It took the kids to lead us in the right direction. Well, count me in. I'm very good with gardening, and I'd be more than happy to cut back those azalea bushes of his and have them lookin' nice again." Miss Dora scanned her gaze around the room. "Okay, we have lots of Garden Club members here. Who else is willing to help me tackle his yard?"

A number of hands shot up in the air.

"Great," I said. "Thank you, Miss Dora, for organizing cleanup for the garden. Mallory, why don't you start writing down names for who's doing what. Okay, now we'll need volunteers to paint the house. And then we have all that trash and junk to deal with . . ."

"I have a large dump truck," Bob Riley from the hardware store said. "I'd be more than happy to make as many trips as necessary to the Levy County dump after we get it filled."

"And I'd like to chip in toward the cost of paint and whatever else we might be needing," somebody else said. "I'll also drive to Lowe's in Gainesville to pick up all the supplies."

"When are we planning to do this?" Grace questioned.

"Well, we have two weeks before Christmas," I told her. "It sure would be great if we could have it all finished by then. So I think we need to get started as soon as possible. I was hoping maybe this Saturday morning we could begin. Between all the people here in the room and the kids, I bet we could have it all done over the weekend. I need everybody to sign up for the days and times that would be good for you to help out."

"I'll provide coffee and muffins in the morning for everybody," Grace said. "But I can't close the shop to come and deliver it."

"I'll come by and pick it up," somebody offered.

"And I'll provide all the lunches for everybody," I heard my mother say from the back of the room. She must have slipped in late because I hadn't seen her arrive. "I'll have Tony's deliver some nice clam chowder and sandwiches. That'll be my donation."

"Thanks, Mom. That's really generous of you."

"Well, this is a very important cause, and I'm very proud of my granddaughter for coming up with an idea to help Mr. Al. So we all have to pitch in and make this happen."

"Hey," Officer Fred said. "Does Mr. Al know anything about this? Do you think he'll be agreeable?"

"He doesn't know anything," I told the group. "But I'm planning to go by his place in the morning and explain it all to him. It might take a bit of coaxing on my part, but in the end I have no doubt he'll be very happy if it means not selling his house and leaving the island. Okay, any other questions?" Heads shook in unison as people lined up to give Mallory their time slots for the weekend. "Good. If you have questions, just give me or Mallory a call. Otherwise, I'll see you Saturday morning at eight sharp in front of Mr. Al's house. And thank you all for coming."

Chapter 8

"Why do you think Mr. Al might not want everyone to help?" Orli asked over breakfast.

"Well, some people consider it charity, and their sense of pride prevents them from taking what's offered."

"Oh, like you do with Grandma?"

This kid was getting too observant.

"I don't do that," I argued.

"Yeah, you do. Like when she bought you the sneakers a few weeks ago."

"Oh . . . well . . . you need to get going or you'll be late for school."

"But you're going to talk to Mr. Al this morning, right?"

"Yup," I told her. "And stop worrying. You worry too much for an eleven-year-old."

Orli came to plant a kiss on my cheek before grabbing her backpack. "See you after school. Love you," she said.

"Love you too."

I began cleaning up the kitchen and gave some thought as to what she'd said. She was right, of course. For eleven years I had made a vain attempt to be independent when it came to accepting help or money from my parents. But if I decided to go through with my plan, that would have to change. I'd require not only financial assistance, but it might be necessary to depend on my mother to look after Orli while I was taking classes.

I'd given a lot of thought to this over the past few days and had come up with a career that not only surprised me, but one that I thought I'd enjoy and would provide a decent salary.

Without pausing to change my mind, I whipped out the Gainesville phone book and instead of looking for the number for the University of Florida, I searched for Sante Fe Community College.

When I reached the correct department and heard a woman say, "Good morning, Division of Nursing, how may I help you?" I almost lost my nerve.

But instead I took a deep breath. "Ah, yes, hello. I was wondering . . . I was wondering how I might go about applying for your registered nurse program. That's a two-year program, right?"

"Yes, it is. Our students receive an associate's degree in nursing. And it does consist of four semesters. I'd be more than happy to send you our brochure with all of the information. We do still have a few openings for the class beginning next fall, but you'd have to have your application in by mid-January."

Wow. I guess I hadn't expected things to move along quite this quickly. "That would be good," I told her. I felt a surge of confidence and said, "Yes, actually, that would be great," and I went on to give her my mailing address and information.

Hanging up the phone I realized my palms were

sweaty. But I also realized that for the first time in a long time I felt *good* about myself. Maybe there was something to that old saying, *success breeds success.* Well, I had taken the first step, and I was about to find out.

"Well, hey, Miss Josie," Al Casey said, opening his back door to my knock. "What a surprise. I never get no visitors."

"I hope you don't mind my dropping by like this. I would have called, but since you don't have a phone . . ."

"No, no. It's fine. Come on in," he said, opening the door wider. "Nah, never did like those contraptions. Besides I really got no need for one. Who would call me?"

I laughed and stepped inside his kitchen. Based on the outside of his house, I was prepared for the worst. Therefore, I was shocked to see a kitchen that would have made Martha Stewart proud. Clean and tidy, with a vase of fresh daisies that matched the yellow hue of his nicely pressed cotton tablecloth. Coffee cup and one plate sat drying in the dish drainer. Three green tomatoes added color on the windowsill, and was that spice I smelled in the air?

As if confirming my olfactory nerve correct, he said, "I'm just ready to take spice bread out of the oven. How 'bout a piece with coffee?"

"That would be great."

"Then have a seat, and it'll just be a minute. Just made a fresh pot before you got here."

I pulled out the kitchen chair and jumped back when a loud whine filled the room. Peeking under the table, I saw a curly dark mass of canine.

Mr. Al laughed. "Hey, Pal, believe it or not we've got company. Come on out and say hello."

The dog inched his way to the middle of the kitchen floor, bowed in a stretch, gave a noisy yawn, and then seemed to notice me. With tail wagging at breakneck speed he came to stand beside me.

"Hey, there, Pal." I patted the top of his dome-shaped head. "You sure are a cute dog."

"Yup, he's my best friend, he is. That's why I named him Pal. Well, that and because I thought it sounded pretty cool when I met people to be able to say 'hi, I'm Al and this is my dog, Pal.' "

I laughed as it occurred to me that I'd never realized Mr. Al had a sense of humor.

He placed a mug of coffee and slice of spice bread in front of me. Next came a beautiful crystal sugar bowl and creamer set.

I took a sip of coffee and found it to be a definite ten on my coffee scale. Yeah, I was a coffee snob and quite picky. Rich, dark, and strong—that's the way coffee is supposed to be. My mother never quite got this, and I always wondered why she didn't just resort to tea, since her coffee was always so weak. A bite of the spice bread and I was convinced there was a lot about Mr. Al that I didn't know.

"Gosh, this is delicious," I told him. "And your coffee—Grace had better watch out. You'll put her out of business."

He laughed and said, "That's my mama's recipe for the spice bread. Figured if I made a lot of the things that she did . . . well . . . it might make her feel a bit closer, ya know?"

I nodded. Yeah, I did know, and I was beginning to understand much more.

"I came to see you for a reason, Mr. Al. There's something I need to talk to you about."

"Oh? And what might that be?"

I proceeded to fill him in on everything that had

transpired over the past couple of days. Finding the paint under Orli's bed, calling everybody together for the meeting, and our plan to help him clean up his property.

"And so," I told him. "Once we get the outside of your yard and your house in decent shape, there won't be a darn thing anybody can do to put you in a nursing home—not even that nephew of yours."

"I sure hope I didn't get your daughter in trouble. When she said her and the other kids wanted to paint my house, well, I figured they were just lookin' for something to do. I offered to pay them too, but they refused, so I don't want ya thinking they came here beggin' for money or nothin'."

"No, no. I know they just wanted to help, and Orli isn't in trouble. Actually . . . that daughter of mine has opened a lot of eyes on this island. We all want to help you, Mr. Al. So will you let us? We've put schedules together, have plenty of volunteers, and we're all set to begin Saturday morning at eight o'clock."

He remained silent for a few moments. Then he dabbed at his eyes and reached over to pat Pal. "Imagine that. Everyone wants to help, Pal. That means you and me can stay right here. We're not goin' nowhere."

He dabbed his eyes again, and when he looked across the table at me I saw the moisture there. "Well," he said. "Seems to me if people went to all the trouble a plannin' this, the least me and Pal can do is to welcome them and say thank you. This sure is mighty kind of you, Miss Josie. You're a very special person."

I felt my own eyes tearing up as I reached across the table to grasp Mr. Al's hand. "No," I said. "It's you that's the special one."

* * *

After I left Mr. Al's house, I rushed to my cleaning job and arrived five minutes late. My client had some extra chores for me, and by the time I got home it was 2:30 and I was starved. Since I'd skipped breakfast, I'd only had the slice of spice bread at Mr. Al's.

Rummaging through the fridge and finding turkey breast and cheese for a sandwich, I was annoyed to hear the doorbell. *Damn, I was hungry.*

So I was more than annoyed when I opened the door to find Ben Sudbury standing on my porch.

"Yes?" I questioned, with one hand on the doorknob while the other gripped a jar of mayonnaise.

A look of apprehension crossed his face, quickly replaced by that killer smile he seemed capable of producing at will.

"Hey, Josie. I hope I'm not interrupting anything . . . but . . . uh . . . I really need to talk to you about something."

What on earth could be so important that it brought him to my front door rather than making a phone call?

"It's about my uncle Al. . . . He won't give me the time of day. I just tried to have a talk with him." Ben ran a hand through his curly hair and sighed.

"Gee, can you blame him?" I snapped as my stomach emitted a low rumble.

"I know, I know. Maybe I took the wrong approach with all of this . . . but you can't blame me. I got the phone call concerning my uncle and even though I'm buried at work right now, I made the effort to get down here and see what I could do."

"Oh, right! Poor you! Forced to leave your ivory tower up there in New York and come back to a place you never wanted to see again. Gee! That's really rough, compared to Mr. Al's being forced to sell his home, give up his dog, and reside in a nursing home."

Ben's tone took on an edge. "There's a lot you don't understand, so you have no right to judge me."

"Then don't come here looking for me to side with you, because that's not going to happen."

"I wasn't looking for you to . . ."

I didn't give him a chance to finish. "If Mr. Al told you to butt out, I'm telling you the same thing," I said, slamming the door and heading back to the kitchen.

Damn him! I thought, as I slathered bread with mayonnaise. How dare he come here and attempt to win me over.

By the time I sat down to dig into my sandwich, I recalled his saying that maybe he had taken the wrong approach, which made me question if I'd been too harsh with him.

Then I remembered his condescending treatment of me at Cook's. *Actually,* I thought, *I wasn't nearly as nasty as I should have been!*

The sandwich certainly hit the spot for my empty stomach. Just as I began cleaning up, the phone rang, and I answered to hear Sydney Webster's voice. "Hey, Miss Syd. What's up?"

"Noah and I just got back from Paris last night. Dora and Monica have brought us up to date about Mr. Al and what's going on. We both want to help, so what can we do?"

"That's really nice of you. Mallory is keeping track of the schedule and who's doing what. Why don't you give her a call? I know she'd be more than happy to add you and Noah to the list."

When I hung up the phone, I felt a smirk covering my face. "So there, Mr. High and Mighty—two more people added to our side."

Chapter 9

The result of the tree trimming party from the night before now stood glittering in our living room. Multi-colored lights sparkled, while ornaments, beads, and garland added to the festive beauty a Christmas tree always brought to a home. Now that it was up and decorated I berated myself for not getting it done sooner. Especially since it was obvious how much Orli was enjoying it.

She lay sprawled on the carpet, chin in hands, quietly gazing at the tree. Clovelly was curled up beside her, and it reminded me of a Hallmark commercial on television.

"Hey, sweetie," I said, thinking this might be a good time to discuss my nursing school plans with her. "I have something I'd like to talk to you about."

Orli sat up clutching her knees to her chest. "About Christmas?"

"No, not Christmas. Actually, it's about what I'm planning to do with the rest of my life. You know you're always the first one I discuss these important decisions with, so I wanted you to know what I've got in mind."

I patted the spot beside me on the sofa, and she came to join me.

"You haven't told Grandma or Mallory yet?"

"Nope. You're the first. Well, you know how I have to work so much? That's because I don't have a very well paying job, so therefore I need to work more hours in order to make more money."

"Oh, so are you saying you're gonna need to work even more hours?"

"No, I don't need more hours. What I need is an education that will enable me to have a career and make a decent salary. It was my choice to quit college to raise you, but I think the time has come for me to return to school and get trained to do something besides waitressing and cleaning."

"Really? You'll be going to school just like me?"

"Just like you, except it'll be college. I've been thinking about it for a while now and . . . I've decided I'd like to become a nurse." I waited for Orli's reaction.

"A nurse? Oh, like Sarah's mom? She works at a hospital in Gainesville."

"Right. And when I graduate I'll be able to get a job right away. Either at a hospital, a clinic, or a doctor's office. There's lots of choices available. The thing is, it'll take me two years to complete the program. Which means it won't be easy. I'll be gone all day to classes and then at night I'll have to study. It's a lot of hard work—but I think it'll be worth it in the long run. What do you think?"

Orli was silent for a few moments. "I think it's a great idea, Mom. You've always told me how important education is. If you forgot how to study, I can help you."

I laughed but realized getting back into the groove of studying wasn't going to be a snap. It would take determination to develop a schedule. But I was motivated, and I felt that was always the first step to any new venture. "Well, I accept your help," I told my daughter. "So you're okay with this? I'm going to have to speak with Grandma because I'll need her help as well. There might be days that I won't be back yet when you get out of school, so you'll have to go to Grandma's house. Would that be okay?"

Orli nodded. "Sure, that'd be fine. I'm sure Grandma will help you, and I will too. Besides, I think you'll make a really good nurse, Mom."

I admired the confidence of a child and wondered why the older we got, the more our confidence seemed to slip away. But I was firm about my decision and my goal. Therefore, I wasn't willing to let my self-assurance disappear.

"Well, thank you. I think I'll enjoy being a nurse and that'll help toward becoming a good one."

"When will you be going?"

"First, I have to apply, so I plan to send the application back to them this week. And then I have to be accepted. The woman I spoke with said there's still a few spots open for next September. So we'll see . . . but I wanted to talk with you about it before I did anything else."

"Well, you have my vote of approval," my daughter told me, and that alone meant everything.

"What a great idea," Mallory said the next morning when I called her with my news. "You'll make a perfect nurse."

I laughed. "That's what Orli said."

"Well, it's true. Remember a couple years ago

when Carter fell off his bike and ended up with a broken arm? I don't know what I'd have done without you. You were so calm and knew exactly what to do until we got him to the pediatrician in Chiefland. Plus, you're good with people, Josie. You seem to instinctively know what people need. You're pleasant to be with—sick people certainly need that."

"Really?" My confidence level just shot up another notch. "Thanks."

"So what's Orli think about all of this?"

I went on to explain our conversation of the night before.

"I'm not surprised at all. She's a smart girl and not just with the books. I'm sure she knows that ultimately this is something that will be good for both of you. So I wish you all the best with it, Josie. You go, girl! Have you told your mother yet?"

"Ah, nope. Was planning to drop by and see her this afternoon."

"Don't you think she'll be excited about your returning to college?"

"Oh, probably. But she might not like my choice of career. She feels I should follow in her footsteps and at least become a journalist even though that doesn't appeal to me at all anymore."

"Hmm. Well, you know your mother."

"Right. Queen of control freaks?"

Mallory laughed. "Hey, good luck. You've made a good choice with nursing."

"So," my mother said, after taking a sip of coffee. "What brings you out here today?"

I picked up on her cool tone of voice and retorted, "Do I have to have a reason?"

"Lately—yes, it seems you do. You never just drop by to visit. You're either in a rush to drop off Orli, or you've been summoned here for dinner."

I was about to say *that's not true* but realized she was right, which gave me my opening.

"Well, that's what I wanted to talk to you about. Working multiple jobs leaves me very little time to do anything else. Especially spending quality time with Orli. She's been really good about it but before I know it, she'll be in high school. She'll be so busy with her own activities it'll leave less time for her and me. So I want to be available for her, and the only way I can do that is by returning to college, getting a degree, and obtaining a decent paying job, rather than working two or three jobs to make ends meet."

My mother's tone of voice changed to excitement. "Finally. You're *finally* going to do it! Of course, it might have been easier when Orli was a baby, but better late than never, I always say. That's wonderful, Josie. So did you get accepted into the journalism program at UF?"

"I'm not going to UF."

"What? Well, it's the closest college around."

"I'm not majoring in journalism. I've decided to pursue a nursing career. I'm applying to Sante Fe Community College in Gainesville for their two-year registered nurse program."

My mother leaned forward on the sofa. "Nursing? You're going to be a *nurse?*" she said, not masking the derogatory inflection on the word "nurse." "Josephine Shelby Sullivan, what on earth are you thinking? Why would you want to choose a back-breaking job where once again you're literally cleaning up for other people?"

The confidence that had notched up with Mallory

was now hovering around minus five on my confidence scale. I remained silent as I gripped the arm of the chair.

"I mean really, Josie. Have you given this any thought whatsoever? Nursing can be a terrible job—putting up with sick people, working all kinds of hours, not to mention being forced to work holidays."

She was right. But I had given it thought. Plenty of thought.

"Yes, true. However, until Orli is off to college, my plan is to work either in a doctor's office, a clinic, or a day surgical unit. They have normal hours, are closed on the holidays, and it will give me some good experience. I think ultimately I'd like to be a critical care nurse, either in the emergency room or intensive care unit. But by then, Orli will be older and have her own life." *Something you refuse to let me have,* I thought.

My mother pushed a strand of hair behind her ear and let out a loud sigh as she flounced back against the sofa cushion. "Well . . . if your mind is made up, guess there isn't much I can do about it. Just like when you were nineteen."

She really knew how to push my buttons, and I could feel anger overtaking me, as I stood up to leave. "First of all," I said, hearing my voice get louder, "I'm not *nineteen* anymore. I may have been young, but I've done pretty damn well raising Orli on my own. You've taken every opportunity you could to throw it in my face that I'm *too* independent—that I never let you help me. Well, today I came here for your help and what do I get? Support? Encouragement? Pride? Hell, no! It's all about you—you've always wanted me to be a journalist. That's what I thought I wanted years ago, but not now. That doesn't matter to *you* though. Shelby Sullivan always maneuvers to make things come out her way. You can do that in your books, Mom, but not with real people. I'm not one of your characters that you can control and mold into what you want." I grabbed my coat and scarf and headed for the front door.

"Josie, wait . . ." I heard my mother call and kept walking.

Before reaching the foyer, I turned around. "I'd really appreciate it if you could tell Dad what my plans are. Maybe *he'll* be happy for me," I said, before slamming the door behind me.

Chapter 10

By the time the Saturday for cleanup at Mr. Al's house arrived I still hadn't heard from my mother. It had been five days. We'd gone longer without speaking but I wondered if maybe this time it was permanent. I also hadn't heard from my father, which made me wonder if my mother had even told him about my visit.

"Come on, Orli," I hollered as I grabbed my jacket. "We don't wanna be late getting to Mr. Al's."

My daughter appeared in the kitchen, a bright smile on her face. "All set. Let's go get Mr. Al's house in shape. We're going to be just like that show on television that does house makeovers. Think we should bring the video camera?"

Even on the most dismal day Orli had a way of bringing laughter to me. "Nah, we'll probably do such a great job that they'll want to hire us, and none of us would want to have to leave Cedar Key for Hollywood."

Orli laughed as we walked outside to the golf cart,

each of us carrying the cans of white paint the children had purchased.

We arrived at Mr. Al's to find a good size crowd had already gathered. I spied Mallory, clipboard in hand, giving out assignments and answering questions.

"Hey," she said, looking up. "Grab yourself some coffee and a donut. We're in the delegating phase at the moment."

"We have a good crowd for the first shift." I poured cream into my coffee and took a sip. "Hmm, good. I could recognize Gracie's coffee anywhere. Where's Mr. Al? Will he be joining us?"

"Oh, yeah. Said he can't have all these people working and him sitting around. He'll be helping Miss Dora with the gardening. Okay, Josie, you're on paint duty. You and Twila Faye will be doing the front of the house. Use the blue for the house and the white for the trim. Orli, join the other kids over there— they're on trash patrol. Grab a garbage bag and pick up any junk on the ground."

"Okay," Orli said as she ran off.

I found the paint cans and brushes and headed to the front of the house. That's when I saw Ben walking from the sidewalk to the yard. He was loaded down with what looked to be huge metal pots.

He caught my eye and hollered, "Mornin', Josie."

"Morning," I called back, wondering what on earth he was doing here. Poor Mr. Al. He wasn't going to be happy, and what was Ben doing bringing those pots?

Twila Faye hadn't arrived yet but I opened my paint can and began swishing the brush up and down, covering the house with a pretty shade of robin's egg blue. I looked up a moment later to see Ben make the same trip to the backyard, this time carrying boxes. What the heck was going on?

When Twila Faye arrived I told her about Ben. She was as surprised as I was.

About ten minutes later we heard a commotion on the side of the house and walked over to see why somebody was clanging a large slotted spoon against the back of a pan. Mr. Al was standing on his back porch, creating the noise, with Ben beside him.

"Just wanna get your attention," Al said. "First off, I wanna thank all of you for coming here to help get my place in order. I sure do appreciate it." He then flung his arm around Ben's shoulders. "As many of you know, this here is my nephew, Ben Sudbury. He's my sister Annie's boy."

I looked around the crowd and saw everyone exchanging bewildered glances.

"Now I know a lotta you didn't take kindly to Ben's coming here to put me in a nursing home. Heck, *I* didn't take kindly to that," he said, which brought a few chuckles.

"But things change and people change. I decided to give Ben a chance when he stopped by again the other day—and I'm glad I did. We had us a long talk, got a lotta things straightened out. Cleared the air, so to speak. This is the Christmas season. A time to show people we care, a time to be a little nicer—and a time to forgive. So I forgive this here nephew of mine for making a mistake." Mr. Al pulled Ben toward him in an embrace. "And I hope all a you can do the same."

Mr. Al removed a large red plaid handkerchief from his pocket and dabbed at his eyes. "Now Ben here would like to say a few words."

"I also want to thank all of you for pitching in to help. I was wrong, and I admit it. I never took the time to really get to know my uncle. But all of you not only knew him, you didn't think twice about coming forward when he needed you. This is a community to be proud of, and all of us should be especially proud of Orli Sullivan, because it was Orli who wasn't about to sit by and let an injustice occur."

I scanned the yard and saw my daughter surrounded by her friends, a smile lighting up her face, as the entire crowd broke into loud applause.

"I also want everybody to know," Ben went on, "the item on the agenda for the City Commission has been dropped. Uncle Al and his dog, Pal, are staying right here where they belong."

This was followed by another loud round of applause and laughter.

"One last thing. My uncle and I would like to show our appreciation by cooking a low country boil for everyone who's helping out. All the work should be completed by next week, just in time for Christmas. So we'd like all of you to join us the day before Christmas Eve if you can. Come around two in the afternoon, and we'll have an old-fashioned Cedar Key gathering. Okay, I think that's it, and now we'd better all get to work."

I glanced over at Mallory. She shrugged her shoulders, raised her eyebrows, and there was no doubt she was thinking, *"Go figure."*

I was thinking about everything Mr. Al and Ben had said as I walked back to the front of the house to resume my painting.

"Josie."

I turned around to see my mother walking toward me. Apparently I'd been so caught up listening to Al and Ben I hadn't seen her arrive. Behind her, I saw my father and three other men putting the old wringer washer on a dolly to deposit in the dump truck waiting at the curb.

"Can I talk to you for a second?" my mother asked.

"Sure."

"I'm not such a big person that I can't admit my mistakes either," she said, fingering the paint brush in her hand. "I was wrong last week when you came to talk to me. I did what I wanted with my life, and you should be able to do the same. I'm sorry for not being more supportive. If being a nurse is what you want— well, then your father and I are very proud, and we want you to know that we'll help you in any way we can."

If you knew my mother, you'd know I could count on one hand the number of times she ever admitted that she was wrong. I knew it took a lot for her to break the ice and say she was sorry—and I also knew that as difficult as she could be, she loved me.

Pulling her into an embrace, I said, "Thanks, Mom. Thanks for understanding because I really *am* going to need your help over the next couple years."

"But, you know, Josie," she said. "Maybe you should consider going for four years and getting your bachelor's degree in nursing."

I shook my head and smiled. She never gave up. If I was a main character in one of her novels, *that* daughter would do precisely that.

"Right, Mom. Maybe I'll think about it," I told her. "But right now, I have to get back to my painting."

Four hours later Twila Faye and I had completed the front of the house, and our shift was over. Standing back to admire our work, I said, "Not bad for two amateurs."

"Hey, speak for yourself. I painted my own house and my mama's house. I came with credentials."

I laughed as I replaced the lid on the paint can. It was when I was taking my brushes to soak in turpentine that I saw Ben face to face for the first time since he'd spoken to the crowd. He was the first to speak.

"I want to thank you and Orli again for your help."

Cripe, did this guy get better looking every time I saw him? "Not a problem," was all I said. I rinsed off the brushes with the faucet attached to the house and began placing them into the can.

"Do you think you'll both be coming to the low country boil?" he asked.

When Ben had announced the invitation, I hadn't given it a second thought. "Oh, I don't think so," I told him.

"Really? Now that doesn't seem very neighborly of you."

I looked up to catch a smile covering his face that quickly broke into a grin, causing me to notice for the first time that he must have paid many visits to an orthodontist as a child. Perfectly straight teeth enhanced his good looks.

"Oh, well . . . I . . . might have to work," I told him, feeling flustered and tongue-tied.

"Aw, you can't be working all day and all night. We'll have the party going till at least nine. So drop by whenever you can. I'm sure your daughter will enjoy it."

"We'll see," is all I said before turning to find Orli and head home.

Chapter 11

I did have to work the morning of the low country boil. A waitress had called in sick at Cook's, and Ida Mae had phoned the night before to see if I could work the seven to noon shift. Since I had no cleaning jobs, I told her yes.

Orli was on Christmas vacation, and school was closed so she'd spent the night before at my mother's where I headed to pick her up.

I rang the bell and walked in to find my mother and Orli at the dining room table wrapping last minute gifts.

"Hi, Mom. Grandma said we should bring a little something for Mr. Al and Ben." She ran over to give me a hug and kiss.

I hadn't told her that we weren't going—but I hadn't said that we were either.

"Oh, well, I'm not sure we'll be going . . ."

"What?" My mother's head shot up as she finished creating an elaborate red satin bow on one of the

packages. "Why, of course you're going. Most everybody will be there, and Orli's really looking forward
to it. Can't remember the last time somebody did a
low country boil."

I actually didn't have a good reason not to go, except . . . I wasn't so sure I wanted to see Ben at a social gathering. Our last encounter had me wondering
if maybe I was becoming attracted to him. Something
I didn't even want to consider.

"Oh, Mom, please," Orli pleaded. "All the kids
from school are going. It'll be so much fun, and
somebody said Mr. Al's going to dress up like Santa."

Orli asked for very little and to deny her the pleasure of going wasn't right. Besides, I could keep my
distance from Ben and just mingle with everybody
else.

"All right. We'll go."

"Yippee!" my daughter yelled, jumping up and
down.

"What time are you and Dad going?" I supposed I
could hang out with my parents for a couple hours.
Between them and Mallory I should be able to effec-
tively avoid Ben.

"We're heading over around three."

"Good. Okay, well, get your things, Orli, and we'll
head home. I need to jump in the shower and change
before we go."

"I know it's casual dress, but you might want to . . ."
my mother started to say. She waved a hand in the air.
"Never mind. We'll see you there."

Stepping out of the shower, my eye went to the bottle of L'Occitane body lotion that Sydney had brought
me from France. I'd only used it once, trying to save it

for as long as possible. The wonderful Verbena fragrance filled the bathroom as I luxuriated in the silkiness on my skin.

I surprised myself by taking extra care with my makeup and styling my hair. Although the afternoon was mild with the temperature hovering in the high sixties, I knew by evening it would be cooler, so I decided to wear my black knit cargo pants that my mother had bought me from Cold Water Creek. They fit me to a "t" and my hand knit red cable pullover went perfectly with them, in addition to being festive.

I glanced in the mirror and smiled appreciatively. "Not bad, Josie girl," I said out loud. It had been so long since I'd taken the time with my personal appearance, I'd forgotten that I could actually look good. My black leather boots added style to my outfit, and, for a finishing touch, I wound the knitted black lace scarf that I'd completed the week before around my neck. *Good to go,* I thought, *not that I'm trying to impress anybody.*

I purposely waited till three-thirty before Orli and I arrived to be sure Mallory and my parents were already there. Parking the golf cart down the street, I heard strains of "Jingle Bells" fill the air. The crowd was having a sing-along.

Walking into Mr. Al's yard I was assaulted with the delicious aroma of sausage, crab, shrimp, clams, potatoes, and corn. All of it was simmering in a gigantic metal pot that had to be two feet around. The pot dangled from a huge metal tripod over a large fire surrounded by rocks that had been assembled beneath it.

I immediately noticed the transformation that had taken place on Mr. Al's property. The entire house had been refurbished. Peeling and cracked shutters had been replaced with pristine white ones, which blended nicely against the soft blue hue of the house. Gone was all the junk that had formerly inhabited the yard. In its place were trimmed bushes, brick walkways that were now visible, large terra cotta pots holding hosta plants, with lawn chairs and tables set up around the yard. It had been a lot of work, and it had all been worth it.

"Josie, there you are."

I turned around to see Mallory. "Yeah, we just got here. Gosh, doesn't this look great? Everybody really worked hard to make this happen."

Before she even had a chance to answer, I heard Ben's voice beside me. "They did, and I hope everybody knows how much my uncle and I appreciate it. I'm glad you decided to come, Josie. It's good to see you."

"Right. Well, ah . . . Orli was anxious to come. Her friends are all here and you know kids . . . They all like to be doing the same thing. So I hated to say no to her . . . You know how it is." He didn't know how it was at all—Ben had no children. I clamped my mouth shut and realized I was babbling as I caught the strange look Mallory was giving me.

Ben smiled, obviously ignoring my chatter. "Well, whatever reason brought you, I'm happy you came. How about a glass of wine?"

"Oh, yes, thank you. That would be nice." Sure, just what I needed—a little alcohol to make me babble more.

As Ben walked away to retrieve the wine, Mallory grabbed my arm. "What the heck is going on with you?" she demanded.

I shook off her hand. "What do you mean?"

"Well, for starters, look at you. All gussied up. I haven't seen you look this good since . . . I can't remember *when*. Your makeup looks like it was professionally applied. Your hair looks super, and that outfit—it looks wonderful on you. And what's with all this babbling with Ben? The last time I remember you doing that was with Chip Blackwell our junior year of high school."

"Don't be silly," I told her as I felt a flush creeping up my neck.

"Oh my God! You like him. You're *attracted* to Ben! Who would have thought," she said and broke out in a giggle.

I spied Ben heading back toward us and glared at Mallory. "Shut *up!* Please!"

"Here ya go," he said, passing me a glass of red wine. "Oh, sorry, Mallory. Did you need a refill?"

"No, no, I'm fine. Actually, I need to go find that son of mine. I thought he was with Troy but I'd better check. Have fun, you two," she said, sending me a wink that I prayed Ben didn't see.

"Well, cheers and Merry Christmas," he said, touching his glass to mine. "You look exceptionally nice today, Josie."

The extra time I'd taken had paid off, but I couldn't remember the last time a male had paid me a sincere compliment, and I ended up muttering, "Yes, Merry Christmas to you too." As if on cue the crowd broke into a rendition of "The Little Drummer Boy."

We stood there silently for a few moments listening. For some reason that Christmas song always brought moisture to my eyes. Maybe it was the simplicity and meaning of the song. It truly was the little things in life that ended up meaning the most. Like a community coming together to help one of their own, making it a very special Christmas for a man who really deserved it.

"I've always liked that song," Ben said.

"Me too."

"I've been meaning to ask you—is there a particular reason you named your daughter Orli? It's very pretty but very unusual. Pronounced like Orly Airport in Paris, right?"

I nodded. "Yes, the same pronunciation. Actually, it's a Hebrew word—it means *you are my light.* Although we're not Jewish, the name fit Orli perfectly. From the moment she was born, she's been the light of my life. I'm sure you know that I've raised her alone. We've always been extremely close."

"That's easy to see. You seem to have a great relationship, and you've certainly done an exceptional job raising her. If not for Orli—well, I'm just not sure where Uncle Al would be right now."

When it came to receiving compliments for my daughter, I always got emotional, and I could feel moisture stinging my eyes.

"You know," he said. "When we were kids—what you used to say was true. It just took me a long time to figure it out."

"What I used to say? What was that?" I asked, dabbing at my eyes.

"Oh, I'd be on my high horse about how I couldn't wait to get out of here and back to New York City and the bright lights and you'd say, 'Yeah, well, New York City might have the bright lights, but Cedar Key has the *magic,*' and you were right, it does."

I smiled. "I still feel that way." I took a sip of wine. "So when are you planning to leave our magical island?"

"I've been giving that a lot of thought. I'm flying back to New York a few days after New Year's—but I'm planning to come back."

"Right. A lot of people say that."

"Well, I mean it. I'm going back to do some rearranging. I plan to make some huge changes in my life."

I was embarking on the same path and looked at him with interest. "Really? Like what?"

"Well, I plan to sublet my apartment beginning June 1. I'll be back here in March for a few weeks to settle things on this end. When I return to New York, I'll be giving my notice at the publishing company."

This *was* a major change. "What? You're leaving? Why? What will you do?" I knew I was bordering on babbling again but I couldn't help it.

Ben laughed. "Yes, I'm leaving the publishing company. It's something I probably should have done a few years ago. Being an editor just doesn't have the same spark of excitement for me that it once did. It's time to move on. New York can be a rat race, and I was like that hamster on a wheel—going around in circles and not knowing what to do or how to change it. But coming back to Cedar Key put everything in perspective for me. Suddenly everything became crystal clear. Being here slowed me down and allowed me to think. Really *think,* for the first time in a long time. And as for what I'm going to do—I'm going to write."

"Write? You mean like my mother writes? Like an author?"

Ben laughed again. "Well, I hope so. I know how difficult it can be getting published. But I have some money put aside, enough to get me through a few years anyway. And so—I'm finally willing to take the risk. I've always wanted to but you know how it is . . . fear of the unknown. My uncle and I have really hit it off, and I enjoy being with him. He's really my last link to family, and I think I need to spend some quality time with him. The last thing I want when I'm his age is to have regrets."

Fear of the unknown—I wondered if perhaps that's what had always held me back from going further in my life. It seemed ironic that both Ben and I had come to the realization that slowing down and having *time* was extremely important in one's life. But even more ironic was the fact that we were both about to step onto a path that would accomplish this for us.

"And so," Ben said, pausing for a second, "since I'm going to be back here in March and then permanently in June . . . do you think it might be possible that I could take you to dinner some evening when I return? That is, if you've forgiven me for being such a jerk as a kid and an even bigger jerk when I arrived here last month."

I turned to look at him. I no longer saw the arrogant and ill-tempered boy who had visited our island every summer and made it clear he didn't want to be here. I didn't see the teen who tried to make us feel we were beneath him and taunted us by bragging about how different his life was in New York, rather than experiencing what the island so freely gave—both in the land and in the people. Suddenly, I saw none of this.

Instead, I now saw an extremely good-looking man who had probably grasped the true meaning of Christmas more than most people. I saw a man who had finally slowed down enough to understand, and, with understanding, exhibited compassion. A man who I knew I'd like to know better.

I smiled and touched the rim of his glass. "Ben Sudbury, I'd love to have dinner with you when you return. And forgive you? Where would my Christmas spirit be if I didn't forgive you? Of course I do. You know what they say—*to err is human, to forgive, divine.*"

Ben threw his head back laughing. "And Josephine Shelby Sullivan—you *are* divine. Merry Christmas!"

I joined his laughter. For some reason, when he verbalized my full, entire name it didn't irk me the way it did when my mother used it.

"Merry Christmas, Ben," I said, knowing that this particular Christmas on Cedar Key had been *magical* indeed.